Christopher Marlowe, Sir Adolphus William Ward

Old English drama, select plays

Christopher Marlowe, Sir Adolphus William Ward

Old English drama, select plays

ISBN/EAN: 9783337305727

Printed in Europe, USA, Canada, Australia, Japan

Cover: Foto ©Andreas Hilbeck / pixelio.de

More available books at **www.hansebooks.com**

Clarendon Press Series

OLD ENGLISH DRAMA

SELECT PLAYS

MARLOWE'S TRAGICAL HISTORY OF

DOCTOR FAUSTUS

AND

GREENE'S HONOURABLE HISTORY OF

FRIAR BACON AND FRIAR BUNGAY

EDITED BY

ADOLPHUS WILLIAM WARD, M.A.

Fellow of Peterhouse, Cambridge, and Professor of History and English Literature in the Owens College, Manchester

Oxford

AT THE CLARENDON PRESS

M DCCC LXXVIII

PREFACE.

It may be well to state that this edition was undertaken before I became aware that my distinguished friend, Professor Wilhelm Wagner of Hamburg, had in the press an edition of Doctor Faustus, which has since been published by Messrs. Longmans, Green, & Co. Of this excellent edition the plan differs in several respects from that of my own; but it would have been a poor compliment to the labours of Professor Wagner not to make such use of them as I could. The special feature of his edition is the Critical Commentary on the Text, which has been of the greatest service to myself. The courtesy of the authorities at the Bodleian, to whom I return my sincere thanks, has however enabled me to supplement Professor Wagner's labours on this head, by means of a personal inspection of the unique copy of the 1604 edition of Doctor Faustus in that Library.

I have also to thank Mr. T. H. Ward, Tutor of Brasenose, and several of my colleagues and friends at Manchester, for information as to various matters on which I consulted them in connexion with the notes to my edition. I am under special obligations to Professor R. Adamson and Mr. T. N. Toller, upon whose learning and kindness I have largely drawn. Mr. Toller was good enough to read through the whole of the proof-sheets of this edition; and much of whatever value it may prove to possess will be due to his suggestions.

A. W. W.

THE OWENS COLLEGE, MANCHESTER,
June 3rd, 1878.

CONTENTS.

INTRODUCTION.

'Doctor Faustus' and 'Friar Bacon and Friar Bungay.' The connexion between the plays, and the *primâ facie* difference between them.

THE internal connexion between the two plays reprinted in this volume is indisputable. There is, as will be seen, no evidence amounting to certain proof as to the priority of either of them to the other in date of composition; and it is highly probable that both were written and performed for the first time, if not within the same year, at least without more than a brief interval between them. Thus as Marlowe was born in 1564 (N.S.), and Greene probably not long before 1560 (for he took his Bachelor of Arts' degree in 1578), the two plays belong to not very different stages in the lives of their respective authors, and offer fair materials for a comparison between their gifts and powers as dramatic poets. While, however, Friar Bacon and Friar Bungay has doubtless come down to us very much as it was written by its author, and has indeed been described by a comparatively early tradition [1] as one of the two plays of which Greene was sole author, the earliest copy we possess of Doctor Faustus contains additions, and possibly other alterations, from other hands than Marlowe's. None of his plays, except Edward II (for Dido Queen of Carthage was written conjointly with Nash), is to be regarded as the unadulterated expression of Marlowe's art [2]; and least of all the tragedy before us. Yet on no other are the marks of his mighty genius more visibly impressed; although it is impossible, were it only for the reason given, to term Doctor

[1] Edward Phillips, in the Theatrum Poetarum, 1675. See R. Simpson, The School of Shakspere, ii. 339. The other play, Faire Em, is almost certainly not by Greene.

[2] See W. Wagner, Emendationen und Bemerkungen zu Marlowe, in Jahrbuch der deutschen Shakespeare-Gesellschaft, xi. (1876) 73–75.

Faustus, what Friar Bacon may be unhesitatingly termed, the masterpiece of the dramatist whose name it bears.

Relations between Greene and Marlowe.

Greene's jealousy of Marlowe not necessarily professional.

That jealousy of rivals which is the bane of all but the highest kinds of artist-life has never raged with greater fury than in Robert Greene. His relations with Christopher Marlowe, who was, like him, University (Cambridge) bred, seem to have varied at different periods in his career. Their plays were mostly written for different companies, in which however the same managers might have an interest; thus Friar Bacon was, so far as we know, first performed by Lord Strange's company, which afterwards became absorbed into the Lord Chamberlain's; while Faustus was probably from the first performed, like most of Marlowe's plays, by the Lord Admiral's (the Earl of Nottingham's) Servants[1]. But the rivalry between the theatrical companies was not clearly marked till the year 1594, from which time two great companies (the Lord Chamberlain's and the Lord Admiral's) included the chief actors and commanded the services of competing dramatists[2]; and our first notice of Doctor Faustus is in a list of plays performed by the Lord Admiral's and the Lord Chamberlain's men, 'beginning at Newington,' where they acted either together, or more probably on alternate days or at different hours in the same day[3]. There is accordingly nothing to show that—after a fashion which afterwards became common, and of which the history of the English theatre continues to this day to furnish examples—either of our two plays was brought out in opposition to the other.

Proofs of Greene's jealousy of Marlowe.

But Greene's jealousy of Marlowe needed no such additional stimulant. The success of Marlowe's Tamburlaine the Great (produced not later than 1587, and probably in 1586, or even in 1585) had suggested the composition of Greene's Comical History of Alphonsus King of Arragon (as to the date of which there seems to be no external evidence), which was incontestably designed to challenge a comparison. Not long

[1] See Henslowe's Diary; and compare Fleay, Shakespeare Manual, p. 88.

[2] R. Simpson, *u.s.*, i. xviii.

[3] See Henslowe's Diary, p. 35 in Collier's edition, and Collier's note.

afterwards in his prose-tract, Perimedes the Blacksmith (1588), Greene, referring to some remarks about a change made by him in the motto which, after the fashion of the time, he was accustomed to append to his publications, wrote as follows:

'I keepe my old course, to palter vp something in prose, vsing mine old poesie still, Omne tulit punctum; although latelye two gentlemen poets made two mad men of Rome beate it out of their paper bucklers, and had it in derision, for that I could not make my verses iet vpon the stage in tragicall buskins, euerie worde filling the mouth like the faburden of Bo-bell, daring God out of heauen with that atheist *Tamburlan*, or blaspheming with the mad priest of the sonne: but let me rather openly pocket vp the asse at Diogenes hand than wantonlye set out such impious instances of intollerable poetrie, such mad and scoffing poets that haue propheticall spirits as bred of Merlins race. If there be anye in England that set the end of scollarisme in an English blanck-verse, I thinke either it is the humor of a nouice that tickles them with selfe-loue, or too much frequenting the hot-house (to use the Germaine prouerbe) hath swet out all the greatest part of their wits, which wasts *gradatim*, as the Italians say poco à poco. If I speake darkely, gentlemen, I craue pardon, in that I but answere in print what they haue offered on the stage[1].'

The reference to Marlowe in this passage explains itself; and it is just possible that the expression 'scollarisme' may have been suggested by the occurrence of that word in the Opening Chorus of Doctor Faustus (16). Greene returned to the attack in the Epistle prefixed to his Farewell to Folly (not known to have been published before 1591, though possibly written earlier[2]). Here his assertion that the whole impression of a previous tract by him, England's Mourning Garment, had been sold, is accompanied by a sneer to

[1] Quoted by Dyce, in the Account of R. Greene and his Writings, in the Works of R. Greene and G. Peele, 35. Compare Simpson, *u. s.*, ii. 351.

[2] See below, p. xciv.

the effect that the pedlar, finding it too dear, had been forced to buy 'the life of Tomlivolin, to wrap up his sweet powders in those unsavoury papers.' In this passage 'Tomlivolin' has been with obvious probability interpreted as a misprint for 'Tamburlan,' which had been first printed in 1590. And, in the Epistle 'to the Gentlemen Students of both Universities' prefixed by Thomas Nash to Greene's Menaphon (1587), there can be little doubt that Nash had rushed in to support the claims of Greene as against Marlowe, and that, while he insinuates a compliment to Greene by inveighing against 'the alchemists of eloquence who (mounted on the stage of arrogance) think to outbrave better pens with swelling bombast of bragging blank-verse[1],' it is to Marlowe he contemptuously alludes as an 'art-master'—a degree which Marlowe had taken at Cambridge in the very year when Nash had been obliged to quit the University in disgrace. Here, again, I will merely point out as curious the choice of the expression 'alchemists,' and the phrase describing these alchemists as 'mounted' on a stage of arrogance, as the alchemist Doctor Faustus in Marlowe's play 'mounts him up to scale Olympus' top.' (Chorus before sc. vii, l. 3.)

His posthumous warning to him.

The bitterness of Greene against Marlowe came to an end —driven out, may be, by that greater bitterness of which the expressions have done more to provoke the ill-will of posterity against Greene's name than all the errors for which he so loudly did penance. In his tract, A Groatsworth of Wit bought with a Million of Repentance, published in 1592 by Henry Chettle soon after its author's miserable death, Greene addresses 'those gentlemen his quondam acquaintance, that spend their wits in making playes,' wishing them 'a better exercise, and wisedome to preuent his extremities.' And the first of those whom, in a passage often quoted, he entreats 'to take heed,' is beyond all doubt Marlowe.

'Wonder not (for with thee will I first beginne), thou famous gracer of tragedians, that Green, who hath said with

[1] See W. Bernhardi, Robert Greene's Leben und Schriften (1874), 48, 49; and compare Collier, History of English Dramatic Poetry, iii. 110-112.

thee, like the foole in his heart, "There is no God," should now giue glorie vnto his greatnesse; for penetrating in his power, his hand lyes heauy vpon me, he hath spoken vnto me with a voyce of thunder, and I haue felt he is a God that can punish enemies. Why should thy excellent wit, his gift, be so blinded that thou shouldest giue no glory to the giuer? Is it pestilent Machiuilian policie that thou hast studied? O peevish follie! what are his rules but meere confused mockeries, able to extirpate in small time the generation of mankinde? for if *sic volo, sic iubeo,* holde in those that are able to commaund, and if it be lawfull *fas et nefas,* to doo any thing that is beneficiall, onely tyrants should possess the earth, and they, striuing to exceed in tiranny, should ech to other be a slaughterman, till, the mightyest outliuing all, one stroke were left for Death, that in one age man's life should end. The brocher of this dyabolicall atheisme is dead, and in his life had neuer the felicitie he aymed at, but, as he beganne in craft, liued in feare, and ended in dispaire. *Quam inscrutabilia sunt Dei judicia!* This murderer of many brethren had his conscience seared like Cayne; this betrayer of him that gaue his life for him inherited the portion of Judas; this apostata perished as ill as Julian; and thou wilt, my friend, be his disciple? Looke vnto mee, by him perswaded to that libertie, and thou shalt finde it an infernall bondage. I know the least of my demerits merit this miserable death; but wilfull striuing against knowne truth exceedeth all the terrors of my soule. Deferre not (with mee) till this last point of extremitie; for little knowest thou how in the end thou shalt be visited[1].'

In a subsequent passage (addressed to Peele) occurred the celebrated attack upon Shakespeare. Both he and Marlowe naturally took offence at the publication, the exhortations in which may have been needed by Marlowe, but are delivered in a ranting tone not surpassed by Tamburlaine or Barabas themselves. Hereupon Chettle, in a statement prefixed to his

and Marlowe's reception of it.

[1] Quoted by Dyce, Some Account of Marlowe and his Writings, Works of C. Marlowe, xxvii.

Kind-Harts Dreame (1592), made a handsome apology to Shakespeare; but Marlowe, after observing that he was not acquainted with him and 'cared not if he neuer be,' merely requests in no very gracious terms to excuse his indiscretion —'For the first, whose learning I reuerence, and, at the perusing of Greenes booke, stroke out what then in conscience I thought he in some diſpleasure writ, or, had it beene true, yet to publish it was intollerable, him I would wish to vse me no worse than I deserve'—pleading haste as his defence[1]. It is known how awful a comment on his unhappy friend's well-meant but not unnaturally ill-taken warnings Marlowe's sudden end was speedily to furnish. On June 1st, 1593, he was killed in a shameful quarrel.

No proof which of the plays was written first.

This summary of the known facts as to the relations between our two dramatists suggests the conclusion, that their two plays before us, which must have been brought out at a time preceding their reconciliation, such as it was, were not written in a spirit of friendly emulation. It likewise, inasmuch as no external evidence as to priority of date exists, suggests that Friar Bacon was written after Doctor Faustus, to which it was in some sense intended to be a rival play. It has indeed been pointed out[2] that a line occurs in Doctor Faustus which seems to have been taken from a passage or passages in Friar Bacon, while there is no similar plagiarism in the latter from Marlowe's tragedy. In Doctor Faustus (i. 86) the hero says:

> 'I'll have them wall all Germany with brass';

in Friar Bacon (ii. 30) Burden says:

> 'Thou mean'st ere many years or days be past
> To compass England with a wall of brass';

and *ib.* (ii. 177) the Friar says himself:

> 'And hell and Hecate shall fail the friar,
> But I will circle England round with brass.'

[1] See Dyce, *ib.*, xxix, and compare Dr. Ingleby's Introduction to Part I. of the Shakspere Allusion-Books printed for the New Shakspere Society, which contains both the Groatsworth of Wit and Kind-Harts Dreame.

[2] By Bernhardi, *u. s.*, 39, who recognises the inadequacy of the evidence, but inclines to the conclusion which he thinks it suggests.

But even if this be regarded as a plagiarism on the part of the one or the other play, the fact manifestly goes for nothing, in the case of a play which like Doctor Faustus is known to have received 'additions,' of which the above passage may be one. But there can be no question of plagiarism in lines expressing in the most natural way, and in similar though not identical terms, a traditional boast which was probably quite familiar from the story-book of Friar Bacon [1].

Probability that Friar Bacon was written after Faustus.

There is accordingly no reason for differing from the generally received view, that Greene's play was suggested by Marlowe's. Coincidences of vocabulary and phraseology were, in consequence of the similarity of their subjects, inevitable in the two plays; but the coincidences go no further than this. On the other hand, it seems going too far to say, that 'just as in his Alphonsus Greene attempted to outdo Tamburlaine, . . . he attempted to outdo Faustus by his Friar Bacon [2].' In a happier moment than that in which he had conceived the possibility not only of out-Heroding Herod (the phrase is not inapposite, for both the Scythian shepherd and the 'haughty Arragon' have a smack of the old mystery-style about them), but of pitting his life-like vigour against the torrent of Marlowe's passion, Greene seems to have resolved upon an altogether distinct treatment of a theme cognate with that of his rival's tragedy. In Faustus (the buffoonery apart, for which Marlowe cannot be held more than partly responsible), awe and terror are inspired by the treatment of the story; in Friar Bacon, as Tieck has observed, joviality is the predominating element, but a joviality refined by a truly poetic vein. Instead of the *terra incognita* of German localities, apparently not familiar in name even to the author himself (or at least to his printer [3]),

Difference of character between the two plays.

[1] In The Jew of Malta, i. 2:

> ''Twould have moved your heart,
> Though countermined with walls of brass, to love,'

the primary allusion is of course to the 'turris ahenea' of Danaë.

[2] See Wagner, Introduction to Doctor Faustus, xxxvii.

[3] Rhodes (Roda); Wertenberg (Wittenberg); Vanholt (Anhalt).

and of a Rome which he knew only at secondhand, we have here English scenery peopled by figures and called by names familiar to the poet's youth; instead of journeys through the air to foreign climes and into the empyrean, postings from Suffolk to Oxford; instead of a tragic catastrophe, a prompt and satisfactory repentance in the hero and a brace of weddings to close the honourable history. Friars Bacon and Bungay are not magicians who would be 'uncanny to meet'; and the representative of Darkness himself is bantered as a 'goodman friend.' On a legend which in itself he treats with so light a touch, Greene has engrafted a charming love-idyll, fresh with the sparkling dew of the meadows; there is nothing sombre in the action, even where it takes us into the Friar's cell; the play 'has all the leisurely beauty of an English summer day, while Marlowe's is like a tropical thunderstorm, intense, brief and unrelieved[1].'

Thus Greene sought rather to rival than to outdo Marlowe; not to surpass Faustus on his own ground, as Friar Bacon surpasses the 'German' Vandermast, but to produce an original play resembling Marlowe's tragedy in nothing but the primary aspect of their main themes. Of plagiarism there is therefore here as little question as of parody; and of essential similarity no question at all. Even in the comic passages there is no imitation; Miles is of the same family as Wagner, but has grown up in his own way. Greene's work is in a word altogether of a distinct kind from Marlowe's, from whose genius his own was widely apart—neither of them coming near to Shakespeare except where they differed altogether from one another. In one point however the two plays agree, namely in the peculiarities of style which help to mark the difference between the group of dramatists to which both Marlowe and Greene belonged, and the great master who was soon to outshine all his predecessors and contemporaries. Both these plays are not only full of bom-

Resemblances of style between them.

[1] I have taken the liberty, and given myself the pleasure, of borrowing one or two phrases from an interesting paper on Greene, entitled 'An Early Rival of Shakespere,' contributed by Professor J. M. Brown to a recent number of the New Zealand Magazine.

bastic diction and ultra-classicality of phrase and figure—the former being a sign of the immaturity which still characterised the poetic style of our dramatists, not yet masters of the secret reasons of their own effectiveness; the latter a conscious endeavour to prove to the world the academical scholarship which seemed the proudest of literary distinctions. But they are also still tinged with an artificiality of manner betraying itself in affectations and oddities of construction and vocabulary which seek to emphasise the difference between the poetic style and the common speech,—such as the omission of the article before the substantive[1], and the formation of new and high-sounding words; and again the habit of making the personages of the action address themselves by their proper names or speak of themselves in the third person, as if conscious of their unreality, instead of simply using the first personal pronoun like living human beings[2]. These are however merely the fashions of a school or of an age, worth noting, but not worth dwelling upon, in comparison with the distinctive characteristics of individual genius which are its own, and which in the case of Marlowe and Greene a critical analysis of these dramas, such as cannot be attempted here, would find occasion to mark in glorious abundance.

Legends of magic and magicians:

The main themes of both these plays are derived from that vast and infinitely interwoven body of legend which deals with magicians—men who have become possessed of

[1] Compare Doctor Faustus, xi. 40; xiii. 90; Friar Bacon, x. 143, 154; xiii. 8.

[2] The late Mr. Simpson has some extremely striking remarks on this practice, of which numerous examples will be found, *passim*, in both our plays, and which is a curious combination of artificiality and childlikeness. Perhaps however he urges a point rather too far when he says: 'With our earlier dramatists the principles of the dumb show, or rather puppet show, affect the whole form of their dramas. As poets, they speak rather like interpreters to the puppets than as dramatists.' See The School of Shakspere, ii. 394. Professor Wagner likewise adverts to the peculiarity of Marlowe's use in Doctor Faustus of 'a proper name where a pronoun would be commonly substituted.' In one passage, iii. 94, the change from the third to the first person has an unpleasingly abrupt effect. Compare also xi. 39-44.

powers and are capable of performances not admitting of explanation by any of the ordinary conditions of humanity. The magician or sorcerer is a conception distinct from that of the witch, who was looked upon as an ignorant instrument in the hands of the Evil One, and whose practices brought with them little but persecution in this world, and damnation in the next [1]. The magician, on the other hand, was usually regarded as having acquired and as exercising his art for purposes of his own, not merely nor essentially from an inclination or tendency towards doing evil and inflicting harm. Hence in the popular belief pre-eminent success in any of the paths which human ambition follows, especially if achieved with extraordinary rapidity or in the teeth of unusual difficulties, was associated with the possession of supernatural powers; while the pursuit of studies and occupations of which the objects and conditions were unintelligible or obscure to the multitude, especially if carried on under conditions of isolation or of other apparent mystery, was similarly accounted for. These notions were not peculiar to the Middle Ages; but in this period they passed through peculiar phases, and took a peculiar colouring from its dominant ideas and ways of life. Pagan antiquity had regarded these supposed supernatural or magical powers as the gift of the gods, and those who exercised them as *theurgi*, human executants of divine works. The prototype of these magicians of Classical antiquity was Pythagoras, to whose mysterious fame both the Doctor Faustus [2] and the Friar Bacon [3] of our plays make appeal. On the overthrow of heathen polytheism, its gods were converted by the Christian world into maleficent daemons, whose agency was controlled but not extinguished by the new Dispensation. The magicians of the earlier Middle Ages were thus regarded as the conscious servants of the Powers of Evil, who, in return for the promise of their souls after death, helped them, or those whom they wished to serve, to the good things of this world. They stood

in pagan antiquity;

in the early Middle Ages.

[1] See T. Wright, Narratives of Sorcery and Magic, i. 1-5.
[2] Compare Doctor Faustus, xiv. 105.
[3] Compare Friar Bacon, ix. 30.

outside Christian life, and were therefore often Jews or Mahometans; while at the same time, mediaeval legend clustered round some of the most popular names of Classical antiquity, such as Hippocrates the physician under the corrupted form of 'Ypocras[1],' and more especially the Roman poets, Horace, Ovid, and above all Vergil[2], and attributed to these sages a variety of magical exploits. It was usually by means of contracts with the Devil, in which Jews were frequently said to have acted as brokers,—occasionally by a close personal relationship with him (that of son to father),—that in a number of mediaeval legends men were said to have obtained a full command over the objects of those passions which it was the task of the Christian religion to repress or expel. Thus men were thought to have been enabled to drink to the dregs the cup of sensual indulgence, to satisfy the cravings of earthly ambition, to glut the accursed hunger for gold and for all that gold can buy, and to gratify the desire for knowledge of all things good and evil and for the power which knowledge ensures. But against this Devil's magic the Christian Church was not deemed to be powerless. Her spells were more potent than those of the Prince of Darkness; her magic outshone with its whiteness the Black Art of her adversary. Her holy offices and her blessed Sacraments offered a sure refuge against the assaults of the Enemy; Guardian Angels hovered round those who trusted in their care; the Saints vouchsafed their protection to the pure, and their aid to the penitent; and the Mother of God mediated between the sinner who prostrated himself at her feet and the Divine wrath provoked by his guiltiness[3].

Legends of contracts with the Devil.

These conceptions pervade a variety of legends, which partly are reproductions of their predecessors, partly attach themselves to historic figures, partly are consciously elaborated by later literary treatment. Among these legends those

[1] Compare note to Doctor Faustus, viii. 21.

[2] Compare note to Doctor Faustus, vii. 13.

[3] For a suggestive treatment of this part of a wide subject, see sect. iv. of a comprehensive essay on Goethe's Faust by Kuno Fischer, in the Deutsche Rundschau for October, 1877.

may here be left aside, which do not contain the element of a contract with the Devil, but account for the possession of supernatural gifts or powers by the supposition of a filial relationship towards him. It is, however, noteworthy that in two of the best-known of this class, in the story of Merlin which belongs to the Arthurian cycle of romance, and in the legend of Robert the Devil, the saving power of Grace is in both cases exercised by the Blessed Virgin. The contract-stories differ from one another as to the objects which in the several instances the human party to the bargain designed to secure by it; but they all adhere to the fundamental idea, that the obligation is invalid against the interposition of the Divine Mercy on behalf of the repentant sinner. Such is the significance of one of the earliest, which also became one of the most widely-spread of these legends [1], and which no commentator on the Faust-legend has failed to notice. Theophilus was a bishop's seneschal or *vice-dominus* at Adana in Cilicia in the reign of the Emperor Justinian. Filled with anger and dismay by unmerited dismissal from his office, he sought through the agency of a Jew the help of the Devil, with whom he sealed a contract, renouncing the Saviour and His Mother, and acknowledging the Devil as his lord. Immediately he was restored to his post. But soon terror of soul fell upon him; for forty nights he fasted and prayed to the Blessed Virgin, till at last she appeared to him at midnight and lent ear to his agony. Assured of a hope of mercy, he proclaimed his penitence and the miracle of his preservation before the congregation; the infernal contract was cast into the flames; soon he passed away in peace, and the Church inscribed his name on the roll of her saints as that of Theophilus the Penitent.

[1] The story, told by Theophilus' pupil Eutychianus as a living witness, was translated into Latin by Paulus Diaconus, and spread in a variety of versions through Eastern and Western Christendom. Hrotsvitha, the learned abbess of Gandersheim, narrated it in leonine hexameters; it was introduced into the Golden Legend; a French trouvère of the thirteenth century brought it on the miracle-stage; it appears in early English narrative and Low German dramatic literature. The *name*, but not the story, of Theophilus, was used by Massinger in his tragedy of The Virgin Martyr.

Of this legend that of Militarius[1] is a reproduction—the story of the soldier who, to prolong a life of jollity, entered (likewise through the agency of a Jew) into a contract with the Devil, but was finally saved by his refusing to renounce the Blessed Virgin, although he had already renounced her Divine Son. In other stories, sensual indulgence re-appears as the motive of the unholy compact; such is, to give only one later example, the significance of the tradition of the original Don Juan (Tenorio), who has a literary history second in interest only to that of Faustus himself, and who was said to have been the associate of King Pedro the Cruel of Castile (1350–1355)[2].

In the legend of Cyprian of Antioch, which seems even earlier in its origin than that of Theophilus, and which early in the seventeenth century Calderon took for the theme of a drama that no student of Marlowe or Goethe will pass by—El Magicó Prodigioso[3]—the thirst for knowledge appears as the primary, though not as the only, motive for Cyprian's contract with the Devil. Still here, as in the Italian Miracolo di Nostra Donna, which belongs to the close of the fourteenth or the beginning of the fifteenth century[4], the conditions of the conflict of which a human soul is the subject are still the same; and that Divine Grace of which the Church is the steward is consistently victorious over its natural enemy.

Legends of ecclesiastics as magicians.

As the course of mediaeval history slowly but surely progressed towards its close, marked in a wide variety of ways by those co-operating but not identical movements which we speak of as the Renascence and the Reformation, the popular conceptions of magic and of magicians were affected both by sentiments which the multitude could not avoid and

[1] It was treated by Gotefridus Thenensis (Gottfried von Thienen) in a narrative in leonine hexameters, of which a specimen is given by Professor von Reichlin-Meldegg in his elaborate treatise reprinted in Scheible's Kloster, xi. 256.

[2] As to Don Juan, see the collection of materials in vol. iii. of Scheible's Kloster.

[3] For analyses of this drama see Lewes' Life of Goethe or Hayward's Translation of Goethe's Faust.

[4] Klein, Geschichte des Drama's, iv. 174.

by phenomena which it could not understand. On the one hand, the worldliness of life and manners exhibited by prelates and popes, and the prominence which they more and more asserted in struggles actually or seemingly directed to the acquisition of secular power,—the profligate lives of many who had taken religious vows, whether as knights or as monks,—and more especially the shortcomings of the latter, with whom the multitude was most familiar,—all these things could not fail to exercise their natural effect. Already of a famous ecclesiastic of the tenth century, Gerbert, it had been told that he had sold himself to the Fiend in return for the promise of the papacy, which he afterwards held under the name of Sylvester II; in his case an Arabian philosopher, with whom Gerbert associated at Toledo, was reported to have acted as intermediary[1]. A still more illustrious occupant of St. Peter's chair—Gregory VII—was believed to have been furnished by the Devil with a magic glass, and to have paid the last penalty of his familiarity with evil arts. That the pious Protestant[2] who assiduously collected a variety of such illustrations for his version of the Faust-legend, should have found no lack of them in the history of the Popes nearer to the Reformation, may hardly seem to warrant a belief in the earlier prevalence of these traditions. But, apart from such well-known historical facts as the charges of diabolic sorcery which, together with other accusations of impiety and crime, served as a pretext for the ruin of the Knights Templars early in the fourteenth century, it is evident that in the popular mind the conviction was gaining ground that the profession of religious vows was frequently combined with the nefarious practice of magic. Old popular fancies may have helped in maturing the idea that the Devil was wont to make his appearance in the shape of a monk[3]; but the association could not have suggested itself to an age full of reverence

[1] See Wright, *u. s.*, 3

[2] Widmann. See the passage in his Commentary in Scheible's Kloster, ii. 770 *seqq.*

[3] See note on Doctor Faustus, iii. 26.

for the monastic orders. The stories of compacts between the Evil One and monks or bishops were by no means the products of the Reformation, though they were eagerly cherished by its champions and adherents. If these tales never found their way to the pre-Reformation stage, this may be easily accounted for by the control which the Church so largely exercised over it. On the other hand, the age of miracles had long passed away in the consciousness of the people; and we know with what suspicion or ridicule popular poetry and fiction treated the vendors of religious charms pretending to mysterious powers. Thus, everything was in readiness for the audacity with which the Reformers proclaimed the existence of a direct connexion between the Black Art and the old ecclesiastical system. The interpretation seemed clear of the warning of Holy Writ[1] against the ministers of the Evil One 'transformed as the ministers of righteousness.' Luther meant no metaphor when he described the clergy of the Church of Rome as the Devil's priests, and the monk's hood as the proper way of Satan himself; and Calvin was in earnest when he termed necromants and magicians the agents of Hell, and the Papists their slavish imitators[2].

Scientific enquiry associated with magic.

It was thus that in an age when the belief in magic and witchcraft not only survived, but was to assume new and more revolting proportions, the popular conceptions of the safe refuge suggested by the Church against these forms of sin had partly grown faint, partly been changed into a feeling of hostility against the system which had formerly found in these beliefs a powerful support of its influence over the minds of men. But long before this, ignorance and superstition had combined their brute forces to associate suspicions and traditions of magical powers with intellectual efforts and tendencies largely indeed in contact with theological speculation and therefore with religious belief and conduct of life, but primarily directed to different ends. It has been seen how the love of knowledge, a passion of all passions the least explicable to the

[1] See ii. Epistle to the Corinthians, xi. 13–15.
[2] See Reichlin-Meldegg, *u. s.*, 239–247.

vulgar, had from an early time been assigned as a motive for supposed compacts with the Powers of Darkness. The history of mediaeval science contains hardly a page without the blot upon it of this long ineradicable popular misconstruction. And in this case aid was not to be sought from the influence of the Church, which would alone have been able to introduce the gentle light of tolerance and kindle from it that of intelligence; it was but fitfully given by the hand of temporal power, rarely extended to protect, oftener to repress; nor was it generally to be found where its proper source should have lain, in the organised and representative seats of learning, the Colleges and Universities of Europe. For besides the ignorance of the ignorant there lay as a stumbling-block in the path of a freer scientific research that unwillingness of the learned to learn new things in new ways, which has often brought the apostles of progress to the verge of despondency. 'Because men,' wrote Roger Bacon, 'do not know the uses of philosophy, they despise many magnificent and beautiful sciences; and they say in derision, and not for information: "What's the worth of this science or of that?" They are unwilling to listen; they shut out, therefore, these sciences from themselves, and despise them. When philosophers are told in these days that they ought to study optics, or geometry, or the languages, they ask with a smile: "What is the use of these things?" insinuating their uselessness. They refuse to hear a word said in defence of their utility; they neglect and condemn the sciences of which they are ignorant. And if it ever happens that some of them profess a willingness to learn, they abandon the task in a few days, because they do not see the use of these things[1].' This apathy on the part of the scholastic philosophisers was a sure ally of the suspicious ignorance of the vulgar, who confounded the search after hidden knowledge with a desire to know forbidden things, and to whom experimental science in particular seemed undistinguishable from the Devil's magic, the Black Art.

[1] Opus Tertium, c. vi. The passage is translated by Brewer, in his Introduction to Fr. Rogeri Bacon Opera Inedita, i. xxi, xxii.

In the Middle Ages, two branches of study, the votaries of which were necessarily to a large extent groping in the dark or unsteadily moving in the twilight, were specially adapted to attract enquiring minds, and to excite the suspicions of the ignorant. These were astrology, which in the terminology of the Middle Ages included what we call astronomy, but which also occupied itself with speculations on the supposed influences of the heavenly bodies upon the inhabitants of the earth and their destinies, as well as with their actual or supposed influences upon the earth itself; and alchemy or chemistry, the speculative part of which treated of the production of all things out of the elements, while the practical part sought to rival or outdo nature in the production of colours and of many other things, but more especially of precious metals. The connexion which both these sciences thus assumed with common life, with its chief events and most cherished objects, could not fail to impress and excite the wild imagination of common men; and the isolation in which these studies have to be carried on, the loneliness of the observatory and the laboratory, added a peculiar element of mystery. In these and in other sciences the instruments used or invented by their professors seemed a machinery of a more than human character and origin. All these studies and their appliances were regarded as magic and as appliances of magic by the vulgar, who could not, like the philosophic mind, distinguish the mighty powers of nature and the still mightier powers of art which uses nature as its instrument, from that which passes beyond the powers of nature and art, and is therefore either suprahuman,—or fiction and imposture. 'For there are persons,' writes the thinker and student already quoted, 'who by a swift movement of their limbs or by changing their voice or by fine instruments or darkness or the cooperation of others produce apparitions, and thus place before mortals marvels which have not the truth of actual existence. Of these the world is full . . . . but in all these things neither is philosophic study concerned, nor does the power of nature consist[1].'

Astrology and alchemy.

Scientific inventions and instruments regarded as magical.

[1] See Roger Bacon's Epistola de Secretis Operibus Artis et Naturae, et

Thus true, though imperfect, science and honest though often misdirected research, were rudely elbowed and discredited by the competition of imposture, and confounded with their counterfeits in the mind of the people.

Roger Bacon.

Wherever, then, in the Middle Ages scientific pursuits, especially of the kinds referred to, sought to assert themselves by the side of the scholastic philosophy and theology which were the ordinary mental *pabulum* of students, there the popular suspicion of magic found an opportunity for introducing itself. One out of many instances of this familiar phenomenon is that of the group or school of enquirers to which Roger Bacon, the hero of the legend on which one of our plays is founded, belonged. In the pages of a narrative of English history unsurpassed as a vivid picture of such episodes in the progress of our national civilisation[1], may be read a summary of Bacon's attempt to give a freer and wider range of culture to the University of Oxford where he resided, and of its failure. The suspicion of magical practices was not indeed the main cause of his persecution, but appears to have contributed to it; and we have his own complaint that to speak to the people of astronomy, was to cause oneself to be immediately clamoured against as a magician, and that not only laymen, but most clerks regarded as wonderful things for which philosophy had a simple explanation[2]. With Roger Bacon the studies he had pursued passed away from his University, and his own name, as will be seen, was long enveloped in the haze of a popular myth.

The historical Roger Bacon.

Of the historical Roger Bacon no more need be said here than will suffice to explain the basis and some of the details of the legend which, at all events in the form in which it supplied Greene with materials for his play, seems to belong to a much later age than that in which the philosopher lived[3]. Roger

de Nullitate Magiae, cap. i. (Brewer, *u. s.*, pp. 523-524). Compare L. Schneider, Roger Bacon, 99.

[1] Mr. J. R. Green's History of the English People, i. 259 *seqq.*

[2] See the references to the Opus Majus and the Epistola de Secretis Operibus Artis et Naturae, in L. Schneider, Roger Bacon, 3; and compare *ib.*, 4.

[3] For the known facts of Roger Bacon's life and for summaries of his

Bacon, born in 1214 near Ilchester in Somersetshire, sprang from a well-to-do family; for he speaks of his brother as wealthy, and was himself able to spend considerable sums on books and instruments. But the troubles of Henry III's reign interfered with the prosperity of the family, and drove some members of it into exile. After carrying on his studies at Oxford and (as is said) taking orders in the year 1233, Bacon resided at Paris, where the rivalry of the Franciscan and Dominican Orders was then attracting public attention. But the theological discussions in which this rivalry found expression, the philosophy which while pretending to base itself upon Aristotle neglected a complete and careful survey of the very author to whom it consistently appealed, and the disregard of experimental methods in the cultivation of so-called physical science, were alike unsatisfactory to his mind; and when, in or before 1250, he returned to Oxford, he may be held to have fully determined upon his own courses and methods of study. It seems to have been about this time that, after taking at Paris the degree of doctor of theology, he entered the Franciscan Order. His fame as a teacher rose so high that, according to the fashion of the age of scholasticism, he was known by the distinctive appellation of '*doctor mirabilis.*' About 1257, however, his lectures were interdicted by the General of his Order, and he was commanded to quit Oxford for Paris, where he was placed under strict supervision, and prohibited from writing for publication. But on the accession in 1265 to the Papacy of Clement IV, that Pope, a friend of the sciences, requested Bacon to send him a treatise on them; and in eighteen months Bacon completed his Opus Majus, Opus Minus, and Opus Tertium, and despatched them by a friendly hand to the Pope. Soon (in 1267)

writings see, in addition to the notices in Mr. Brewer's Introduction to the Opus Tertium and other previously unpublished works of the philosopher, E. Charles, Roger Bacon, sa vie, ses ouvrages et ses doctrines (Paris, 1861); L. Schneider, Roger Bacon Ord. Min. (Augsburg, 1873); and Professor R. Adamson's article on Roger Bacon in the new edition of the Encyclopædia Britannica, which last I have used without ceremony.

permission was given to him to return to Oxford, where he continued his studies, and in 1271 produced his Compendium Studii Philosophiae. The attacks contained in this work, not only upon the insufficiency of the existing studies, but upon the ignorance and vices of the clergy and monks, were the main cause of the persecution which now befell him. His books were condemned by the General of his Order, and in 1278 he was thrown into prison, where he appears to have remained for fourteen years. In the year of his release, 1292, he produced what is probably his latest work, the Compendium Studii Theologiae; and it would seem that two years afterwards he died.

To the two later periods of Bacon's residence at Oxford, from 1250 to 1257, and from 1268 to his imprisonment, may be assigned the origin of such local legends as came to cluster round his name, and of his popular fame in England at large. Among those with whom he had been intimate as a student was the famous Robert Grosseteste, afterwards Bishop of Lincoln, whom popular tradition asserted to have been like Bacon the inventor of a Brazen Head[1]; and among the faithful companions of his researches was Friar Thomas or John de Bungaye[2], whose name is coupled with that of Friar Bacon in the fictions of the Elizabethan story-book. Friar Bacon's connexion with Brasenose College, on the other hand, must be mythical—for the best of reasons. Brasenose College was not in existence in the thirteenth century[3]; but there is no reason why Bacon should not be supposed to have resided in or near one of the halls out of which the College grew. These halls or houses may have been of very ancient date, and it is just possible that one of them may have already in Bacon's time borne the name of Brasin- or Brazen-house. In any case, already in the Elizabethan age, Miles Windsore, whose manuscript notes Hearne reproduced in a volume of his

Traditional connexion of Bacon with Brasenose.

[1] So Butler in Hudibras, Part II. canto iii, speaks of 'Old Hodge Bacon and Bob Grosted.' (The same satirist refers to Friar Bacon's 'noddle of brass,' *ib.*, canto i.)

[2] See FRIAR BUNGAY in notes on Dramatis Personae of Friar Bacon.

[3] See as to Brasenose College, note on Friar Bacon, ii. 11.

Diary[1], connected the story of Friar Bacon's wonderful Brazen Head with the well-known 'brazen nose' in the face over Brasenose College gate, from which nose the college was supposed to have derived its name; and reported that a likeness, either of Bacon or of the Head, was kept in the secret recesses of the *Aula*, i. e. the *Aula Philosophiae*, which once occupied part of the site of the present Brasenose College. His chemical studies the Friar was said to have carried on in one of the secluded places of retreat then common at Oxford, and his astrological in an observatory in the tower of the church in the neighbouring village of Sunningwell. See Hearne's Diary, vol. civ. pp. 166-169:

His places of study in and near Oxford.

'*The second commaundment is ffore this werk* [chemica ars] *thou haue a specialle priue place from mennes sight with* 2. *chambres or* 3. *to make these sublimations fixations calcinations solutions distillations and congelations.* Such private places were common in Oxford. ffryer Bacon always desired such retirement, whenever he searched into the secrets of nature. 'tis true, the place, in the South suburbs of Oxford, is now very common, but in his time it was much more private; tho' after all I do not think that at that place he carryed on any chymical Experiments, or even the Machines for wch he hath been so famous ever since, even among the vulgar, who daily speak of his brazen Head, a thing wch nevertheless others were noted for performing, as well as he, as the famous Mr. Thomas Allen, of Gloucester-Hall, hath sufficiently shown in a MS. of the Bodleian Library. Unless I am mistaken, the Place, known now by the name of his Study (the lower part whereof is certainly very old) was used by him chiefly for his

[1] See Hearne's Diary, MSS. Bodleian., vol. cxxxii. pp. 73, 74. After the passage quoted in the above note the Diary continues: 'Cujus Baconem mathematicum praedicat antiquitas authorem eo loci artibus mathematicis exstinctum. Cujus simulacrum in imis aulae penetralibus sopitum in umbras repositum fertur. At penes authorem fides esto.' The construction of the first of these sentences is the reverse of transparent; but it seems impossible to doubt that the antecedent of the *cujus* with which it begins is 'imago aenea facie' in the previous sentence; and that it is either to the same word or to 'Baconem' that the 'cujus' of the next sentence refers.

Astronomical Studies, and here I believe he penned many of his writings, that any thing related to that Subject, whilst what he did in Chymistry was carried on by him in places more private, sometimes in the Suburbs . . . in wch there was also a fine grove of trees, now a bare meadow, and sometimes at Sunningwell, then much more retired than even at this time, abundance of woods having been destroyed thereabouts. . . . At Sunningwell they have the tradition of ffryer Bacon's studying there to this day, where (according to the same tradition) he had an Observatory, and that too upon the Tower of the Church. There is always some ground for such sort of Tradition, and 'tis not therefore to be despised. 'Tis very likely that he might often go up to the top of that Tower and make his observations, tho' (as I take it) the Church and the Tower have been much altered since his day. . . . Other Scholars of Oxford had, in those times, likewise their retiring Places, in imitation of ffryer Bacon, whose Example was much followed, he being indeed a Prodigy of Learning, wch made him so much taken notice of by all sorts of people, that he was prosecuted as a magician, tho' he writ against that practice.'

Popular ideas on the studies of Bacon. His supposed inventions.

Of the real nature of Bacon's studies, and of the method by which he sought to give unity to them, the popular mind necessarily had no conception. 'His fame in popular estimation,' says Professor Adamson, 'has always rested on his mechanical discoveries,' although 'careful research has shown that very little in this department can with accuracy be ascribed to him. He certainly describes a method of constructing a telescope, but not so as to lead one to conclude that he was in possession of that instrument. Gunpowder, the invention of which has been claimed for him on the ground of a passage in one of his works, which fairly interpreted at once disposes of any such claim, was already known to the Arabs. Burning-glasses were in common use, and spectacles it does not appear he made, although he was probably acquainted with the principle of their construction.' As to the invention of gunpowder, the popular story-book in which the legend of Friar Bacon was stereotyped is, oddly enough, silent. As to the telescope, the statement of Bacon in his work on Perspective that by refraction the Sun, and Moon, and Stars might (by being represented as nearer) be made to *appear* to descend, may have given rise to a belief in possessing a power ascribed to magic from a very early date[1]. But, the 'glass prospective,' commemorated both in the story-book and in our play, seems to be a combination in the popular mind of the *camera obscura* and burning-glass and the telescope, all of which Bacon was supposed to have invented or used. In his Opus Majus he states that by artificial condensation of the air and arrangement of several mirrors a variety of '*appericationes*' can be produced, whereby the foes of the realm and the infidels may be terrified; the apparition of camps of soldiers and of armies in the air (*visio reflexiva*[2]), *i.e.* the so-called *fata morgana*, he says, is regarded by some as diabolical sorcery, whereas such phenomena have a perfectly natural explanation. Julius Caesar, he continues, used large mirrors in Gaul, in order to discover the position of the enemy; burning-glasses in particular are very useful in war, and in time to come the Devil will by such means set fire to town, villages, etc. Hence Bacon calls the burning-glass (*speculum comburens*) a miraculous work[3]. The vulgar of course connected the use of these instruments with the practices of magic, in which it was thought feasible 'to make a spirit appear in a crystal[4]'—more especially angels, who

The Magical Glass.

[1] See note to Doctor Faustus, iii. 38.

[2] A mirror producing such results was made by the enchanter Virgil 'of his clergie,' in which the Romans might behold their enemies 'by thritty mile about.' See Gower's Confessio Amantis, bk. v. A magical mirror was, as has been seen, also attributed to Pope Gregory VII; compare Görres in Scheible's Kloster, ii. 30.

[3] See Schneider, *u. s.*, 82, 83.

[4] See R. Scot's Discovery of Witchcraft, bk. xv. ch. xvii. Compare the glass borne by the last of the Eight Kings who appear before Macbeth, and see Jonson's Alchemist, i. 1, where Face mentions among other tricks that of 'taking in of shadows with a glass.' This mode of divination was very common, and was 'usually conducted by confederacy; for the possessor of the glass seldom pretended to see the angels or hear their answers. His part was to mumble over some incomprehensible prayers; after which a *speculatrix*, a virgin of pure life, was called in

entered into the glass and gave responses, as the English astrologer William Lilley reports, 'in a voice like the Irish, much in the throat'; whence also the allegorical fancy of wonderful glasses showing 'all things in their degree,' as they have been, are, or should be[1]. Of Bacon's reputation as an astrologer Mr. Adamson says that 'his wonderful predictions (in the De Secretis) must be taken cum grano salis; and it is not to be forgotten that he believed in astrology, in the doctrine of signatures, and in the philosopher's stone, and *knew* that the circle had been squared.' There appears to be little doubt that it was partly in consequence of his occupation with *astrologia judiciaria*, thoroughly as his notions in this respect agreed with those of his age, that Bacon acquired a popular notoriety sufficient to furnish a popular pretext for his persecution, the real cause of which was his spirit of liberty and reform. The belief in his powers of forecast long survived, and finds expression in a very pleasing poem of a later age (1604), by William Terilo, entitled A Piece of Friar Bacons Brazen-heads Prophesie,—a satire on the degeneracy of the times[2]. Of necromancy Bacon was an avowed opponent, and one of his lesser works[3] was directed against it.

His relations to astrology; and necromancy.

The Brazen Head.

As for the famous tradition of the Brazen Head itself, which may possibly have suggested the tradition of Roger Bacon's supposed connexion with Brasenose College, it is not peculiar to the legendary history of the Friar, but reappears in many other stories of magic and magicians. The enchanter Virgilius was said to have made certain images of the gods upon the Capitol at Rome, which by their motions and the 'clynking' of bells prepared the citizens for hostile attacks[4]. William

to inspect the crystal.' See Cunningham's note *l. c.*, and quotation from Lilly's Life.—As to the belief in magical mirrors among the ancient Greeks and Romans, see Maury, La Magie et l'Astrologie, etc., 437, 438.—The magic mirror is introduced in the scene of the Witches' Kitchen in Goethe's Faust.

[1] See Gascoigne's The Steel Glas, 55 *seqq.* in Arber's reprint.

[2] Printed in the Percy Society's Publications, vol. xv.

[3] De mirabili potestate Artis et Naturae. See Charles, *u. s.*, 45.

[4] See The Lyfe of Virgilius in Thoms' Early Prose Romances, ii. 20.

of Malmesbury relates how Gerbert (Sylvester II) owned a magical head, founded of metal, which prophesied. A similar head was said to have belonged to the illustrious Albertus Magnus[1]. A brazen head which could speak is reported by Gower to have been constructed by Roger Bacon's early friend Robert Grosseteste[2]. Nor, if Bacon's Brazen Head was not the first, was it the last of the series. Stow mentions a story of a head of clay made at Oxford in the reign of Edward II, which at a time appointed spake the mystic words: '*Caput decidetur;—Caput elevabitur;—Pedes elevabuntur supra caput*[3].' A similar head was said to have been made at Madrid by Henry de Villeine, which was afterwards taken to pieces by order of King John II of Castile (who died in 1450)[4]. And, from an earlier period, we may finally recall the idol or head said to have been worshipped by the Knights Templars—according to some made 'in figuram Baffometi,' and thence regarded as a proof that the Templars had secretly embraced Mahometanism[5]. Thus there is no need to take

[1] See the Introduction to the History of Friar Bacon, v, in Thoms' Early Prose Romances, iii. As to Albertus Magnus, see note on Doctor Faustus, i. 152.

[2] See Confessio Amantis, book iii:

'For of the grete clerk Grostest
I rede how busy that he was
Upon the clergie an heved of bras
To forge—and make it for to telle
Of suche thinges as befelle.
And seven yeres besinesse
He laide, but for the lachesse
Of half a minute of an houre
Fro firste he began laboure
He lost all that he hadde do.'

[3] See Thoms, *u. s.*

[4] *Ib.*

[5] See Wright's Sorcery and Magic, i. 60.—In Greene's Alphonsus King of Arragon, act iv, Mahomet speaks out of a brazen head to the priests and princely ambassadors.—I may add that in Sir Henry Taylor's drama, St. Clement's Eve, iii. 2, the two Austin Fathers, Buvulan and Betizan (agents employed to inflame the bigotry of the Paris populace, and to circumvent the rival of the Duke of Burgundy), are discovered in 'an apartment in the Château St. Antoine furnished with a brazen head fixed on a skeleton, crystal globes, magic mirrors, and celestial squares.'

refuge in the ingenious alchemistic 'explanation' of Sir Thomas Browne in his History of Vulgar Errors, bk. vii. ch. xvii:

'Every ear is filled with the story of Friar Bacon, that made a Brazen Head to speak these words, *Time is.* Which though there went not the like relations, is surely too literally received, and was but a mystical fable concerning the philosopher's great work, wherein he eminently laboured: implying no more by the copper head, than the vessel wherein it was wrought; and by the words it spake, than the opportunity to be watched, about the *tempus ortus*, or birth of the magical child, or philosophical King of Lullius, the rising of the *terra foliata* of Arnoldus; when the earth, sufficiently impregnated with the water, ascendeth white and splendent. Which not observed, the work is irrecoverably lost, according to that of Petrus Bonus, "Ibi est operis perfectio aut annihilatio; quoniam ipsâ die oriuntur elementa simplicia depurata, quae egent statim compositione, antequam volent ab igne." Now letting slip the critical opportunity, he missed the intended treasure: which had he obtained, he might have made out the tradition of making a brazen wall about England: that is, the most powerful defence or strongest fortification which gold could have effected.'

The story of Friar Bacon's Brazen Head became a favourite subject of allusion in popular literature; it is more than once referred to by the Elizabethan dramatists [1]; and the Friar's great namesake on a memorable occasion pointed with it the advice he offered to his royal mistress [2]. The version of it

[1] So in Jonson's Every Man in his Humour, i. 4, Cob says: 'Oh, an' my house were the Brasen-head now!' (so that this may have been a popular sign for a house), 'faith it would e'en speak *Mo' fools yet.*' Compare also in Greene's Tu Quoque, or The City Gallant (printed in 1614, but said to have been acted before Queen Elizabeth):—

'Look to yourself, sir;
The brazen head has spoke, and I must leave you.'

[2] See Bacon's Apology concerning the Earl of Essex (of his advice to the Queen as to taking proceedings against Essex for his conduct in Ireland), Spedding's Letters and Life of Bacon, iii. 152: 'Whereunto I said (to the end utterly to divert her), Madam, if you will have me to speak to you in this argument, I must speak to you as Friar Bacon's head

referred to on which Greene founded his play will be cited below, when I give the requisite extracts from the story-book in question, which was probably written towards the close of the sixteenth century.

The theosophy of Renascence.

The life of Roger Bacon is almost conterminous with the thirteenth century. In the next are already perceptible the beginnings of the long and manifold movement known as the Renascence, which was in the end to join its current to that of the Reformation. Its earliest home was Italy; and a new impulse was here first given to it by the study of Greek, facilitated by the consequences of the final overthrow of the Eastern Empire. In times which had accustomed themselves to clothe their theological studies in philosophical forms and to take these forms from the Greek philosopher Aristotle, this study could not fail to turn with special energy to Greek philosophy. The Platonic Academy of Florence resumed the speculations of the Platonic Academy of Athens which the Emperor Justinian had suppressed; and the last endeavours on the part of Pagan speculation to conceive of the world as an emanation of the Deity became the beginnings of the *theosophy* of the Renascence. Eager to find a dogmatic exposition of mystic conceptions incomprehensible to the outer multitude—for nothing is more characteristic of the Renascence than its 'Odi profanum vulgus et arceo'—leading spirits of the Renascence both in Italy and in Germany sought refuge in the Cabbalistic or secret books in which Jewish learning had developed its ideas of the system of the Universe and its Divine government, and had sanctified them by an appeal to primitive revelation[1]. To penetrate into the inner life of Nature, to learn her hidden truths, to

Cabbalistic studies

spake, that said first, *Time is*, and then *Time was*, and *Time would never be;* for certainly (said I) it is now far too late, the matter is cold and hath taken too much wind.' It was certainly a maxim that Queen Elizabeth needed being reminded of on many occasions, which Bacon clothed in the form of the old story, and which Goethe has repeated in his wise lines beginning,

'Niemand versteht zur rechten Zeit.'

[1] See note to Friar Bacon, ii. 106.

understand the conflict of the powers at work in her system, was the aim of what at once sought to be a religious, and to become a natural, philosophy. And here more than ever it was inevitable that the conceptions and practices of magic should associate themselves with such cravings and studies; that astrology and alchemy should re-assert their endeavours to lay bare the secrets of Nature; and that she should be called upon to reveal of all her powers those which men most thirsted to control—the power of making gold and that of giving life[1].

The *scholastici vagantes.*

The Renascence movement, which bridged so wide a distance of time, likewise, in conjunction with the geographical discoveries of the fifteenth century, and the love of travel and adventure everywhere engendered, did much to throw down the barriers of place. Formerly students had migrated in masses or whole bodies of doctrine had been carried from University to University, transplanting as it were part of Paris to Oxford and Oxford to Prague; now the individual has become cosmopolitan, and we are in the age of the *scholastici vagantes*, the knights-errant of the New Learning, possessed of and practising a multitude of arts, and masters of a mysterious variety of knowledge. They are seen at the courts of kings and princes, in the rapidly multiplying Universities, in the houses and homes of every class of men. They are famous physicians, like Theophrastus Paracelsus, academical lecturers like Giordano Bruno, knights whose pen is ready to be turned into a sword like Ulrich von Hutten. In Germany more especially, which the Renascence and the Reformation are combining to make the centre of the intellectual life of Europe, and where the art of printing is first used as an agency working upon the mind of the people at large, a whole succession of scholars whom the multitude is apt to regard, and the Church is willing to see regarded, as sorcerers, hurriedly carry the torch from hand to hand. The South-west, whence the national highroad of the Rhine flows past seat after seat of clerical and learned life, whence communication is easiest with France and Switzerland and Italy,—the

The German South-west.

[1] See Kuno Fischer, *u. s.*, pp. 62, 63.

home of the High-German tongue and of its ancient literary glories, the birth-place of the new art of printing and the foster-mother of the Reformation,—is the region most favourable to the growth of speculative genius. Here Reuchlin taught in the University of Tübingen and gained his victory over the Obscure Men of Cologne; here Johann Tritheim was born (1462) in the village from which he took his name on the left bank of the Mosel, and after many wanderings pursued his studies at Heidelberg, and spent his latter years as abbot of the Benedictine monastery of Sponheim, which he exchanged for another abbacy at Würzburg, where he died in 1516. Encouraged by the goodwill of the Emperor Maximilian I, he wrote on many subjects and in many branches of literature, especially theology, but his studies likewise extended to the physical and metaphysical speculations, and in his Steganographia he approached the boundary-line between cabbalism and magic. Though he condemned necromancy and witchcraft, the vulgar persisted in believing him a magician; and stories virtually identical with some afterwards told of Doctor Faustus were told of him[1]. Tritheim was the reputed master of Paracelsus and of Cornelius Agrippa von Nettesheim, a native of Cologne, whose life is sketched elsewhere[2]. All these personages popular report represented as magicians, and upon the lives and characters of all it fastened features which reappear in the popular legend of the last of the great magicians, Doctor Faustus.

Tritheim.

His pupils.

It had long been the practice of orthodoxy to proclaim the connexion which is thus expressed by a Catholic[3] of the sixteenth century: '*Crescit cum magia hæresis, cum hæresi magia.*' But undoubtedly the influence of the Reformation movement, which had widely sapped the popular belief in the remedy which the miracles of the Church provided against the machinations of the Devil, itself increased the

Increase of popular belief in sorcery and witchcraft in the Reformation and following ages.

[1] Compare note on Doctor Faustus, ix. 68 (Tritheim summons the shadow of Mary of Burgundy before the Emperor Maximilian). As to the life and writings of Tritheim, see Scheible's Kloster, iii. 1012-1064.

[2] See CORNELIUS in notes on Dramatis Personae of Doctor Faustus.

[3] Thomas Stapleton (Bellarmine's tutor). See Maury, *u. s.*, 192.

popular belief in these perils. The century of the Reformation and that which succeeded to it were the period in which the belief in necromancy and witchcraft reached its height. Warning voices were indeed not wanting to protest against the perils of popular credulity; some of these, as has been seen, were those of the very men who were decried or persecuted as sorcerers. In England, says an eminent historian[1], 'the belief in the reality of witchcraft was strongly rooted in the minds of the population. James I, in his book on Dæmonology, had only echoed opinions which were accepted freely by the multitude, and were tacitly admitted without enquiry by the first intellects of the day. Bacon and Raleigh alike took the existence of witches for granted. In 1584, indeed, Reginald Scot[2], wise before his time, had discoursed to ears that would not hear on the shallowness of the evidence by which charges of witchcraft were sustained, but even Reginald Scot did not venture to assert that witchcraft itself was a fiction. A few years later, Harsnet[3], who rose to be Bishop of Norwich and Archbishop of York, charged certain Jesuits and priests with imposture in pretending to eject devils from possessed persons, in sheer forgetfulness of the fact that these priests did no more than take in sober earnestness the belief which was all around them. That the tide, however, was beginning to turn, there is a slight indication in The Witch of Edmonton[4], a play produced on the London stage about 1622, the authors of which directed the compassion of their hearers to an old woman accused of having entered into a league with Satan. . . Yet

England.

[1] Gardiner, Personal Government of Charles I, i. 28, 29.

[2] Discovery of Witchcraft; and also A Discourse upon Divels and Spirits; both of which I have several times cited in my notes in this volume.—George Giffard's Dialogue concerning Witches and Witchcraft (reprinted in the Percy Society's Publications, vol. viii) is likewise noticeable as showing a critical and temperate spirit in the author, who however does not present himself as a disbeliever in the superstition itself.

[3] From Harsnet's book Shakespeare took some hints for the scene in King Lear (iii. 4) where Edgar appears 'disguised as a madman.'

[4] By Ford, Dekker, and (according to the publishers) William Rowley (not Samuel, who made 'additions' to Doctor Faustus).

even here the old woman was treated as being in actual possession of the powers which she claimed.' The accession of a king who not only gave credit to the fiction of dæmonology, but rejoiced in proclaiming his belief, could not but intensify the popular sentiment. The law making witchcraft punishable by death was not repealed in England till 1736[1]. It is needless to add that our Elizabethan and early Stuart dramatic literature largely deals with themes concerned with practices of witchcraft[2], astrology[3], and alchemy[4]; while a hellish sorcerer is a prominent figure in the great allegorical epic of the Elizabethan age[5]. The idea of an actual compact between the Devil and a sorcerer, however, in the later plays of this period only appears as a satiric allusion[6], or is converted into a theme for comic treatment[7], as indeed it is in one popular comedy improperly (as it seems to me) ascribed to Shakespeare—The Merry Devil of Edmonton[8]. In following the shameful tradition which attributed the glorious achievements of the Maid of Orleans to a compact with the Powers of Hell, Shakespeare, if he was the author of these passages in 1 Henry VI, adhered to the belief kept alive in English minds by a popular chronicler[9].

Testimony of the English drama.

[1] See Lecky, History of England in the Eighteenth Century, i. 267.

[2] See especially Macbeth; Middleton's The Witch; and Heywood and Brome's The Lancashire Witches, besides Jonson's The Sad Shepherd and the Mask of Queens.

[3] See Tomkis's Albumazar, which is not however original.

[4] See above all Jonson's The Alchemist, where the treatment is of course satirical, as it is in Fletcher's The Chances.

[5] Archimago in the Faerie Queene.

[6] So in C. Tourneur's The Atheist's Tragedie, iv. 3.

[7] See Jonson's The Devil is an Ass.—The Birth of Merlin, which was published in 1662 as the work of Shakespeare and William Rowley, is a different kind of play, which of course follows the old legend.

[8] The legend of Peter Fabel of Edmonton, who sells his soul to the Evil One, but contrives to outwit the purchaser, is said to be identical with the German popular story, afterwards turned into English verse under the title of The Smith of Apolda, and thus published in The Original, and reprinted in Thoms' Lays and Legends of Germany. This I have not at hand; but it is noticeable that in the English legend the hero is a University man (of the age of Henry VII)—I regret to say, educated at the most ancient College in Cambridge.

[9] Holinshed, who in one of his versions of the end of Joan states

Germany. On the continent, and especially in Germany, the popular belief in the infernal origin of practices of sorcery attached itself to a wide variety of personages—from the *scholastici vagantes* of whom Hans Sachs had already brought an example on the stage[1], to an Elector of the Empire such as Joachim II of Brandenburg (1535–1571). In France charges of this kind were even brought against a king (Henry III) and his royal mother (Catharine de' Medici). But if princes were the patrons of necromancy (as they were more especially of alchemy), they likewise persecuted its practice with the utmost severity; thus we find an edict of the Elector Augustus of Saxony (of the year 1572), proclaiming the penalty of death by fire against whosoever 'in forgetfulness of his Christian faith shall have entered into a compact, or hold converse or intercourse, with the Devil, *albeit such person by magic may do no harm to any one*[2].' The clause I have italicised strikes me as particularly significant. In vain did a writer such as Johannes Wierus (Wier or Weiher) seek, in the spirit of Reginald Scot, to stem the tide of popular prejudice, and to vindicate the memory of those whose fame, like that of Cornelius Agrippa, had by that prejudice been converted into infamy. Wierus' noble effort (1583[3]) in the cause of reason, and the partial protest of his contemporary Augustine Lercheimer (1585[4]), were outclamoured by eager

that she was found, at the enquiry conducted by the Bishop of Beauvais, 'all damnably faithless to be a pernicious instrument to hostility and bloodshed in devilish witchcraft and sorcery.'

[1] See his Der Fahrende Schüler mit dem Teufelspannen (The Scholar-Errant with the Devil's bans).

[2] The *constitutiones* of the Elector Augustus were drawn up on the basis of the Carolina (the code of the Emperor Charles IV, who appears occasionally to have patronised magicians). See R. Calinich, Aus dem sechszehnten Jahrhundert, 289, 290.

[3] See Scheible's Kloster, ii. 187–205.

[4] See *ib.*, v. 263–348; and compare Düntzer, Die Sage von Faust, 73. Lercheimer protests against the prevalent treatment of witches, who, he says, should be taken to the physician and the sacristan rather than to the judge and the magistrate. He, however, advocates a more rigorous treatment of sorcerers, conjurors, and jugglers than they have hitherto received.

witnesses to the truth of the popular superstitions and of the narratives by which they were supported, such as above all Bodinus (1591)[1], whom Fischart translated into German, and Hondorff (1572)[2]. Thus fostered, these beliefs flourished in Germany through the sixteenth and part of the seventeenth century, the troubles of which furnished them with new materials. But of these all notice must be left aside. The neighbouring countries were not in advance of Germany; the last personage widely believed to have entered into a compact with the Evil One was the French Marshal Luxembourg (1628–1695), whose Dialogues in the Kingdom of the Dead with Doctor Faustus were a catchpenny of the year 1733[3]; and if Germany had its Faustus in the sixteenth century, Bohemia had had its Zytho in the fifteenth (in the age of Charles IV), and Poland had its Twardowski, said to have been a contemporary of the German magician, of whose legend his is a reflexion or a singularly close parallel[4]. How the story of Faustus found a ready welcome in the Netherlands and in France, as it did in England, will be immediately shown.

Neighbouring countries.

The supposition[5], first put forward as early as 1621 by the Tübingen theologian Schickard, that the story of Faustus is a legendary fiction pure and simple, invented as a warning against practices of magic, is altogether untenable. Faust or Faustus was a real personage. His original German surname may be uncertain; for the Latin form 'Faustus' in which his

Faustus a real person.

The name 'Faustus' or 'Faust.'

[1] See Scheible's Kloster, ii. 218–232.

[2] See *ib.*, 233–242.

[3] See *ib.*, v. 574–637.

[4] See *ib.*, xi. 526 *seqq.* Mr. Sutherland-Edwards has introduced the Polish Faust to English readers in a paper in Macmillan's Magazine, July, 1876.

[5] The literature on Faust and the Faust-legend has swelled to proportions so enormous that even an enumeration of its principal works is quite out of question here. Most of it is collected in vols. ii, iii, v, and xi of Scheible's Kloster, an uncouth repertory of odd learning indispensable to every student of the subject. Most of the information summarised in my text is taken from Düntzer's Die Sage von Doctor Johannes Faust, printed both in Schieble, vol. v, and in a separate edition, or from Baron von Reichlin-Meldegg's Die deutschen Volksbücher von Johann Faust und Christoph Wagner, &c., printed in Scheible, vol. xi; but I have also referred to a variety of other authorities.

name occasionally appears already in the oldest German literary version of the legend is obviously either a Latinisation of a native name, or a name bestowed on account of its significance. In the latter case 'Faust' would only be a Germanisation of 'Faustus,' which would mean much the same as 'Fortunatus,' a name familiar to mediæval legend and thence transplanted into the Elizabethan drama[1]. In the other, and more probable, case we may suppose the original German form to have been 'Faust,' or possibly 'Fust.' But the notion that Faustus or Faust the magician and Fust the printer are the same person, cannot be accepted. It was suggested by Dürr, an Altdorf professor of theology, in a letter written in 1676, but not published till 1726; and has since been adopted by various writers, including the German dramatists Klinger and Klingemann, who wrote plays on the subject, Heinrich Heine, F. V. Hugo (the French translator of Marlowe's tragedy), and no less an authority than the late Karl Simrock. But it must be rejected nevertheless. It rests primarily on the specious assumption, that the art of printing was regarded as an invention of the Evil One by the people, or decried as such by the monks. But of this there is no satisfactory proof. The story that the printer Johann Fust, who was in Paris in 1466, was there looked upon as a conjuror, has no historical foundation; just as there is no reason to attribute the dispersion of Fust and Schöffer's printing-establishment at Mainz in 1462 to any cause but the sack of the city by Archbishop Adolf of Nassau and its natural effects. The printer Fust in his Latin colophons never assumed the name of 'Faustus'; and there is no basis whatever for the ingenious fancy which identified or identifies him with the necromant[2].

Doctor Faustus not identical with the printer Fust.

[1] See Dekker's Olde Fortunatus. Hans Sachs has a 'Tragedia' on the same subject (1553). In one of the German puppet-plays on the story of Faustus, the hero asks for a purse which shall never be empty—Fortunatus's purse. See Simrock, Faust. Das Volksbuch und das Puppenspiel, 208.

[2] Mr. Sutherland-Edwards, I observe, thinks it 'just possible' that the printer may have been the father of the professor of the Black Art. This useless suggestion does not absolutely disagree, but does not very well tally, with the probable dates of the life and death of the latter.

Faust or Faustus shared his surname in its Latin form with several Christian ecclesiastics of the early Middle Ages, two of whom were canonised by the Church of Rome, while a third (Faustus Reiensis, i. e. bishop of Riez) was accounted a heretic by strict Augustinian orthodoxy[1]. The Christian name of the magician is in the legend with all but unvarying consistency given as John (Johannes or Johann), and is the same in several of the authentic notices of him as an actual personage[2]. But, oddly enough, there exist two notices of unquestioned authenticity, in which, under a distinct, but not altogether different, form of appellation, mention is made of a strolling necromant of precisely the same kind as the Doctor Johannes Faustus of other authentic notices and of the legend. In the year 1507 the already mentioned Tritheim informs a friend that in an inn at Gelnhausen (in the countship of Hanau) he had found traces of a personage to whose acquaintance Tritheim's friend had been looking forward with eager curiosity. On Tritheim's approach the impostor had decamped, but he had left behind him a card for a citizen of Gelnhausen identical with one he had sent to Tritheim's friend, and bearing his name (without his address) and 'additions' as follows:

The Christian name of Doctor Faustus.

Who was 'Georgius' Sabellicus or 'Faustus'?

'Magister Georgius Sabellicus, Faustus junior, fons necromanticorum, magus secundus, chiromanticus, agromanticus [query aeromanticus?], pyromanticus, in hydra arte secundus.'

This worthy, whom in another passage of his letter Tritheim calls simply 'Georgius Sabellicus,' he proceeds to describe as having at Würzburg blasphemously boasted his power to equal the miracles of Christ, and having in this year 1507 through the good offices of Franz von Sickingen (the famous

[1] A mention of this Faustus by Sebastian Frank (1531) is rather misleadingly quoted by Scheible, ii. 271.

[2] Is it worth noticing that the name of Tritheim (said to have been Faust's instructor) was Johann?—The Christian name of Goethe's Faust is Henry; because neither in Goethe's day nor at the present could a German reader or audience tolerate a 'Johann' as taking part in any but a *comic* love-scene.

knight of that name) obtained a post as schoolmaster at Kreuznach. Soon, however, he had to quit the place in haste, having been guilty of the most shameful immorality. A few years later (in 1513 or 1514), another witness of unimpeachable trustworthiness, the celebrated humanist and friend of Reuchlin and Melanchthon, Mutianus Rufus (Conrad Mudt), writes to a friend that 'a week ago there came to Erfurt a chiromant, by name Georgius Faustus Helmitheus Hedebergensis, a mere braggart and fool. His art, like that of all sorcerers, is vain, and such a physiognomy is lighter than a water-spider (*typula*, i. e. *tippula*). The ignorant marvel thereat. The theologians should rise against him, instead of seeking to annihilate Reuchlin. I heard him jabber at the inn; I did not chastise his ignorance; for what is the folly of others to me?' It would therefore appear that by this time the adventurer in question, whoever he was, called himself Faustus without adding the word 'junior,' but using epithets which can hardly have any other signification than 'semi-divine' (ἡμίθεος[1]), and 'of the University of Heidelberg'—then a seat of learning of specially high repute. The question arises whether this personage (for Tritheim's and Mutianus's man are manifestly the same) is to be regarded as identical with the Doctor *Johannes* Faustus or John Faust, of whom there is no trace before the year 1525, and to whom it would therefore be surprising if a competing necromant had as early as 1507 sought to compare himself as 'junior' or 'secundus.' Was this man's surname really Faust, or was it Sabellicus? The latter can hardly have been, as has been thought, a mere Latinisation, but must surely have been adopted in allusion to the Sabine magic mentioned by the Roman poets—and indeed Widmann speaks of the hero of his narrative, Johannes Faustus, as having studied among other books 'Sabellicum Ennead[2].' If George and John Faust were one and the same

[1] Hemithea, it may be worth noticing, was a goddess who, as Diodorus Siculus states, in the Thracian Chersonnese exercised the same miraculous powers as those ascribed to Isis. See Maury, *u. s.*, 239.

[2] Part I. chap. iv; Scheible's Kloster, ii. 297. The Enneades are a collection of treatises by Plotinus.

person, then it is not absolutely impossible that George may have assumed the name of John in memory either of the printer John Fust or Faust, or of some earlier necromant of note bearing that name. But there is no obvious connexion between the reputation of the printer and the sort of notoriety a strolling charlatan endeavoured to acquire; while of an earlier necromant John Faust or Faustus no real evidence whatever exists. On the other hand, there is no improbability in the supposition of George and John Faust having been competitors, although the evidence of the notoriety of John is later in date than that of the vagabond who called himself 'junior' and in some branches of his profession 'secundus.' The unwarranted assumption by popular entertainers of a name to which they have no birth-right has, I believe, been a common practice in much later times than those in question; and if a 'Johannes Faustus,' who according to the Heidelberg registers took his degree there as bachelor of divinity in 1509, was the same person as the famous Doctor, Georgius may perchance have decorated himself not only with the surname of Johannes, but also with the name of his University. But this is quite uncertain, more especially as the register attaches to the name the letter '*d*,' signifying '*dedit*,' i. e. he paid his fees.

Evidence as to the real (Johannes) Faustus.

Passing by the statement of the Württemberg historian Sattler, that according to 'trustworthy information,' which he does not cite, a Doctor Faust in the year 1516 visited his fellow-countryman and good friend the Abbot Johann Entenfuss in his monastery at Maulbronn (in Württemberg), we come to the well-authenticated notices of the real Faust or Faustus by persons who were actually or nearly contemporary with him. In these can hardly be included the famous inscriptions in Auerbach's Cellar, an ancient wine-tavern and vault at Leipzig. One of these inscriptions appears to make reference (by the words 'at this time,' '*zu dieser Frist*') to a date, 1525, twice written on the wall, where a fresco still recalls the magician's exploit of riding out of the cellar on a wine-butt, and another represents him as treating a party of students with its contents[1]. The date 1525 is said to be of

[1] These pictures are described and the inscriptions quoted in a note to

proved authenticity, and is unhesitatingly adopted in Vogel's Leipzig Annals, published in 1714. It was possibly from the Leipzig legend that Widmann, in his version of the story of Faustus,—where, on the evidence of a book 'with concealed letters,' he states Faustus's contract with the Devil to have been sealed in 1521,—took the date of 1525 as that of the beginning of the conjuror's public career.

Contemporary notices.

The first known writer who mentions Faustus as a real personage is Dr. Philip Begardi, physician to the Free Imperial City of Worms, in his Index Sanitatis of 1539. He there speaks of 'Faustus' as a famous necromant and medical quack, who 'a few years ago' travelled about 'through all countries, principalities and kingdoms, and made his name known by everyone there.' He made, says Begardi, no secret of it himself, adding to it the title of 'philosophus philosophorum.' In 1545, another medical writer, Conrad Gesner of Zurich, mentions a 'Faustus quidam' as famous among the 'scholastici vagantes' who practised magic, and as not long since dead. In the second edition, 1548, of a book of historical anecdotes of which the first volume was published in its first edition in 1543, the Protestant theologian Johann Gast relates two stories of Faustus's marvellous doings; the scene of one being laid in the Palatinate, that of the other, which Gast narrates as an eye-witness, in the Great College at Basel. Gast mentions the wonderful dog which, together with a similarly uncanny horse, attended Faustus, and the magician's terrible death—but these things only on hearsay. A still more remarkable piece of evidence is furnished by the Locorum Communium Collectanea, published at Basel in 1562 by Manlius (Johann Mennel of Ausbach), a pupil of Melanchthon, of whose sayings the collection professes to a great extent to consist. In this book Melanchthon (for it is clearly he who is supposed to be speaking) says that he was acquainted with one of the name of Faustus, of Kundling, a small town near his own native place[1], who studied and learnt

Hayward's Translation of Goethe's Faust (6th edition, 186), in which the scene in Auerbach's Cellar is immortalised.

[1] Melanchthon was born at Bretten in the Lower Palatinate.

magic at Cracow, and practised his devilish art at Venice and elsewhere. 'A few years ago' he met with his death 'in a village of the Duchy of Württemberg,' having predicted a terrible event for the night in which he died, and being found in the morning dead in his bed with his face twisted, 'so the devil had killed him.' Melanchthon proceeds to mention that this Faustus, whom he call 'Johannes,' had a dog 'who was the Devil'; and that he twice made his escape from impending imprisonment, on one occasion from 'our town of Wittenberg,' where 'the excellent prince, Duke John' had ordered his arrest, and on another from Nürnberg. He adds that 'this conjuror Faustus, an infamous *bestia*, a *cloaca* of many devils,' boasted that all the victories gained by the Imperial armies in Italy were due to his magic, 'which,' adds Manlius, 'for the sake of the young, lest they should at once give credit to such fellows,' 'was the emptiest of lies.' Melanchthon is likewise said to mention Faustus in his letters; but the passage has not proved discoverable. On the other hand, in Luther's Table-Talk (*Tischreden*) published posthumously in 1566, it is stated that the conversation one evening at supper turned on a necromant called Faustus, whereupon Doctor Martin solemnly said: 'The Devil doth not use the services of the magicians against me: had he been able and strong enough to do harm to me, he would have done so long ago. He has in truth more than once had me by the head; but yet he was constrained to let me go.' This shows that the name of Faustus was well known at Wittenberg, and confirms the statement of his visit there attributed by Manlius to Melanchthon, whose own residence at Wittenberg lasted from 1518 to his death in 1560. Shortly after this, in 1561, the learned Conrad Gesner mentions Faust as a magician of the kind which had its origin at Salamanca, and called *fahrende Schüler*, and as a personage whose fame was extraordinary and who died 'not so very long since.' The next witness is the worthy and liberal-minded Wierus, in an edition of whose work De praestigiis daemonum &c., bearing date 1583, are found copied the statements reported by Manlius concerning the University studies and death of Faustus, and it is stated (possibly on the aûthority of Begardi) that Faustus practised magic shortly before 1540 in different parts of Germany. Wierus adds some stories of the conjuror's tricks, of one of which the scene is laid at Batenberg on the Maas, and of another at Goslar in the Harz. The Batenberg story is related on the personal authority of the chaplain 'Dr. Johann Dorst' who was the subject of the experiment (he was induced to shave himself by a fomentation of arsenic instead of a razor, and the consequences were very unpleasant). Another story is likewise given by Wierus on the authority of a man 'mihi non incognitus,' to whom in it an insulting speech is made by Faustus.

Appeals to contemporary evidence.

The theologian Heinrich Bullinger, who died in 1575, in his work against the Black Art speaks of the necromant Faustus as having lived 'in our times'; and in 1570 Bullinger's son-in-law, Ludwig Lavater, refers to the marvellous stories about the magical arts of 'the German Faustus'; while a contemporary or rather later writer on exorcism, Leonhard Thurnheisser, touches on the poverty and misery suffered by the magicians, mentioning Doctor Faustus as one of several instances seen 'in our times' of these 'wretched monsters.' In 1572 Andreas Hondorff in his Promptuarium Exemplorum repeats the statements in Manlius as to Johann Faustus's visits to Nürnberg and Wittenberg, and as to his death in a Würtemberg village; and they again re-appear in a work (1615) by the learned jurist Philip Camerarius, who says that he has 'heard many proofs of Johann Faust's eminence in magic from persons who were well acquainted with that impostor,' and tells a story (which afterwards re-appeared in the *Faustbuch*) of his conjuring up a vine full of grapes in the middle of winter, and deluding the company in the manner in which Mephistophiles befools the students at the close of the scene in the Cellar in Goethe's play. In 1585 appeared the Considerations on Magic of Augustine Lercheimer, a pupil of Melanchthon, in which occur several notices of Faustus, doubtless of Wittenberg origin. Lercheimer calls him 'Johann Faust of Knütlingen,' and tells stories of his doings at Wittenberg, at Salzburg, and at 'M.' (which Düntzer conjectures to be Magdeburg). He relates an interview between Faustus and Melanchthon, with a repartee of the divine to the vapourings of the sorcerer in Luther's robustest style, and gives the story of the attempted conversion of Faustus by an Old Pious Man, which found its way, together with some of Lercheimer's tales about *other* conjurors, into the *Faustbuch*, and thence into Marlowe's play.

We are now near the date at which the story of Doctor Faustus was to be made the theme of a popular story-book, and near the end of the list of notices possessing more or less value as historical evidence of the actual man. To this list may perhaps be added the statement cited from an old Erfurt chronicle by a later author, Motschmann, in his Erfordia Literata Continuata, as to the attempted conversion of Dr. Faust at Erfurt by the Guardian of the Franciscans Dr. Kling (who actually lived there from 1520 to 1556), of Faust's recalcitrance, and of his consequent expulsion from the city [1]. Probably, however, this incident was borrowed by the compiler of the old chronicle from an episode in the later edition of the popular story-book with which it almost verbatim agrees. The first edition of the story-book was, as will be immediately seen, published in 1587; and the statement in its Second Preface ('to the Christian Reader'), that Dr. Johann Faust 'lived within the memory of men,' is the last of such notices of him appealing to contemporary evidence as appear to be discoverable.

Dates of the public life of the real Faustus.

The writer of this story-book annotates the account of Faustus's dealings with Sultan Soliman (chap. xxvi) by the remark that 'Solimannus began his reign in 1519'; and it is therefore clear that he considers the life of Faustus to have been spent in the earlier half, and partly in the first quarter, of the sixteenth century. This agrees as well with the evidence as to chronology already cited, as with the dates on the wall at Leipzig, and with those given by Widmann, the author of a later literary version of the legend. But Widmann's dates fail to tally with the notices of Georgius

[1] Compare note to Doctor Faustus, xiii. 36.

Sabellicus or Faustus; and whether or not we assume him to have been a different person from the real Doctor Johannes Faustus, it will be safe to assign the public life of the latter to some time between the years 1510 and 1540. The places in which one or the other is stated to have made his appearances are, as has been seen, numerous already in the historical notices, which likewise mention as such Würzburg, Gotha, Meissen, and Prague; their number was largely increased by the legend, and was doubtless in the case of the actual Faustus very large and multifarious. Such comment as appears requisite in the case of one or two of these places, will be made further on, after some of the variations offered by the legend have been mentioned. It may here be added, that the various writings on magic attributed to the actual Doctor Faustus are all palpable forgeries. These tractates, of which the earliest is the famous 'Doctor Faustus's Triple Charm of Hell' (*Dreifacher Höllenzwang*), pretending to have been printed at Lyons in 1469, begin with the end of the sixteenth, or the early part of the seventeenth, century, and continue into the eighteenth[1]. The name of Faustus had by this time become, in one way or another, indispensable for every publication of the sort. Nor, on the other hand, will any value be attached to the assertion by Widmann in a passage of his commentary[2], that he is citing rhymes composed by Doctor Faustus himself, when he quotes some verses developing in German the sentiment:

Places in which he is said to have appeared.

His supposed writings

'Credite mortales, noctis potatio mors est;'

(which verses Doctor Faustus, he asserts, bore as his *symbolum* or motto when a student of medicine),—and a Latin distich, with its German translation, impressing a similar maxim and said to have been inscribed by Doctor Faustus 'in a physic book.' Almost as readily might we regard the

[1] See Reichlin-Meldegg, *u. s.*, xi. 549 *seqq.* Most, if not all, of this curious rubbish will be found in Scheible's earlier volumes.

[2] On Part I, chap. xiv; Scheible's Kloster, ii. 371, 372; compare Reichlin-Meldegg, *ib.*, xi. 726.

Doctor's narrative of his journey among the stars, which the old *Faustbuch* (chap. xxv) professes to copy from a manuscript written by Faustus himself and dedicated to his friend Jonas Victor, a physician of Leipzig,—or his second Contract with the Devil, which 'was found left behind him after his death,'—as genuine documents. Lastly, the personal appearance of the man must be left to the imagination, to which faculty doubtless already Rembrandt owed his conception of the famous magician, apparently varied by the great painter in at least three several etchings[1].

and pretended portraits.

In the latter part of the sixteenth century the name and story of Doctor Faustus had thus in Germany and its vicinity become typical of the figure and career of the strolling magician, who after selling his soul to the Evil One and thus acquiring the supernatural powers of which he gave evidence in the practice of his arts, had to pay the penalty of his bargain in a violent death. They were at the same time the name and story, not indeed of the last of the necromants, astrologers, and alchemists, but of the last of the cosmopolitan type of *scholastici vagantes* famed for their magical powers and doings. And thus it came to pass that all the wonderful tales which—some of them for centuries—had floated about among the people were fathered upon this the last representative of the mediaeval magicians. There is accordingly hardly one, if any, incident or feature in the legend of Faustus to which a parallel may not be found in one or more of the legends of his predecessors. His tricks are the old tricks; his adventures the old adventures; his canine companion is the dog of Agrippa and Friar Bungay; his death is the magician's traditional doom. Hence too the double nature of the purpose of Faustus's contract with the Devil. It is not knowledge only, or pleasure only, but both ends intermixed, to compass which he barters his soul. But the sixteenth century impresses a character of its own—and this in more than one respect—upon its condensation into a single collective legend of all these con-

The collective legend of Doctor Faustus.

General characteristics.

[1] See Moehsen's statement in Scheible, ii. 254. A coarse, but telling, woodcut 'after Rembrandt' accompanies this volume.

tributory stories. In the first place, the colour of the Faust-legend is altogether anti-Papal or anti-Roman; for the age of the Reformation delights in casting derision upon monks and priests, upon cardinals and upon the pope himself. Yet this age was far from being a rationalistic age; and as there has never been a firmer believer in the Devil than Luther himself was, so the fancy of the infernal compact never flourished with more vital vigour than in these times, when it was by no means confined to the uses of fiction [1]. It was an age which held most devoutly the doctrine of eternal punishment, and entertained no doubts as to the inevitable consequences of an obstinate revolt against the ordinances of religion. The greater *seriousness* distinguishing the age of the Reformation from those which had preceded it, gives a tragic dignity to its conception of the revolt of a human being against his God, and at the same time invests the spirit of such a defiance with what has been truly called a Titanic character [2]. The individual is contending against the Divine Order of things; and thus the legend of Faustus begins to acquire a significance, which later poetic genius was to develope, in a sense resembling that of the ancient Prometheus-myth [3].

The old Faust-buch.

The first, so far as we know, and for the purpose of the present enquiry the one important, form in which the legend of Faustus made its appearance in literature is the 'Historia of Dr. Johann Faust, the widely-noised conjuror and master of the Black Art, How he sold himself to the Devil against a fixed time, What in the meanwhile were the strange ad-

[1] See the notice in R. V. Mohl's account of the manners and behaviour of the students of the University of Tübingen in the sixteenth century (p. 70, 2nd edition), as to the proceedings of the Senate against a student of the name of Leipziger, said to have sold himself to the Devil when in want of 'a little money,' in the year 1596. This curious incident is particularly apposite, on account of the connexion of Tübingen with the literary history of the Faust-legend noticed below.

[2] See Kuno Fischer, *u. s.*, 65.

[3] I cannot help referring with astonishment to a passage touching upon this familiar parallel in Mr. W. Watkiss Lloyd's interesting work The Age of Pericles, i. 334,—which passage must be left to the judgment of other critics.

ventures he witnessed, himself set on foot and practised, until at last he received his well-merited reward. Mostly collected and put in print from his own writings left by him, as a terrific instance and horrible example, and as a friendly warning to all arrogant, insolent-minded and godless men'; with the motto from the Epistle of St. James (iv. 7): 'Submit yourselves to God. Resist the devil, and he will flee from you.' This book, 'printed at Frankfort-on-the-Main by Johann Spies, in the year 1587,' is the *editio princeps* of the famous *Faustbuch* (as it is usually called, and as I have called it in the present volume), on which Marlowe founded his tragedy. The printer, in his Preface, states that the story was 'recently communicated and sent' to him 'through a good friend from Speyer' (in the Rhenish Palatinate).

Editio princeps and later editions.

Of this edition only a single copy exists in the Imperial Library at Vienna[1]. A second edition of the same year 1587 exists in two copies, one at Ulm and another at Wolfenbüttel; it differs to some extent in arrangement and is enlarged by some additional stories taken from Lercheimer. At least three editions exist of the year 1588; one of 1589; and one of 1590, which contains six additional chapters, taken from the old Erfurt Chronicle already mentioned, or (as seems more probable) taken by the Chronicle from this edition of the Faustbuch. There exist, or are mentioned, a number of later editions, among which that of 1598 is noticeable as professing in its title (for the edition itself has not been discovered) to narrate the doings of the three famous conjurors, Dr. Johann Faust, Christophorus Wagner, and Jacobus Scholtus. Of Wagner we shall hear more; 'Scholtus' is another form of Schotus, who on the title of the Wagnerbuch adverted to below appears as its author under the name of Fridericus Schotus Tolet (i. e. Toletanus,

[1] An exact and critical reprint of the *editio princeps* of the Faustbuch, with the variations of the edition of 1590, and Introduction and Notes, has been published by Dr. August Kühne, Zerbst, 1868. To this my quotations refer, and not to Scheible's reprint in vol. ii. of his Kloster, which is from the second edition, likewise of the year 1587.

of Toledo)—the name of a real man; for Professor Gindely has discovered notices of an alchemist named Scotus, who practised his art in the Netherlands, at Prague, and in different parts of Germany early in the seventeenth century [1].

The Wagnerbuch.

The popularity of the Faustbuch was in 1593 interfered with by the publication of the Wagnerbuch—an imitation or continuation professing to give an account of the doings of Doctor Faustus's famulus Wagner, whose adventures were of course a mere copy or expansion of those of Doctor Faustus himself [2]. Meanwhile already in 1588 had appeared a rhymed version of the Faustbuch [3]; and at some unknown, but doubtless early date a ballad on the story of Faustus, which is preserved in 'a broadside from Cologne,' was in circulation [4].

Rhymed Faustbuch and Ballad.

The supposition that in Germany the subject had likewise at once been treated in a dramatic shape seems to rest on a mistake [5]. A notice in the protocols of the Senate of the University of Tübingen, stating that by resolution of the Senate, dated April 18th, 1587, the printer Hock and the '*autores* of the *historia Fausti*' were to be arrested, and that the '*autor comoediae nuper habitae*' was to be put in the *carcer* (University prison), was misread [6], so as to identify the comedy with the history. What the comedy was is unknown; the '*historia Fausti*' must have been the rhymed version of the Faustbuch, published by Alexander Hock at Tübingen early in 1588 (with the date 1587). Whether a non-extant Latin drama, '*Justi Placidii: Infelix prudentia*' (Leipzig, 1598) treated the story of Faustus, or some other theme of the same kind, is unknown [7]. No play on the subject of Faustus can

Earliest German plays on Faustus.

[1] See Kühne's Introduction, xviii–xx.

[2] Compare WAGNER in notes on Dramatis Personae of Doctor Faustus.

[3] Reprinted in Scheible's Kloster xi. 1–211.

[4] See Düntzer, 223. This ballad was reprinted in the famous collection Des Knaben Wunderhorn by Arnim and Brentano, and is given in Scheible's Kloster, ii. 120–123.

[5] See W. Creizenach, Versuch einer Geschichte des Volksschauspiels vom Doctor Faust (Halle, 1878), 34–36.

[6] By Mohl, *u. s.*, 57.

[7] See Creizenach, *u. s.*, 36–40. The title 'Infelix Sapientia' was afterwards taken by a popular puppet-play on the story of Faustus.

be shown to have been produced on the German stage before the 'Tragoedia von Dr. Faust,' acted by the 'English Comedians' at Dresden in 1626, which was clearly Marlowe's[1]. From the latter part of the seventeenth century onwards the story of Faust frequently appeared on the German stage,—the first known instance being at Danzig in 1668, from which year we have the report of a performance recalling in its main features Marlowe and the Faustbuch[2]. Out of these popular dramas again arose that long succession of popular puppet-plays on the story of Faustus, which form the most interesting series of a branch of the German popular drama deserving, for reasons which cannot here be explained, the attention of all students of the history of dramatic literature or of the German national life[3].

Puppet-plays.

Meanwhile the legend of Faustus in its narrative form had courted a new class of readers in Germany, since in 1599 G. R. Widmann, a literary man of much (including a good deal of useless and even under the circumstances pernicious) learning and an ardent Lutheran, had published his greatly enlarged version of the story, accompanied by a commentary replete with examples and precepts more or less directly suggested by the text. This didactic version of the story was in 1674 jointly elaborated by a doctor of medicine, J. N. Pfitzer, and a doctor of divinity, C. W. Platz; and their version again was condensed into a shorter and more popular form in 1726 by an author who called himself 'one of Christian purpose' ('ein Christlich Meynender'), under which

Elaborations of the Faustbuch. Widmann, &c.

[1] See Creizenach, *u. s.*, 45.

[2] *Ib.*, 47.

[3] For a history of this treatment of the Faust-legend the reader must be referred to the work of W. Creizenach cited in a previous note (which only reached me as these pages were passing through the press), to the Introduction to C. Engel's Das Volksschauspiel Doctor Johann Faust (Oldenburg, 1874), where one of these plays is reprinted from the MS., and to Simrock's Faust. Das Volksbuch und das Puppenspiel (Frankfort-on-the-Main, 1877). In this last the endeavour—for which few were qualified like Simrock—is made to restore the old puppet-play from memory and from the reports of others. In an altered form the puppet-play of Faustus is said to be still performed on the most popular stages of this humble description.

designation he is known in the bibliography of the subject. This book is of importance, as the first smaller book on the Faust-legend in its most elaborate version, and as one which, together with its larger original, was read by Goethe in his youth. It is said still to be sold at fairs in Germany; and with it the growth of the popular legend as such in Germany may be held to close.

The Faustbuch and its story in other continental countries.

But from its native Germany the legend, as put into some sort of literary shape by the printer Spiess in 1587, had with extraordinary rapidity passed into the popular literature of other countries. A Low-German version had appeared at Lübeck in 1588; and thus it was easy for a Dutch translation to follow in 1592, which has no additions of note except a characteristic precision in the matter of dates—informing the reader for instance that the Evil One carried off Faustus in the night from the 23rd to the 24th of October, 1538, between the hours of 12 and 1 a.m. A close French translation had been put forth already in 1589 by Victor Palma Cayet, whose end according to tradition was the same as that of Doctor Faustus himself. There seems a trace, though an uncertain one, of the existence, in Holberg's day, of a popular version of the legend on the Danish stage; on the other hand there can be little doubt that the Polish story of Twardowski, already noticed, was elaborated with the help of the German Faustbuch. A Czechish puppet-play on the subject is also mentioned, but without a date. The Wagnerbuch was in its turn translated and adapted in several Dutch editions, the interest excited by it in the Netherlands doubtless arising from the circumstances that it professed to be by a Spanish author, and that the scene of its adventures was mostly laid in Spain. In France Wagner never attained to a similar popularity.

The story of Faustus in England.

At last we come to what for us possesses a more direct importance, the English versions of the legend of Doctor Faustus; and this brings us at once to what there is good reason to regard as the earliest of these versions, viz. Mar-

Date of Marlowe's tragedy.

lowe's tragedy itself. Now, though the earliest extant edition of this tragedy is the quarto of 1604, we find the following entry in the Registers of the Stationers' Company of London under date the 7th of January, 1600—i. e. 1601 N.S.: External evidence.

'7 Januarij

Thomas Bushell Entred for his copye under the handes of master Doctor BARLOWE and the Wardens a booke called *the plaie of Doctor FAUSTUS*[1].'

And between six and seven years before this, under the date of September 30th, 1594, we find in Henslowe's Diary[2] the first of a long series of notices of his share of receipts from this play. This first notice is a remarkable one, for it appears that Henslowe on this occasion

'R^{d} at Doctor Fustose . . . . iij^{li} xjj^{s},'

being the largest sum except one which, so far as I have observed, Henslowe ever notes as received by him as his share after a performance[3]. Between this date and the end of October, 1597, Henslowe has not less than 23 notices of receipts 'at Doctor Faustus,' most of which attest the popularity of the play, though by December, 1596, the receipts sink to 'ix^{s},' and by the January following to 'v^{s},' till one more repetition—in October—appears to bring in nothing at all. Now, though these entries by Henslowe begin as far back as February, 1592 (N.S.), when the first play entered is 'fryer bacone,' Doctor Faustus is not mentioned as acted before September 30th, 1594, and the amount of the receipts on this occasion certainly point to the performance having proved specially attractive. Henslowe does not however append to his mention of it the letters '*ne*' (new), as he usually does in the case of plays performed for the first time; and it is in itself unlikely, even supposing Doctor Faustus not to have been brought out in Marlowe's lifetime, that an unacted posthumous play by him should not have been performed till more than a year after his death,

[1] See Arber's Transcript of the Stationers' Registers, iii. 67 *b*.

[2] Collier's edition, 42.

[3] Oddly enough, 'the taner of Denmarke,' on account of which Henslowe on May 23, 1592, received 'iij^{li} xiij^{s} vj^{d}' as his share, and which he marks as a new play, does not appear to have been repeated. Tamburlaine brings in good sums on several occasions.

The performance in September, 1594, probably a revival with additions.

which occurred on June 1st, 1593. The conjecture is therefore not hazardous, that Henslowe and his company took advantage of the notoriety which that death had attracted to 'revive' a play which had for some time previously remained unacted, and which was not yet on sale as a book; and that very possibly it was already on this occasion—in September, 1594—produced with additions from other hands. Certainly the reference to Doctor Lopez (xi. 46) would have been specially effective in September, 1594, as this would-be poisoner had been executed not longer ago than the previous June[1]; and it could not have been made at a much earlier date. Again, if a line in the quarto of Doctor Faustus of 1616 cited below be imitated from the old Taming of a Shrew (which was entered in the Stationers' Registers in 1594), this would indicate that Marlowe's play had before 1597 received additions from some other hand; for the line occurs in a scene which was certainly not by Marlowe[2].

The Ballad of Doctor Faustus.

This would not in itself take us very far back, especially as Henslowe's register of plays does not begin earlier than February, 1592. But already in the year 1589 (N.S.) there occurs another entry in the Stationers' Registers, dated 'ultimo die Februarij':

> 'Ric. Jones   Allowed vnto him for his Copie, A ballad of the life and deathe of Doctor *FFAUSTUS* the great Cunngerer. Allowed vnder the hand of the Bishop of London, and master warden Denhams hand beinge to the copie . . . vjd.' [3]

There is of course nothing to *prove* that the ballad (which, it need hardly be said, has no connexion with the German ballad mentioned above) was later in date than Marlowe's play, on which it *need* not have been founded, especially as

[1] See note on the passage in Doctor Faustus.

[2] See Dyce, Some Account of Marlowe and his Writings, xxi-xxii. The line in the 1616 edition of Doctor Faustus is:

'Or hew'd this flesh and blood as small as sand';

in the old Taming of a Shrew it runs:

'And hew'd thee smaller than the Libian sandes.'

The same play contains another passage corresponding to one in the first quarto of Doctor Faustus; see note on sc. iv; and others, according to Dyce, *u. s.*, li-lii, corresponding to passages in Tamburlaine.

[3] Arber's Transcript, ii. 241 *b*.

there are certain discrepancies between the form in which the ballad has been preserved, and the tragedy; though I think too much importance has been attached to these differences[1]. But, whether or not the ballad entered in 1589 was identical with that which we now have, it is certainly more *probable* that it should have been founded on the play than *vice versâ*. The usual process of the Elizabethan age was no doubt for dramas to be founded on favourite stories, and for popular ballads or other brief treatments of the kind to summarise the incidents and morals of favourite plays[2]; and I cannot see sufficient reason for supposing the sequence to have been different in the present instance.

Internal evidence as to the date of Marlowe's tragedy.

This would place the probable date of the first performance of Marlowe's tragedy some time before February, 1589, and very possibly in 1588 or even in 1587; by which year Tamburlaine had certainly been performed[3]. Such internal evidence as the play of Doctor Faustus furnishes agrees with this assumption. It has been pointed out with some force[4] that the reference to the Prince of Parma as the oppressor of the Netherlands (i. 91), assuming it, as there is no reason to doubt, to have formed part of the original text, would best suit the time when 'this Prince's hand was still lying heavy upon them,' viz. before 1590, in which year his attention

[1] The ballad makes Faustus to be born at 'Wittenburge,' and not at 'Rhodes'; and 'of good degree,' instead of 'of parents base of stock.' It likewise states him to have been brought up by his 'uncle,' who left him 'all his wealth,' instead of 'chiefly by kinsmen.' Again, it represents Faustus as unrepentant till his end; designates as his sole motive for entering into the compact the desire 'to live in peace' (i. e. pleasure); and omits one of the principal features in the tragedy, the episode of Helen. See Wagner's Introduction, xxiii–xxvi.

[2] Compare Dyce's Introduction, xxii, xx. As an example I may notice the entry of 'The twooe comicall discourses of Tomberlein the Cithian shepparde' in the Stationers' Registers under August 13th, 1590 (Arber's Transcript, ii. 262*b*). So again the ballad of The murtherous life and terrible deathe of the rich Jew of Malta is entered May 16th, 1594 (Arber, ii. 307).

[3] See Collier, History of English Dramatic Poetry, iii. 108-112.

[4] By Dr. J. H. Albers, in an article on Marlowe's Faustus in the Jahrbuch für romanische und englische Sprache und Literatur, Neue Folge, vol. iii. (1876).

began to be principally turned to France, and at all events before his death in December, 1592. On the other hand, the reference to the destruction of the Antwerp bridge (i. 94) shows that the play must have been written *after* the spring of 1585. The same critic who makes the above suggestion seeks an allusion in the passage (i. 80–83)

'I'll have them fly to India for gold,' &c.

to the entertainment given by Thomas Cavendish to Queen Elizabeth on shipboard after his return in the autumn of 1588[1] from his voyage round the world; and such may possibly be the case, though the passage does not require to be interpreted as containing any special allusion. It is of more importance that the evidence of versification points to Doctor Faustus having been the play composed by Marlowe next after Tamburlaine. Mr. Collier has shown[2] how the habit of 'terminating nearly all the lines with monosyllables' and letting 'each line run as if a rhyme were wanting' (so that, it may be added, the verse occasionally, as it were, slips into rhyme[3]) is exchanged for greater variety of endings to the lines in the middle, and for still greater towards the conclusion of the tragedy; and that, though of course it is impossible to speak decisively in the case of a play which we have in a form that has received so many alterations, the appearance is as if the poet had 'improved his blank-verse as he proceeded.' I think that in Edward II, which is clearly one of Marlowe's latest works, the versification may fairly be described as freer throughout; and the number of double-endings in that play is twice as great as that in either Part of Tamburlaine, and much further exceeds that in Doctor Faustus[4].

The English History of Doctor Faustus.

Neither before nor in 1589 were there, so far as we know, any literary materials in existence of which Marlowe could have availed himself, except the editions which had already

[1] Not 1587, as Albers gives the date. Cavendish was said to have amassed wealth sufficient 'to buy a fair earldom.'

[2] *u. s.*, iii. 129–131.

[3] See v. 86–87, 89–90.

[4] See the table in Mr. Fleay's edition of Edward II.

appeared of the German Faustbuch. It is true that an English translation of the German book soon made its appearance under the title of 'The History of the Damnable Life and deserved Death of Doctor Johann Faustus. Newly Printed and in convenient Places impertinent Matter amended, according to the true Copy, Printed at Frankfort; and translated into English, by P. R. Gent. London, printed by R. C. Brown.' But the date of this publication[1], or that of the work of which it was a reprint, is unknown; it is not, so far as I can find, entered in the Stationers' Registers; and the arrangement of its chapters shows that it is a version not of the Faustbuch of 1587, but of that of 1590[2]. On the other hand, it is proper to state that Marlowe's tragedy in the quarto of 1604 includes *none* of the additions made to the story in the Faustbuch of 1590[3]; and that the verbal agreement between at least one salient passage in the play and the text of the English History is indisputable[4]. The balance of probability is therefore strongly in favour of the conclusion that Marlowe took the story of his play direct from one of the editions of the German Faustbuch published before 1590; though I confess that I see no impossibility in the assumption that he had seen the English Translation—but this assumption is not *necessary*.

The Faustbuch of 1587 the source of Marlowe's play.

The name Vanholt.

In all the copies we possess of Marlowe's tragedy there

[1] Two copies of this are in the Bodleian Library; and it is reprinted in Thoms's Early Prose Romances, vol. iii. R. C. Brown is not mentioned in the Provisional List of London Printers and Publishers in the latter half of Queen Elizabeth's reign, given by Mr. Arber in vol. ii. of his Transcript.

[2] Düntzer, 96. Thoms mentions an edition of 1626 of the English History; Dyce's quotations are from that of 1648.

[3] The incident of Faustus eating the load of hay, which occurs in the German Faustbuch but not in the English History, is adduced by van der Velde as a proof that Marlowe did not use the latter. But the scene in which this incident is introduced occurs neither in the quarto of 1604 nor in that of 1609, while it appears in that of 1616, and was therefore manifestly a later addition to the drama.

[4] The passage is the third article of the contract (v. 99–100), where, as Dyce notes, the History has: 'That Mephistophiles should bring him any thing, and doe for him whatsoever.' This is in the edition of 1648; 'a later edition adds, "he desired."' Compare Wagner's note, 117.

is a curious instance of divergence both from the Faustbuch and from the English History, which would seem at first sight to indicate that he had come across the story, if not in a Dutch version, at least through a narrator who had heard it, or a passage of it, told in the Netherlands. Or why should the Duke of *Anhalt*, as the name of the Duchy is written in the German book (it is '*Anholt*' in the English translation), become in the play the Duke of *Vanholt*?

The English comedians in Germany and the Netherlands, as probable intermediaries.

This oddity is I think best to be reconciled with the other circumstances of the case by the supposition that the German Faustbuch was brought over to England in one of its early editions (before that of 1590) by some person or persons who had travelled both in Germany and in the Netherlands; that through them it came into Marlowe's hands in the shape of a MS. English translation; and that this MS. translation was very probably used by 'P. R.' or whoever was the 'gentleman' who wrote the English History. Marlowe himself can hardly have been in the Netherlands, at all events as late as 1587.

Who, then, were the person or persons in question? It has been happily conjectured by van der Velde[1]—and the conjecture is adopted by Professor Wagner[2]—that they were English comedians who had performed in Germany before the year 1588. In a work[3] of which the interest and importance for the study of the English as well as the German drama have been generally recognised, Mr. A. Cohn has shown that on October 16th, 1586, Duke Christian of Saxony appointed five Englishmen 'fiddlers and instrumentalists to play music and exhibit their art in "leaping and other graceful things that they have learnt";' and that this company of comedians included the names, afterwards well known in the annals of the English stage, of Thomas Pope and George Bryan. He considers that it hardly admits of doubt that this Thomas Pope was the only actor of that name known

[1] Marlowe's Faust (German translation), Introduction, 23.

[2] Introduction, xxxi.

[3] Shakespeare in Germany in the XVIth and XVIIth Centuries, xxv–xxvii.

to us as belonging to this period,—the same Thomas Pope who was afterwards the associate of Shakespeare, and who before 1588 had taken part in Tarlton's play of the Second Part of The Seven Deadly Sins, which has a special interest for us in connexion with Marlowe's tragedy[1]. 'The above-mentioned Englishmen,' he continues, 'are not met with again in the Dresden Archives after 1586, though other "Jumpers and Dancers" are named at a later period, as *e.g.* in 1588. It is therefore probable that these Englishmen quitted the Saxon service soon after 1586, and returned to England. On the London stage Thomas Pope had played the parts of the "rustic clowns," and there is nothing surprising therefore in the supposition that at an earlier period of his life he had condescended to still more subordinate arts. It appears that in 1593 he belonged to the same company as Edward Alleyn. . . . As to George Bryan . . . his connexion with the London theatres may be traced back to a period prior to 1588, as he also took part in The Second Part of the Seven Deadly Sins.' On their way back to England—in 1587 or 1588—these men would naturally pass through the Netherlands, where, as early as 1585, at least one English actor had appeared in the suite of the Earl of Leicester[2], and where afterwards the performances of the 'English comedians' were as common as they were in Germany itself. It is a curious coincidence that the name of the manager of the only company of English comedians (besides that which Leicester may have brought with him in 1585) which is known to have played in the Netherlands in the sixteenth century, when it gave performances in 1590 at Leyden, was Robert Browne[3], and that an 'R. C. Brown' printed the English History of Doctor Faustus.

Here, then, we have a link suggested between Marlowe and Germany, and an easy way for him to have become acquainted with the German Faustbuch in the very year

[1] See sc. vi; and compare **The Seven Deadly Sins** in notes on Dramatis Personae of Doctor Faustus.

[2] Cohn, *u. s.*, xxii–xxiii.

[3] See F. von Hellwald, Geschichte des holländischen Theaters, 7.

of its first publication, or in that immediately succeeding it, through men who had in all probability passed through the Netherlands and had there learnt to begin names with '*van*.' With these men Marlowe can hardly have failed to come into immediate contact in London, and two of them were concerned in the performance of a play to which, as an episode in the tragedy of Doctor Faustus (due in all probability to Marlowe's own insertion) shows, the poet cannot have been a stranger.

The existence of any German Faust-drama before Marlowe's not proved.

The Faustbuch then may be assumed to have been the source of Marlowe's tragedy. For he can hardly be supposed to have had a model in any German drama, since there is no sufficient reason for supposing that any such existed at so early a date. A weighty authority—Simrock[1]—has indeed held it probable that some such German play existed and was known to Marlowe, who elaborated his tragedy out of it with the help of the Faustbuch. The essential point which Marlowe's tragedy has in common with the puppet-plays, based on an early German drama or dramas, is to be found, as Simrock says, in the apparitions of the Good and the Evil Angel,—allegorical figures familiar to German legend, but not appearing in the story-book. I cannot think the fact of this parallelism, striking as it is, strong enough to make us look for the original of Marlowe's tragedy in an unknown German drama, of which the very existence rests on pure conjecture. To the Faustbuch his debt is in any case undeniable. Before making the extracts necessary for establishing this fact, it will however be convenient to complete the data as to the history of the legend of Doctor Faustus in our Elizabethan literature, by stating that in 1594 was published in London 'The Second Report of Doctor John Faustus, containing his appearances and the deeds of Wagner. Written by an English Gentleman student in Wittenberg an Vniuersity of Germany in Saxony. Published for the delight of all those who desire Nouelties by a frend of the same Gentleman[2].' This English

The English Wagner-book.

[1] *u. s.*, 224–227.

[2] This publication, of which there is a copy in the Bodleian Library, is reprinted by Thoms, *u. s.*, vol. iii.

version of the Wagnerbuch is preceded by a preface 'unto them which would know the Trueth,' in which they are apprised of some remarkable instances in support of the fact that Faustus was a real man. 'First, there is yet remaining the ruins of his house not farre from Melanchthon's at Wittenberg. Secondly, there is his tree, a great hollow Tree wherein he vsed to read Nigromancy to his schollers, not farre from the towne in a very remote place. . . . Next, his tomb at Mars Temple a three miles beyond the cittie, upon which is written on a Marble stone by his owne hand this Epitaph, which is somewhat old by reason of his small skill in graving:

"Hic iaceo Iohannes Faustus, Doctor diuini iuris indignissimus, qui pro amore magiae Diabolicae scientiae vanissimè cecidi ab amore Dei: O Lector pro me miserrimo damnato nomine ne preceris, nam preces non iuvant quem Deus condemnavit: O pie Christiane memento mei, et saltem vnam pro infiducia mea lachrymulam exprime, et cui non potes mederi, eius miserere, et ipse caue."

The Stone was found in his Study, and his wil was fulfilled, and he lieth betwixt a heap of three and thirty fir trees in the foot of the Hill in a great hole where this is erected.'

For further testimony to convince the incredulous, he repeats (with their manifest errors) the statements of Wierus; and with this circumstantial evidence conscientiously offered by an Englishman who, faithful to the character of his nation, has scorned to see with any but his own eyes, I may close my sketch of the early history of the Faust-legend; for later English translations of German magical works attributed to Faustus have no significance for the present purpose, any more than their German originals.

Discrepancies as to localities between the Faustbuch and Marlowe, and other authorities.

The following are the passages in the first edition of the Faustbuch of 1587, which Marlowe has obviously used in his tragedy. I have throughout sought to translate as literally as possible, only here and there borrowing a phrase from the English History as given by Thoms, which is a very loose rendering indeed of the German original. It will be noticed that both by the Faustbuch and by Marlowe 'Rod' or 'Rhodes' is mentioned as the birthplace of the magician. This is Roda in the Duchy of Saxe-Altenburg, situate between the towns of Jena and Gera, and therefore 'near Weinmar' (Weimar). Widmann gives Anhalt as the country of Faustus's birth, and the mark Sondwedel, i. e. Salzwedel, as the place of his parents' abode. But we have seen that the older and contemporary authorities stated him to have been born at Knütlingen (i.e. Knittlingen)—or, as several of them, following Manlius's report of Melanchthon's discourse, mis-spelt the name, 'Kundling'—in Würthemberg[1]. The connexion of Faustus with Wittenberg led to a confusion between the names of the Duchy and of the Saxon University town by Marlowe or the transcribers of his play, in the first two extant editions of which Wittenberg is constantly called 'Wertemberg' or 'Wirtenberg[2].' I have seen no reason for retaining this error, which is merely confusing. Again, in the Faustbuch, and in Marlowe, the student life of Faustus is passed at Wittenberg only; Widmann makes him study at Ingolstadt, a University of great celebrity, where Reuchlin was professor. In the Faustbuch the summoning of the Devil takes place in 'a thick wood'—'a hidden grove' in Marlowe—which the author calls 'the Spesser Wald,' and which has been thought identifiable with a kind of bosquet near Wittenberg called the 'Specke,' a locality where Luther is known to have taken his exercise[3]. Lastly, in the Faustbuch the village of Rimlich near Wittenberg, and in Marlowe Wittenberg itself, is the scene of Faustus's death; according to Melanchthon it occurred in a village of Faustus's native country (Württemberg). Other places contended for the notoriety of having seen the last of the famous sorcerer—among them another village near Wittenberg called Praten, the castle of Wærdenberg, and the towns Maulbronn

[1] According to the 'Second Report' 'in Silesia.'

[2] This is noted by Professor Wagner, and I have verified it in the case of the quarto of 1604. Oddly enough, the converse blunder occurs in R. Scot's Discovery of Witchcraft, book vi. chapter iv (edition of 1654): 'Wierus telleth a notable story. . . . There was (saith he) in the dukedom of *Wittneberge*, not far from *Tubing*, a butcher,' &c.

[3] See Kühne's quotation from Luther's Table-Talk in his edition of the Faustbuch, 156. The 'Spesser Wald' had been thought to be a synonym for the Spesshart mountains.

and Cologne. The rest of the geography of the Faustbuch and Marlowe must be left to account for itself.

CHAPTER I. *The Historia of Doctor John Faustus, the widely-noised conjuror's, birth and studia.* Doctor Faustus was the son of a peasant, born at Rod, near Weinmar, who had a great number of kinsfolk at Wittenberg; his parents also were godly and Christian people; and indeed his cousin, who was settled at Wittenberg, was a burgher and well-to-do, who brought up Faustus, and kept him as if he had been his own child. For whereas he was without heirs, he adopted this Faustus as his child and heir, also sent him to the School [i.e. University], to study *Theologiam;* but he departed from this godly intent and misused the Word of God. . . . . . .

Extracts from the Faustbuch

Inasmuch as Dr. Faust having a very docile and quick head was qualified and inclined for studying, he afterwards came so far in his *Examine* before the *Rectores*, that he was examined for the Magistratus [i.e. for the Master's or Doctor's degree], and with him 16 *Magistri* also; these he overcame and vanquished in the *vivâ voce*[1], in questions and in cleverness, so that he [was held to have] studied sufficiently for his part, and accordingly became *Doctor Theologiae.* At the same time he also had an obstinate[2], senseless and arrogant head, insomuch that he was always called the speculator[3]; he fell into evil company, cast Holy Writ behind the door and under the bench, lived recklessly and godlessly (as from this History hereafter sufficiently shall appear); for it is a true proverb: None can hold or prevent that will to the Devil. Moreover Dr. Faustus met with his like, who were seen in Chaldaean, Persian, Arabic and Greek words, *figuris, characteribus, coniurationibus, incantationibus*, and whatever such books, words and names may be called. This pleased Dr. Faustus well; he studies and speculates night and day therein; would after this not allow himself any more to be called a *theologus*, waxed a worldly man[4], called himself a *Doctor Medicinae*, became an *Astrologus* and *Mathematicus*, and for a pretext[5]

[1] *Gehör.* [2] *thumm.* [3] *Specu*l*erier.* [4] *Weltmensch.* [5] *zum Glimpff.*

he became a physician; at first helped many people with medicine, with herbs, roots, waters, draughts and receipts; and at the same time he was in good sooth[1] affable[2], well proved in God's Scripture; he well knew the rule of Christ: he that knoweth his Master's will, and doeth it not, is worthy to be beaten with many stripes. *Item*, No man can serve two masters. *Item*, thou shalt not tempt the Lord thy God. All this he threw in the wind, and made his soul for a time of no estimation[3]; therefore there shall be no excuse for him.

CHAPTER II. *Doctor Faustus a Physician, and how he conjured the Devil.* As has been told before, the mind[4] of Dr. Faustus stood towards loving that which was not to be loved; on this he studies day and night; took unto him the wings of an eagle; and thought to study all secrets[5] in heaven and earth; for his insolence, liberty and recklessness pricked and itched him so that he proposed unto himself at one time to set on foot and try some magical *vocabula, figuras, characteres* and *coniurationes*, wherewith he might summon the Devil before him. Accordingly he came to a thick wood, as some also relate, which lies near to Wittenberg, called the Spesser Wood[6], as indeed Dr. Faustus himself did thereafter confess. In this wood towards the west[7], at the crossing of four ways he drew around with a wand some circles, and two beside[8], so that the two uppermost were included in the great circle. Thus he conjured the Devil in the night, between 9 and 10 of the clock. . . . . When Dr. Faustus conjured the Devil, the Devil bore himself as if he were unwilling to come to the point and into court[9]; insomuch that the Devil began so great a rumour in the wood, as if all things were to come to an end, so that the trees bowed their tops to the ground. Then the Devil bore himself as if the wood were full of devils, who soon after appeared in the midst of and beside the circle of Dr. Faustus, as if the place were full of

[1] *ohne Ruhm.* [2] *Redsprechig.* [3] *setzte seine Seel ein weil vber die Vberthür.* [4] *Datum.* [5] *Gründ.* [6] *Spesser Wald.* [7] Or, towards the evening (*gegen Abend*). [8] *neben zween.* [9] *an den Reyen* (to the dance?).

naught but waggons. After this from the four corners of the wood there came towards the circle bolts and rays [of thunder and lightning]; soon thereafter a great, report of a gun; whereupon a brightness appeared, and there were heard in the wood many delightful instruments, music and songs. Also some dances, and thereupon some tournaments with spears and swords, so that Dr. Faustus waxed so tired of it all, that he thought of running out of the circle. At the last he again takes a godless and daring resolve, and rests or stood in his former *condition*, let God see to it what may result therefrom. He began as before to conjure the Devil again; whereupon the Devil made such a strange noise[1] before his eyes, as follows: It seemed as if above the circle a griffin or dragon hovered, and fluttered; whenever then Dr. Faustus used his conjuration, the beast made a horrible grunting[2]; soon after, there fell from a height of three or four fathom a fiery star, which changed into a fiery ball, at which Dr. Faustus also was very greatly afraid, but he held fast to his intent, thinking it of high esteem, that the Devil should be subject unto him. . . . . Therefore he conjured this star for the first, the second and the third time; whereupon there went up a stream of fire as high as a man, let itself down again, and hereupon were seen six small lights; now one light sprang aloft, then the other fell down, till at last it changed and formed the figure of a fiery man, who walked round the circle for the time of a quarter of an hour. Soon after the Devil and Spirit changes himself into the shape of a Grey Friar, came to speech with Faustus, and asked what he desired. Hereupon the desire of Dr. Faustus was, that he should appear to him to-morrow at 12 of the clock at night in his house, which for a while the Devil refused. But Dr. Faustus conjured him in the name of his master, that he should fulfil his desire and accomplish it. Which at last the Spirit agreed to, and granted.

CHAPTER III. *Follows the Conference*[3] *of Dr. Faustus with the Spirit.* . . . . Dr. Faustus begins

[1] *Geplerr.* [2] *kirrete jämmerlich.* [3] *Disputation.*

his tricks again, conjured him anew, and proposes to the Spirit certain articles.

First, that he shall be subject and obedient to him, in all that he requested, asked or required of him, throughout the life and up to the death of him, Faustus.

Moreover, he should not keep back from him whatsoever he might enquire of him.

Also, that he should not make any untrue responses to any of his interrogatories.

Whereupon the Spirit denied him this, and refused it, giving as his reason therefor, that he had no complete power, except in so far as he could obtain it from his master who ruled over him, and said: Dear Fauste, to fulfil your desire, stands not in my choice and power, but in the hands of the god of hell. Answer of Dr. Faustus to this: How am I to understand that, are you not possessed enough of this power? The Spirit answers, No. Says Faustus again to him, Friend[1], tell me the reason why. Thou must know, Fauste, said the Spirit, that with us there is a kingdom and government even as on earth, for we have our rulers and regents and servants, as I also am one, and our kingdom we call the Legion. For although Lucifer the rejected one, brought about his own fall by pride and arrogance, he has set up a Legion and a kingdom over many devils; whom we call the Oriental Prince, for he had his dominion in the rising sun. So there is also a dominion in *Meridie*, *Septentrione* and *Occidente*; and whereas Lucifer, the fallen angel, has his dominion and principality under the heavens also, we must change our shape, come among men, and be subject unto them; for otherwise man with all his power and arts could not make Lucifer subject unto him, unless he send a Spirit as I am sent. We have not indeed revealed unto man the true foundation of our abode, or of our kingdom and dominion, except after the death of the condemned man, who comes to understand and have experience of it. Dr. Faustus was terrified thereat, and said: And yet I will not be damned, for thy sake. . . .

. . . . When then the Spirit was fain to escape, Dr.

[1] *Lieber*.

Faustus at once fell into another doubtful mind, and entreated him to appear unto him again there at vesper-time and listen to what he would further say unto him. Which the Spirit granted unto him, and thus vanished from before him. . . .

CHAPTER IV. *The Second Conference of Faustus with the Spirit, which is called Mephostophiles.* [Mephistophiles re-appears with full powers from his Chief, and the bases of the contract are settled between him and Faustus. The latter demands:] First, that he might also have and receive to himself the cunning[1], form and shape of a spirit. Secondly, that the Spirit shall do all that he demands, and may desire from him. Thirdly, that he shall be assiduous, subject and obedient to him, as a servant. Fourthly, that he shall at all times, whenever he called and summoned him, be to be found in his house. Fifthly, that he shall rule in his house invisibly and not let himself be seen by any but him [Faustus], unless it were his will and behest. And lastly, that he shall appear unto him as often as he summons him, and in the shape which he shall impose upon him.

[The Spirit assents to these conditions, and asks his own in return:] First, that he, Faustus, shall promise and swear that he will belong to him, the Spirit, as his own property. Secondly, that for further confirmation he shall attest this with his own blood, and thus make himself over to him. Thirdly, that he will be a foe to all men of Christian faith. Fourthly, that he will renounce the Christian faith. Fifthly, that he will not allow himself to be seduced, if any one should desire to convert him. In return, the Spirit would appoint a number of years as a term for him; when these had expired, he should be fetched by him. And provided he should keep such articles, he should have all that his heart craved and desired, and should soon perceive that he would have the form and manner of a spirit. Dr. Faustus in his pride and arrogance was so daring, although he took thought with himself for a while, that he would not consider the salvation of his soul, but agreed to the conditions of the Evil Spirit, and promised to keep all the articles. He thought the Devil was not so

[1] Skill (*Geschickligkeit*).

black as he was painted, and hell not so hot as it was said to be.

CHAPTER V. *The third Colloquium of Dr. Faustus with the Spirit as to his promise.* After Dr. Faustus had made this promise, on the following day at early morning he summoned the Spirit, and bade him, as often as he summoned him, appear unto him in the shape and dress of a Franciscan monk, with a little bell, and before appearing give unto him some signals, so that he might know, from the ringing of the bell, when he was on his way to him. Thereupon he asked the Spirit what was his name, and how he was called. The Spirit made answer, he was named Mephostophiles. In this very hour the ungodly man falls away from his God aad Creator who has created him, yea he becomes a limb of the sorry Devil[1]; and this falling-away is naught else, than his proud arrogance, despair, daring and insolence, as it was with the Giants, whereof the poets feign, that they carried together the mountains, and were fain to war against God, yea as it was with the Evil Angel, who set himself against God, wherefore he was on account of his arrogance and insolence rejected by God. Thus whoso seeketh to mount high, he also falleth low.

After this Dr. Faustus, in his great daring and insolence, draws up for the Evil Spirit his instrument, recognition, formal document[2], and confession. This was a loathsome and awful work, and this Obligation was after his miserable departure found in his dwelling. . . . . When these two parties had agreed with one another, Dr. Faustus took a sharp-pointed knife, pricked open a vein in his left hand, and it is truly said, that in this hand was seen a graven and bloody writing, *O Homo fuge, id est,* O man flee from him and do what is right.

CHAPTER VI. *Dr. Faustus lets his blood drop in a chafer[3], sets it on warm coals, and writes as followeth:* I Johannes Faustus Dr. do openly acknowledge with my own hand, for the confirmation, and by virtue of this letter, that after I re-

[1] *dess leydigen Teuffels.* [2] *brieffliche Urkund.* [3] *Tiegel.*

solved to study[1] the *Elementa*, but from the gifts which have been bestowed upon me from above and mercifully granted unto me, do not find such cunning in my head, and may not learn such from men, So I have subjected myself to the Spirit sent [to me and] now present, and have also chosen the same unto myself, to report and teach such things unto me, who hath also bound himself to me, to be subject and obedient in all things. In return I on the other hand bind and promise myself to him, that when twenty-four years from the date of this bill have gone round and past, he shall have full power to deal with me, govern, rule and conduct me after his manner and fashion, as he may choose, with all, even with body, soul, flesh, blood and estate, and that into eternity. On this I renounce[3] all those who are living, all the Hosts of Heaven, and all men, and it shall be so. As a sure document and for further confirmation, I have written this bill[4] with my own hand, subscribed it, and with my own blood pressed out for this purpose, being in [command of] my senses, head, thoughts and will, have tied, sealed and attested it.

O LORD[2] God forbid[2].

Subscriptio,

John Faustus, the expert[5]
in the Elements, and
Doctor of the Spirituals[6].

[In Chapter VIII Faustus, with the help of his familiar spirit, who now appears 'quite cheerful,' makes various conjurations'—among the rest that of a lion and a dragon, who fight with one another. In Chapter IX we read of other tricks and adventures, and are introduced to 'Dr. Fausti *famulus*':]

Dr. Faustus abode in the house of his pious cousin, as the latter had left it to him in his will; in the house with him he had daily a young scholar as *famulus*, a greedy scamp[7], named Christoph Wagner, who well liked this game; forasmuch as his master bade him be of good cheer, he would make of him a man of high experience and cunning, and as youth is by

[1] *speculieren.* [2] *Sic* in margin. [3] *absage.*
[4] *Recess.* [5] *der Erfahrne.* [6] *der Geistlichen.*
[7] *ein verwegener Lecker* (Thoms, 'an unhappy wag').

nature more inclined to the evil than to the good, so with this one . . . . .

CHAPTER X. *Doctor Faustus wished to marry*; [but was prevented by Mephistophiles].

CHAPTER XI. *Question of Doctor Faustus to his spirit Mephostophiles.* . . . . Soon his Spirit gives to him a large book, concerning all kinds of magic and *Nigromantia*, wherein he found amusement. . . Soon being pricked by insolence of mind, he summons his Spirit *Mephostophilem*, with whom he desired to hold a colloquy, and says to the Spirit: My servant, tell me, what kind of spirit art thou? To him the Spirit made answer and said: My lord Fauste, I am a spirit, and a flying spirit, ruling under the heavens. But how did Lucifer thy lord come to fall? The Spirit said, Master, as my lord Lucifer, a beautiful angel, created by God, was a creature of bliss, so I know so much of him, that such angels are called *Hierarchiae*, and of these there were three[1]. . . . So Lucifer also was one of the fair and Arch-Angels among them, and called Raphael, the other two Gabriel and Michael. . . .

[In Chapter XII hell is briefly described; but the Spirit confesses that 'we devils cannot know in what form and manner hell was created, nor how it was founded and built by God; for it has neither end nor bottom; and this is my brief report.' In Chapter XIII follows an exposition of the constitution of the infernal government; and this account and a further discussion on the former beauty and gloriousness of Lucifer in Chapter XIV inspire Faustus with a feeling of remorse, and a desire to 'turn, and cry to God for grace and pardon; for never to do, is a long penance'; and he would have gone to church and followed the sacred teaching, thus saving his soul although he must leave his body to the Devil, had he not again waxed full of doubt, and want of faith and hope. Further conferences follow, in one of which, in Chapter XVI, Mephistophiles answers the question, whether the condemned are ever received back again into grace, with No: 'For all, who are in hell, and whom God has rejected, they must eternally burn in the wrath and displeasure of God,

[1] The passage following is probably corrupt.

forasmuch as there is nevermore no hope. Yea, if they could come to the grace of God, like us spirits, who hope and wait at all hours, they would rejoice and sigh for such a time. But as little as the devils in hell can hope to come to grace from their fall and rejection, so little can the damned, for there is no hope.' . . . And, in the next chapter, being asked what would be his course of conduct if he were created a man in place of Faustus, the Spirit avows he would serve God, and recover grace notwithstanding his former sins. 'Then,' says Faustus, 'for me also there is time, if I should repent.' 'It is too late now,' rejoins the Spirit, 'the wrath of God lies upon thee.' 'Leave me in peace,' exclaims Faustus; and the Spirit retorts: 'Then leave me also in peace henceforth with thy questions.'

This concludes the First Part of the story: in the next Faustus appears as an *Astronomus* or *Astrologus*, and a calendar-maker. He addresses a series of enquiries to the Spirit on the subject of these studies and pursuits; but it is unnecessary to make any extracts from the information imparted by Mephistophiles in reply, as Marlowe has not followed these passages in detail. Then begins the adventurous part of the narrative. After all the spirits of hell have been introduced to Faustus—among them seven of the highest rank named by their names—(Chapter XXIII), he himself visits the lower regions, from which he is carried aloft again in a chariot drawn by two dragons (Chapter XXIV). He next (Chapter XXV) mounts into the heavens on his dragon's car, which had 'four wheels, that made a rushing noise as if I' (for a written narrative of Faustus is here quoted) 'were driving in the country, but in their course the wheels ever gave out streams of fire.' Next, 'in the 16th year,' he undertakes 'a journey or pilgrimage,' for the purpose of which 'Mephostophiles had turned and changed himself into a horse, but he had wings like a dromedary, and thus passed whithersoever Dr. Faustus landed him' (Chapter XXVI). Their journeys take them to a wide variety of countries; but I need only make the following extracts from this part of the narrative:]

CHAPTER XXVI. . . . [He] came to the neighbourhood of

Trier, when it first occurred to him to behold this city, because it was so old-fashioned [1] to look upon; where he saw nothing very remarkable, except a palace, wonderfully built, which was made of baked bricks, and so strong that they have to fear no foe. Thereafter he saw the church, wherein Simeon and the Bishop Pepo were buried, which is made out of incredibly large stones welded together with iron. Thereafter he turns towards Pariss in France, and was well pleased with the Studia and the High School. Whatsoever towns and countries now come into Faust's mind, through these he journeys. So among others also Meyntz (Mainz), where the Main flows into the Rhine. But here he delays not long, but came to Campania, into the city Neapolis (Naples), wherein he saw many monasteries and churches, more than can be told, and houses so large, high and gloriously decorated, that he admired thereat. . . . Soon Venice occurred to him; he is astonished to find it lying with the sea all round it. . . . He also saw the wide houses and high towers and the beauty of the churches and buildings founded and set up in the midst of the water. Further he journeys in Welschlandt (Italy &c.) to Padua, to visit the School there. This city is fortified with a threefold wall, with manifold fosses and waters running round; therein is a citadel and fastness, and the buildings thereof are manifold, for it also has a fine church with a tower, and a town-hall which is so fine that none in the world is said to be comparable unto this. A church is there called S. Anthonij, the like whereof is not to be found in all Italia. Further he came to Rome, which lies by a river called Tyberis, which flows through the middle of the city, and on the further side of the right side, the city comprises seven hills around it, has eleven portals and gates, *Vaticanum*, a hill whereon stands the minster or dome [2] of St. Peter. Near it stands the Pope's palace, which is beautifully surrounded by a pleasure-garden. . . . . He also came invisible before the Pope's palace, where he saw many servants and court-followers [3], and what courses and meats were being served to the Pope, and

[1] *altfränckisch.* [2] *Thumb.* [3] *Hoffschrantzen.*

such superfluity, that Dr. Faustus afterwards said to his Spirit: Fie, why has the Devil not made me also a Pope? . . . . And forasmuch as he had heard much of Rome, he remained three days and nights in the Pope's palace, being invisible by his magic, and good Master Faustus has since that time not had much that was good to eat or drink. So once he stood invisible before the Pope; when the Pope was about to eat, he crossed himself; as often as this happened, Dr. Faustus blew into his face. Once Dr. Faustus laughed, so that it was heard through the whole hall, then he wept, as if he were doing it seriously, and the serving-men knew not what it was. The Pope persuaded the serving-men that it was a condemned soul praying for an indulgence, whereupon the Pope imposed a penance upon it accordingly. Doctor Faustus laughed thereat, and was well pleased with this delusion. But when the last courses and dishes came on the Pope's table, and he, Dr. Faustus, was hungry, he, Faustus, lifted up his hand; immediately courses and meats, together with the dishes, flew into his hand; wherewith he vanished, together with his Spirit, to a hill at Rome called Capitolium, and thus enjoyed his dinner. He also sent his Spirit back there, who had to bring him the best wine from the Pope's table, with the silver cups and candles[1]. When the Pope had seen all this that had been stolen from him, in the same night he caused all the bells to ring together, and masses and prayers to be held for the deceased soul, and in his wrath sentenced and condemned Faustum, or the departed soul, into purgatory. But Dr. Faustus had made a good sweep[2] of the Pope's meats and drink. This silver plate was found left behind him after his death. . . . .

[Faustus journeys to many other places, including Cracow, Constantinople, and the islands Britannia (Chapter XXVII), Crete and Caucasus, whence he beholds Paradise. The remainder of this Part of the Faustbuch contains further conferences of Faustus with Mephistophiles, chiefly as to astronomical and meteorological difficulties. The Third and Last Part turns to

[1] *Kanten.* [2] *Fegen.*

'the doings and effects of Faustus with his *Nigromantia* at the Courts of Potentates,' and lastly also reports 'his miserable and terrible end and departure [1].' Here Marlowe found the following materials:]

CHAPTER XXXIII. *A Historia of Dr. Faustus and Emperor Carolus Quintus.* The Emperor Carolus the Fifth of this name, was come with his court to Innsbruck, whither Dr. Faustus also repaired. . . . . . Whom the Emperor Carolus espied, and took notice of him, who he was? Then he was told, it was Dr. Faustus. Whereupon the Emperor was silent, till after dinner; this was in the summer, after St. Philip and St. James. Then the Emperor summoned Faustus into his chamber, put it to him, how he knew that he was an expert in the Black Art, and had a sorcerer spirit [2]; wherefore he desired, that he would let him see an example, nothing should happen to him, this he promised by his Imperial Crown. Thereupon Dr. Faustus offered most humbly to obey his Imperial Majesty. Well then listen to me, said the Emperor; once upon a time in my court [3] I stood in thought, how before me my forefathers and ancestors rose to so high a degree and authority, which I and my successors might yet possibly equal [4], and specially how among all monarchs the high and mighty Emperor Alexander Magnus, a shining light [5] and glory of all emperors, as may be read in the Chronicles, brought under him so great riches, so many kingdoms and dominions, that I and my successors will find it a hard matter to accomplish the same [4]. Therefore it is my gracious desire to have brought before me his, Alexander's, and his consort's form, figure, walk, features, as they were in life, so that I may find thee to be an experienced master of thy art. Most gracious lord, said Faustus, in order most humbly to obey your Imperial Majesty's desire by producing the person Alexander Magni and of his consort, in form and shape as they were in their lifetime, I will, so far as by my Spirit I am able, cause the same visibly to appear: but your Majesty should know, that their mortal bodies cannot rise again from the dead, or be present,

[1] *Abschiedt.* [2] *einen Warsager Geist.* [3] *Läger.* [4] *entspringen.* [5] *Lucern.*

forasmuch as this is impossible. But the primitive[1] Spirits, which saw Alexandrum and his consort, they can take upon them such form and shape, and change themselves into it; through these I will let your Majesty see Alexandrum in truth. Hereupon Faustus went out of the Emperor's chamber, to confer with his Spirit; after this he went in again to the Emperor, announces to him how he is ready herein to obey him, but on the condition, that his Imperial Majesty is to ask no questions nor say aught: which the Emperor granted him. Dr. Faustus opened the door. Soon the Emperor Alexander came in, in the very shape and form as he was seen in life. Namely, a well-built[2], fat little man, with a red or all-yellow[3] and thick beard, red cheeks, and a severe countenance, as if he had the eyes of a basilisk. He entered in a whole complete suit of armour to the Emperor Carolus, and bows with a deep salute[4]. The Emperor was accordingly about to rise, and receive him, but this Dr. Faustus would not allow. Soon after, when Alexander had bowed again, and was going out at the door, his consort at once comes in towards him; she also bowed to the Emperor; she was in a complete suit of blue velvet, adorned with golden embroidery and pearls; she was also exceeding beautiful and red-cheeked, like milk and blood, rather tall, and of a round face. Herein the Emperor thought, now have I see two persons, whom I have long desired to see, and it cannot well be but that the Spirit has changed into these forms, and does not deceive me, like as the woman awakened from the dead the Prophet Samuel. And in order that he might know this the more surely, the Emperor thought to himself, Now I have often heard, that she had at the back of her neck a great mole; and went up to see whether this was also to be found in this figure[5]; and accordingly found the mole, for she stood stock-still before him, and after this vanished away again; herewith the Emperor's desire was fulfilled.

CHAPTER XXXIV. *Dr. Faustus conjured a stag's horns upon*

[1] *vhralte.* [2] *wolgesetztes.* [3] *gleichfalben.* [4] *Reverentz.* [5] *Bild.*

the head of a knight. When Dr. Faustus had fulfilled the Emperor's desire, as has been told, he lay down at eventide, after at the court the trumpet had sounded for table, upon a turret, to see the court servants come out and in. Then Faustus sees over the way in the lodgings[1] of the knights one lying asleep under the window (for it was very hot that same day); the person who had so fallen asleep, I do not wish to name, for he was a knight and baron born, although these adventures made him to be mocked, yet the Spirit Mephostophiles diligently and faithfully gave aid to his master thereunto, and thus conjured on his head, while he was asleep, a stag's horns. When he then awoke, and bent his head under the window, he perceived the trick; now who was more frightened than this good lord? For the windows were shut, and with his stag's horns he could neither move backwards nor forwards, which the Emperor observed, laughed thereat, and was well pleased therewith, till at last Dr. Faustus removed the magic again from him.

Erat Baro ab Hardeck[2].

[Interspersed are some adventures in humble company, among them:]

CHAPTER XXXIX. *Dr. Faustus deceives a horse-courser.* He played the same trick upon a horse-courser at a fair; for he made for himself a fine splendid horse, on which he rode to a fair, called Pfeiffering, and had many buyers offering for it; in the end he sold it for forty florins, having before told the horse-courser not to ride it into any water. The horse-courser wished to see what in the world he could mean by this, so he rode into a place of watering, when the horse vanished and he found himself sitting upon a bundle of hay, so that he had nigh been drowned. The buyer knew still very well at what inn his seller lay, went thither in wrath, found Dr. Faustum lying in a bed, asleep and snoring. The horse-courser seized him by the foot, meaning to pull him down, when the foot came off, and the horse-courser fell down with it in the chamber. Then Dr. Faustus began to cry Ho! Murder! The horse-courser was afraid, took to his heels and made off, thinking not otherwise than that he

[1] *Losament.*

[2] *Sic* in margin.

had pulled the man's foot off; so Dr. Faustus recovered his money.

CHAPTER XLIV. *What adventures Dr. Faustus carried on at the court of the Prince of Anhalt.* Dr. Faustus came at one time to the Count of Anhalt, who are nowadays princes, who showed him every gracious kindness; this happened in January. When supper had been brought in, and sweetmeats[1] were served, Faustus said to the Countess: Gracious lady, I pray your Grace not to withhold from me what you would desire to have to eat. She answered him: Master Doctor, truly I will not withhold it from you, what I would at this moment desire. Namely, if that it were the season of autumn, I should like to eat my fill of fresh grapes and fruit. Dr. Faustus on this said: Gracious lady, that is easy for me to perform, and in half an hour the desire of your Grace shall be satisfied. He took speedily two silver dishes, and placed them out before the window. And when the time had come he put his hand out of the window, and took the dishes in again, in which were red and white grapes, similarly in the other dish apples and pears, but of a foreign sort and as from a remote land, placed these before the Countess, and says, I pray your Grace not to be frightened hereat against eating [of them], for they are of a sort from a foreign land far away, at that side [of the earth[2]] where the summer is about to end. So the Countess ate of all the fruit and grapes with delight and great astonishment. The Prince of Anhalt could not refrain from asking, what had been the manner and occasion with the grapes and fruit. Dr. Faustus answers: Gracious lord, your Grace must know, that the year is divided into two circles of the world, so that when now it is with us winter, it is summer in Orient and Occident, for the heavens are round, and the sun has at present mounted to his greatest height, so that at this time we have the short days and winter, but in Orient and Occident, as in Saba, India and the right East[3], there the sun is going down, and in those places they have summer, and twice in the year corn and fruit. *Item,* when it is night with us, the day begins with them. For the sun has gone down

[1] *Specerey.* [2] *der Enden.* [3] *recht Morgenland.*

under the earth, and it is therewith as with this other matter[1]: the sea is and rises higher than [the surface of] the earth lies; now if the sea were not obedient to the Most High, it could spoil the world in a moment; so now the sun is ascending with them, and descending with us. On such report, gracious lord, I sent thither my Spirit, who is a swift and flying Spirit, can change himself in a moment, he has conquered these grapes and fruit. To this the Prince listened with great astonishment.

CHAPTER L. *On White Sunday*[2] *of the enchanted Helena*. On White Sunday the aforesaid students came unexpectedly again into the house of Doctor Faustus to supper, bringing with them their meat and drink, who were pleasant guests. Now when the wine was brought in, the talk at table was of fair women, when one of them began to say, that there was no other woman he would rather behold than the fair *Helenam* of *Graecia*, for whose sake the fair city of Troy had been destroyed; she must have been fair, because she had been carried away from her husband, on which account such a disturbance had arisen. Dr. Faustus answered, Forasmuch then as you are so desirous to see the fair form of the Queen *Helena*, the house-wife *Menelai*, or daughter *Tyndari* and *Lædæ*, *Castoris* and *Pollucis* sister (said to have been the fairest in *Graecia*), I will present the same to you, so that you may personally see her spirit in form and shape, as she was in life; even as I obeyed the desire of Emperor *Carolus Quintus*, by presenting *Alexandrum Magnum* and his consort. Hereupon Dr. Faustus forbade that none should say naught, nor arise from table, or venture to receive her; and goes out of the chamber. When he comes in again, the Queen *Helena* followed his footsteps, so wondrously fair, that the students knew not whether they were in their senses or not, so confused and ardent were they. This *Helena* appeared in a costly black purple robe, her hair she wore hanging down, which shone fair and glorious with a hue of gold, and so long

[1] *ist dessen ein Gleichnuss;* i. e. both things are equally wonderful instances of Providence.

[2] *Dominica Alba* or *Quasimodogeniti*, the First Sunday after Easter.

that it descended down to her knees, with beautiful coal-black eyes, a lovely countenance, with a round little head, her lips red as cherries, with a small little mouth, a neck like a white swan, red little cheeks like a rose-bud[1], an exceeding fair shining[2] face, a rather tall erect straight person[3]. In summa there was no fault to find in her . . . .

CHAPTER LIII. *Of an Old Man, that wished to warn off and convert Dr. Faustus from his godless life, also what ingratitude he therein received.* A Christian pious God-fearing physician, and lover of Holy Writ, a neighbour too of Dr. Faustus . . . resolved by his exhortations to bring Dr. Faustum from his devilish godless ways, and for this purpose in Christian zeal summoned him into his house. Faustus came to him, and over meat the Old Man thus addressed Faustus: My dear Master Neighbour, I have to you a friendly Christian prayer, that you will not take and receive my zealous speech unkindly or in anger, and at the same time not despise this slender entertainment, but kindly be content with it, as the good God has bestowed it. Dr. Faustus thereupon requested that he would explain to him his intent, he would do courteous obedience to him. Then the kind friend[4] began, My dear Master Neighbour, you know your resolve, that you have renounced God and all the Saints, and given yourself up to the Devil, whereby you have fallen into the utmost anger and wrath of God, and from a Christian have become a real heretic and devil. Alas, why do you charge[5] your soul? It is not the body alone that is in question, but the soul also, thus are you lying in the eternal punishment[6] and wrath of God; well then, Master, it is not yet too late, if only you turn and seek grace and pardon with God, as you see the example in the Acts of the Apostles . . . . therefore, Master, do you too listen to my sermon, and let it be a hearty Christian admonition to you. Now is to be sought penance, grace and pardon, of which you have many fine examples . . . . . This speech I beg you, Master, to take to heart, and pray God for forgiveness, for Christ's sake, and

[1] *Rösslin.* [2] *gleissend.*
[3] *eine länglichte auffgerichte gerade Person.* [4] *der Patron.*
[5] *was zeiht jhr.* [6] *in der ewigen Pein.*

at the same time abandon your evil resolve, for magic is against the commandments of God . . . . . Dr. Faustus listened diligently to him and said that he was well pleased with the doctrine, and gave thanks for it to the Old Man on account of his good intent, and promised to obey it in so far as he could; therewith he took his leave. Now when he came home, he thought diligently on this doctrine and admonition, reflected with what he had charged himself and his soul, that he had thus given himself up to the sorry Devil; he wished to do penance, and to renounce his promise to the Devil.

The Devil is not idle[1].

In such thoughts his Spirit appears to him, tries to lay hold of him[2], as if he were about to twist round his head, and reproachfully reminded him of what had moved him to give himself up to the Devil, namely his insolent perversity[3]. Moreover he had promised to be an enemy to God and to all men; this promise he was now not keeping, (but) wished to follow the sly old fellow[4], to be in kindness with a man and with God, when it was already too late and he belonged to the Devil, who had good power to fetch him, as indeed he now commanded, and for this reason he was there, that he should put an end to him[5],—otherwise, let him speedily sit down and bind himself anew by a contract signed with his blood, and promise that he would no more allow himself to be warned and tempted by any man; and as to this he must now speedily declare himself, whether he would do it or not. Dr. Faustus utterly terrified, grants him his wish anew, sits down, and writes with his blood as follows, which bill was accordingly found, after his death, left behind him.

[In Chapter LIV the Second Contract is given *verbatim*; and the story then returns to the Old Man:]

After this damnable and godless contract, he became so wroth with the good Old Man, that he sought to take away his life; but his Christian prayers and conduct dealt such a blow to the Fiend that he could not get at him[6]. For not more than two days after, when the pious man was going to bed, he heard in the house a great disturbance[7], which he

[1] *Sic* in margin. [2] *tappet nach jm.* [3] *Mutwillen.* [4] *dem alten Lauren.* [5] *jme den gar auss machen.* [6] *jm beykommen.* [7] *Gerömpel.*

had never heard before; it enters his chamber, grunted[1] like a sow, and carried this on for a long time. Hereupon the Old Man began to mock at the Spirit, and says: Ah of a truth that is a rustic *Musica*, a fine song indeed from a ghost, like a fine song of praise by an Angel, who could not remain two days in Paradise; he busies himself[2] in other folks' houses, and could not remain in his own lodging. With such mockery he had driven away the Spirit. Dr. Faust asked him, how he had dealt with the Old Man? Answered the Spirit, he had been unable to get at him, for he was in armour—meaning prayer. So he had over and above mocked him, which the Spirits or devils cannot bear, especially when they are reproached with their Fall. Thus God protects all pious Christians, such as give themselves up and commend themselves to God against the Evil Spirit.

[After some further magical tricks of Faustus, and an account of his life with Helena of Greece, who bore unto Faustus a son whom he called *Iustum Faustum*, we come at last to 'the doings of Doctor Faustus with his Spirit and others in his last year's term, which was the twenty-fourth and last year of his contract.' First we have the account of his last will, in which he left all his house-property (which is specified), a rent of 1600 florins, a peasant's farm, and cash, ornaments and plate collected by him in his travels, to his famulus Wagner, of whose early days another sketch is given (Chapter LXI); and who is promised a Spirit of his own after his master's death (Chapter LXII). Then, only a month now remaining between Faustus and his doom, begins a series of his lamentations and despairing soliloquies; 'for he was terrified, weeps and continues talking to himself, fumbles with his hands[3], groans and sighs, lost flesh and henceforth would allow himself to be but rarely seen or not at all, and would not see or bear his Spirit any more to be in his company' (Chapter LXIII). The Spirit however thrusts himself into his presence, and attacks him in his sorrow with strange jests and proverbs (Chapter LXVI). Faustus resumes his lamentations; and then the catastrophe is at hand.]

[1] *kürrete.* [2] *vexiert sich.* [3] *fantasiert mit den Händen.*

CHAPTER LXVIII. *Here follows* [the account] *of Dr. Fausti horrible and awful end, from which every Christian may take a sufficient example to himself*[1], *and guard himself against it.* The twenty-four years of Doctor Faustus had gone[2], and in this very week the Spirit appeared unto him, presents to him his bill and contract, at the same time announces to him that in the next night the Devil will fetch his body, for which let him be prepared. Doctor Faustus lamented and wept the whole night, so that the Spirit again appeared to him in this night, and comforted him: My Fauste, prithee be not so faint-hearted; although thou mayest lose thy body, yet it is a long time before thou shalt come to judgment; in the end thou must after all die, although thou shouldest live many hundred years. . . . Doctor Faustus who knew not otherwise than that he must pay the promise or contract with his person[3], on this very day when the Spirit had announced to him that the Devil would fetch him, goes to his intimate companions, Magistri, Baccalaurei and other students, who had heretofore often visited him; these he prays to take a walk[4] with him into the village of Rimlich, half a mile distant from Wittenberg, and there hold a repast with him, which they promised to do. So they go thither together, and eat a morning-repast, with many costly courses, of meat and wine, which the host served. Dr. Faustus was merry with them, but not from his very heart; prays them all again that they would so far favour him, and sup with him, and remain through the night with him. He had (he said) something of moment to tell them; which they again granted to him, and also partook of the repast. Now when the posset[5] had also been finished, Dr. Faustus pays the host, and begged of the students that they would go with him into another chamber, he wished to say something to them; this was done. Dr. Faustus spoke to them as follows:

CHAPTER LXIX. *Oratio Fausti ad Studiosos.* My dear intimate and most loving masters, the cause why I have called you here is this, that you have known of me for

[1] *ab welchem sich gnugsam zu spiegeln.* [2] *waren erschienen.* [3] *mit der Haut.* [4] *spatzieren.* [5] *Schlafftrunck.*

many years, what manner of man I was, experienced in many arts and magic, which however come from no other source, than from the Devil; to which devilish joy neither has any one brought me but the bad company which dealt in such like tricks; next my naughty[1] flesh and blood, my obstinate and godless will, and high-flying[2] devilish thoughts, which I proposed unto myself, wherefore I had to promise myself to the Devil, namely in twenty-four years, my body and soul. Now these years all but this night are run out, and the hour-glass stands before my eyes, so that I must watch, when it runs out, and he shall fetch me this night, forasmuch as I have contracted body and soul to him for a second time at so dear a price with my own blood; therefore I have called you, kind loving dear masters, to me before my end, and desired to drink with you a loving-cup[3] for a fare-well, and wished to conceal from you my decease. Whereupon I pray you, kind dear brethren and masters, you will salute all those belonging to me, and those who think of me in a friendly way, fraternally and kindly from me, at the same time not take anything in ill part from me, and wherein-soever I have offended you heartily forgive it me. But as to what concerns the adventures which I have carried on in these twenty-four years, this you will find all left in writing behind me; and let my awful end be for all your days an example and admonition, that ye may desire to have God before your eyes, and pray Him to guard you from the guile and craft of the Devil, and not to lead you into temptation, on the contrary to cling to Him, and least of all[5] to fall away from Him, as I godless and condemned man (have done), who have contemned and renounced Baptism, the Sacrament of Christ, God Himself, all the Heavenly Host, and man—a God who desireth not that any one shall be lost. Let not evil company seduce you, as it is with and hath happened to me. Go to church with diligence and zeal, conquer and fight at all times against the Devil, being stablished[6] with a good faith in Christ, and a godly conduct of life.

The Devil's brethren[4].

[1] *nichtwerdes* (worthless). [2] *fliegende.* [3] *Johanns trunck.*
[4] *Sic* in margin. [5] *nicht so gar.* [6] *gericht.*

Lastly now and in conclusion, it is my kindly request, that you will betake yourselves to bed, sleep in quiet, and let it not trouble you, even if you hear a loud noise and tumult [1] in the house, do not by any means be frightened thereat, no harm shall happen to you, do not rise from bed; and should you find my body dead, let it be buried in the earth. For I die as a bad and good Christian,—a good Christian, forasmuch as I have a hearty repentance, and in my heart am ever praying for grace, that my soul may be saved; a bad Christian, forasmuch as I know that the Devil desires to have my body, and this I will gladly let him have, let him but leave my soul in quiet [3]. Hereupon I pray you, you would betake yourselves to bed, and wish you a good night, but to me a troublous, evil and terrible one.

Judas repentance [2].

This declaration and narration Doctor Faustus made in a courageous mood, lest he should make them timorous, afraid and dispirited. But the students were utterly astonished, that he had been so daring, and had only for the sake of pleasure, arrogance of mind and magic entered into such a danger of life and soul; they were heartily grieved, for they loved him, and said: Alas Master Fauste, what have you charged yourself with, that you were silent so long, and have not revealed this to us; we would through learned theologos have saved and torn you out of the Devil's net, but now it is too late, and hurtful to your body and soul. Doctor Faustus answers: He had not been allowed to do it, although he had often wished to go to pious persons, and seek counsel and aid, as indeed my neighbour addressed me hereon, that I should follow his doctrine, abandon magic, and be converted. And when thereupon I was also willing to do this, the Devil came and said: So soon as I should accept conversion to God, he would make an end of me. When they learnt this from Doctor Faustus, they said to him: Since then naught else was to be hoped for, let him call upon God, pray for His forgiveness for the sake of His dear Son Jesus Christ, and say: O God, be merciful to me a miserable sinner, and enter not

[1] *Gepölter vnd Vngestümb.* [2] *Sic* in margin. [3] *zu frieden.*

into judgment with me, for I cannot stand before Thee. Although I must leave my body to the Devil, yet Thou be willing to preserve my soul—whether perchance God would interpose [1]. This he promised them to do; he sought to pray, but it would not come from his heart [2]; as with Cain, who also said, that his sins were greater than that they could be forgiven him. So he likewise ever had it in his thoughts, that he had done too heavy a piece of work [3] with his contract. These students and good gentlemen, when they had blessed Faustus, they wept and embraced one another. But Dr. Faustus remained in the chamber, and when the gentlemen had gone to bed, not one of them could sleep well, for they desired to hear the issue. But it happened between twelve and one o'clock in the night, that there blew against the house a great violent wind, which environed the house on all sides, as if everything were to perish and the wind were about to tear down the house to its foundations. At this the students were terrified in mind, sprang out of bed, and began to comfort one another, and would not leave the chamber. The host ran out of his house into another. The students lay near to the chamber wherein was Dr. Faustus; they heard an awful whistling and hissing, as if the house were full of snakes, adders and other noxious worms; at that moment the door in the chamber of Dr. Faustus opens; who began to cry Help! and Murder!—but scarce with half his voice, and soon after he was heard no more. When after this the day came, and the students had not slept the whole night, they went into the chamber wherein Dr. Faustus had been; but they saw no Faustus there any longer and naught but the chamber spattered full of blood. The brain was cleaving to the wall, for the Devil had beaten him from one wall to the other. His eyes also and some toes lay there, a loathsome and terrible spectacle. Then the students began to lament and weep for him, and sought him everywhere, and at last they found lying outside the door

[1] *etwas wirckenwolte.* [2] *jhme eingehen.*
[3] *hette es zu grob gemacht.*

of the house by the mixen his body, which was loathsome to look upon, for the head and all the limbs were quivering.

The aforesaid magistri and students, who were present at Fausti death, obtained so much that he was buried in this village; after this they went home to Wittenberg. . . .

[The closing passages relate how this Fausti Historia was found in his house at Wittenberg, and how the masters and students added to it the account of his death. The enchanted Helena with her son had vanished; but Wagner the famulus remained, and received a visit from the Spirit of his master, whose house henceforth stood empty, an object of mystery and awe. The book ends with an admonition and a text from Holy Writ.]

Ballad of Doctor Faustus.

To these extracts from the Faustbuch I append the text of the ballad already mentioned, as printed by Dyce from a copy in the Roxburghe Collection in the British Museum:—

'*The Judgment of God shewed upon one John Faustus, Doctor in Divinity.*

Tune of Fortune, my Foe.

All Christian men, give ear awhile to me,
How I am plung'd in pain, but cannot die:
I liv'd a life the like did none before,
Forsaking Christ, and I am damn'd therefore.

At Wittenburge, a town in Germany,
There was I born and bred of good degree;
Of honest stock, which afterwards I sham'd;
Accurst therefore, for Faustus was I nam'd.

In learning, loe, my uncle brought up me,
And made me Doctor in Divinity;
And, when he dy'd, he left me all his wealth,
Whose cursed gold did hinder my souls health.

Then did I shun the holy Bible-book,
Nor on Gods word would ever after look;
But studied accursed conjuration,
Which was the cause of my utter damnation.

The devil in fryars weeds appear'd to me,
And streight to my request he did agree,
That I might have all things at my desire:
I gave him soul and body for his hire.

Twice did I make my tender flesh to bleed,
Twice with my blood I wrote the devils deed,
Twice wretchedly I soul and body sold,
To live in peace and do what things I would.

For four and twenty years this bond was made,
And at the length my soul was truly paid:
Time ran away, and yet I never thought
How dear my soul our Saviour Christ had bought.

Would I had first been made a beast by kind!
Then had not I so vainly set my mind;
Or would, when reason first began to bloom,
Some darksome den had been my deadly tomb!

Woe to the day of my nativity!
Woe to the time that once did foster me!
And woe unto the hand that seal'd the bill!
Woe to myself, the cause of all my ill!

The time I past away, with much delight,
'Mongst princes, peers, and many a worthy knight:
I wrought such wonders by my magick skill,
That all the world may talk of Faustus still.

The devil he carried me up into the sky,
Where I did see how all the world did lie;
I went about the world in eight daies space,
And then return'd unto my native place.

What pleasure I did wish to please my mind
He did perform, as bond and seal did bind;
The secrets of the stars and planets told,
Of earth and sea, with wonders manifold.

When four and twenty years was almost run,
I thought of all things that was past and done;
How that the devil would soon claim his right,
And carry me to everlasting night.

Then all too late I curst my wicked deed,
The dread whereof doth make my heart to bleed;
All daies and hours I mourned wondrous sore,
Repenting me of all things done before.

I then did wish both sun and moon to stay,
All times and seasons never to decay;
Then had my time nere come to dated end,
Nor soul and body down to hell descend.

At last, when I had but one hour to come,
I turn'd my glass, for my last hour to run,
And call'd in learned men to comfort me;
But faith was gone, and none could comfort me.

By twelve a clock my glass was almost out:
My grieved conscience then began to doubt;
I wisht the students stay in chamber by;
But, as they staid, they heard a dreadful cry.

Then present, lo, they came into the hall,
Whereas my brains was cast against the wall;
Both arms and legs in pieces torn they see,
My bowels gone: this was an end of me.

You conjurors and damned witches all,
Example take by my unhappy fall;
Give not your souls and bodies unto hell,
See that the smallest hair you do not sell.

But hope that Christ his kingdom you may gain,
Where you shall never fear such mortal pain;
Forsake the devil and all his crafty ways,
Embrace true faith that never more decays.

Printed by and for A. M. and sold by the Booksellers of London.'

Notices of additions to Marlowe's Doctor Faustus by other hands.

Marlowe's The Tragical History of Doctor Faustus, as preserved to us in the earliest extant copy, is not the play in its original form. This fact is proved by two entries in Henslowe's Diary. The first (Collier's edition, 71) runs as follows:

'P[d] unto Thomas Dickers the 20 of Desembr 1597, for adycyons to Fostus twentie shellinges, and fyve shellinges for a prolog to Marloes Tamberlen, so in all I payde twenty fyve shellinges';

and the second (*ib.* 228):

'Lent unto the companye, the 22 of novembr 1602, to paye unto W[m] Birde and Samwell Rowley for their adicyones in Docter Fostes, the some of . . . . iiij[li].'

The company in which Henslowe and his partner Edward Alleyn were chiefly interested (though they also had an interest in others) was that 'indifferently called the Earl of Nottingham's or the Lord Admiral's Servants' (who became 'the Prince's Servants' in 1603)[1]. This company from June 1594 to July 1596 occupied the Newington Theatre jointly with the Lord Chamberlain's Servants, or possibly played there in combination with them; they also played, first at 'the Theatre'

[1] These data are given from a comparison of the statements in Henslowe's Diary and Mr. Collier's notes with the chapter on the earliest English Theatrical Companies in Mr. Fleay's Shakspere Manual.

and at the Curtain (on the stage of which an early ballad asserted that Marlowe 'in his early age' was a player and 'brake his leg'), and then at the Rose; whence after Alleyn had in 1600 built the Fortune they moved to this house, where they continued till it was burnt down in 1621. In the 'Enventary tacken of all the properties for my Lord Admeralles men, the 10 of Marche 1598,' given by Henslowe (Collier's edition, 273), occurs the item 'j dragon in fostes.' Alleyn himself at one time performed the hero of Marlowe's tragedy, as appears from a passage cited by Collier from S. Rowland's Knave of Clubs, 1600:

'The gull gets on a surplis
With crosse upon his breast,
Like Allen playing Faustus;
In that manner he was drest;'

and an inventory of Alleyn's theatrical apparel includes 'Faustus Jerkin, his cloke[1].'

Estimate of these revisions.

Now, it has been seen that the play had probably received additions from other hands than the author's already on its production—which was probably a revival—by the Lord Admiral's men in 1594; and thus we have the probability of three, and the certainty of two, revisions before the date of the printing of the play in its first extant edition, of 1604. Of these three revisions it is clear that the last, that of 1602, must have contained extensive alterations; or so large a sum as £4 would not have been risked on the bargain. It is of course possible that the later revision or revisions restored parts or passages which the earlier had omitted; it is likewise possible that parts or passages omitted in one or more of the revisions were re-inserted in the printed editions of the play, of which the third and following contain much that is not in the first and second extant editions. There is the third possibility (which is assumed by Ulrici[2]), that the edition of 1604 contains the play as it was performed from 1597 onwards with the additions by Dekker, and the edition of 1616

[1] Cited by Dyce, xx, from Collier's Memoirs of Alleyn, 20.

[2] Christopher Marlowe und Shakespeare's Verhältniss zu ihm, in the Jahrbuch der deutschen Shakespeare-Gesellschaft, i. (1865) 64-65.

the play as it was performed from 1602 onwards with the additions by Birde and S. Rowley [1]. Dekker was, not indeed a dramatist fitted for improving Marlowe,—as a comparison between Doctor Faustus and Olde Fortunatus would suffice to show,—but a capable playwright of the better sort, devoid neither of comic humour nor of elements of tragic power, whom it would be pleasant to be able to pronounce guiltless of the worthless additions, as nearly all of them are [2], of the third quarto. Of William Birde, or Borne, we have nothing of his own left; Samuel Rowley, to judge from the one of his two extant plays with which I am acquainted [3], was a writer resembling Thomas Heywood in his least refined vein—the very man to write down a play to the level of a popular audience.

I shall make no attempt to distinguish between the original work of Marlowe, and the additions of other playwrights. Marlowe, though a writer not altogether devoid of humour [4], is far from being distinguished by this quality; and he may

[1] This supposition is rendered probable by the fact that a passage printed in the quartos of 1604 and 1609 is omitted in that of 1616; which passage, as has been acutely pointed out by Dr. Albers, *u. s.*, 380, seems like an addition of the year 1597. It is the Clown's contemptuous comparison of the value of French crowns to that of English counters (iv. 36-37). 'In the year 1595 an active and considerable commerce arose between England and France. England commenced to export a large quantity "d'objets de première nécessité" to France, and this commerce together with the reimbursement of the large sums which Queen Elizabeth had lent to Henry IV, drew a large quantity of French money to England; but this was not the case in the days of Marlowe, and the allusion in question in his days would have been rather incomprehensible. Five years later—in 1602—when Birde and Rowley revised the play, Sully had already improved the French finances so much, that the allusion was omitted as antiquated.'

[2] Professor Wagner has marked as an exception two passages towards the close of the tragedy. See note on sc. xiv.

[3] When You See Me You Know Me, or the Famous Chronicle Historie of King Henrie the Eight, etc.

[4] There is a touch of it in Gaveston in Edward II. The Friars in the Jew of Malta are coarsely satirical rather than humorous figures, and they may not be altogether from Marlowe's hand; the Nurse in Dido (who probably suggested the Nurse in Romeo and Juliet) is humorously drawn, but *may* be Nash's invention.

not have scrupled to meet the tastes of his audience by a reproduction of comic passages of the story-book in an appropriately vulgar form. He had introduced scenes of this kind into the original Tamburlaine, which the printer of that tragedy in 1590 states that he has purposely omitted. But it is on the other hand bare justice to the genius of a great tragic poet to present one of its noblest productions without passages and scenes which are nearly all worthless in themselves, and which, as in the case of those absent from the first and second quartos, there is every probability to regard as additions by other hands. For this reason The Tragical History of Doctor Faustus has in the present volume been unhesitatingly reprinted from the text of the first extant quarto.

The first three quartos of the play; and later editions.

This is the quarto, preserved in the Bodleian Library, bearing the date of 1604. A second quarto, 'almost throughout the same' as the first, is that of 1609, belonging to the Town Library of Hamburg. A third edition is that of 1616, in which it is noteworthy that several expressions likely to give offence are changed, and certain lines are even altogether omitted, apparently for the same reason[1]. With this 'the later editions of 1620, 1624, 1631 and 1663 are generally in agreement; but all these are interpolated.' (In the edition of 1663 a scene at Babylon is inserted, which contains an allusion to the story of The Jew of Malta[2].) A careful comparison of the texts will be found in the Critical Commentary in Professor W. Wagner's admirable edition of the play; the text of 1616 is reprinted as well as that of 1604 in Dyce's edition of Marlowe's Works. In my notes I have adverted to some of the more important variations which the text of 1616 presents; for my text I have collated Dyce's edition of the 1604 quarto with that quarto itself, without thinking

[1] Thus i. 106–107 are omitted; in iii. 53 'all godliness' is substituted for 'the Trinity'; for xiv. 96–98 is substituted the one line,

'O, if my soul must suffer for my sin';

and in the same scene the word 'heaven' repeatedly takes the place of the Divine name.

[2] See Dyce, xxii, note.

it desirable to alter Dyce's modernised spelling. In the stage-directions and headings of scenes I have usually followed Dyce, while allowing myself occasional liberties of my own.

References to the play in our early literature.

The references to Marlowe's tragedy in our dramatic and other early literature are, so far as I am aware, very few. Besides the notice of Alleyn's performance of the principal character already quoted, Professor Wagner has mentioned two further passages in point. A play called The Devil's Charter, performed before King James I at Christmas 1606-7 and in October 1607 [1], and printed at London in the latter year, which treats of the life and death of Pope Alexander VI (I have not seen this play; but the story is in Widmann's Commentary), contains a scene of the signing of a contract between Alexander and a 'diuill' disguised as a pronotary; which scene is clearly copied from the corresponding one (v.) in Doctor Faustus [2]. In a collection of Satires by 'R. C. Gent.' written between the years 1614 and 1616 occurs a passage referring, as the modern editor of these Satires suggests, 'to the story of the play of Faustus, although it may be said the story was common enough for "R. C." to have got it elsewhere [3].' The late Mr. R. Simpson, in a letter to The Academy, October 17th, 1874, observes, in reference to the indications of a rivalry between Shakespeare and Marlowe mentioned by him in his remarks on Marlowe, Greene and Shakespeare [4], that he 'should have added Shakspere's lxxxvi^th Sonnet, which, as Mr. Massey shows, refers to some such relation. Marlowe perhaps, like Shak-

[1] See Collier, History of English Dramatic Poetry, i. 368, 435. The author of this play was B. Barnes.

[2] Wagner, Introduction, xxxviii-xxxix.

[3] *Ib.* xxxix-xl. The passage occurs p. 53 of Mr. J. W. Cowper's edition of this collection of Satires in the Early English Text Society's Publications, 1871. Mr. Cowper (Introduction, xxi) observes that two lines in the same satire appear to be 'another form of one of the opinions "of one Christofer Marlaye," namely, "that the first beginning of religion was only to keep men in awe."'

[4] Reprinted from The Academy, April 11th, 1874, as a Supplement to Dr. Ingleby's General Introduction to the Shakspere Allusion Books, Part I (New Shakspere Society's Publications, 1874).

spere, intended to dedicate his poem to Southampton; Sonnet lxxx:

> "O how I faint when I of you do write,
> Knowing a better spirit doth use your name";

and Sonnet lxxxvi:

> "Was it his spirit, by spirits taught to write
> Above a mortal pitch, that struck me dead?
> No, neither he, nor his compeers by night
> Giving him aid, my verse astonishèd.
> He, nor that affable familiar ghost
> Which nightly gulls him with intelligence,
> As victors of my silence cannot boast."

Mr. Massey with great probability argues that Shakspere here alludes to Marlowe under the mask of Faustus, with Mephistophiles his familiar[1].' Perhaps, too, a special allusion to Marlowe's authorship may be sought in the last two lines of the fine passage in which the author of The Returne from Parnassus (a play acted before Queen Elizabeth, though not printed till 1606) contrasts the genius of Marlowe with his 'life and end':

> 'Our theater hath lost, Pluto hath got,
> A tragick penman for a driery plot.'

Marlowe's play in Germany.

So popular a stage-play as Marlowe's Doctor Faustus could hardly fail to be carried into Germany by the English comedians who, as already noticed, performed in that country in the latter part of the sixteenth and the early part of the seventeenth century. When therefore among the plays acted at the Dresden Court by the English comedians in 1626 we find mentioned a 'Tragœdia von Dr. Faust,' we can hardly doubt that this is Marlowe's tragedy[2]. Thus Marlowe, who

[1] Shakespeare alludes to the *story* of Doctor Faustus in The Merry Wives of Windsor, iv. 5. 71, where Bardolph says: 'As soon as I came beyond Eton, they threw me off from behind one of them, in a slough of mire: and set spurs and away, like three German devils, three Doctor Faustuses.' But neither this nor the use of the name 'Mephistophilus' in the same comedy, i. 1. 132, need be regarded as alluding to the *play*.

[2] See above, p. xlvii; and compare Cohn, *u. s.*, cxv, cxvii, and R. Genée, Geschichte der Shakespeare'schen Dramen in Deutschland, 41. A 'Barrabas,' clearly a reproduction of Marlowe's The Jew of Malta, occurs in the same list.

had derived his subject from a German source, seems in his turn to have influenced, if not to have given rise to, the treatment of the same theme by the German popular drama. 'That our old plays,' writes Lessing[1], 'really contain much that is English, I could prove to you with very little trouble. To name only the best-known among them: Doctor Faust has a number of scenes, which only a Shakespearean genius was capable of conceiving. And how thoroughly in love Germany was, and partly still is, with her Doctor Faust!'

Later dramatic treatments of the subject in England;

Here it is necessary to break off. For it would carry me beyond the proper sphere of this Introduction, were I to pursue the history of the literary treatments of the story of Faustus beyond the period of the direct influence of Marlowe's tragedy. It must suffice to observe, on the one hand, that in England no dramatic version of the theme has been attempted after Marlowe's worthy of notice by its side. Neither an English puppet-play produced by Powell at the Haymarket Theatre in 1710[2], nor a series of harlequinades on the subject from 1724 onwards, requires to be dwelt upon; and of W. Montfort's Life and Death of Doctor Faustus (a farce produced at Dorset Gardens between 1684 and 1688, and published in 1697) two-thirds were borrowed from Marlowe, the fame of whose Faustus-tragedy had survived the dark age of the English theatre[3], and the rest was harlequinade[4]. Later English dramatic versions of the story are based partly on the old legend and on Marlowe, partly on Goethe, and have in no case aimed at more than the delectation of theatrical audiences[5]. What little a work of a very different kind—Byron's Manfred—owed to Marlowe's Faustus, it owed

[1] Quoted by Kuno Fischer, *u. s.*, 78.

[2] See Engel, *u. s.*, 30.

[3] See Geneste's History of the Drama and Stage in England, ii. 450–451.

[4] Sir William D'Avenant in his The Playhouse to be Let (written about 1673) refers to Faustus as a popular play of the old times. See Collier, iii. 424.

[5] The curious will find a list of English Faust-plays in the notes to Hayward's Translation of Goethe's Faust (6th edition). This list might be easily enlarged.

indirectly through Goethe. In Germany, on the other hand, the story of Faustus has been the theme of a numberless series of dramatic treatments, of which many are in different degrees memorable in the national poetic literature. Two of the greatest names of that literature are, but again each in a different measure, associated with the subject. Lessing drew up two plans of a drama on Faust; but has left only a single scene. Thus it remained for Goethe to make the subject his own. On Goethe's Faust, which may be said to have been the inseparable companion of nearly the whole of the poet's literary life, research and criticism have expended and will continue to expend their most elaborate efforts, but —in so far at least as the First Part is concerned—no research will really elucidate and no criticism correctly judge the poem which fail to regard and treat it as a gradual but not systematic growth. A comparison between Marlowe's Doctor Faustus and Goethe's Faust would be out of place here, and the direct debt owing by the latter to the former can easily be estimated with the aid of a few incidental hints which will be given in my notes. This direct debt is trifling; the indirect can only be judged by an examination of Goethe's as well as of Marlowe's tragedy [1]. Goethe himself, when spoken to on the subject of Marlowe's Doctor Faustus, 'burst out with an exclamation of praise: How greatly is it all planned! He had thought of translating it. He was fully aware that Shakespeare did not stand alone [2]!'

And in Germany. *Lessing.* *Goethe.*

Of other German writers who have treated the subject it will be enough to mention, among the poets of the earlier and later growths of the Romantic School, Friedrich (called 'Maler,' i.e. painter) Müller and Klinger, and (these after

Other German dramatists.

[1] It is pleasing to be able to direct attention to an article by M. Foucher de Careil, in the Revue Politique et Littéraire (No. 51, June 16th, 1877), in which the contrast drawn by certain other French critics between Marlowe's and Goethe's Fausts as the living man and the philosophic symbol is discriminatingly weighed.

[2] H. Crabb Robinson's Diary, ii. 434, under the year 1829, quoted by Cunningham in the Introductory Notice to his edition of Marlowe's Works, xiv.

the publication of the First Part of Goethe's tragedy) Klingemann, Grabbe, Baggesen (a Dane who wrote, however, in German), Heine in his 'dance-poem' written for performance in London [1], the popular dramatist Karl von Holtei, and the gifted but ill-fated Lenau [2]. Goethe's drama has received musical illustration from many hands; and there are several operas on the subject, of which the last and most successful—the Frenchman Gounod's—is at this day a familiar favourite. The Faust-story has long been a favourite theme of the pictorial art in almost every conceivable form; it has employed the vivid fancy of Retzsch and the comprehensive genius of Kaulbach, and the varied powers of innumerable competitors. But since Marlowe, its chosen home has been the stage, whence its chief figures, increased with an incomparable addition by the genius of Goethe, are unlikely to be banished so long as a theatre exists.

Faustus in other arts.

Translations of Marlowe's tragedy.

Of translations of Marlowe's Doctor Faustus I am acquainted with three. Two are in German verse and prose—the one by Wilhelm Müller, published with an interesting preface by Achim von Arnim and notes by F. Notter in 1818 [3]; the other A. von der Velde's, 1870. The third is in French, by the late F. V. Hugo, 1858.

Greene's Friar Bacon.

External evidence as to date.

A very few notes will suffice as a summary of all that is known concerning the sources and history of Greene's Honourable History of Friar Bacon and Friar Bungay. This comedy was certainly performed as early as February 19th, 1592 (N.S.), as appears from the following entry in Henslowe's Diary (Collier's edition, 20):

'R^d at fryer bacone, the 19 of febrary, satterdaye . . xvij^s iij^d.'

Friar Bacon is the first play of the performance of which Henslowe states his share of receipts, and heads a list of plays performed by 'my lord Stranges mene,' the company

[1] See Mr. Sutherland-Edwards's paper How Dr. Faust became a Dancer, in Macmillan's Magazine, March, 1877. A ballet Doctor Faust was actually performed at Vienna in 1730.

[2] As to these see Reichlin-Meldegg, *u. s.*, xi. 750 *seqq.*

[3] Reprinted in Scheible's Kloster, vol. v.

which was probably the same as that which had formerly borne the name of Lord Strange's father Lord Derby, and which seems to have acted at the Rose. Henslowe does not mark Friar Bacon as a new play, nor is there any reason to conclude it to have been such. He mentions its performance by Lord Strange's and by Lord Sussex's company (which latter had also borne the name of the Lord Chamberlain's men till the appointment of Lord Hunsdon to that office in 1582) on eight subsequent occasions, ending with April 5th, 1593; but the receipts are usually moderate, though in one instance Henslowe's share rises to 'xxxiiis[1].'

The play was first published in 1594, in which year we find in the Stationers' Registers[2]:

> 'xiiii^to^ die Maij
>
> ~~Adam Islip~~ Entred for his Copie vnder th[e h]andes of bothe Edward White the wardens a booke entituled the *Historye of fryer BACON and ffryer BOUNGAY* . . . . vi^d^ c.' Sic crossed through

It was reprinted in 1599, 1630, and 1655; and of the first of these reprints (that of 1599) I have compared the copy in the Bodleian Library with Dyce's text, which is modernised like that of Doctor Faustus. The comedy was revived for performance at the Court in 1602, when we find this notice in Henslowe (Collier, 228):

> 'Lent unto Thomas Downton, the 14 of desember 1602, to paye unto Mr. Mydelton for a prologe and epeloge for the playe of Bacon for the corte, the some of . . . . v^s^.'

The prologue and epilogue for which the dramatist Thomas Middleton was so scantily remunerated[3] are not, so far as I know, preserved.

Internal evidence.

There is no direct internal evidence to fix the date of the composition of Friar Bacon. The insufficiency on this head of two passages in the comedy which a line in Doctor Faustus resembles, has been already pointed out[4]. The allusion to the Statute (xv. 27), which Bernhardi thought might

[1] See Collier's Henslowe's Diary, and compare Fleay, *u. s.*

[2] Arber's Transcript, ii. 307.

[3] According to Mr. Bell, in Dryden's day popular authors received a regular *honorarium* of five or six guineas for such contributions.

[4] Above, p. vi.

possibly be of value for the purpose will not help us; for the Act of Elizabeth regulating apparel was 5 Elizabeth, c. 6 (1563). Bernhardi[1] has also directed attention to the similarity between the opening scenes of Friar Bacon and of A Pleasant Comedie of Faire Em, the Millers Daughter of Manchester; with the Love of William the Conqueror. This play, which has (but I am convinced, wrongly) been attributed to Greene, must, whoever was its author, have been written after, and not before, Friar Bacon; of which its first scene certainly imitates the opening, but, as Simpson justly remarks, in an inferior way[2]. The title of the piece was very possibly suggested by the designation of the Keeper's Daughter in Friar Bacon as 'the Fair Maid of Fressingfield.' Moreover, the Epistle 'to the Gentlemen Students of both Universities' prefixed by Greene to his Farewell to Folly contains sarcastic allusions to two passages in Faire Em[3]. The tract in question was registered June 11th, 1587; it is however not known to have been printed till 1591. The allusions in the Epistle to Greene's Mourning Garment (registered July 1st, 1590, as 'England's mourninge gowne[4],' and first printed in that year), and to the published Tamburlaine (1590), show that the Epistle at all events cannot have been published with the Farewell to Folly till 1590 or 1591. On the other hand, the occurrence in Greene's Penelope's Web (received for printing June 19th, 1587, but not extant in any earlier edition than that of 1601) of a passage similar in tone to the sneer against Faire Em and its author in the Epistle[5], can hardly be regarded as a proof that the Epistle was written already in 1587.

Probable date.

I thus arrive at the conclusion that there is no reason against the assumption that Friar Bacon was written before February, 1589—very possibly in 1588, or even already in

[1] *u. s.*, 38.

[2] Sir R. Simpson's Introduction to Faire Em in The School of Shakspere, ii.

[3] See Simpson, *u. s.*, ii. 377–379. The passage is also cited in Collier's History of English Dramatic Poetry, ii. 441–442.

[4] Arber's Transcript, ii. 260.

[5] See Simpson, ii. 350.

1587; after, and if so, doubtless very soon after, Doctor Faustus had been produced on the stage.

Friar Bacon is not like Doctor Faustus a play following the thread of a single narrative in which serious and comic scenes are intermixed, but is constructed on the basis of a narrative of the same kind, with the addition of an underplot, or rather of a combination of two underplots. The chief of these underplots and the link between it and the other are manifestly Greene's own invention. The former is the story of Prince Edward's love for the Fair Maid of Fressingfield, and his resignation of her to the favoured messenger of his suit, Lacy. The notion of this story, which lacks all historical foundation, recurs with variations in other plays, illustrating in different fashions the maxim of Claudio in Much Ado about Nothing (ii. 1. 182–185), that

Sources of Friar Bacon.

The double underplot. Parallels.

> 'Friendship is constant in all other things
> Save in the office and affairs of love:
> Therefore all hearts in love use their own tongues;
> Let every eye negotiate for itself
> And trust no agent.'

In 1 Henry VI, Suffolk woos Margaret for the King—and for himself at the same time. In Faire Em the Marquis Lubeck is sent as William's emissary to Blanche, but in this instance the agent prefers his friendship to his love; while in Lord Orrery's 'heroic' play, The History of Henry V, Owen Tudor loyally renounces his passion for the Princess Catharine in the interest of his sovereign, in whose name he has been sent to court her[1]. Parallel passages to the magnanimous resignation of his passion by the Prince have been pointed out elsewhere[2]. The story of the enmity between the two neighbours and former friends, and of its fatal results for themselves and for their sons, Greene took from the same source as that

[1] Longfellow has treated a theme similar to that of Greene's underplot in his poem The Courtship of Miles Standish; and a similar story, said to be founded on the experience of two illustrious German scholars —brothers between whom the issue never affected a close friendship immortal in the world of letters—was some years ago brought on the German stage in a harmless but pleasant little piece.

[2] See note on Friar Bacon, viii. 120.

of Friar Bacon itself; but he has ingeniously connected it with the chief underplot by making a rival passion for the Fair Maid of Fressingfield the cause of the quarrel. The poet has laid the scene of his double underplot in Suffolk, with the localities and scenery of which, as a native of the neighbouring county (born at Norwich), he was doubtless well acquainted.

The Elizabethan story-book.

The story of Friar Bacon and his friend and associate Friar Bungay was taken by Greene from a popular story-book probably written towards the end of the sixteenth century, and founded upon the accretions of the legendary history of Friar Bacon already noticed. The title of the book, which has since been republished and is reprinted by Mr. Thoms [1], runs as follows: 'The Famous Historie of frier Bacon: containing the wonderful things that he did in his life: also the Manner of his death, with the Lives and Deaths of the two Conjurers, Bungye and Vandermast.' My extracts from this book are (with one exception) taken from this reprint, which I have compared with another in a duodecimo, published by J. Hollis in London, apparently in the last or about the beginning of the present century. This story-book does not mention the tradition of Bacon's contract with the Devil containing a clause that the Devil was to have the Friar's soul provided he died either in the church or out of it, which issue the Friar evaded by causing a cell to be constructed neither in nor out of the church, but in its wall, wherein he both died and was buried [2]; but it makes him die in such a cell, where he had lived for two years 'a true Penitent Sinner and an Anchorite.' The address of Friar Bacon to his friends and scholars before burning his books and withdrawing into a religious retreat, was very possibly suggested by the '*Oratio Fausti ad Studiosos*' in the Faustbuch [3]. To other incidents in the narrative it would be easy to find parallels in similar

[1] Early Prose Romances, vol. ii.

[2] See Thoms's Introduction to the Famous Historie, etc., *ib.* viii. A similar trick is related of Pope Silvester II by Widmann; see Schieble's Kloster, ii. 772.

[3] Compare above, pp. lxxviii *seqq.*

legends and traditions[1], and in the story of Faustus itself. For the rest, it is obvious that the author of the story-book was not altogether acquainted with some of the facts in the life of the real Roger Bacon, and more especially with the titles at least of one or more of his works, though here again he deviates into at least one allusion to a famous work of another philosopher and supposed magician—the De Incertitudine et Vanitate Scientiarum et Artium of Cornelius Agrippa.

Extracts from the story-book.

'The Famous Historie of Fryer Bacon' begins with a fictitious account of Roger Bacon's parentage and early days, showing how his father, a wealthy farmer in the west part of England, would not take the advice of the parson of the town with whom Roger was put to school to send him to Oxford, and how in the end 'young Bacon' 'gave his Father the slip and went to a Cloyster some twenty miles off, where he was entertained, and so continued his learning, and in a small time came to be so famous, that he was sent for to the University of Oxford, where he long time studied, and grew so excellent in the secrets of Art and Nature, that not England only, but all Christendome, admired him.'

CHAPTER II, '*How the King sent for Fryer Bacon, and of the wonderful things he showed the King and Queene*,' probably suggested the summoning of the Hostess of the Bell in order to confound Master Burden in the play (sc. ii); but the resemblance is not very close. Chapter IV I quote at length from Dyce, who has reprinted it at the close of the play:

CHAPTER IV. '*How Fryer Bacon made a Brasen Head to speake, by the which hee would have walled England about with brasse.* Fryer Bacon, reading one day of the many conquests of England, bethought himselfe how he might keepe it hereafter from the like conquests, and so make himselfe famous hereafter to all posterities. This, after great study, hee found could be no way so well done as one; which was to make a head of brasse, and if he could make this head to speake, and heare it when it speakes, then might hee be able

[1] The notion of Miles conjuring for meat has been compared to a similar episode in The Friars of Berwick, a Scottish poem which has been attributed to Dunbar. See Thoms, *u. s.*, vi.

to wall all England about with brasse. To this purpose hee got one Fryer Bungey to assist him, who was a great scholler and a magician, but not to bee compared to Fryer Bacon: these two with great study and paines so framed a head of brasse, that in the inward parts thereof there was all things like as in a naturall mans head. This being done, they were as farre from perfection of the worke as they were before, for they knew not how to give those parts that they had made motion, without which it was impossible that it should speake: many bookes they read, but yet could not finde out any hope of what they sought, that at the last they concluded to raise a spirit, and to know of him that which they could not attaine to by their owne studies. To do this they prepared all things ready, and went one evening to a wood thereby, and after many ceremonies used, they spake the words of coniuration; which the Devill straight obeyed, and appeared unto them, asking what they would? "Know," said Fryer Bacon, "that wee have made an artificiall head of brasse, which we would have to speake, to the furtherance of which wee have raised thee; and being raised, wee will here keepe thee, unlesse thou tell to us the way and manner how to make this head to speake." The Devill told him that he had not that power of himselfe. "Beginner of lyes," said Fryer Bacon, "I know that thou dost dissemble, and therefore tell it us quickly, or else wee will here bind thee to remaine during our pleasures." At these threatenings the Devill consented to doe it, and told them, that with a continuel fume of the six hotest simples it should have motion, and in one month space speak; the time of the moneth or day hee knew not: also hee told them, that if they heard it not before it had done speaking, all their labour should be lost. They being satisfied, licensed the spirit for to depart.

'Then went these two learned fryers home againe, and prepared the simples ready, and made the fume, and with continuall watching attended when this brasen head would speake. Thus watched they for three weekes without any rest, so that they were so weary and sleepy that they could not any longer refraine from rest: then called Fryer Bacon his man

Miles, and told him, that it was not unknown to him what paines Fryer Bungey and himselfe had taken for three weekes space, onely to make, and to heare the Brazen-head speake, which if they did not, then had they lost all their labour, and all England had a great losse thereby; therefore hee intreated Miles that he would watch whilst that they slept, and call them if the head speake. "Feare not, good master," said Miles, "I will not sleepe, but harken and attend upon the head, and if it doe chance to speake, I will call you; therefore I pray take you both your rests and let mee alone for watching this head." After Fryer Bacon had given him a great charge the second time, Fryer Bungy and he went to sleepe, and Miles, alone to watch the brasen head. Miles, to keepe him from sleeping, got a tabor and pipe, and being merry disposed, sung this song to a northern tune of

"*Cam'st thou not from Newcastle?*"[1]

'With his owne musicke and such songs as these spent he his time, and kept from sleeping at last. After some noyse the head spake these two words, TIME IS. Miles, hearing it to speake no more, thought his master would be angry if hee waked him for that, and therefore he let them both sleepe, and began to mocke the head in this manner; "Thou brazen-faced head, hath my master tooke all these paines about thee, and now dost thou requite him with two words, TIME IS? Had hee watched with a lawyer so long as he hath watched with thee, he would have given him more and better words than thou hast yet. If thou canst speake no wiser, they shal sleepe till doomes day for me: TIME IS! I know Time is, and that you shall heare, Goodman Brazen-face:—

'*To the tune of* "*Daintie, come thou to me.*"[2]

"Time is for some to eate,
Time is for some to sleepe,
Time is for some to laugh,
Time is for some to weepe.

[1] I omit this unpretentious lyric.
[2] Of this effort two stanzas will suffice.

Time is for some to sing,
Time is for some to pray,
Time is for some to creepe,
That have drunke all the day.

'"Do you tell us, copper-nose, when TIME IS? I hope we schollers know our times, when to drinke drunke, when to kisse our hostes, when to goe on her score, and when to pay it,—that time comes seldome." After halfe an houre had passed, the head did speake againe, two words, which were these, TIME WAS. Miles respected these words as little as he did the former, and would not wake them, but still scoffed at the brazen head, that it had learned no better words, and have such a tutor as his master: and in scorne of it sung this song;

'To the tune of "A Rich Merchant-man."

"Time was when thou, a kettle,
wert fill'd with better matter;
But Fryer Bacon did thee spoyle
when he thy sides did batter.

Time was when conscience dwellèd
with men of occupation;
Time was when lawyers did not thrive
so well by mens vexation.

Time was when kings and beggers
of one poore stuffe had being;
Time was when office kept no knaves,——
that time it was worth seeing.

Time was a bowle of water
did give the face reflection;
Time was when women knew no paint,
Which now they call complexion[1].

'"TIME WAS! I know that, brazen-face, without your telling, I know Time was, and I know what things there was when Time was; and if you speake no wiser, no master shall be waked for mee." Thus Miles talked and sung till another halfe-houre was gone: then the brazen head spake again these words, TIME IS PAST; and therewith fell downe, and

[1] Compare Terilo's Satire, A Piece of Friar Bacons Brazen-heads Prophesie, noticed above, p. xxiv.

presently followed a terrible noyse, with strange flashes of fire, so that Miles was halfe dead with feare. At this noyse the two Fryers awaked, and wondred to see the whole roome so full of smoake; but that being vanished, they might perceive the brazen head broken and lying on the ground. At this sight they grieved, and called Miles to know how this came. Miles, halfe dead with feare, said that it fell downe of itselfe, and that with the noyse and fire that followed he was almost frighted out of his wits. Fryer Bacon asked him if hee did not speake? "Yes," quoth Miles, "it spake, but to no purpose: Ile have a parret speake better in that time that you have been teaching this brazen head." "Out on thee, villaine!' said Fryer Bacon; "thou hast undone us both: hadst thou but called us when it did speake, all England had been walled round about with brasse, to its glory and our eternal fames. What were the words it spake? "Very few," said Miles, "and those were none of the wisest that I have heard neither: first he said, TIME IS." "Hadst thou call'd us then," said Fryer Bacon, "we had been made for ever." "Then," said Miles, "half-an-hour after it spake againe and said, TIME WAS.' "And wouldst thou not call us then?" said Bungey. "Alas," said Miles, "I thought he would have told me some long tale, and then I purposed to have called you: then half-an-houre after he cried, TIME IS PAST, and made such a noyse that hee hath waked you himselfe, mee thinkes." At this Fryer Bacon was in such a rage that hee would have beaten his man, but he was restrained by Bungey: but neverthelesse, for his punishment, he with his art struck him dumbe for one whole months space. Thus the greate worke of these learned fryers was overthrown, to their great griefes, by this simple fellow.'

CHAPTER VI, '*How Fryer Bacon, by his Art, took a towne, when the King had lyen before it three months without doing any hurt,*' contains a long account given to the King by the Friar of the wonderful inventions of his Art, in which he describes how by 'the figuration of Art there may be made instruments of navigation, without men to rowe in them, as great ships to brooke the sea, only with one man to steere them, and they shall sayle far more swiftly than if they were full of men; also chariots that shall move with an unspeakable force, without any living creature to stirre them'; flying-engines; and an instrument 'of three fingers high, and three fingers broad,' by which 'a man may rid himself and others from all imprisonment: yea, such an instrument may be easily made, whereby a man may violently draw unto him a thousand men, will they, nill they, or any other thing. By Art also an instrument may bee made, where with men may walke in the bottom of the sea or rivers without bodily danger: this Alexander the Great used (as the Ethnick philosopher reporteth), to the end he might behold the secrets of the seas. But physicall figurations are farre more strange: for by that may be framed perspects and looking-glasses, that one thing shall appeare to be many, as one man shall appeare to be a whole army, and one sunne or moone shall seem divers. Also perspects may be so framed, that things farre off shall seem most nigh unto us: with one of these did Iulius Cæsar from the sea coasts in France marke and observe the situation of the castles in England. Bodies may also be so framed that the greatest thinges shall appeare to be the least, the highest lowest, the most secret to bee the most manifest, and in such like sort the contrary. Thus did Socrates perceive, that the dragon which did destroy the citie and countrey adioyning, with his noisome breath, and contagious influence, did lurke in the dens between the mountains: and thus may all things that are done in cities or armies be discovered by the enemies. Againe, in such wise may bodies be framed, that venomous and infectious influences may be brought whither a man will: in this did Aristotle instruct Alexander; through which instruction the poyson of a basiliske, being lift up upon the wall of a Citie, the poison was convayed into the Citie, to the destruction thereof: also perspects may be made to deceive the sight, as to make a man beleeve that he seeth great store of riches, when that there is not any. But it appertaineth to a higher power of figuration, that beams should be brought and assembled by divers flexions and reflexions in any distance that we will, to burne any thing that is opposite unto it, as it is witnessed by those perspects or glasses that burne before and behinde: but the greatest and chiefest of all figurations and things figured, is to describe the heavenly bodies, according to their length and breadth in a corporall figure, wherein they may corporally move with a daily motion. These things are worth a kingdom to a wise man. These may suffise, my royall lord, to show what Art can do: and these, with many things more as strange, I am able by Art to performe.'

CHAP. VII contains the narrative of '*How Fryer Bacon over-came the German coniurer Vandermast, and made a spirit of his owne carry him into Germany*,' on which sc. ix of our play is founded; and which runs as follows: 'Presently after the King of France sent an Ambassadour to the King of England for to intreat a peace betweene them. This Ambassadour being come to the King, he feasted him (as it is the manner of princes to doe) and with the best sports as he had then, welcomed him. The Ambassadour seeing the King of England so free in his love, desired likewise to give him some taste of his good liking, and to that intent sent for one of his fellowes (being a Germane, and named Vandermast) a famous Coniurer, who being come, hee told the King, that since his Grace had been so bountiful in his love to him, he would shew him (by a servant of his) such wonderfull things that his Grace had never seene the like before. The King demaunded of him of what nature those things were that hee would doe: the Ambassadour answered that they were things done by the Art of Magicke. The King hearing of this, sent straight for Fryer Bacon, who presently came, and brought Fryer Bungey with him.

'When the banquet was done, Vandermast did aske the King, if he desired to see the spirit of any man deceased: and if that hee did, hee would raise him in such manner and fashion as he was in when that he lived. The King told him, that above all men he desired to see Pompey the Great, who could abide no equall. Vandermast by his Art raised him, armed in such a manner as hee was when he was slaine at the battell of Pharsalia; at this they were all highly contented. Fryer Bacon presently raised the ghost of Julius Cæsar, who could abide no superiour, and had slaine this Pompey at the battell of Pharsalia: at the sight of him they were all amazed, but the King, who sent for Bacon; and Vandermast said, there was some man of Art in that presence, whom he desired to see. Fryer Bacon then shewed himselfe, saying, It was I, Vandermast, that raised Cæsar, partly to give content to this royall presence, but chiefely for to conquer thy Pompey, as he did once before, at that great battell of Pharsalia, which he now againe shall doe. Then presently began a fight between Cæsar and Pompey, which continued a good space, to the content of all, except Vandermast. At last Pompey was overcome and slaine by Cæsar: then vanished they both away.

'My Lord Ambassadour, (said the King), me thinks that my Englishman hath put down your German: hath he no better cunning than this? Yes, answered Vandermast, your Grace shall see me put downe your Englishman ere that you goe from hence: and therefore Fryer prepare thy selfe with thy best of Art to withstand me. Alas, said Fryer Bacon, it is a little thing will serve to resist thee in this kind. I have here one that is my inferior, (shewing him Fryer Bungey), try thy Art with him; and if thou doe put him to the worst, then will I deale with thee, and not till then.

'Fryer Bungey then began to shew his Art: and after some turning and looking in his booke, he brought up among them the Hysperian Tree, which did beare golden apples; these apples were kept by a waking Dragon that lay under the tree. He having done this, bid Vandermast finde one that durst gather the fruit. Then Vandermast did raise the ghost of Hercules in his habit that he wore when he was living, and with his club on his shoulder: Here is one, said Vandermast, that shall gather fruit from this tree: this is Hercules, that in his life time gathered of this fruit, and made the Dragon crouch: and now againe shall hee gather it in spight of all opposition. As Hercules was going to plucke the fruit, Fryer Bacon held up his wand, at which Hercules stayed and seemed fearful. Vandermast bid him for to gather of the fruit, or else he would torment him. Hercules was more fearfull, and said, I cannot, nor I dare not: for great Bacon stands, whose charms are farre more powerful than thine, I must obey him Vandermast. Hereat Vandermast curst Hercules, and threatned him: But Fryer Bacon laughed, and bid him not to chafe himself ere that his journey was ended: for seeing (said he) that Hercules will doe nothing at your command, I will have him doe you some service at mine: with that he bid Hercules carry him home into Germany. The Devill obeyed him, and tooke Vandermast on his backe, and went away with him in all their sights. Hold Fryer, cried the Ambassadour, I will not loose Vandermast for half my land. Content yourself my Lord, answered Fryer Bacon, I have but sent him home to see his wife, and ere long he may returne. The King of England thanked Fryer Bacon, and forced some gifts on him for his service that he had done for him: for Fryer Bacon did so little respect money, that he never would take any of the King.'

In other chapters Miles and Vandermast re-appear; but the incidents of these have not been borrowed by Greene, though the scene of Miles's conjuring (sc. xv) was probably suggested by chapters xii, in which Miles 'coniures for Meat,' and xv, in which he 'one day finding his Master's study open, stole out of it one of his coniuring-bookes; with this booke would Miles needs coniure for some money'; but in the story the Fiend proves the stronger, and Miles is so frightened by the fire hurled about by his visitor, that he is made to 'leape from off the leades' and break his leg. The twofold use of the 'glass prospective,' in scenes vi and xiii, is however borrowed from chapter xiii, '*How Fryer Bacon did helpe a Young Man to his Sweet-heart, which Fryer Bungye would have married to another,*' etc., and from chapter xvi. In the former the following is the passage in question:

'Fryer Bacon (knowing him for a vertuous Gentleman) pittyed him; and to give his griefes some release, shewed him a glasse, wherein any one might see any thing done (within fifty miles space) that they desired: so soone as he looked in the glasse, hee saw his love Millisant with her father, and the Knight, ready to be married by Fryer Bungye; at the sight of this hee cryed out that he was undone, for now should he lose his life in losing of his love. Fryer Bacon bids him take comfort, for he would prevent the marriage; so taking this gentleman in his armes, he set himselfe downe in an enchanted chaire, and suddenly they were carried through the ayre to the chappell. Just as they came in, Fryer Bungye was ioyning their hands to marry them: but Fryer Bacon spoyled his speech, for he strucke him dumbe, so that he could not speake a worde. Then raised he a myst in the chappell, so that neither the father could see his daughter, nor the daughter her father, nor the Knight either of them. Then tooke he Millisant by the hand, and led her to the man she most desired: they both wept for ioy, that they so happily once more had met, and kindly thanked Fryer Bacon.'

Chapter xvi, as will be seen, contains the story from which Greene took the plot of the hatred (in the play a rivalry in love) between Lambert and Serlsby and of its fatal results to them and to their sons (sc. xiii), and the suggestion of the catastrophe having caused the Friar's repentance. With this and the following (and last) chapter of the story-book, which suggested to Greene the one serious speech given to Friar Bacon in the play (xiii. 86 *seqq.*), I conclude my extracts:

CHAPTER XVI. '*How two young Gentlemen that came to Fryer Bacon to know how their Father did, killed one another; and how Fryer Bacon for griefe, did breake his rare Glasse, wherein he could see any thing that was done within fifty miles about him.* It is spoken of before now, that Fryer Bacon had a glasse, which was of that excellent nature, that any man might behold any thing that he desired to see within the compasse of fifty miles round about him: with this glasse he had pleasured divers kinds of people: for fathers did oftentimes desire to see (thereby) how their children did, and children how their parents did; one friend how another did; and one enemy (sometimes) how his enemy did: so that from far they would come to see this wonderfull glasse. It happened one day, that there came to him two young gentlemen (that were countrey men, and neighbors children) for to know of him by his glasse, how their fathers did: Hee being no niggard of his cunning, let them see his glasse, wherein they straight beheld their wishes, which they (through their owne follies) bought at their lives losse, as you shall heare.

'The fathers of these two gentlemen (in their sonnes absence) were become great foes: this hatred betweene them was growne to that height, that wheresoever they met, they had not onely wordes, but blowes. Just at that time, as it should seeme, that their sonnes were looking to see how they were in health, they were met, and had drawne, and were together by the eares. Their sonnes seeing this, and having been alwayes great friends, knew not what to say to one another, but beheld each other with angry lookes. At last, one of the fathers, as they might perceive in the Glasse, had a fall, and the other, taking advantage, stood over him ready to strike him. The sonne of him that was downe, could then containe himselfe no longer, but told the other young man, that his father had received wrong. He answered againe, that it was faire. At last there grew such foule words betweene them, and their bloods were so heated, that they presently stabbed one the other with their daggers, and so fell downe dead.

'Fryer Bacon seeing them fall, ranne to them, but it was too late, for they were breathlesse ere he came. This made him to grieve exceedingly: he iudging that they had received the cause of their deaths by this Glasse, tooke the Glasse in his hand, and uttered words to this effect:

'Wretched Bacon, wretched in thy knowledge, in thy understanding wretched; for thy Art hath beene the ruine of these two Gentlemen. Had I been busied in those holy things, the which mine Order tyes me to, I had not had that time that made this wicked Glasse: wicked I may well call it, that is the causer of so vile an act: would it were sensible, then should it feele my wrath; but being as it is, Ile ruin it for ruining of them: and with that he broke his rare and wonderfull Glasse, the like of it the whole world had not. In this grief of his, came there newes to him of the deaths of Vandermast and Fryer Bungey: This did increase his griefe, and made him sorrowfull, that in three days he would not eat any thing, but kept his Chamber.'

CHAPTER XVII. '*How Fryer Bacon burnt his books of Magick, and gave himselfe to the study of Divinity only; and how he turned Anchorite.* In the time that Fryer Bacon kept his Chamber, hee fell into divers meditations: sometimes into the vanity of Arts and Sciences: then would hee condemne himselfe for studying of those things that were so contrary to his Order and soules health; and would say, That magicke made a man a Devill: sometimes would hee meditate on divinity; then would he cry out upon himselfe, for neglecting the study of it, and for studying magick: sometime would he meditate on the shortnesse of mans life, then would he condemne himselfe for spending a time so short, so ill as he had done his: so would he goe from one thing to another and in all condemne his former studies.

'And that the world should know how truly he did repent his wicked life, he caused to be made a great fire; and sending for many of his friends, schollers, and others, he spake to them after this manner: My good friends and fellow students, it is not unknowne to you, how that through my Art I have attained to that credit, that few men living ever had: of the wonders that I have done, all England can speak, both King and Commons: I have unlocked the secrets of Art and Nature, and let the world see those things, that have layen hid since the death of Hermes, that rare and profound philosopher: my studies have found the secrets of the Starres; the bookes that I have made of them, doe serve for presidents to our greatest Doctors, so excellent hath my judgment beene therein. I likewise have found out the secrets of Trees, Plants and Stones, with their several uses; yet all this knowledge of mine I esteeme so lightly, that I wish that I were ignorant, and knew nothing: for the knowledge of these things, (as I have truly found,) serveth not to better a man in goodnesse, but onely to make him proude and thinke too well of himselfe. What hath all my knowledge of Natures secrets gained me? Onely this, the losse of a better knowledge, the losse of Divine Studies, which makes the immortall part of man (his soule) blessed. I have found, that my knowledge has beene a heavy burden, and has kept downe my good thoughts: but I will remove the cause, which are these Bookes: which I doe purpose here before you all to burne. They all intreated him to spare the bookes, because in them there were those things that after-ages might receive great benefit by. He would not hearken unto them, but threw them all into the fire, and in that flame burnt the greatest learning in the world. Then did he dispose of all his goods; some part he gave to poor schollers, and some he gave to other poore folkes: nothing left he for himselfe: then caused he to be made in the Church-Wall a Cell, where he locked himselfe in, and there remained till his Death. His time hee spent in prayer, meditation, and such divine exercises, and did seeke by all means to perswade men from the study of magicke. Thus lived he some two yeeres space in that Cell, never comming forth: his meat and drink he received in at a window, and at that window he did discourse with those that came to him; his grave he digged with his owne nayles, and was there layed when he dyed. Thus was the Life and Death of this famous Fryer, who lived most part of his life a Magician, and dyed a true Penitent Sinner and an Anchorite.'

Similarities between Greene's Friar Bacon and other Elizabethan plays.

Mr. Collier observes[1] that Greene's Friar Bacon was one of the last instances in which a devil appeared on the English stage. But in Jonson's The Devil is an Ass both 'the great' and 'the less' representatives of the Lower Regions are characters; and after the Restoration, Wilson, in his Belphegor, or the Marriage of the Devil, a revival of an old English theme (that of Grim the Collier of Croydon, though Wilson followed an Italian model), brought 'Belzebub and Puggs' on the stage once more. Grim the Collier of Croydon had moreover been already re-introduced to the stage by 'I. T.' in a play said to have been printed as early as 1599, though the first extant edition is of a much later date. But the days

[1] History of English Dramatic Poetry, iii. 91.

of the *naïf* devil of the Mysteries were certainly on the wane[1].

Anthony Munday's comedy John a Kent and John a Cumber (1598)[2], so called from the two rival magicians who intervene in the action, bears some resemblance to our play in general conception. Henslowe's Diary has several notices, under the year 1601, of a play of which the full title seems to have been 'Friar Rush and the Proud Woman of Antwerp,' by Haughton and Day; but the famous legend of Friar Rush essentially differs from that of Friar Bacon, since in the former the Fiend takes service as under-cook in a monastery, and there plays his pranks as Friar Rush—

'Quis non legit
Quae Frater Rauschius egit[3]?'

'Friar Fox,' 'Friar Francis,' and 'Friar Spendleton' or 'Pendleton' likewise occur in Henslowe's Diary as the eponymous heroes of contemporary dramas; but some of these personages may possibly have been of the 'Friar Tuck' type, with which we have no concern here.

Greene's Friar Bacon on the German

Whether Greene's Friar Bacon ever made its way with the English comedians to the continent, I cannot say; but it is not impossible, as in a recent paper on the performances of these players at Cologne[4], where they appeared first in 1592, and again in 1600 and in later years, I find the conjecture that among the *comœdiæ* presented by them were the favourite plays of Greene. The history of the play on the later English stage seems to be exhausted by the mention of a pantomime, Friar Bacon, or Harlequin's Adventures in Lilliput, Brobdingnag, &c., by the popular Irish dramatist O'Keefe, said to have been produced in 1783, but never printed[5].

and later English stage.

[1] Among later appearances of the Devil on the English stage may be noticed that in Foote's 'comedy' of The Devil upon Two Sticks (1768).

[2] Edited by Collier for the (old) Shakespeare Society, 1851.

[3] See Thoms, Early Prose Romances, vol. ii, where the English story-book of 1620 is reprinted; and compare for the German and Danish versions of this famous legend, Scheible's Kloster, xi. 1070-1118.

[4] The first of a series of articles on 'Englische Schauspieler in Köln,' by Dr. Ennen, in the Stadt-Anzeiger der Kölnischen Zeitung, No. 320, November 17th, 1877.

[5] Biographia Dramatica (1812), ii. 251.

Thus the great historic memory of Friar Bacon is only through a degrading legend associated with one master-piece of our early comic drama; while the name of Doctor Faustus, in history a miserable charlatan, has, partly with the aid of an English tragedy of genius, obtained a place second to no other in the poetic literature of the world. Conclusion.

THE TRAGICAL HISTORY OF

DOCTOR FAUSTUS.

DRAMATIS PERSONÆ.

THE POPE.
CARDINAL OF LORRAIN.
THE EMPEROR OF GERMANY.
DUKE OF VANHOLT.
FAUSTUS.
VALDES, } friends to FAUSTUS.
CORNELIUS, } friends to FAUSTUS.
WAGNER, servant to FAUSTUS.
Clown.
ROBIN.
RALPH.
Vintner.
Horse-courser.
A Knight.
An Old Man.
Scholars, Friars, and Attendants.
DUCHESS OF VANHOLT.
LUCIFER.
BELZEBUB.
MEPHISTOPHILIS.
Good Angel.
Evil Angel.
The Seven Deadly Sins.
Devils.
Spirits in the shapes of ALEXANDER THE GREAT, of his Paramour, and of HELEN.
Chorus.

Enter Chorus.

Chorus. Not marching now in fields of Thrasimene,
Where Mars did mate the Carthaginians;
Nor sporting in the dalliance of love;
In courts of kings where state is overturn'd;
Nor in the pomp of proud audacious deeds,
Intends our Muse to vaunt his heavenly verse:
Only this, gentlemen,—we must perform
The form of Faustus' fortunes, good or bad:
To patient judgments we appeal our plaud,
And speak for Faustus in his infancy.
Now is he born, his parents base of stock,
In Germany, within a town call'd Rhodes:
Of riper years, to Wittenberg he went,
Whereas his kinsmen chiefly brought him up.
So soon he profits in divinity,
The fruitful plot of scholarism grac'd,
That shortly he was grac'd with doctor's name,
Excelling all whose sweet delight disputes

In heavenly matters of theology;
Till swoln with cunning, of a self-conceit,
His waxen wings did mount above his reach,
And, melting, heavens conspir'd his overthrow;
For, falling to a devilish exercise,
And glutted now with learning's golden gifts,
He surfeits upon cursèd necromancy;
Nothing so sweet as magic is to him,
Which he prefers before his chiefest bliss:
And this the man that in his study sits. [*Exit.*

SCENE I. *Faustus's study.*

FAUSTUS *discovered.*

Faust. Settle thy studies, Faustus, and begin
To sound the depth of that thou wilt profess:
Having commenc'd, be a divine in shew,
Yet level at the end of every art,
And live and die in Aristotle's works.
Sweet Analytics, 'tis thou hast ravish'd me!
Bene disserere est finis logices.
Is, to dispute well, logic's chiefest end?
Affords this art no greater miracle?
Then read no more; thou hast attain'd that end:
A greater subject fitteth Faustus' wit:
Bid Economy farewell, and Galen come,
Seeing, *Ubi desinit philosophus, ibi incipit medicus:*
Be a physician, Faustus; heap up gold,
And be etèrniz'd for some wondrous cure:
Summum bonum medicinae sanitas,
The end of physic is our body's health.
Why, Faustus, hast thou not attain'd that end?
Is not thy common talk found aphorisms?
Are not thy bills hung up as monuments,
Whereby whole cities have escap'd the plague,
And thousand desperate maladies been eas'd?
Yet art thou still but Faustus, and a man.
Couldst thou make men to live eternally,

Or, being dead, raise them to life again,
Then this profession were to be esteem'd.
Physic, farewell! Where is Justinian? [*Reads.*
Si una eademque res legatur, duobus, alter rem, alter valorem rei, etc.
A pretty case of paltry legacies! [*Reads.*
Exhaereditare filium non potest pater, nisi, etc.
Such is the subject of the institute,
And universal body of the law:
His study fits a mercenary drudge,
Who aims at nothing but external trash;
Too servile and illiberal for me.
When all is done, divinity is best:
Jerome's Bible, Faustus; view it well. [*Reads.*
Stipendium peccati mors est. Ha! *Stipendium, etc.*
The reward of sin is death: that 's hard. [*Reads.*
Si peccasse negamus, fallimur, et nulla est in nobis veritas;
If we say that we have no sin, we deceive ourselves, and there 's no truth in us.
Why, then, belike we must sin, and so consequently die:
Ay, we must die an everlasting death.
What doctrine call you this, *Che sera, sera,*
What will be, shall be? Divinity, adieu!
These metaphysics of magicians,
And necromantic books are heavenly;
Lines, circles, scenes, letters, and characters;
Ay, these are those that Faustus most desires.
O, what a world of profit and delight,
Of power, of honour, of omnipotence,
Is promis'd to the studious artizan!
All things that move between the quiet poles
Shall be at my command: emperors and kings
Are but obeyèd in their several provinces,
Nor can they raise the wind, or rend the clouds;
But his dominion that exceeds in this,
Stretcheth as far as doth the mind of man;
A sound magician is a mighty god:
Here, Faustus, tire thy brains to gain a deity.

Enter WAGNER.

Wagner, commend me to my dearest friends,
The German Valdes and Cornelius;
Request them earnestly to visit me.

Wag. I will, sir. [*Exit.*

Faust. Their conference will be a greater help to me
Than all my labours, plod I ne'er so fast.

Enter Good Angel *and* Evil Angel.

G. Ang. O, Faustus, lay that damnèd book aside,
And gaze not on it, lest it tempt thy soul,
And heap God's heavy wrath upon thy head!
Read, read the Scriptures:—that is blasphemy.

E. Ang. Go forward, Faustus, in that famous art
Wherein all Nature's treasure is contain'd:
Be thou on earth as Jove is in the sky,
Lord and commander of these elements. [*Exeunt* Angels.

Faust. How am I glutted with conceit of this!
Shall I make spirits fetch me what I please,
Resolve me of all ambiguities,
Perform what desperate enterprise I will?
I'll have them fly to India for gold,
Ransack the ocean for orient pearl,
And search all corners of the new-found world
For pleasant fruits and princely delicates;
I'll have them read me strange philosophy,
And tell the secrets of all foreign kings;
I'll have them wall all Germany with brass,
And make swift Rhine circle fair Wittenberg;
I'll have them fill the public schools with silk,
Wherewith the students shall be bravely clad;
I'll levy soldiers with the coin they bring,
And chase the Prince of Parma from our land,
And reign sole king of all our provinces;
Yea, stranger engines for the brunt of war,
Than was the fiery keel at Antwerp's bridge,
I'll make my servile spirits to invent.

Enter VALDES *and* CORNELIUS.

Come, German Valdes, and Cornelius,
And make me blest with your sage conference.
Valdes, sweet Valdes, and Cornelius,
Know that your words have won me at the last
To practise magic and concealèd arts:
Yet not your words only, but mine own fantasy,
That will receive no object; for my head
But ruminates on necromantic skill.
Philosophy is odious and obscure;
Both law and physic are for petty wits;
Divinity is basest of the three,
Unpleasant, harsh, contemptible, and vile:
'Tis magic, magic, that hath ravish'd me.
Then, gentle friends, aid me in this attempt;
And I, that have with concise syllogisms
Gravell'd the pastors of the German church,
And made the flowering pride of Wittenberg
Swarm to my problems, as the infernal spirits
On sweet Musaeus when he came to hell,
Will be as cunning as Agrippa was,
Whose shadows made all Europe honour him.

Vald. Faustus, these books, thy wit, and our experience,
Shall make all nations to canònize us.
As Indian Moors obey their Spanish lords,
So shall the subjects of every element
Be always serviceable to us three;
Like lions shall they guard us when we please;
Like Almain rutters with their horsemen's staves,
Or Lapland giants, trotting by our sides;
Sometimes like women, or unwedded maids,
Shadowing more beauty in their airy brows
Than have the white breasts of the queen of love:
From Venice shall they drag huge argosies,
And from America the golden fleece
That yearly stuffs old Philip's treasury;
If learnèd Faustus will be resolute.

Faust. Valdes, as resolute am I in this
As thou to live: therefore object it not.

Corn. The miracles that magic will perform
Will make thee vow to study nothing else.
He that is grounded in astrology,
Enrich'd with tongues, well seen in minerals,
Hath all the principles magic doth require:
Then doubt not, Faustus, but to be renowm'd,
And more frequented for this mystery
Than heretofore the Delphian oracle.
The spirits tell me they can dry the sea,
And fetch the treasure of all foreign wrecks,
Ay, all the wealth that our forefathers hid
Within the massy entrails of the earth:
Then tell me, Faustus, what shall we three want?

Faust. Nothing, Cornelius. O, this cheers my soul!
Come, shew me some demonstrations magical,
That I may conjure in some lusty grove,
And have these joys in full possession.

Vald. Then haste thee to some solitary grove,
And bear wise Bacon's and Albanus' works,
The Hebrew Psalter, and New Testament;
And whatsoever else is requisite
We will inform thee ere our conference cease.

Corn. Valdes, first let him know the words of art;
And then, all other ceremonies learn'd,
Faustus may try his cunning by himself.

Vald. First I'll instruct thee in the rudiments,
And then wilt thou be perfecter than I.

Faust. Then come and dine with me, and, after meat,
We'll canvass every quiddity thereof;
For, ere I sleep, I'll try what I can do:
This night I'll conjure, though I die therefore. [*Exeunt.*

SCENE II. *Before Faustus's house.*

Enter Two Scholars.

First Schol. I wonder what 's become of Faustus, that was wont to make our schools ring with *sic probo.*

Sec. Schol. That shall we know; for see, here comes his boy.

Enter WAGNER.

First Schol. How now, sirrah! where 's thy master?

Wag. God in heaven knows.

Sec. Schol. Why, dost not thou know?

Wag. Yes, I know; but that follows not.

First Schol. Go to, sirrah! leave your jesting, and tell us where he is.

Wag. That follows not necessary by force of argument, that you, being licentiates, should stand upon 't: therefore acknowledge your error, and be attentive.

Sec. Schol. Why, didst thou not say thou knewest?

Wag. Have you any witness on 't?

First Schol. Yes, sirrah, I heard you.

Wag. Ask my fellow if I be a thief.

Sec. Schol. Well, you will not tell us?

Wag. Yes, sir, I will tell you: yet, if you were not dunces, you would never ask me such a question; for is not he *corpus naturale*? and is not that *mobile*? then wherefore should you ask me such a question? But that I am by nature phlegmatic, slow to wrath, it were not for you to come within forty foot of the place of execution, although I do not doubt to see you both hanged the next sessions. Thus having triumphed over you, I will set my countenance like a precisian, and begin to speak thus:—Truly, my dear brethren, my master is within at dinner, with Valdes and Cornelius, as this wine, if it could speak, it would inform your worships: and so, the Lord bless you, preserve you, and keep you, my dear brethren, my dear brethren! [*Exit.*

First Schol. Nay, then, I fear he is fallen into that damned art for which they two are infamous through the world.

Sec. Schol. Were he a stranger, and not allied to me, yet should I grieve for him. But, come, let us go and inform the Rector, and see if he by his grave counsel can reclaim him.

First Schol. O, but I fear me nothing can reclaim him!

Sec. Schol. Yet let us try what we can do. [*Exeunt.*

SCENE III. *A grove.*

Enter FAUSTUS *to conjure.*

Faust. Now that the gloomy shadow of the earth,
Longing to view Orion's drizzling look,
Leaps from th' antarctic world unto the sky,
And dims the welkin with her pitchy breath,
Faustus, begin thine incantations,
And try if devils will obey thy hest,
Seeing thou hast pray'd and sacrific'd to them.
Within this circle is Jehovah's name,
Forward and backward anagrammatiz'd,
The breviated names of holy saints,
Figures of every adjunct to the heavens,
And characters of signs and erring stars,
By which the spirits are enforc'd to rise:
Then fear not, Faustus, but be resolute,
And try the uttermost magic can perform.—
Sint mihi dei Acherontis propitii! Valeat numen triplex Jehovae! Ignei, aerii, aquatani spiritus, salvete! Orientis princeps Belzebub, inferni ardentis monarcha, et Demogorgon, propitiamus vos, ut appareat et surgat Mephistophilis, quod tumeraris: per Jehovam, Gehennam, et consecratam aquam quam nunc spargo, signumque crucis quod nunc facio, et per vota nostra, ipse nunc surgat nobis dicatus Mephistophilis!

Enter MEPHISTOPHILIS.

I charge thee to return, and change thy shape;
Thou art too ugly to attend on me:
Go, and return an old Franciscan friar;
That holy shape becomes a devil best. [*Exit* MEPHISTOPHILIS.
I see there 's virtue in my heavenly words:
Who would not be proficient in this art?
How pliant is this Mephistophilis,
Full of obedience and humility!
Such is the force of magic and my spells:
No, Faustus, thou art conjuror laureat,
That canst command great Mephistophilis:
Quin regis Mephistophilis fratris imagine.

Re-enter MEPHISTOPHILIS *like a Franciscan friar.*

Meph. Now, Faustus, what wouldst thou have me do?

Faust. I charge thee wait upon me whilst I live,
To do whatever Faustus shall command,
Be it to make the moon drop from her sphere,
Or th' ocean to overwhelm the world.

Meph. I am a servant to great Lucifer,
And may not follow thee without his leave:
No more than he commands must we perform.

Faust. Did not he charge thee to appear to me?

Meph. No, I came hither of mine own accord.

Faust. Did not my conjuring speeches raise thee? speak.

Meph. That was the cause, but yet *per accidens*;
For, when we hear one rack the name of God,
Abjure the Scriptures and his Saviour Christ,
We fly, in hope to get his glorious soul;
Nor will we come, unless he use such means
Whereby he is in danger to be damn'd.
Therefore the shortest cut for conjuring
Is stoutly to abjure the Trinity,
And pray devoutly to the prince of hell.

Faust. So Faustus hath
Already done; and holds this principle,

There is no chief but only Belzebub;
To whom Faustus doth dedicate himself.
This word 'damnation' terrifies not him,
For he confounds hell in Elysium:
His ghost be with the old philosophers!
But, leaving these vain trifles of men's souls,
Tell me what is that Lucifer thy lord?

Meph. Arch-regent and commander of all spirits.

Faust. Was not that Lucifer an angel once?

Meph. Yes, Faustus, and most dearly lov'd of God.

Faust. How comes it, then, that he is prince of devils?

Meph. O, by aspiring pride and insolence;
For which God threw him from the face of heaven.

Faust. And what are you that live with Lucifer?

Meph. Unhappy spirits that fell with Lucifer,
Conspir'd against our God with Lucifer,
And are for ever damn'd with Lucifer.

Faust. Where are you damn'd?

Meph. In hell.

Faust. How comes it, then, that thou art out of hell?

Meph. Why, this is hell, nor am I out of it:
Think'st thou that I, who saw the face of God,
And tasted the eternal joys of heaven,
Am not tormented with ten thousand hells,
In being depriv'd of everlasting bliss?
O, Faustus, leave these frivolous demands,
Which strike a terror to my fainting soul!

Faust. What, is great Mephistophilis so passionate
For being deprivèd of the joys of heaven?
Learn thou of Faustus manly fortitude,
And scorn those joys thou never shalt possess.
Go bear these tidings to great Lucifer:
Seeing Faustus hath incurr'd eternal death
By desperate thoughts against Jove's deity,
Say, he surrenders up to him his soul,
So he will spare him four and twenty years,

Letting him live in all voluptuousness;
Having thee ever to attend on me,
To give me whatsoever I shall ask,
To tell me whatsoever I demand,
To slay mine enemies, and aid my friends,
And always be obedient to my will.
Go and return to mighty Lucifer,
And meet me in my study at midnight,
And then resolve me of thy master's mind.

Meph. I will, Faustus. [*Exit.*

Faust. Had I as many souls as there be stars,
I'd give them all for Mephistophilis.
By him I'll be great emperor of the world,
And make a bridge thorough the moving air,
To pass the ocean with a band of men;
I'll join the hills that bind the Afric shore,
And make that country continent to Spain,
And both contributory to my crown:
The Emperor shall not live but by my leave,
Nor any potentate of Germany.
Now that I have obtain'd what I desir'd,
I'll live in speculation of this art,
Till Mephistophilis return again.

SCENE IV. *A street.*

Enter WAGNER *and* Clown.

Wag. Sirrah boy, come hither.

Clown. How, boy! swowns, boy! I hope you have seen many boys with such pickadevaunts as I have: boy, quotha!

Wag. Tell me, sirrah, hast thou any comings in?

Clown. Ay, and goings out too; but you may see else.

Wag. Alas, poor slave! see how poverty jesteth in his nakedness! the villain is bare and out of service, and so hungry, that I know he would give his soul to the devil for a shoulder of mutton, though it were blood-raw.

Clown. How! my soul to the devil for a shoulder of mutton, though 'twere blood-raw! not so, good friend: by'r lady, I had need have it well roasted, and good sauce to it, if I pay so dear.

Wag. Well, wilt thou serve me, and I'll make thee go like *Qui mihi discipulus?*

Clown. How, in verse?

Wag. No, sirrah; in beaten silk and staves-acre.

Clown. How, how, knaves-acre! ay, I thought that was all the land his father left him. Do ye hear? I would be sorry to rob you of your living.

Wag. Sirrah, I say in staves-acre.

Clown. Oho, oho, staves-acre! why, then, belike, if I were your man, I should be full of vermin.

Wag. So thou shalt, whether thou beest with me or no. But, sirrah, leave your jesting, and bind yourself presently unto me for seven years, or I'll turn all the lice about thee into familiars, and they shall tear thee in pieces.

Clown. Do you hear, sir? you may save that labour; they are too familiar with me already: swowns, they are as bold with my flesh as if they had paid for their meat and drink.

Wag. Well, do you hear, sirrah? hold, take these guilders. [*Gives money.*

Clown. Gridirons, what be they?

Wag. Why, French crowns.

Clown. Mass, but for the name of French crowns, a man were as good have as many English counters. And what should I do with these?

Wag. Why, now, sirrah, thou art at an hour's warning, whensoever or wheresoever the devil shall fetch thee.

Clown. No, no; here, take your gridirons again.

Wag. Truly, I'll none of them.

Clown. Truly, but you shall.

Wag. Bear witness I gave them him.

Clown. Bear witness I give them you again.

Wag. Well, I will cause two devils presently to fetch thee away.—Baliol and Belcher!

Clown. Let your Baliol and your Belcher come here, and I'll knock them, they were never so knocked since they were devils: say I should kill one of them, what would folks say? 'Do ye see yonder tall fellow in the round slop? he has killed the devil.' So I should be called Kill-devil all the parish over.

Enter two Devils; *and the* Clown *runs up and down crying.*

Wag. Baliol and Belcher,—spirits, away! [*Exeunt* Devils.

Clown. What, are they gone? a vengeance on them! they have vile long nails. There was a he-devil and a she-devil: I'll tell you how you shall know them; all he-devils has horns, and all she-devils has cloven feet.

Wag. Well, sirrah, follow me.

Clown. But, do you hear? if I should serve you, would you teach me to raise up Banios and Belcheos?

Wag. I will teach thee to turn thyself to any thing, to a dog, or a cat, or a mouse, or a rat, or any thing.

Clown. How! a Christian fellow to a dog, or a cat, a mouse, or a rat! no, no, sir; if you turn me into any thing, let it be in the likeness of a little pretty frisking flea, that I may be here and there and everywhere.

Wag. Well, sirrah, come.

Clown. But, do you hear, Wagner?

Wag. How!—Baliol and Belcher!

Clown. O Lord, I pray, sir, let Banio and Belcher go sleep.

Wag. Villain, call me Master Wagner, and let thy left eye be diametarily fixed upon my right heel, with *quasi vestigias nostras insistere.* [*Exit.*

Clown. God forgive me, he speaks Dutch fustian. Well, I'll follow him; I'll serve him, that 's flat. [*Exit.*

SCENE V. *Faustus's study.*

FAUSTUS *discovered.*

Faust. Now, Faustus, must
Thou needs be damn'd, and canst thou not be sav'd:
What boots it, then, to think of God or heaven?
Away with such vain fancies, and despair;
Despair in God, and trust in Belzebub:
Now go not backward; no, Faustus, be resolute:
Why waver'st thou? O, something soundeth in mine ears,
'Abjure this magic, turn to God again!'
Ay, and Faustus will turn to God again.
To God? he loves thee not;
The god thou serv'st is thine own appetite,
Wherein is fix'd the love of Belzebub:
To him I'll build an altar and a church,
And offer lukewarm blood of new-born babes.

Enter Good Angel *and* Evil Angel.

G. Ang. Sweet Faustus, leave that execrable art.

Faust. Contrition, prayer, repentance—what of them?

G. Ang. O, they are means to bring thee unto heaven!

E. Ang. Rather illusions, fruits of lunacy,
That makes men foolish that do trust them most.

G. Ang. Sweet Faustus, think of heaven and heavenly things.

E. Ang. No, Faustus; think of honour and of wealth.
[*Exeunt* Angels.

Faust. Of wealth!
Why, the signiory of Embden shall be mine.
When Mephistophilis shall stand by me,
What god can hurt thee, Faustus? thou art safe:
Cast no more doubts.—Come, Mephistophilis,
And bring glad tidings from great Lucifer;—
Is 't not midnight?—come, Mephistophilis,
Veni, veni, Mephistophile!

Enter MEPHISTOPHILIS.

Now tell me what says Lucifer, thy lord?

Meph. That I shall wait on Faustus while he lives,
So he will buy my service with his soul.

Faust. Already Faustus hath hazarded that for thee.

Meph. But, Faustus, thou must bequeath it solemnly,
And write a deed of gift with thine own blood;
For that security craves great Lucifer.
If thou deny it, I will back to hell.

Faust. Stay, Mephistophilis, and tell me, what good
Will my soul do thy lord?

Meph. Enlarge his kingdom.

Faust. Is that the reason why he tempts us thus?

Meph. *Solamen miseris socios habuisse doloris.*

Faust. Why, have you any pain that torture others?

Meph. As great as have the human souls of men.
But tell me, Faustus, shall I have thy soul?
And I will be thy slave, and wait on thee,
And give thee more than thou hast wit to ask.

Faust. Ay, Mephistophilis, I give it thee.

Meph. Then, Faustus, stab thine arm courageously,
And bind thy soul, that at some certain day
Great Lucifer may claim it as his own;
And then be thou as great as Lucifer.

Faust. [*Stabbing his arm*] Lo, Mephistophilis, for love of thee,
I cut mine arm, and with my proper blood
Assure my soul to be great Lucifer's,
Chief lord and regent of perpetual night!
View here the blood that trickles from mine arm,
And let it be propitious for my wish.

Meph. But, Faustus, thou must
Write it in manner of a deed of gift.

Faust. Ay, so I will [*Writes*]. But, Mephistophilis,
My blood congeals, and I can write no more.

Meph. I'll fetch thee fire to dissolve it straight. [*Exit.*

Faust. What might the staying of my blood portend?
Is it unwilling I should write this bill?
Why streams it not, that I may write afresh?
Faustus gives to thee his soul: ah, there it stay'd!
Why shouldst thou not? is not thy soul thine own?
Then write again, *Faustus gives to thee his soul.*

Re-enter MEPHISTOPHILIS *with a chafer of coals.*

Meph. Here 's fire; come, Faustus, set it on.

Faust. So, now the blood begins to clear again;
Now will I make an end immediately. [*Writes.*

Meph. O, what will not I do to obtain his soul? [*Aside.*

Faust. *Consummatum est*; this bill is ended,
And Faustus hath bequeath'd his soul to Lucifer.
But what is this inscription on mine arm?
Homo, fuge: whither should I fly?
If unto God, he'll throw me down to hell.
My senses are deceiv'd; here 's nothing writ:—
I see it plain; here in this place is writ,
Homo, fuge: yet shall not Faustus fly.

Meph. I'll fetch him somewhat to delight his mind.
[*Aside, and then exit.*

Re-enter MEPHISTOPHILIS *with* Devils, *who give crowns and rich apparel to* FAUSTUS, *dance, and then depart.*

Faust. Speak, Mephistophilis, what means this show?

Meph. Nothing, Faustus, but to delight thy mind withal,
And to shew thee what magic can perform.

Faust. But may I raise up spirits when I please?

Meph. Ay, Faustus, and do greater things than these.

Faust. Then there 's enough for a thousand souls.
Here, Mephistophilis, receive this scroll,
A deed of gift of body and of soul:
But yet conditionally that thou perform
All articles prescrib'd between us both.

Meph. Faustus, I swear by hell and Lucifer
To effect all promises between us made!

Faust. Then hear me read them. [*Reads*]

On these conditions following. First, that Faustus may be a spirit in form and substance. Secondly, that Mephistophilis shall be his servant, and at his command. Thirdly, that Mephistophilis shall do for him, and bring him whatsoever [*he desires*]. *Fourthly, that he shall be in his chamber or house invisible. Lastly, that he shall appear to the said John Faustus, at all times, in what form or shape soever he please. I, John Faustus, of Wittenberg, Doctor, by these presents, do give both body and soul to Lucifer prince of the east, and his minister Mephistophilis; and furthermore grant unto them, twenty-four years being expired, the articles above written inviolate, full power to fetch or carry the said John Faustus, body and soul, flesh, blood, or goods, into their habitation wheresoever. By me,* JOHN FAUSTUS.

Meph. Speak, Faustus, do you deliver this as your deed?

Faust. Ay, take it, and the devil give thee good on 't!

Meph. Now, Faustus, ask what thou wilt.

Faust. First will I question with thee about hell.
Tell me, where is the place that men call hell?

Meph. Under the heavens.

Faust. Ay, but whereabout?

Meph. Within the bowels of these elements,
Where we are tortur'd and remain for ever:
Hell hath no limits, nor is circumscrib'd
In one self place; for where we are is hell,
And where hell is, there must we ever be:
And, to conclude, when all the world dissolves,
And every creature shall be purified,
All places shall be hell that are not heaven.

Faust. Come, I think hell 's a fable.

Meph. Ay, think so still, till experience change thy mind.

Faust. Why, think'st thou, then, that Faustus shall be damn'd?

Meph. Ay, of necessity, for here 's the scroll
Wherein thou hast given thy soul to Lucifer.

Faust. Ay, and body too: but what of that?
Think'st thou that Faustus is so fond to imagine
That, after this life, there is any pain?
Tush, these are trifles and mere old wives' tales.

Meph. But, Faustus, I am an instance to prove the contrary;
For I am damn'd, and now in hell.

Faust. How! now in hell!
Nay, an this be hell, I'll willingly be damn'd here:
What! walking, disputing, etc.
But, leaving off this, let me have a wife,
The fairest maid in Germany.

Meph. How! a wife!
I prithee, Faustus, talk not of a wife.

Faust. Nay, sweet Mephistophilis, fetch me one; for I will have one.

Meph. Well, thou wilt have one? Sit there till I come:
I'll fetch thee a wife in the devil's name. [*Exit.*

Re-enter MEPHISTOPHILIS *with a* Devil *drest like a* Woman, *with fire-works.*

Meph. Tell me, Faustus, how dost thou like thy wife?

Faust. A plague on her!

Meph. Tut, Faustus,
Marriage is but a ceremonial toy;
If thou lovest me, think no more of it.
She whom thine eye shall like, thy heart shall have,
Be she as chaste as was Penelope,
As wise as Saba, or as beautiful
As was bright Lucifer before his fall.
Hold, take this book, peruse it thoroughly: [*Gives book.*
The iterating of these lines brings gold;
The framing of this circle on the ground
Brings whirlwinds, tempests, thunder, and lightning;
Pronounce this thrice devoutly to thyself,
And men in armour shall appear to thee,
Ready to execute what thou desir'st.

Faust. Thanks, Mephistophilis; yet fain would I have a book wherein I might behold all spells and incantations, that I might raise up spirits when I please.

Meph. Here they are in this book. [*Turns to them.*

Faust. Now would I have a book where I might see all characters and planets of the heavens, that I might know their motions and dispositions.

Meph. Here they are too. [*Turns to them.*

Faust. Nay, let me have one book more,—and then I have done,—wherein I might see all plants, herbs, and trees, that grow upon the earth.

Meph. Here they be.

Faust. O, thou art deceived.

Meph. Tut, I warrant thee. [*Turns to them.*

SCENE VI. *In the house of Faustus.*

Faust. When I behold the heavens, then I repent,
And curse thee, wicked Mephistophilis,
Because thou hast depriv'd me of those joys.

Meph. Why, Faustus,
Thinkest thou heaven is such a glorious thing?
I tell thee, 'tis not half so fair as thou,
Or any man that breathes on earth.

Faust. How prov'st thou that?

Meph. 'Twas made for man, therefore is man more excellent.

Faust. If it were made for man, 'twas made for me:
I will renounce this magic and repent.

Enter Good Angel *and* Evil Angel.

G. Ang. Faustus, repent; yet God will pity thee.

E. Ang. Thou art a spirit; God cannot pity thee.

Faust. Who buzzeth in mine ears I am a spirit?
Be I a devil, yet God may pity me;
Ay, God will pity me, if I repent.

E. Ang. Ay, but Faustus never shall repent.

[*Exeunt* Angels.

Faust. My heart 's so harden'd, I cannot repent:
Scarce can I name salvation, faith, or heaven,
But fearful echoes thunder in mine ears,
'Faustus, thou art damn'd!' then swords, and knives,
Poison, guns, halters, and envenom'd steel
Are laid before me to despatch myself;
And long ere this I should have slain myself,
Had not sweet pleasure conquer'd deep despair.
Have not I made blind Homer sing to me
Of Alexander's love and Oenon's death?
And hath not he, that built the walls of Thebes
With ravishing sound of his melodious harp,
Made music with my Mephistophilis?
Why should I die, then, or basely despair?
I am resolv'd; Faustus shall ne'er repent.—
Come, Mephistophilis, let us dispute again,
And argue of divine astrology.
Tell me, are there many heavens above the moon
Are all celestial bodies but one globe,
As is the substance of this centric earth?

Meph. As are the elements, such are the spheres,
Mutually folded in each other's orb,
And, Faustus,
All jointly move upon one axletree,
Whose terminine is term'd the world's wide pole;
Nor are the names of Saturn, Mars, or Jupiter
Feign'd, but are erring stars.

Faust. But, tell me, have they all one motion, both *situ et tempore?*

Meph. All jointly move from east to west in twenty-four hours upon the poles of the world; but differ in their motion upon the poles of the zodiac.

Faust. Tush,
These slender trifles Wagner can decide:
Hath Mephistophilis no greater skill?

Who knows not the double motion of the planets? The first is finish'd in a natural day; The second thus: as Saturn in thirty years; Jupiter in twelve; Mars in four; the Sun, Venus, and Mercury in a year; the Moon in twenty-eight days. Tush, these are freshmen's suppositions. But, tell me, hath every sphere a dominion or *intelligentia*?

Meph. Ay.

Faust. How many heavens or spheres are there?

Meph. Nine; the seven planets, the firmament, and the empyreal heaven.

Faust. Well, resolve me in this question: why have we not conjunctions, oppositions, aspects, eclipses, all at one time, but in some years we have more, in some less?

Meph. *Per inaequalem motum respectu totius.*

Faust. Well, I am answered. Tell me who made the world?

Meph. I will not.

Faust. Sweet Mephistophilis, tell me.

Meph. Move me not, for I will not tell thee.

Faust. Villain, have I not bound thee to tell me any thing?

Meph. Ay, that is not against our kingdom; but this is. Think thou on hell, Faustus, for thou art damned.

Re-enter Good Angel *and* Evil Angel.

G. Ang. Think, Faustus, upon God that made the world.

Meph. Remember this. [*Exit.*

Faust. Ay, go, accursèd spirit, to ugly hell!
'Tis thou hast damn'd distressèd Faustus' soul.
Is 't not too late?

E. Ang. Too late.

G. Ang. Never too late, if Faustus can repent.

E. Ang. If thou repent, devils shall tear thee in pieces.

G. Ang. Repent, and they shall never raze thy skin.

[*Exeunt* Angels.

Faust. Ay, Christ, my Saviour,
Seek to save distressèd Faustus' soul!

Enter LUCIFER, BELZEBUB, *and* MEPHISTOPHILIS.

Luc. Christ cannot save thy soul, for he is just:
There 's none but I have interest in the same.

Faust. O, who art thou that look'st so terrible?

Luc. I am Lucifer,
And this is my companion-prince in hell.

Faust. O, Faustus, they are come to fetch away thy soul!

Luc. We come to tell thee thou dost injure us;
Thou talk'st of Christ, contráry to thy promise:
Thou shouldst not think of God: think of the devil,
And of his dam too.

Faust. Nor will I henceforth: pardon me in this,
And Faustus vows never to look to heaven,
Never to name God, or to pray to him,
To burn his Scriptures, slay his ministers,
And make my spirits pull his churches down.

Luc. Do so, and we will highly gratify thee.
Faustus, we are come from hell to shew thee some pastime: sit down, and thou shalt see all the Seven Deadly Sins appear in their proper shapes.

Faust. That sight will be as pleasing unto me,
As Paradise was to Adam, the first day
Of his creation.

Luc. Talk not of Paradise nor creation; but mark this show: talk of the devil, and nothing else.—Come away!

Enter the Seven Deadly Sins.

Now, Faustus, examine them of their several names and dispositions.

Faust. What art thou, the first?

Pride. I am Pride. I disdain to have any parents. I am like Ovid's flea; I can creep into every corner; sometimes, like a perriwig, I sit upon a wench's brow; or, like a fan of feathers, I kiss her lips. But, fie, what a scent is here! I'll not speak another word, except the ground were perfumed, and covered with cloth of arras.

Faust. What art thou, the second?

Covet. I am Covetousness; and, might I have my wish, I would desire that this house and all the people in it were turned to gold, that I might lock you up in my good chest, O my sweet gold!

Faust. What art thou, the third?

Wrath. I am Wrath. I had neither father nor mother: I leapt out of a lion's mouth when I was scarce half-an-hour old; and ever since I have run up and down the world with this case of rapiers, wounding myself when I had nobody to fight withal. I was born in hell; and look to it, for some of you shall be my father.

Faust. What art thou, the fourth?

Envy. I am Envy, born of a chimney-sweeper and an oyster-wife. I cannot read, and therefore wish all books were burnt. I am lean with seeing others eat. O, that there would come a famine through all the world, that all might die, and I live alone! then thou shouldst see how fat I would be. But must thou sit, and I stand? come down, with a vengeance!

Faust. Away, envious rascal!—What art thou, the fifth?

Glut. Who I, sir? I am Gluttony. My parents are all dead, and the devil a penny they have left me, but a bare pension, and that is thirty meals a-day and ten bevers,—a small trifle to suffice nature. O, I come of a royal parentage! my grandfather was a Gammon of Bacon, my grandmother a Hogshead of Claret-wine; my godfathers were these, Peter Pickle-herring and Martin Martlemas-beef; O, but my godmother, she was a jolly gentlewoman, and well beloved in every good town and city; her name was Mistress Margery March-beer. Now, Faustus, thou hast heard all my progeny; wilt thou bid me to supper?

Faust. No, I'll see thee hanged; thou wilt eat up all my victuals.

Glut. Then the devil choke thee!

Faust. Choke thyself, glutton!—What art thou, the sixth?

Sloth. I am Sloth. I was born on a sunny bank, where I have lain ever since; and you have done me great injury to bring me from thence: let me be carried thither again by Gluttony and Lechery. I'll not speak another word for a king's ransom.

Faust. What are you, Mistress Minx, the seventh and last?

Lechery. Who, I, sir? The first letter of my name begins with L.

Luc. Away, to hell, to hell! [*Exeunt the* Sins.] Now, Faustus, how dost thou like this?

Faust. O, this feeds my soul!

Luc. Tut, Faustus, in hell is all manner of delight.

Faust. O, might I see hell, and return again,
How happy were I then!

Luc. Thou shalt; I will send for thee at midnight.
In meantime take this book; peruse it throughly,
And thou shalt turn thyself into what shape thou wilt.

Faust. Great thanks, mighty Lucifer!
This will I keep as chary as my life.

Luc. Farewell, Faustus, and think on the devil.

Faust. Farewell, great Lucifer. Come, Mephistophilis.
[*Exeunt omnes.*

Enter Chorus.

Chor. Learnèd Faustus,
To know the secrets of astronomy
Graven in the book of Jove's high firmament,
Did mount himself to scale Olympus' top,
Being seated in a chariot burning bright,
Drawn by the strength of yoky dragons' necks.
He now is gone to prove cosmography,
And, as I guess, will first arrive at Rome,

To see the Pope and manner of his court,
And take some part of holy Peter's feast,
That to this day is highly solemniz'd. [*Exit.*

SCENE VII. *The Pope's privy-chamber.*

Enter FAUSTUS *and* MEPHISTOPHILIS.

Faust. Having now, my good Mephistophilis,
Pass'd with delight the stately town of Trier,
Environ'd round with airy mountain-tops,
With walls of flint, and deep-entrenchèd lakes,
Not to be won by any conquering prince;
From Paris next, coasting the realm of France,
We saw the river Maine fall into Rhine,
Whose banks are set with groves of fruitful vines;
Then up to Naples, rich Campania,
Whose buildings fair and gorgeous to the eye,
The streets straight forth, and pav'd with finest brick,
Quarter the town in four equivalents;
There saw we learnèd Maro's golden tomb,
The way he cut, an English mile in length,
Thorough a rock of stone, in one night's space;
From thence to Venice, Padua, and the rest,
In one of which a sumptuous temple stands,
That threats the stars with her aspiring top.
Thus hitherto hath Faustus spent his time:
But tell me now what resting-place is this?
Hast thou, as erst I did command,
Conducted me within the walls of Rome?

Meph. Faustus, I have; and, because we will not be unprovided, I have taken up his Holiness' privy-chamber for our use.

Faust. I hope his Holiness will bid us welcome.

Meph. Tut, 'tis no matter, man; we'll be bold with his good cheer.
And now, my Faustus, that thou may'st perceive

What Rome containeth to delight thee with,
Know that this city stands upon seven hills
That underprop the groundwork of the same:
Just through the midst runs flowing Tiber's stream,
With winding banks that cut it in two parts;
Over the which four stately bridges lean,
That make safe passage to each part of Rome:
Upon the bridge call'd Ponte Angelo
Erected is a castle passing strong,
Within whose walls such store of ordnance are,
And double cannons fram'd of carvèd brass,
As match the days within one cómplete year;
Besides the gates, and high pyramides,
Which Julius Caesar brought from Africa.

Faust. Now, by the kingdoms of infernal rule,
Of Styx, of Acheron, and the fiery lake
Of ever-burning Phlegethon, I swear
That I do long to see the mountains
And situation of bright-splendent Rome:
Come, therefore, let 's away.

Meph. Nay, Faustus, stay: I know you'd fain see the Pope,
And take some part of holy Peter's feast,
Where thou shalt see a troop of bald-pate friars,
Whose *summum bonum* is in belly-cheer.

Faust. Well, I'm content to compass then some sport,
And by their folly make us merriment.
Then charm me, that I
May be invisible, to do what I please,
Unseen by any whilst I stay in Rome.

[MEPHISTOPHILIS *charms him.*

Meph. So, Faustus; now
Do what thou wilt, thou shalt not be discern'd.

Sound a Sonnet. Enter the POPE *and the* CARDINAL OF LORRAIN *to the banquet, with* Friars *attending.*

Pope. My Lord of Lorrain, will 't please you draw near?

Faust. Fall to, and the devil choke you, an you spare!

Pope. How now! who 's that which spake?—Friars, look about.

First Friar. Here 's nobody, if it like your Holiness.

Pope. My lord, here is a dainty dish was sent me from the Bishop of Milan.

Faust. I thank you, sir. [*Snatches the dish.*

Pope. How now! who 's that which snatched the meat from me? will no man look?—My lord, this dish was sent me from the Cardinal of Florence.

Faust. You say true; I 'll ha 't. [*Snatches the dish.*

Pope. What, again?—My lord, I'll drink to your grace.

Faust. I'll pledge your grace. [*Snatches the cup.*

C. of Lor. My lord, it may be some ghost, newly crept out of Purgatory, come to beg a pardon of your Holiness.

Pope. It may be so.—Friars, prepare a dirge to lay the fury of this ghost.—Once again, my lord, fall to.

[*The* POPE *crosses himself.*

Faust. What, are you crossing of yourself?
Well, use that trick no more, I would advise you.

[*The* POPE *crosses himself again.*

Well, there 's the second time. Aware the third;
I give you fair warning.

[*The* POPE *crosses himself again, and* FAUSTUS *hits him a box of the ear; and they all run away.*

Come on, Mephistophilis; what shall we do?

Meph. Nay, I know not: we shall be cursed with bell, book, and candle.

Faust. How! bell, book, and candle,—candle, book, and bell,—
Forward and backward, to curse Faustus to hell!
Anon you shall hear a hog grunt, a calf bleat, and an ass bray,
Because it is Saint Peter's holiday.

Re-enter all the Friars *to sing the Dirge.*

First Friar. Come, brethren, let 's about our business with good devotion.

They sing.

Cursed be he that stole away his Holiness' meat from the table! maledicat Dominus!

Cursed be he that struck his Holiness a blow on the face! maledicat Dominus!

Cursed be he that took Friar Sandelo a blow on the pate! maledicat Dominus!

Cursed be he that disturbeth our holy dirge! maledicat Dominus!

Cursed be he that took away his Holiness' wine! maledicat Dominus!

Et omnes Sancti! Amen!

[MEPHISTOPHILIS *and* FAUSTUS *beat the* Friars, *and fling fire-works among them; and so exeunt.*

Enter Chorus.

Chor. When Faustus had with pleasure ta'en the view
Of rarest things, and royal courts of kings,
He stay'd his course, and so returnèd home;
Where such as bear his absence but with grief,
I mean his friends and near'st companions,
Did gratulate his safety with kind words,
And in their conference of what befell,
Touching his journey through the world and air,
They put forth questions of astrology,
Which Faustus answer'd with such learnèd skill
As they admir'd and wonder'd at his wit.
Now is his fame spread forth in every land:
Amongst the rest the Emperor is one,
Carolus the Fifth, at whose palace now
Faustus is feasted 'mongst his noblemen.
What there he did, in trial of his art,
I leave untold; your eyes shall see['t] perform'd. [*Exit.*

SCENE VIII. *Near an inn.*

Enter ROBIN *the Ostler, with a book in his hand.*

Robin. O, this is admirable! here I ha' stolen one of Doctor Faustus' conjuring-books, and, i'faith, I mean to search some circles for my own use.

Enter RALPH, *calling* ROBIN.

Ralph. Robin, prithee, come away; there's a gentleman tarries to have his horse, and he would have his things rubbed and made clean: he keeps such a chafing with my mistress about it; and she has sent me to look thee out; prithee, come away.

Robin. Keep out, keep out, or else you are blown up, you are dismembered, Ralph: keep out, for I am about a roaring piece of work.

Ralph. Come, what doest thou with that same book? thou canst not read?

Robin. Yes, my master and mistress shall find that I can read.

Ralph. Why, Robin, what book is that?

Robin. What book! why, the most intolerable book for conjuring that e'er was invented by any brimstone devil.

Ralph. Canst thou conjure with it?

Robin. I can do all these things easily with it; first, I can make thee drunk with ippocras at any tabern in Europe for nothing; that's one of my conjuring works.

Ralph. Our Master Parson says that 's nothing.

Robin. True, Ralph: and more, Ralph, if thou hast any mind to Nan Spit, our kitchenmaid,—

Ralph. O, brave, Robin! shall I have Nan Spit? On that condition I'll feed thy devil with horse-bread as long as he lives, of free cost.

Robin. No more, sweet Ralph; let's go and make clean our boots, which lie foul upon our hands, and then to our conjuring in the devil's name. [*Exeunt.*

SCENE IX. *The same.*

Enter ROBIN *and* RALPH *with a silver goblet.*

Robin. Come, Ralph: did I not tell thee, we were for ever made by this Doctor Faustus' book? *ecce, signum!* here 's a simple purchase for horse-keepers: our horses shall eat no hay as long as this lasts.

Ralph. But, Robin, here comes the Vintner.

Robin. Hush! I'll gull him supernaturally.

Enter Vintner.

Drawer, I hope all is paid; God be with you!—Come, Ralph.

Vint. Soft, sir; a word with you. I must yet have a goblet paid from you, ere you go.

Robin. I a goblet, Ralph, I a goblet!—I scorn you; and you are but a, etc. I a goblet! search me.

Vint. I mean so, sir, with your favour. [*Searches* ROBIN.

Robin. How say you now?

Vint. I must say somewhat to your fellow.—You, sir!

Ralph. Me, sir! me, sir! search your fill. [Vintner *searches him.*] Now, sir, you may be ashamed to burden honest men with a matter of truth.

Vint. Well, tone of you hath this goblet about you.

Ralph. You lie, drawer, 'tis afore me [*Aside*].—Sirrah you, I'll teach you to impeach honest men;—stand by;—I'll scour you for a goblet;—stand aside you had best, I charge you in the name of Belzebub.—Look to the goblet, Ralph [*Aside to* RALPH].

Vint. What mean you, sirrah?

Robin. I'll tell you what I mean. [*Reads from a book*] *Sanctobulorum Periphrasticon*—nay, I'll tickle you, Vintner.—Look to the goblet, Ralph [*Aside to* RALPH].—[*Reads*] *Polypragmos Belseborams framanto pacostiphos tostu, Mephistophilis, etc.*

Enter MEPHISTOPHILIS, *sets squibs at their backs, and then exit. They run about.*

Vint. *O, nomine Domini!* what meanest thou, Robin? thou hast no goblet.

Ralph. *Peccatum peccatorum!*—Here's thy goblet, good Vintner. [*Gives the goblet to* Vintner, *who exit.*

Robin. *Misericordia pro nobis!* what shall I do? Good devil, forgive me now, and I'll never rob thy library more.

Re-enter MEPHISTOPHILIS.

Meph. Monarch of hell, under whose black survey
Great potentates do kneel with awful fear,
Upon whose altars thousand souls do lie,
How am I vexèd with these villains' charms!
From Constantinople am I hither come,
Only for pleasure of these damnèd slaves.

Robin. How, from Constantinople! you have had a great journey: will you take sixpence in your purse to pay for your supper, and be gone?

Meph. Well, villains, for your presumption, I transform thee into an ape, and thee into a dog; and so be gone. [*Exit.*

Robin. How, into an ape! that's brave: I'll have fine sport with the boys; I'll get nuts and apples enow.

Ralph. And I must be a dog.

Robin. I' faith, thy head will never be out of the pottage-pot. [*Exeunt.*

SCENE X. *The Emperor's Court at Innsbruck.*

Enter EMPEROR, FAUSTUS, *and a* Knight, *with* Attendants, *among whom* MEPHISTOPHILIS.

Emp. Master Doctor Faustus, I have heard strange report of thy knowledge in the black art, how that none in my empire nor in the whole world can compare with thee for the rare effects of magic: they say thou hast a familiar spirit, by whom thou canst accomplish what thou list. This, therefore, is my request, that thou let me see some proof of thy skill, that mine eyes may be witnesses to confirm what mine ears have heard reported: and here I swear to thee, by the honour of mine imperial crown, that, whatever thou doest, thou shalt be no ways prejudiced or endamaged.

Knight. I' faith, he looks much like a conjurer. [*Aside.*

Faust. My gracious sovereign, though I must confess myself far inferior to the report men have published, and nothing answerable to the honour of your imperial majesty, yet, for that love and duty binds me thereunto, I am content to do whatsoever your majesty shall command me.

Emp. Then, Doctor Faustus, mark what I shall say.
As I was sometime solitary set
Within my closet, sundry thoughts arose
About the honour of mine ancestors,
How they had won by prowess such exploits,
Got such riches, subdu'd so many kingdoms,
As we that do succeed, or they that shall
Hereafter possess our throne, shall
(I fear me) ne'er attain to that degree
Of high renown and great authority:
Amongst which kings is Alexander the Great,
Chief spectacle of the world's pre-eminence,
The bright shining of whose glorious acts
Lightens the world with his reflecting beams,
As when I hear but motion made of him,
It grieves my soul I never saw the man:
If, therefore, thou, by cunning of thine art,
Canst raise this man from hollow vaults below,
Where lies entomb'd this famous conqueror,
And bring with him his beauteous paramour,
Both in their right shapes, gesture, and attire
They us'd to wear during their time of life,
Thou shalt both satisfy my just desire,
And give me cause to praise thee whilst I live.

Faust. My gracious lord, I am ready to accomplish your request, so far forth as by art and power of my spirit I am able to perform.

Knight. I' faith, that 's just nothing at all. [*Aside.*

Faust. But, if it like your grace, it is not in my ability to present before your eyes the true substantial bodies of those deceased princes, which long since are consumed to dust.

Knight. Ay, marry, Master Doctor, now there 's a sign of grace in you, when you will confess the truth. [*Aside.*

Faust. But such spirits as can lively resemble Alexander and his paramour shall appear before your grace, in that manner that they both lived in, in their most flourishing estate; which I doubt not shall sufficiently content your imperial majesty.

Emp. Go to, Master Doctor; let me see them presently.

Knight. Do you hear, Master Doctor? you bring Alexander and his paramour before the Emperor!

Faust. How then, sir?

Knight. I' faith, that 's as true as Diana turned me to a stag.

Faust. No, sir; but, when Actaeon died, he left the horns for you.—Mephistophilis, be gone. [*Exit* MEPHISTOPHILIS.

Knight. Nay, an you go to conjuring, I'll be gone. [*Exit.*

Faust. I'll meet with you anon for interrupting me so.—Here they are, my gracious lord.

Re-enter MEPHISTOPHILIS *with* Spirits *in the shapes of* ALEXANDER *and his* Paramour.

Emp. Master Doctor, I heard this lady, while she lived, had a wart or mole in her neck: how shall I know whether it be so or no?

Faust. Your highness may boldly go and see.

Emp. Sure, these are no spirits, but the true substantial bodies of those two deceased princes. [*Exeunt* Spirits.

Faust. Will 't please your highness now to send for the knight that was so pleasant with me here of late?

Emp. One of you call him forth. [*Exit* Attendant.

Re-enter the Knight *with a pair of horns on his head.*

How now, sir knight! Feel on thy head.

Knight. Thou damnèd wretch and execrable dog,
Bred in the concave of some monstrous rock,
How dar'st thou thus abuse a gentleman?
Villain, I say, undo what thou hast done!

Faust. O, not so fast, sir! there's no haste: but, good, are you remembered how you crossed me in my conference with the Emperor? I think I have met with you for it.

Emp. Good Master Doctor, at my entreaty release him: he hath done penance sufficient.

Faust. My gracious lord, not so much for the injury he offered me here in your presence, as to delight you with some mirth, hath Faustus worthily requited this injurious knight; which being all I desire, I am content to release him of his horns:—and, sir knight, hereafter speak well of scholars.—Mephistophilis, transform him straight. [MEPHISTOPHILIS *removes the horns.*]—Now, my good lord, having done my duty, I humbly take my leave.

Emp. Farewell, Master Doctor: yet, ere you go,
Expect from me a bounteous reward.

[*Exeunt* EMPEROR, Knight, *and* Attendants.

SCENE XI. *A green; afterwards the house of Faustus.*

Faust. Now, Mephistophilis, the restless course
That time doth run with calm and silent foot,
Shortening my days and thread of vital life,
Calls for the payment of my latest years:
Therefore, sweet Mephistophilis, let us
Make haste to Wittenberg.

Meph. What, will you go on horse-back or on foot?

Faust. Nay, till I'm past this fair and pleasant green,
I'll walk on foot.

Enter a Horse-courser.

Horse-c. I have been all this day seeking one Master Fustian: mass, see where he is!—God save you, Master Doctor!

Faust. What, horse-courser! you are well met.

Horse-c. Do you hear, sir? I have brought you forty dollars for your horse.

Faust. I cannot sell him so. If thou likest him for fifty, take him.

Horse-c. Alas, sir, I have no more!—I pray you speak for me.

Meph. I pray you, let him have him: he is an honest fellow, and he has a great charge, neither wife nor child.

Faust. Well, come, give me your money [Horse-courser *gives* FAUSTUS *the money*]: my boy will deliver him to you. But I must tell you one thing before you have him; ride him not into the water, at any hand.

Horse-c. Why, sir, will he not drink of all waters?

Faust. O, yes, he will drink of all waters; but ride him not into the water: ride him over hedge or ditch, or where thou wilt, but not into the water.

Horse-c. Well, sir.—Now am I made man for ever: I'll not leave my horse for forty: if he had but the quality of hey-ding-ding, hey-ding-ding, I'd make a brave living on him: he has a buttock as slick as an eel [*Aside*].—Well, God b'wi'ye sir: your boy will deliver him me: but, hark you, sir; if my horse be sick or ill at ease, you'll tell me what it is?

Faust. Away, you villain! what, dost think I am a horse-doctor? [*Exit* Horse-courser.

What art thou, Faustus, but a man condemn'd to die?
Thy fatal time doth draw to final end;
Despair doth drive distrust into my thoughts:
Confound these passions with a quiet sleep:
Tush, Christ did call the thief upon the Cross;
Then rest thee, Faustus, quiet in conceit.
[*Sleeps in his chair.*

Re-enter Horse-courser, *all wet, crying.*

Horse-c. Alas, alas! Doctor Fustian, quoth a? mass, Doctor Lopus was never such a doctor: has given me a purgation, has purged me of forty dollars; I shall never see them more. But yet, like an ass as I was, I would not be ruled by him, for he bade me I should ride him into no water: now I, thinking my horse had had some rare quality that he would not have had me known of, I, like a venturous youth, rid him into the deep pond at the town's end. I was no sooner in the middle of the pond, but my horse vanished away, and I sat upon a bottle of hay, never so near drowning in my life. But I'll seek out my doctor, and have my forty dollars again, or I'll make it the dearest horse!—O, yonder is his snipper-snapper.—Do you hear? you, heypass, where 's your master?

Meph. Why, sir, what would you? you cannot speak with him.

Horse-c. But I will speak with him.

Meph. Why, he 's fast asleep: come some other time.

Horse-c. I'll speak with him now, or I'll break his glass-windows about his ears.

Meph. I tell thee, he has not slept this eight nights.

Horse-c. An he have not slept this eight weeks, I'll speak with him.

Meph. See, where he is, fast asleep.

Horse-c. Ay, this is he.—God save you, Master Doctor, Master Doctor, Master Doctor Fustian! forty dollars, forty dollars for a bottle of hay!

Meph. Why, thou seest he hears thee not.

Horse-c. So-ho, ho! so-ho, ho! [*Holla's in his ear.*] No, will you not wake? I'll make you wake ere I go. [*Pulls* FAUSTUS *by the leg, and pulls it away.*] Alas, I am undone! what shall I do?

Faust. O, my leg, my leg!—Help, Mephistophilis! call the officers!—My leg, my leg!

Meph. Come, villain, to the constable.

Horse-c. O Lord, sir, let me go, and I'll give you forty dollars more!

Meph. Where be they?

Horse-c. I have none about me: come to my ostry, and I'll give them you.

Meph. Be gone quickly. [Horse-courser *runs away.*

Faust. What, is he gone? farewell he! Faustus has his leg again, and the Horse-courser, I take it, a bottle of hay for his labour: well, this trick shall cost him forty dollars more.

Enter WAGNER.

How now, Wagner! what 's the news with thee?

Wag. Sir, the Duke of Vanholt doth earnestly entreat your company.

Faust. The Duke of Vanholt! an honourable gentleman, to whom I must be no niggard of my cunning.—Come, Mephistophilis, let 's away to him. [*Exeunt.*

SCENE XII. *The court of the Duke of Vanholt.*

Enter the DUKE OF VANHOLT, *the* DUCHESS, *and* FAUSTUS.

Duke. Believe me, Master Doctor, this merriment hath much pleased me.

Faust. My gracious lord, I am glad it contents you so well.—But it may be, madam, you take no delight in this. I have heard that women do long for some dainties or other: what is it, madam? tell me and you shall have it.

Duchess. Thanks, good Master Doctor: and, for I see your courteous intent to pleasure me, I will not hide from you the thing my heart desires; and, were it now summer, as it is January and the dead time of the winter, I would desire no better meat than a dish of ripe grapes.

Faust. Alas, madam, that 's nothing!—Mephistophilis, be gone. [*Exit* MEPHISTOPHILIS.] Were it a greater thing than this, so it would content you, you should have it.

Re-enter MEPHISTOPHILIS *with grapes.*

Here they be, madam: will 't please you taste on them?

Duke. Believe me, Master Doctor, this makes me wonder above the rest, that being in the dead time of winter and in the month of January, how you should come by these grapes.

Faust. If it like your grace, the year is divided into two circles over the whole world, that, when it is here winter with us, in the contrary circle it is summer with them, as in India, Saba, and farther countries in the east; and by means of a swift spirit that I have, I had them brought hither, as you see.—How do you like them, madam? be they good?

Duchess. Believe me, Master Doctor, they be the best grapes that e'er I tasted in my life before.

Faust. I am glad they content you so, madam.

Duke. Come, madam, let us in, where you must well reward this learned man for the great kindness he hath shewed to you.

Duchess. And so I will, my lord; and, whilst I live, rest beholding for this courtesy.

Faust. I humbly thank your grace.

Duke. Come, Master Doctor, follow us, and receive your reward. [*Exeunt.*

SCENE XIII. *A room in the house of Faustus.*

Enter WAGNER.

Wag. I think my master means to die shortly,
For he hath given to me all his goods:
And yet, methinketh, if that death were near,
He would not banquet, and carouse, and swill
Amongst the students, as even now he doth,
Who are at supper with such belly-cheer
As Wagner ne'er beheld in all his life.
See, where they come! belike the feast is ended. [*Exit.*

Enter FAUSTUS *with two or three* Scholars, *and* MEPHISTOPHILIS.

First Schol. Master Doctor Faustus, since our conference

about fair ladies, which was the beautifulest in all the world, we have determined with ourselves that Helen of Greece was the admirablest lady that ever lived: therefore, Master Doctor, if you will do us that favour, as to let us see that peerless dame of Greece, whom all the world admires for majesty, we should think ourselves much beholding unto you.

Faust. Gentlemen,
For that I know your friendship is unfeign'd,
And Faustus' custom is not to deny
The just requests of those that wish him well,
You shall behold that peerless dame of Greece,
No otherways for pomp and majesty
Than when Sir Paris cross'd the seas with her,
And brought the spoils to rich Dardania.
Be silent, then, for danger is in words.

[*Music sounds, and* HELEN *passeth over the stage.*

Sec. Schol. Too simple is my wit to tell her praise,
Whom all the world admires for majesty.

Third Schol. No marvel though the angry Greeks pursu'd
With ten years' war the rape of such a queen,
Whose heavenly beauty passeth all compare.

First Schol. Since we have seen the pride of Nature's works,
And only paragon of excellence,
Let us depart; and for this glorious deed
Happy and blest be Faustus evermore!

Faust. Gentlemen, farewell: the same I wish to you.

[*Exeunt* Scholars.

Enter an Old Man.

Old Man. Ah, Doctor Faustus, that I might prevail
To guide thy steps unto the way of life,
By which sweet path thou may'st attain the goal
That shall conduct thee to celestial rest!
Break heart, drop blood, and mingle it with tears,
Tears falling from repentant heaviness
Of thy most vile and loathsome filthiness,

The stench whereof corrupts the inward soul
With such flagitious crimes of heinous sin
As no commiseration may expel,
But mercy, Faustus, of thy Saviour sweet,
Whose blood alone must wash away thy guilt.

Faust. Where art thou, Faustus? wretch, what hast thou done?
Damn'd art thou, Faustus, damn'd; despair and die!
Hell calls for right, and with a roaring voice
Says, 'Faustus, come; thine hour is almost come;'
And Faustus now will come to do thee right.

[MEPHISTOPHILIS *gives him a dagger.*

Old Man. Ah, stay, good Faustus, stay thy desperate steps!
I see an angel hovers o'er thy head,
And, with a vial full of precious grace,
Offers to pour the same into thy soul:
Then call for mercy, and avoid despair.

Faust. Ah, my sweet friend, I feel
Thy words to comfort my distressèd soul!
Leave me a while to ponder on my sins.

Old Man. I go, sweet Faustus; but with heavy cheer,
Fearing the ruin of thy hopeless soul. [*Exit.*

Faust. Accursèd Faustus, where is mercy now?
I do repent; and yet I do despair:
Hell strives with grace for conquest in my breast:
What shall I do to shun the snares of death?

Meph. Thou traitor, Faustus, I arrest thy soul
For disobedience to my sovereign lord:
Revolt, or I'll in piece-meal tear thy flesh.

Faust. Sweet Mephistophilis, entreat thy lord
To pardon my unjust presumption,
And with my blood again I will confirm
My former vow I made to Lucifer.

Meph. Do it, then, quickly, with unfeignèd heart,
Lest greater danger do attend thy drift.

[FAUSTUS *stabs his arm, and writes on a paper with his blood.*

Faust. Torment, sweet friend, that base and crooked age,
That durst dissuade me from thy Lucifer,
With greatest torments that our hell affords.

Meph. His faith is great; I cannot touch his soul;
But what I may afflict his body with
I will attempt, which is but little worth.

Faust. One thing, good servant, let me crave of thee,
To glut the longing of my heart's desire,—
That I might have unto my paramour
That heavenly Helen which I saw of late,
Whose sweet embracings may extinguish clean
These thoughts that do dissuade me from my vow,
And keep mine oath I made to Lucifer.

Meph. Faustus, this, or what else thou shalt desire,
Shall be perform'd in twinkling of an eye.

Re-enter HELEN.

Faust. Was this the face that launch'd a thousand ships,
And burnt the topless towers of Ilium?—
Sweet Helen, make me immortal with a kiss.— [*Kisses her.*
Her lips suck forth my soul: see where it flees!—
Come, Helen, come, give me my soul again.
Here will I dwell, for heaven is in these lips,
And all is dross that is not Helena.
I will be Paris, and for love of thee,
Instead of Troy, shall Wittenberg be sack'd;
And I will combat with weak Menelaus,
And wear thy colours on my plumèd crest;
Yes, I will wound Achilles in the heel,
And then return to Helen for a kiss.
O, thou art fairer than the evening air
Clad in the beauty of a thousand stars;
Brighter art thou than flaming Jupiter
When he appear'd to hapless Semele;
More lovely than the monarch of the sky
In wanton Arethusa's azur'd arms;
And none but thou shalt be my paramour! [*Exeunt.*

Enter the Old Man.

Old Man. Accursèd Faustus, miserable man,
That from thy soul exclud'st the grace of heaven,
And fly'st the throne of his tribunal-seat!

Enter Devils.

Satan begins to sift me with his pride:
As in this furnace God shall try my faith,
My faith, vile hell, shall triumph over thee.
Ambitious fiends, see how the heavens smile
At your repulse, and laugh your state to scorn!
Hence, hell! for hence I fly unto my God.
[*Exeunt,—on one side* Devils, *on the other* Old Man.

Scene XIV. *The same.*

Enter Faustus, *with* Scholars.

Faust. Ah, gentlemen!

First Schol. What ails Faustus?

Faust. Ah, my sweet chamber-fellow, had I lived with thee, then had I lived still! but now I die eternally. Look, comes he not? comes he not?

Sec. Schol. What means Faustus?

Third Schol. Belike he is grown into some sickness by being over-solitary.

First Schol. If it be so, we'll have physicians to cure him.—'Tis but a surfeit; never fear, man.

Faust. A surfeit of deadly sin, that hath damned both body and soul.

Sec. Schol. Yet, Faustus, look up to heaven; remember God's mercies are infinite.

Faust. But Faustus' offence can ne'er be pardoned: the serpent that tempted Eve may be saved, but not Faustus. Ah, gentlemen, hear me with patience, and tremble not at my speeches! Though my heart pants and quivers to remember that I have been a student here these thirty years, O, would

I had never seen Wittenberg, never read book! and what wonders I have done, all Germany can witness, yea, all the world; for which Faustus hath lost both Germany and the world, yea, heaven itself, heaven, the seat of God, the throne of the blessed, the kingdom of joy; and must remain in hell for ever, hell, ah, hell, for ever! Sweet friends, what shall become of Faustus, being in hell for ever?

Third Schol. Yet, Faustus, call on God.

Faust. On God, whom Faustus hath abjured! on God, whom Faustus hath blasphemed! Ah, my God, I would weep! but the devil draws in my tears. Gush forth blood, instead of tears! yea, life and soul—O, he stays my tongue! I would lift up my hands; but see, they hold them, they hold them!

All. Who, Faustus?

Faust. Lucifer and Mephistophilis. Ah, gentlemen, I gave them my soul for my cunning!

All. God forbid!

Faust. God forbade it, indeed; but Faustus hath done it: for vain pleasure of twenty-four years hath Faustus lost eternal joy and felicity! I writ them a bill with mine own blood: the date is expired; the time will come, and he will fetch me.

First Schol. Why did not Faustus tell us of this before, that divines might have prayed for thee?

Faust. Oft have I thought to have done so; but the devil threatened to tear me in pieces, if I named God, to fetch both body and soul, if I once gave ear to divinity: and now 'tis too late. Gentlemen, away, lest you perish with me.

Sec. Schol. O, what shall we do to save Faustus?

Faust. Talk not of me, but save yourselves, and depart.

Third Schol. God will strengthen me; I will stay with Faustus.

First Schol. Tempt not God, sweet friend; but let us into the next room, and there pray for him.

Faust. Ay, pray for me, pray for me; and what noise soever ye hear, come not unto me, for nothing can rescue me.

Sec. Schol. Pray thou, and we will pray that God may have mercy upon thee.

Faust. Gentlemen, farewell: if I live till morning, I'll visit you; if not, Faustus is gone to hell.

All. Faustus, farewell.

[*Exeunt* Scholars.—*The clock strikes eleven.*

Faust. Ah, Faustus,
Now hast thou but one bare hour to live,
And then thou must be damn'd perpetually!
Stand still, you ever-moving spheres of heaven,
That time may cease, and midnight never come;
Fair Nature's eye, rise, rise again, and make
Perpetual day; or let this hour be but
A year, a month, a week, a natural day,
That Faustus may repent and save his soul!
O lente, lente currite, noctis equi!
The stars move still, time runs, the clock will strike,
The devil will come, and Faustus must be damn'd.
O, I'll leap up to my God!—Who pulls me down?—
See, see, where Christ's blood streams in the firmament!
One drop would save my soul, half a drop: ah, my Christ!—
Ah, rend not my heart for naming of my Christ!
Yet will I call on him: O, spare me, Lucifer!—
Where is it now? 'tis gone: and see, where God
Stretcheth out his arm, and bends his ireful brows!
Mountains and hills, come, come, and fall on me,
And hide me from the heavy wrath of God!
No, no!
Then will I headlong run into the earth:
Earth, gape! O, no, it will not harbour me!
You stars that reign'd at my nativity,
Whose influence hath allotted death and hell,
Now draw up Faustus, like a foggy mist,
Into the entrails of yon labouring clouds,
That, when you vomit forth into the air,

My limbs may issue from your smoky mouths,
So that my soul may but ascend to heaven!

[*The clock strikes the half-hour.*

Ah, half the hour is past! 'twill all be past anon.
O God,
If thou wilt not have mercy on my soul,
Yet for Christ's sake, whose blood hath ransom'd me,
Impose some end to my incessant pain;
Let Faustus live in hell a thousand years,
A hundred thousand, and at last be sav'd!
O, no end is limited to damnèd souls!
Why wert thou not a creature wanting soul?
Or why is this immortal that thou hast?
Ah, Pythagoras' metempsychosis, were that true,
This soul should fly from me, and I be chang'd
Unto some brutish beast! all beasts are happy,
For, when they die,
Their souls are soon dissolv'd in elements;
But mine must live still to be plagu'd in hell.
Curs'd be the parents that engender'd me!
No, Faustus, curse thyself, curse Lucifer
That hath depriv'd thee of the joys of heaven.

[*The clock strikes twelve.*

O, it strikes, it strikes! Now, body, turn to air,
Or Lucifer will bear thee quick to hell!

[*Thunder and lightning.*

O soul, be chang'd into little water-drops,
And fall into the ocean, ne'er be found!

Enter Devils.

My God, my God, look not so fierce on me!
Adders and serpents, let me breathe a while!
Ugly hell, gape not! come not, Lucifer!
I'll burn my books!—Ah, Mephistophilis!

[*Exeunt* Devils *with* FAUSTUS.

Enter Chorus.

Chor. Cut is the branch that might have grown full straight,
And burnèd is Apollo's laurel-bough,
That sometime grew within this learnèd man.
Faustus is gone: regard his hellish fall,
Whose fiendful fortune may exhort the wise
Only to wonder at unlawful things,
Whose deepness doth entice such forward wits
To practise more than heavenly power permits. [*Exit.*

Terminat hora diem; terminat auctor opus.

THE HONOURABLE HISTORY OF

FRIAR BACON AND FRIAR BUNGAY.

DRAMATIS PERSONÆ.

KING HENRY THE THIRD.
EDWARD, Prince of Wales, his son.
EMPEROR OF GERMANY.
KING OF CASTILE.
LACY, Earl of Lincoln.
WARREN, Earl of Sussex.
ERMSBY, a gentleman.
RALPH SIMNELL, the King's Fool.
FRIAR BACON.
MILES, Friar Bacon's poor scholar.
FRIAR BUNGAY.
JAQUES VANDERMAST.
BURDEN, MASON, CLEMENT, Doctors of Oxford.
LAMBERT, SERLSBY, gentlemen.
Two Scholars, their sons.
Keeper.
THOMAS, RICHARD, clowns.
Constable.
A Post.

Lords, Clowns, &c.

ELINOR, daughter to the King of Castile.
MARGARET, the Keeper's daughter, the Fair Maid of Fressingfield.
JOAN, a country wench.
Hostess of the Bell at Henley.

A DEVIL.
Spirit in the shape of HERCULES.

SCENE I. *Near Framlingham.*

Enter PRINCE EDWARD *malcontented, with* LACY, WARREN, ERMSBY, *and* RALPH SIMNELL.

Lacy. Why looks my lord like to a troubled sky
When heaven's bright shine is shadow'd with a fog?
Alate we ran the deer, and through the lawnds
Stripp'd with our nags the lofty frolic bucks
That scudded 'fore the teasers like the wind:
Ne'er was the deer of merry Fressingfield
So lustily pull'd down by jolly mates,
Nor shared the farmers such fat venison,
So frankly dealt, this hundred years before;
Nor have
I seen my lord more frolic in the chase,
And now chang'd to melancholy dump.

War. After the prince got to the Keeper's lodge,
And had been jocund in the house awhile,
Tossing off ale and milk in country cans,
Whether it was the country's sweet content,
Or else the bonny damsel fill'd us drink,
That seem'd so stately in her stammel red,
Or that a qualm did cross his stomach then,
But straight he fell into his passions.

Erms. Sirrah Ralph, what say you to your master,
Shall he thus all amort live malcontent?

Ralph. Hearest thou, Ned?—Nay, look if he will speak to me!

P. Edw. What say'st thou to me, fool?

Ralph. I prithee, tell me, Ned, art thou in love with the Keeper's daughter?

P. Edw. How if I be, what then?

Ralph. Why, then, sirrah, I'll teach thee how to deceive Love.

P. Edw. How, Ralph?

Ralph. Marry, Sirrah Ned, thou shalt put on my cap and my coat and my dagger, and I will put on thy clothes and thy sword: and so thou shalt be my fool.

P. Edw. And what of this?

Ralph. Why, so thou shalt beguile Love; for Love is such a proud scab, that he will never meddle with fools nor children. Is not Ralph's counsel good, Ned?

P. Edw. Tell me, Ned Lacy, didst thou mark the maid,
How lovely in her country-weeds she look'd?
A bonnier wench all Suffolk cannot yield:—
All Suffolk! nay, all England holds none such.

Ralph. Sirrah Will Ermsby, Ned is deceived.

Erms. Why, Ralph?

Ralph. He says all England hath no such, and I say, and I'll stand to it, there is one better in Warwickshire.

War. How provest thou that, Ralph?

Ralph. Why, is not the abbot a learned man, and hath

read many books, and thinkest thou he hath not more learning than thou to choose a bonny wench? yes, warrant I thee, by his whole grammar.

Erms. A good reason, Ralph.

P. Edw. I tell thee, Lacy, that her sparkling eyes
Do lighten forth sweet love's alluring fire;
And in her tresses she doth fold the looks
Of such as gaze upon her golden hair;
Her bashful white, mix'd with the morning's red,
Luna doth boast upon her lovely cheeks;
Her front is beauty's table, where she paints
The glories of her gorgeous excellence;
Her teeth are shelves of precious margarites,
Richly enclos'd with ruddy coral cleeves.
Tush, Lacy, she is beauty's over-match,
If thou survey'st her curious imagery.

Lacy. I grant, my lord, the damsel is as fair
As simple Suffolk's homely towns can yield;
But in the court be quainter dames than she,
Whose faces are enrich'd with honour's taint,
Whose beauties stand upon the stage of fame,
And vaunt their trophies in the courts of love.

P. Edw. Ah, Ned, but hadst thou watch'd her as myself,
And seen the secret beauties of the maid,
Their courtly coyness were but foolery.

Erms. Why, how watch'd you her, my lord?

P. Edw. Whenas she swept like Venus through the house,
And in her shape fast folded up my thoughts,
Into the milk-house went I with the maid,
And there amongst the cream-bowls she did shine
As Pallas 'mongst her princely huswifery:
She turn'd her smock over her lily arms,
And div'd them into milk to run her cheese;
But, whiter than the milk, her crystal skin,
Checkèd with lines of azure, made her blush
That art or nature durst bring for compare.
Ermsby,

If thou hadst seen, as I did note it well,
How beauty play'd the huswife, how this girl,
Like Lucrece, laid her fingers to the work,
Thou wouldst, with Tarquin, hazard Rome and all
To win the lovely maid of Fressingfield.

Ralph. Sirrah Ned, wouldst fain have her?

P. Edw. Ay, Ralph.

Ralph. Why, Ned, I have laid the plot in my head; thou shalt have her already.

P. Edw. I'll give thee a new coat, an learn me that.

Ralph. Why, sirrah Ned, we'll ride to Oxford to Friar Bacon: O, he is a brave scholar, sirrah; they say he is a brave necromancer, that he can make women of devils, and he can juggle cats into costermongers.

P. Edw. And how then, Ralph?

Ralph. Marry, sirrah, thou shalt go to him: and because thy father Harry shall not miss thee, he shall turn me into thee; and I'll to the court, and I'll prince it out; and he shall make thee either a silken purse full of gold, or else a fine wrought smock.

P. Edw. But how shall I have the maid?

Ralph. Marry, sirrah, if thou be'st a silken purse full of gold, then on Sundays she'll hang thee by her side, and you must not say a word. Now, sir, when she comes into a great prease of people, for fear of the cutpurse, on a sudden she'll swap thee into her plackerd; then, sirrah, being there, you may plead for yourself.

Erms. Excellent policy!

P. Edw. But how if I be a wrought smock?

Ralph. Then she'll put thee into her chest and lay thee into lavender, and upon some good day she'll put thee on.

Lacy. Wonderfully wisely counselled, Ralph.

P. Edw. Ralph shall have a new coat.

Ralph. God thank you when I have it on my back, Ned.

P. Edw. Lacy, the fool hath laid a perfect plot;
For why our country Margaret is so coy,

And stands so much upon her honest points,
That marriage or no market with the maid.
Ermsby, it must be necromantic spells
And charms of art that must enchain her love,
Or else shall Edward never win the girl.
Therefore, my wags, we'll horse us in the morn,
And post to Oxford to this jolly friar:
Bacon shall by his magic do this deed.

War. Content, my lord; and that 's a speedy way
To wean these headstrong puppies from the teat.

P. Edw. I am unknown, not taken for the prince;
They only deem us frolic courtiers,
That revel thus among our liege's game:
Therefore I have devis'd a policy.
Lacy, thou know'st next Friday is Saint James',
And then the country flocks to Harleston fair:
Then will the Keeper's daughter frolic there,
And over-shine the troop of all the maids
That come to see and to be seen that day.
Haunt thee disguis'd among the country-swains,
Feign thou'rt a farmer's son, not far from thence,
Espy her loves, and who she liketh best;
Cote him, and court her to control the clown;
Say that the courtier 'tirèd all in green,
That help'd her handsomely to run her cheese,
And fill'd her father's lodge with venison,
Commends him, and sends fairings to herself.
Buy something worthy of her parentage,
Not worth her beauty; for, Lacy, then the fair
Affords no jewel fitting for the maid:
And when thou talk'st of me, note if she blush:
O, then she loves; but if her cheeks wax pale,
Disdain it is. Lacy, send how she fares,
And spare no time nor cost to win her loves.

Lacy. I will, my lord, so execute this charge
As if that Lacy were in love with her.

P. Edw. Send letters speedily to Oxford of the news.

Ralph. And, Sirrah Lacy, buy me a thousand thousand million of fine bells.

Lacy. What wilt thou do with them, Ralph?

Ralph. Marry, every time that Ned sighs for the Keeper's daughter, I'll tie a bell about him: and so within three or four days I will send word to his father Harry, that his son, and my master Ned, is become Love's morris-dance[r].

P. Edw. Well, Lacy, look with care unto thy charge,
And I will haste to Oxford to the friar,
That he by art and thou by secret gifts
Mayst make me lord of merry Fressingfield.

Lacy. God send your honour your heart's desire.

[*Exeunt.*

SCENE II. *Friar Bacon's cell at Brasenose.*

Enter FRIAR BACON, *and* MILES *with books under his arm;* BURDEN, MASON, *and* CLEMENT.

Bacon. Miles, where are you?

Miles. *Hic sum, doctissime et reverendissime doctor.*

Bacon. *Attulisti nos libros meos de necromantia?*

Miles. *Ecce quam bonum et quam jucundum habitare libros in unum!*

Bacon. Now, masters of our academic state,
That rule in Oxford, viceroys in your place,
Whose heads contain maps of the liberal arts,
Spending your time in depths of learnèd skill,
Why flock you thus to Bacon's secret cell,
A friar newly stall'd in Brazen-nose?
Say what's your mind, that I may make reply.

Burd. Bacon, we hear that long we have suspect,
That thou art read in magic's mystery;
In pyromancy, to divine by flames;
To tell, by hydromancy, ebbs and tides;
By aeromancy to discover doubts,
To plain out questions, as Apollo did.

Bacon. Well, Master Burden, what of all this?

Miles. Marry, sir, he doth but fulfil, by rehearsing of these names, the fable of the Fox and the Grapes: that which is above us pertains nothing to us.

Burd. I tell thee, Bacon, Oxford makes report,
Nay, England, and the court of Henry says,
Thou'rt making of a brazen head by art,
Which shall unfold strange doubts and aphorisms,
And read a lecture in philosophy;
And, by the help of devils and ghastly fiends,
Thou mean'st, ere many years or days be past,
To compass England with a wall of brass.

Bacon. And what of this?

Miles. What of this, master! why, he doth speak mystically; for he knows, if your skill fail to make a brazen head, yet Mother Waters' strong ale will fit his turn to make him have a copper nose.

Clem. Bacon, we come not grieving at thy skill,
But joying that our acadèmy yields
A man suppos'd the wonder of the world;
For if thy cunning work these miracles,
England and Europe shall admire thy fame,
And Oxford shall in characters of brass,
And statues, such as were built up in Rome,
Etérnize Friar Bacon for his art.

Mason. Then, gentle friar, tell us thy intent.

Bacon. Seeing you come as friends unto the friar,
Resolve you, doctors, Bacon can by books
Make storming Boreas thunder from his cave,
And dim fair Luna to a dark eclipse.
The great arch-ruler, potentate of hell,
Trembles when Bacon bids him, or his fiends,
Bow to the force of his pentageron.
What art can work, the frolic friar knows;
And therefore will I turn my magic books,
And strain out necromancy to the deep.
I have contriv'd and fram'd a head of brass
(I made Belcephon hammer out the stuff),

And that by art shall read philosophy:
And I will strengthen England by my skill,
That if ten Cæsars liv'd and reign'd in Rome,
With all the legions Europe doth contain,
They should not touch a grass of English ground:
The work that Ninus rear'd at Babylon,
The brazen walls fram'd by Semiramis,
Carv'd out like to the portal of the sun,
Shall not be such as rings the English strand
From Dover to the market-place of Rye.

Burd. Is this possible?

Miles. I'll bring ye two or three witnesses.

Burd. What be those?

Miles. Marry, sir, three or four as honest devils and good companions as any be in hell.

Mason. No doubt but magic may do much in this;
For he that reads but mathematic rules
Shall find conclusions that avail to work
Wonders that pass the common sense of men.

Burd. But Bacon roves a bow beyond his reach,
And tells of more than magic can perform,
Thinking to get a fame by fooleries.
Have I not pass'd as far in state of schools,
And read of many secrets? yet to think
That heads of brass can utter any voice,
Or more, to tell of deep philosophy,
This is a fable Æsop had forgot.

Bacon. Burden, thou wrong'st me in detracting thus;
Bacon loves not to stuff himself with lies.
But tell me 'fore these doctors, if thou dare,
Of certain questions I shall move to thee.

Burd. I will: ask what thou can.

Miles. Marry, sir, he'll straight be on your pick-pack, to know whether the feminine or the masculine gender be most worthy.

Bacon. Were you not yesterday, Master Burden, at Henley upon the Thames?

Burd. I was: what then?

Bacon. What book studied you thereon all night?

Burd. I! none at all; I read not there a line.

Bacon. Then, doctors, Friar Bacon's art knows naught.

Clem. What say you to this, Master Burden? doth he not touch you.

Burd. I pass not of his frivolous speeches.

Miles. Nay, Master Burden, my master, ere he hath done with you, will turn you from a doctor to a dunce, and shake you so small, that he will leave no more learning in you than is in Balaam's ass.

Bacon. Masters, for that learn'd Burden's skill is deep,
And sore he doubts of Bacon's cabalism.
I'll show you why he haunts to Henley oft:
Not, doctors, for to taste the fragrant air,
But there to spend the night in alchemy,
To multiply with secret spells of art;
Thus private steals he learning from us all.
To prove my sayings true, I'll show you straight
The book he keeps at Henley for himself.

Miles. Nay, now my master goes to conjuration, take heed.

Bacon. Masters,
Stand still, fear not, I'll show you but his book. [*Conjures.*
Per omnes deos infernales, Belcephon!

Enter Hostess *with a shoulder of mutton on a spit, and a* Devil.

Miles. O, master, cease your conjuration, or you spoil all; for here 's a she-devil come with a shoulder of mutton on a spit: you have marred the devil's supper; but no doubt he thinks our college fare is slender, and so hath sent you his cook with a shoulder of mutton, to make it exceed.

Hostess. O, where am I, or what 's become of me?

Bacon. What art thou?

Hostess. Hostess at Henley, mistress of the Bell.

Bacon. How cam'st thou here?

Hostess. As I was in the kitchen 'mongst the maids,
Spitting the meat 'gainst supper for my guess,
A motion mov'd me to look forth of door:
No sooner had I pried into the yard,
But straight a whirlwind hoisted me from thence,
And mounted me aloft unto the clouds.
As in a trance I thought nor fearèd naught,
Nor know I where or whither I was ta'en,
Nor where I am nor what these persons be.

Bacon. No? know you not Master Burden?

Hostess. O yes, good sir, he is my daily guest.—
What, Master Burden! 'twas but yesternight
That you and I at Henley play'd at cards.

Burd. I know not what we did.—A plague of all conjuring friars!

Clem. Now, jolly friar, tell us, is this the book
That Burden is so careful to look on?

Bacon. It is.—But, Burden, tell me now,
Think'st thou that Bacon's necromantic skill
Cannot perform his head and wall of brass,
When he can fetch thine hostess in such post?

Miles. I'll warrant you, master, if Master Burden could conjure as well as you, he would have his book every night from Henley to study on at Oxford.

Mason. Burden,
What, are you mated by this frolic friar?—
Look how he droops; his guilty conscience
Drives him to 'bash, and makes his hostess blush.

Bacon. Well, mistress, for I will not have you miss'd,
You shall to Henley to cheer up your guests
'Fore supper gin.—Burden, bid her adieu;
Say farewell to your hostess 'fore she goes.—
Sirrah, away, and set her safe at home.

Hostess. Master Burden, when shall we see you at Henley?

Burd. The devil take thee and Henley too.
[*Exeunt* Hostess *and* Devil.

Miles. Master, shall I make a good motion?

Bacon What 's that?

Miles. Marry, sir, now that my hostess is gone to provide supper, conjure up another spirit, and send Doctor Burden flying after.

Bacon. Thus, rulers of our academic state,
You have seen the friar frame his art by proof;
And as the college callèd Brazen-nose
Is under him, and he the Master there,
So surely shall this head of brass be fram'd,
And yield 'forth strange and uncouth aphorisms;
And hell and Hecate shall fail the friar,
But I will circle England round with brass.

Miles. So be it *et nunc et semper*; amen. [*Exeunt.*

SCENE III. *Harleston Fair.*

Enter MARGARET *and* JOAN; THOMAS, RICHARD, *and other* Clowns; *and* LACY *disguised in country apparel.*

Thom. By my troth, Margaret, if this weather hold, we shall have hay good cheap, and butter and cheese at Harleston will bear no price.

Mar. Thomas, maids when they come to see the fair
Count not to make a cope for dearth of hay:
When we have turn'd our butter to the salt,
And set our cheese safely upon the racks,
Then let our fathers prize it as they please.
We country sluts of merry Fressingfield
Come to buy needless naughts to make us fine,
And look that young men should be frank this day,
And court us with such fairings as they can.
Phoebus is blithe, and frolic looks from heaven,
As when he courted lovely Semele,
Swearing the pedlers shall have empty packs,
If that fair weather may make chapmen buy.

Lacy. But, lovely Peggy, Semele is dead,
And therefore Phoebus from his palace pries,
And, seeing such a sweet and seemly saint,
Shows all his glories for to court yourself.

Mar. This is a fairing, gentle sir, indeed,
To soothe me up with such smooth flattery;
But learn of me, your scoff's too broad before.—
Well, Joan, our duties must abide their jests;
We serve the turn in jolly Fressingfield.

Joan. Margaret,
A farmer's daughter for a farmer's son:
I warrant you, the meanest of us both
Shall have a mate to lead us from the church.
[LACY *whispers* MARGARET *in the ear.*
But, Thomas, what's the news? what, in a dump?
Give me your hand, we are near a pedler's shop;
Out with your purse, we must have fairings now.

Thom. Faith, Joan, and shall: I'll bestow a fairing on you, and then we will to the tavern, and snap off a pint of wine or two.

Mar. Whence are you, sir? of Suffolk? for your terms
Are finer than the common sort of men.

Lacy. Faith, lovely girl, I am of Beccles by,
Your neighbour, not above six miles from hence,
A farmer's son, that never was so quaint
But that he could do courtesy to such dames.
But trust me, Margaret, I am sent in charge
From him that revell'd in your father's house,
And fill'd his lodge with cheer and venison,
'Tirèd in green: he sent you this rich purse,
His token that he help'd you run your cheese,
And in the milkhouse chatted with yourself.

Mar. To me?

Lacy. You forget yourself:
Women are often weak in memory.

Mar. O, pardon, sir, I call to mind the man:
'Twere little manners to refuse his gift,

And yet I hope he sends it not for love;
For we have little leisure to debate of that.

Joan. What, Margaret! blush not: maids must have their loves.

Thom. Nay, by the mass, she looks pale as if she were angry.

Rich. Sirrah, are you of Beccles? I pray, how doth Goodman Cob? my father bought a horse of him.—I'll tell you, Margaret, 'a were good to be a gentleman's jade, for of all things the foul hilding could not abide a dung-cart.

Mar. [*aside.*] How different is this farmer from the rest
That erst as yet have pleas'd my wandering sight!
His words are witty, quickened with a smile,
His courtesy gentle, smelling of the court;
Facile and debonair in all his deeds;
Proportion'd as was Paris, when, in grey,
He courted Œnon in the vale by Troy.
Great lords have come and pleaded for my love:
Who but the Keeper's lass of Fressingfield?
And yet methinks this farmer's jolly son
Passeth the proudest that hath pleas'd mine eye.
But, Peg, disclose not that thou art in love,
And show as yet no sign of love to him,
Although thou well wouldst wish him for thy love;
Keep that to thee till time doth serve thy turn,
To show the grief wherein thy heart doth burn.—
Come, Joan and Thomas, shall we to the fair?—
You, Beccles man, will not forsake us now?

Lacy. Not whilst I may have such quaint girls as you.

Mar. Well, if you chance to come by Fressingfield,
Make but a step into the Keeper's lodge,
And such poor fare as woodmen can afford,
Butter and cheese, cream and fat venison,
You shall have store, and welcome therewithal.

Lacy. Gramercies, Peggy; look for me ere long.

[*Exeunt.*

SCENE IV. *The Court at Hampton-House.*

Enter KING HENRY THE THIRD, *the* EMPEROR, *the* KING OF CASTILE, ELINOR, *and* VANDERMAST.

K. Hen. Great men of Europe, monarchs of the west,
Ring'd with the walls of old Oceanus,
Whose lofty surge is like the battlements
That compass'd high-built Babel in with towers,
Welcome, my lords, welcome, brave western kings,
To England's shore, whose promontory-cleeves
Show Albion is another little world;
Welcome says English Henry to you all;
Chiefly unto the lovely Elinor,
Who dar'd for Edward's sake cut through the seas,
And venture as Agenor's damsel through the deep,
To get the love of Henry's wanton son.

K. of. Cast. England's rich monarch, brave Plantagenet.
The Pyren Mounts swelling above the clouds,
That ward the wealthy Castile in with walls,
Could not detain the beauteous Elinor;
But hearing of the fame of Edward's youth,
She dar'd to brook Neptunus' haughty pride,
And bide the brunt of froward Æolus:
Then may fair England welcome her the more.

Elin. After that English Henry by his lords
Had sent Prince Edward's lovely counterfeit,
A present to the Castile Elinor,
The comely portrait of so brave a man,
The virtuous fame discoursèd of his deeds,
Edward's courageous resolution,
Done at the Holy Land 'fore Damas' walls,
Led both mine eye and thoughts in equal links,
To like so of the English monarch's son,
That I attempted perils for his sake.

Emp. Where is the prince, my lord?

K. Hen. He posted down, not long since, from the court,

To Suffolk side, to merry Framlingham,
To sport himself amongst my fallow deer:
From thence, by packets sent to Hampton-house,
We hear the prince is ridden, with his lords,
To Oxford, in the acadėmy there
To hear dispute amongst the learnèd men.
But we will send forth letters for my son,
To will him come from Oxford to the court.

Emp. Nay, rather, Henry, let us, as we be,
Ride for to visit Oxford with our train.
Fain would I see your universities,
And what learn'd men your acadėmy yields.
From Hapsburg have I brought a learnèd clerk
To hold dispute with English orators:
This doctor, surnam'd Jaques Vandermast,
A German born, pass'd into Padua,
To Florence and to fair Bologna,
To Paris, Rheims, and stately Orleans,
And, talking there with men of art, put down
The chiefest of them all in aphorisms,
In magic, and the mathematic rules:
Now let us, Henry, try him in your schools.

K. Hen. He shall, my lord; this motion likes me well.
We'll prógress straight to Oxford with our trains,
And see what men our acadėmy brings.—
And, wonder Vandermast, welcome to me:
In Oxford shalt thou find a jolly friar,
Call'd Friar Bacon, England's only flower:
Set him but nonplus in his magic spells,
And make him yield in mathematic rules,
And for thy glory I will bind thy brows,
Not with a poet's garland made of bays,
But with a coronet of choicest gold.
Whilst then we set to Oxford with our troops,
Let 's in and banquet at our English court. [*Exeunt.*

SCENE V. *Oxford.*

Enter RALPH SIMNELL *in* PRINCE EDWARD'S *apparel; and* PRINCE EDWARD, WARREN, *and* ERMSBY, *disguised.*

Ralph. Where be these vagabond knaves, that they attend no better on their master?

P. Edw. If it please your honour, we are all ready at an inch.

Ralph. Sirrah Ned, I'll have no more post-horse' to ride on: I'll have another fetch.

Erms. I pray you, how is that, my lord?

Ralph. Marry, sir, I'll send to the Isle of Ely for four or five dozen geese, and I'll have them tied six and six together with whip-cord: now upon their backs will I have a fair field-bed with a canopy; and so, when it is my pleasure, I'll flee into what place I please. This will be easy.

War. Your honour hath said well: but shall we to Brazen-nose College before we pull off our boots?

Erms. Warren, well motion'd; we will to the friar
Before we revel it within the town.—
Ralph, see you keep your countenance like a prince.

Ralph. Wherefore have I such a company of cutting knaves to wait upon me, but to keep and defend my countenance against all mine enemies? have you not good swords and bucklers?

Erms. Stay, who comes here?

War. Some scholar; and we'll ask him where Friar Bacon is.

Enter FRIAR BACON *and* MILES.

Bacon. Why, thou arrant dunce, shall I never make thee a good scholar? doth not all the town cry out and say, Friar Bacon's subsizer is the greatest blockhead in all Oxford? why, thou canst not speak one word of true Latin.

Miles. No, sir? yet, what is this else? *Ego sum tuus homo*, 'I am your man'; I warrant you, sir, as good Tully's phrase as any is in Oxford.

Bacon. Come on, sirrah; what part of speech is *Ego*?

Miles. *Ego*, that is 'I'; marry, *nomen substantivo.*

Bacon. How prove you that?

Miles. Why, sir, let him prove himself an 'a will; I can be heard, felt, and understood.

Bacon. O gross dunce! [*Beats him.*

P. Edw. Come, let us break off this dispute between these two.—Sirrah, where is Brazen-nose College?

Miles. Not far from Coppersmith's Hall.

P. Edw. What, dost thou mock me?

Miles. Not I, sir: but what would you at Brazen-nose?

Erms. Marry, we would speak with Friar Bacon.

Miles. Whose men be you?

Erms. Marry, scholar, here 's our master.

Ralph. Sirrah, I am the master of these good fellows; mayst thou not know me to be a lord by my reparrel?

Miles. Then here 's good game for the hawk; for here 's the master-fool and a covey of coxcombs: one wise man, I think, would spring you all.

P. Edw. Gog's wounds! Warren, kill him.

War. Why, Ned, I think the devil be in my sheath; I cannot get out my dagger.

Erms. Nor I mine: swones, Ned, I think I am bewitched.

Miles. A company of scabs! the proudest of you all draw your weapon if he can.—[*Aside.*] See how boldly I speak, now my master is by.

P. Edw. I strive in vain; but if my sword be shut
And conjur'd fast by magic in my sheath,
Villain, here is my fist. [*Strikes* MILES *a box on the ear.*

Miles. O, I beseech you conjure his hands too, that he may not lift his arms to his head, for he is light-fingered!

Ralph. Ned, strike him; I'll warrant thee by mine honour.

Bacon. What means the English prince to wrong my man?

P. Edw. To whom speak'st thou?

Bacon. To thee.

P. Edw. Who art thou?

Bacon. Could you not judge when all your swords grew fast,
That Friar Bacon was not far from hence?
Edward, King Henry's son and Prince of Wales,
Thy fool disguis'd cannot conceal thyself:
I know both Ermsby and the Sussex Earl,
Else Friar Bacon had but little skill.
Thou com'st in post from merry Fressingfield,
Fast-fancied to the Keeper's bonny lass,
To crave some succour of the jolly friar:
And Lacy, Earl of Lincoln, hast thou left
To treat fair Margaret to allow thy loves;
But friends are men, and love can baffle lords;
The earl both woos and courts her for himself.

War. Ned, this is strange; the friar knoweth all.

Erms. Apollo could not utter more than this.

P. Edw. I stand amaz'd to hear this jolly friar
Tell even the very secrets of my thoughts.—
But, learnèd Bacon, since thou know'st the cause
Why I did post so fast from Fressingfield,
Help, friar, at a pinch, that I may have
The love of lovely Margaret to myself,
And, as I am true Prince of Wales, I'll give
Living and lands to strength thy college-state.

War. Good friar, help the prince in this.

Ralph. Why, servant Ned, will not the friar do it? Were not my sword glued to my scabbard by conjuration, I would cut off his head, and make him do it by force.

Miles. In faith, my lord, your manhood and your sword is all alike; they are so fast conjured that we shall never see them.

Erms. What, doctor, in a dump! tush, help the prince,
And thou shalt see how liberal he will prove.

Bacon. Crave not such actions greater dumps than these?
I will, my lord, strain out my magic spells;
For this day comes the earl to Fressingfield,
And 'fore that night shuts in the day with dark,
They'll be betrothèd each to other fast.
But come with me; we'll to my study straight,
And in a glass prospective I will show
What's done this day in merry Fressingfield.

P. Edw. Gramercies, Bacon; I will quite thy pain.

Bacon. But send your train, my lord, into the town:
My scholar shall go bring them to their inn;
Meanwhile we'll see the knavery of the earl.

P. Edw. Warren, leave me:—and, Ermsby, take the fool;
Let him be master, and go revel it,
Till I and Friar Bacon talk awhile.

War. We will, my lord.

Ralph. Faith, Ned, and I'll lord it out till thou comest: I'll be Prince of Wales over all the blackpots in Oxford.

[*Exeunt* WARREN, ERMSBY, RALPH SIMNELL, *and* MILES.

SCENE VI. *Friar Bacon's cell.*

Enter FRIAR BACON *and* PRINCE EDWARD.

Bacon. Now, frolic Edward, welcome to my cell;
Here tempers Friar Bacon many toys,
And holds this place his consistory-court,
Wherein the devils plead homage to his words.
Within this glass prospective thou shalt see
This day what's done in merry Fressingfield
'Twixt lovely Peggy and the Lincoln Earl.

P. Edw. Friar, thou glad'st me: now shall Edward try
How Lacy meaneth to his sovereign lord.

Bacon. Stand there and look directly in the glass.

Enter MARGARET *and* FRIAR BUNGAY.

What sees my lord?

P. Edw. I see the Keeper's lovely lass appear,
As brightsome as the paramour of Mars,
Only attended by a jolly friar.

Bacon. Sit still, and keep the crystal in your eye.

Mar. But tell me, Friar Bungay, is it true
That this fair courteous country swain,
Who says his father is a farmer nigh,
Can be Lord Lacy, Earl of Lincolnshire?

Bun. Peggy, 'tis true, 'tis Lacy for my life,
Or else mine art and cunning both do fail,
Left by Prince Edward to procure his loves;
For he in green, that holp you run your cheese,
Is son to Henry, and the Prince of Wales.

Mar. Be what he will, his lure is but for lust:
But did Lord Lacy like poor Margaret,
Or would he deign to wed a country lass,
Friar, I would his humble handmaid be,
And for great wealth quite him with courtesy.

Bun. Why, Margaret, dost thou love him?

Mar. His personage, like the pride of vaunting Troy,
Might well avouch to shadow Helen's rape:
His wit is quick and ready in conceit,
As Greece afforded in her chiefest prime:
Courteous, ah friar, full of pleasing smiles!
Trust me, I love too much to tell thee more;
Suffice to me he's England's paramour.

Bun. Hath not each eye that view'd thy pleasing face
Surnamèd thee Fair Maid of Fressingfield?

Mar. Yes, Bungay; and would God the lovely earl
Had that in *esse* that so many sought.

Bun. Fear not, the friar will not be behind
To show his cunning to entangle love.

P. Edw. I think the friar courts the bonny wench:
Bacon, methinks he is a lusty churl.

Bacon. Now look, my lord.

Enter LACY *disguised as before.*

P. Edw. Gog's wounds, Bacon, here comes Lacy!

Bacon. Sit still, my lord, and mark the comedy.

Bun. Here's Lacy, Margaret; step aside awhile.
[*Retires with* MARGARET.

Lacy. Daphne, the damsel that caught Phoebus fast,
And lock'd him in the brightness of her looks,
Was not so beauteous in Apollo's eyes
As is fair Margaret to the Lincoln Earl.
Recant thee, Lacy, thou art put in trust:
Edward, thy sovereign's son, hath chosen thee,
A secret friend, to court her for himself,
And dar'st thou wrong thy prince with treachery?
Lacy, love makes no exception of a friend,
Nor deems it of a prince but as a man.
Honour bids thee control him in his lust;
His wooing is not for to wed the girl,
But to entrap her and beguile the lass.
Lacy, thou lov'st, then brook not such abuse,
But wed her, and abide thy prince's frown;
For better die than see her live disgrac'd.

Mar. Come, friar, I will shake him from his dumps.—
[*Comes forward.*
How cheer you, sir? a penny for your thought:
You're early up, pray God it be the near.
What, come from Beccles in a morn so soon?

Lacy. Thus watchful are such men as live in love,
Whose eyes brook broken slumbers for their sleep.
I tell thee, Peggy, since last Harleston fair
My mind hath felt a heap of passions.

Mar. A trusty man, that court it for your friend:
Woo you still for the courtier all in green?
I marvel that he sues not for himself.

Lacy. Peggy,
I pleaded first to get your grace for him;

But when mine eyes survey'd your beauteous looks,
Love, like a wag, straight div'd into my heart,
And there did shrine the idea of yourself.
Pity me, though I be a farmer's son,
And measure not my riches, but my love.

Mar. You are very hasty; for to garden well,
Seeds must have time to sprout before they spring:
Love ought to creep as doth the dial's shade,
For timely ripe is rotten too-too soon.

Bun. [*coming forward.*] *Deus hic;* room for a merry friar!
What, youth of Beccles, with the Keeper's lass?
'Tis well; but tell me, hear you any news?

Lacy. No, friar: what news?

Bun. Hear you not how the pursuivants do post
With proclamations through each country-town?

Lacy. For what, gentle friar? tell the news.

Bun. Dwell'st thou in Beccles, and hear'st not of these news?
Lacy, the Earl of Lincoln, is late fled
From Windsor court, disguisèd like a swain,
And lurks about the country here unknown.
Henry suspects him of some treachery,
And therefore doth proclaim in every way,
That who can take the Lincoln Earl shall have,
Paid in the Exchequer, twenty thousand crowns.

Lacy. The Earl of Lincoln! Friar, thou art mad:
It was some other; thou mistak'st the man.
The Earl of Lincoln! why, it cannot be.

Mar. Yes, very well, my lord, for you are he:
The Keeper's daughter took you prisoner.
Lord Lacy, yield, I'll be your gaoler once.

P. Edw. How familiar they be, Bacon!

Bacon. Sit still, and mark the sequel of their loves.

Lacy. Then am I double prisoner to thyself:
Peggy, I yield. But are these news in jest?

Mar. In jest with you, but earnest unto me;

For why these wrongs do wring me at the heart.
Ah, how these earls and noblemen of birth
Flatter and feign to forge poor women's ill!

Lacy. Believe me, lass, I am the Lincoln Earl:
I not deny but, 'tirèd thus in rags,
I liv'd disguis'd to win fair Peggy's love.

Mar. What love is there where wedding ends not love?

Lacy. I mean, fair girl, to make thee Lacy's wife.

Mar. I little think that earls will stoop so low.

Lacy. Say shall I make thee countess ere I sleep?

Mar. Handmaid unto the earl, so please himself:
A wife in name, but servant in obedience.

Lacy. The Lincoln Countess, for it shall be so:
I'll plight the bands, and seal it with a kiss.

P. Edw. Gog's wounds, Bacon, they kiss! I'll stab them.

Bacon. O, hold your hands, my lord, it is the glass!

P. Edw. Choler to see the traitors gree so well
Made me [to] think the shadows substances.

Bacon. 'Twere a long poniard, my lord, to reach between
Oxford and Fressingfield; but sit still and see more.

Bun. Well, Lord of Lincoln, if your loves be knit,
And that your tongues and thoughts do both agree,
To avoid ensuing jars, I'll hamper up the match.
I'll take my portace forth and wed you here.

Lacy. Friar, content.—Peggy, how like you this?

Mar. What likes my lord is pleasing unto me.

Bun. Then hand-fast hand, and I will to my book.

Bacon. What sees my lord now?

P. Edw. Bacon, I see the lovers hand in hand,
The friar ready with his portace there
To wed them both: then am I quite undone.
Bacon, help now, if e'er thy magic serv'd;
Help, Bacon; stop the marriage now,
If devils or necromancy may suffice,
And I will give thee forty thousand crowns.

Bacon. Fear not, my lord, I'll stop the jolly friar
For mumbling up his orisons this day.

Lacy. Why speak'st not, Bungay? Friar, to thy book.
[BUNGAY *is mute, crying,* 'Hud, hud.'

Mar. How look'st thou, friar, as a man distraught?
Reft of thy senses, Bungay? show by signs,
If thou be dumb, what passions holdeth thee.

Lacy. He 's dumb indeed. Bacon hath with his devils
Enchanted him, or else some strange disease
Or apoplexy hath possess'd his lungs:
But, Peggy, what he cannot with his book,
We'll 'twixt us both unite it up in heart.

Mar. Else let me die, my lord, a miscreant.

P. Edw. Why stands Friar Bungay so amaz'd?

Bacon. I have struck him dumb, my lord; and, if your honour please,
I'll fetch this Bungay straight from Fressingfield,
And he shall dine with us in Oxford here.

P. Edw. Bacon, do that, and thou contentest me.

Lacy. Of courtesy, Margaret, let us lead the friar
Unto thy father's lodge, to comfort him
With broths, to bring him from this hapless trance.

Mar. Or else, my lord, we were passing unkind
To leave the friar so in his distress.

Enter a Devil, *who carries off* BUNGAY *on his back.*

O, help, my lord! a devil, a devil, my lord!
Look how he carries Bungay on his back!
Let 's hence, for Bacon's spirits be abroad.
[*Exit with* LACY.

P. Edw. Bacon, I laugh to see the jolly friar
Mounted upon the devil, and how the earl
Flees with his bonny lass for fear.
As soon as Bungay is at Brazen-nose,
And I have chatted with the merry friar,
I will in post hie me to Fressingfield,
And quite these wrongs on Lacy ere 't be long.

Bacon. So be it, my lord: but let us to our dinner;
For ere we have taken our repast awhile,
We shall have Bungay brought to Brazen-nose. [*Exeunt.*

SCENE VII. *The Regent-house at Oxford.*

Enter BURDEN, MASON, *and* CLEMENT.

Mason. Now that we are gather'd in the Regent-house,
It fits us talk about the king's repair;
For he, troopèd with all the western kings,
That lie alongst the Dantzic seas by east,
North by the clime of frosty Germany,
The Almain monarch, and the Saxon duke,
Castile and lovely Elinor with him,
Have in their jests resolv'd for Oxford town.

Burd. We must lay plots of stately tragedies,
Strange comic shows, such as proud Roscius
Vaunted before the Roman emperors,
To welcome all the western potentates.

Clem. But more; the king by letters hath foretold
That Frederick, the Almain emperor,
Hath brought with him a German of esteem,
Whose surname is Don Jaques Vandermast,
Skilful in magic and those secret arts.

Mason. Then must we all make suit unto the friar,
To Friar Bacon, that he vouch this task,
And undertake to countervail in skill
The German; else there's none in Oxford can
Match and dispute with learnèd Vandermast.

Burd. Bacon, if he will hold the German play,
Will teach him what an English friar can do:
The devil, I think, dare not dispute with him.

Clem. Indeed, Mas doctor, he [dis]pleasur'd you,
In that he brought your hostess with her spit,
From Henley, posting unto Brazen-nose.

Burd. A vengeance on the friar for his pains!
But leaving that, let 's hie to Bacon straight,
To see if he will take this task in hand.

Clem. Stay, what rumour is this? The town is up in a mutiny: what hurly-burly is this?

Enter a Constable, *with* RALPH SIMNELL, WARREN, ERMSBY, *all three disguised as before, and* MILES.

Cons. Nay, masters, if you were ne'er so good, you shall before the doctors to answer your misdemeanour.

Burd. What 's the matter, fellow?

Cons. Marry, sir, here 's a company of rufflers, that, drinking in the tavern, have made a great brawl, and almost killed the vintner.

Miles. *Salve*, Doctor Burden!
This lubberly lurden,
Ill-shap'd and ill-fac'd,
Disdain'd and disgrac'd,
What he tells unto *vobis*
Mentitur de nobis.

Burd. Who is the master and chief of this crew?

Miles. *Ecce asinum mundi*
Figura rotundi,
Neat and fine,
As brisk as a cup of wine.

Burd. What are you?

Ralph. I am, father doctor, as a man would say, the bell-wether of this company: these are my lords, and I the Prince of Wales.

Clem. Are you Edward, the king's son?

Ralph. Sirrah Miles, bring hither the tapster that drew the wine, and, I warrant, when they see how soundly I have broke his head, they'll say 'twas done by no less man than a prince.

Mason. I cannot believe that this is the Prince of Wales.

War. And why so, sir?

Mason. For they say the prince is a brave and a wise gentleman.

War. Why, and think'st thou, doctor, that he is not so?
Dar'st thou detract and derogate from him,
Being so lovely and so brave a youth?

Erms. Whose face, shining with many a sugar'd smile,
Bewrays that he is bred of princely race.

Miles. And yet, master doctor,
To speak like a proctor,
And tell unto you
What is veriment and true;
To cease of this quarrel,
Look but on his apparel;
Then mark but my talis,
He is great Prince of Walis,
The chief of our *gregis*,
And *filius regis*:
Then 'ware what is done,
For he is Henry's white son.

Ralph. Doctors, whose doting night-caps are not capable of my ingenious dignity, know that I am Edward Plantagenet, whom if you displease, [I] will make a ship that shall hold all your colleges, and so carry away the niniversity with a fair wind to the Bankside in Southwark.—How sayest thou, Ned Warren, shall I not do it?

War. Yes, my good lord; and, if it please your lordship, I will gather up all your old pantofles, and with the cork make you a pinnace of five-hundred ton, that shall serve the turn marvellous well, my lord.

Erms. And I, my lord, will have pioners to undermine the town, that the very gardens and orchards be carried away for your summer-walks.

Miles. And I, with *scientia*
And great *diligentia*,
Will conjure and charm,
To keep you from harm;

That *utrum horum mavis*,
Your very great *navis*,
Like Barclay's ship,
From Oxford do skip
With colleges and schools,
Full-loaden with fools.
Quid dicis ad hoc,
Worshipful *Domine* Dawcock?

Clem. Why, hare-brain'd courtiers, are you drunk or mad,
To taunt us up with such scurrility?
Deem you us men of base and light esteem,
To bring us such a fop for Henry's son?—
Call out the beadles and convey them hence
Straight to Bocardo: let the roisters lie
Close clapt in bolts, until their wits be tame.

Erms. Why, shall we to prison, my lord?

Ralph. What sayest, Miles, shall I honour the prison with my presence?

Miles. No, no: out with your blades,
And hamper these jades;
Have a flurt and a crash,
Now play revel-dash,
And teach these sacerdos
That the Bocardos,
Like peasants and elves,
Are meet for themselves.

Mason. To the prison with them, constable.

War. Well, doctors, seeing I have sported me
With laughing at these mad and merry wags,
Know that Prince Edward is at Brazen-nose,
And this, attirèd like the Prince of Wales,
Is Ralph, King Henry's only lovèd fool;
I, Earl of Sussex, and this Ermsby,
One of the privy-chamber to the king;
Who, while the prince with Friar Bacon stays,
Have revell'd it in Oxford as you see.

Mason. My lord, pardon us, we knew not what you were:
But courtiers may make greater scapes than these.
Will 't please your honour dine with me to-day?

War. I will, Master doctor, and satisfy the vintner for his hurt; only I must desire you to imagine him all this forenoon the Prince of Wales.

Mason. I will, sir.

Ralph. And upon that I will lead the way; only I will have Miles go before me, because I have heard Henry say that wisdom must go before majesty. [*Exeunt.*

SCENE VIII. *Fressingfield.*

Enter PRINCE EDWARD *with his poniard in his hand,* LACY, *and* MARGARET.

P. Edw. Lacy, thou canst not shroud thy traitorous thoughts,
Nor cover, as did Cassius, all thy wiles;
For Edward hath an eye that looks as far
As Lynceus from the shores of Graecia.
Did not I sit in Oxford by the friar,
And see thee court the maid of Fressingfield,
Sealing thy flattering fancies with a kiss?
Did not proud Bungay draw his portace forth,
And joining hand in hand had married you,
If Friar Bacon had not struck him dumb,
And mounted him upon a spirit's back,
That we might chat at Oxford with the friar?
Traitor, what answer'st? is not all this true?

Lacy. Truth all, my lord; and thus I make reply.
At Harleston fair, there courting for your grace,
Whenas mine eye survey'd her curious shape,
And drew the beauteous glory of her looks
To dive into the centre of my heart,
Love taught me that your honour did but jest,

That princes were in fancy but as men;
How that the lovely maid of Fressingfield
Was fitter to be Lacy's wedded wife
Than concubine unto the Prince of Wales.
P. Edw. Injurious Lacy, did I love thee more
Than Alexander his Hephæstion?
Did I unfold the passions of my love,
And lock them in the closet of thy thoughts?
Wert thou to Edward second to himself,
Sole friend, and partner of his secret loves?
And could a glance of fading beauty break
Th' enchainèd fetters of such private friends?
Base coward, false, and too effeminate
To be corrival with a prince in thoughts!
From Oxford have I posted since I din'd,
To quite a traitor 'fore that Edward sleep.
Mar. 'Twas I, my lord, not Lacy stept awry:
For oft he su'd and courted for yourself,
And still woo'd for the courtier all in green;
But I, whom fancy made but over-fond,
Pleaded myself with looks as if I lov'd;
I fed mine eye with gazing on his face,
And still bewitch'd lov'd Lacy with my looks;
My heart with sighs, mine eyes pleaded with tears,
My face held pity and content at once,
And more I could not cipher out by signs,
But that I lov'd Lord Lacy with my heart.
Then, worthy Edward, measure with thy mind
If women's favours will not force men fall,
If beauty, and if darts of piercing love,
Are not of force to bury thoughts of friends.
P. Edw. I tell thee, Peggy, I will have thy loves:
Edward or none shall conquer Margaret.
In frigates bottom'd with rich Sethin planks,
Topt with the lofty firs of Lebanon,
Stemm'd and incas'd with burnish'd ivory,
And over-laid with plates of Persian wealth,
Like Thetis shalt thou wanton on the waves,

And draw the dolphins to thy lovely eyes,
To dance lavoltas in the purple streams;
Sirens, with harps and silver psalteries,
Shall wait with music at thy frigate's stem,
And entertain fair Margaret with their lays.
England and England's wealth shall wait on thee;
Britain shall bend unto her prince's love,
And do due homage to thine excellence,
If thou wilt be but Edward's Margaret.

Mar. Pardon, my lord: if Jove's great royalty
Sent me such presents as to Danaë;
If Phoebus, 'tirèd in Latona's webs,
Came courting from the beauty of his lodge;
The dulcet tunes of frolic Mercury,
Nor all the wealth heaven's treasury affords,
Should make me leave Lord Lacy or his love.

P. Edw. I have learn'd at Oxford, then, this point of schools,—
Ablata causa, tollitur effectus:
Lacy, the cause that Margaret cannot love
Nor fix her liking on the English prince,
Take him away, and then th' effects will fail.
Villain, prepare thyself; for I will bathe
My poniard in the bosom of an earl.

Lacy. Rather than live, and miss fair Margaret's love,
Prince Edward, stop not at the fatal doom,
But stab it home: end both my loves and life.

Mar. Brave Prince of Wales, honour'd for royal deeds,
'Twere sin to stain fair Venus' courts with blood;
Love's conquest ends, my lord, in courtesy:
Spare Lacy, gentle Edward; let me die,
For so both you and he do cease your loves.

P. Edw. Lacy shall die as traitor to his lord.

Lacy. I have deserv'd it, Edward; act it well.

Mar. What hopes the prince to gain by Lacy's death?

P. Edw. To end the loves 'twixt him and Margaret.

Mar. Why, thinks King Henry's son that Margaret's love
Hangs in th' uncertain balance of proud time?
That death shall make a discord of our thoughts?
No, stab the earl, and, 'fore the morning sun
Shall vaunt him thrice over the lofty east,
Margaret will meet her Lacy in the heavens.

Lacy. If aught betides to lovely Margaret
That wrongs or wrings her honour from content,
Europe's rich wealth nor England's monarchy
Should not allure Lacy to over-live.
Then, Edward, short my life, and end her loves.

Mar. Rid me, and keep a friend worth many loves.

Lacy. Nay, Edward, keep a love worth many friends.

Mar. An if thy mind be such as fame hath blaz'd,
Then, princely Edward, let us both abide
The fatal resolution of thy rage:
Banish thou fancy, and embrace revenge,
And in one tomb knit both our carcases,
Whose hearts were linkèd in one perfect love.

P. Edw. [*aside.*] Edward, art thou that famous Prince of Wales,
Who at Damasco beat the Saracens,
And brought'st home triumph on thy lance's point?
And shall thy plumes be pull'd by Venus down?
Is't princely to dissever lovers' leagues,
To part such friends as glory in their loves?
Leave, Ned, and make a virtue of this fault,
And further Peg and Lacy in their loves:
So in subduing fancy's passion,
Conquering thyself, thou gett'st the richest spoil.—
Lacy, rise up. Fair Peggy, here's my hand:
The Prince of Wales hath conquer'd all his thoughts,
And all his loves he yields unto the earl.
Lacy, enjoy the maid of Fressingfield;
Make her thy Lincoln Countess at the church,
And Ned, as he is true Plantagenet,
Will give her to thee frankly for thy wife.

Lacy. Humbly I take her of my sovereign,
As if that Edward gave me England's right,
And rich'd me with the Albion diadem.

Mar. And doth the English prince mean true?
Will he vouchsafe to cease his former loves,
And yield the title of a country maid
Unto Lord Lacy?

P. Edw. I will, fair Peggy, as I am true lord.

Mar. Then, lordly sir, whose conquest is as great,
In conquering love, as Cæsar's victories,
Margaret, as mild and humble in her thoughts
As was Aspasia unto Cyrus self,
Yields thanks, and, next Lord Lacy, doth enshrine
Edward the second secret in her heart.

P. Edw. Gramercy, Peggy:—now that vows are past,
And that your loves are not to be revolt,
Once, Lacy, friends again. Come, we will post
To Oxford; for this day the king is there,
And brings for Edward Castile Elinor.
Peggy, I must go see and view my wife:
I pray God I like her as I lov'd thee.
Beside, Lord Lincoln, we shall hear dispute
'Twixt Friar Bacon and learn'd Vandermast.
Peggy, we'll leave you for a week or two.

Mar. As it please Lord Lacy: but love's foolish looks
Think footsteps miles and minutes to be hours.

Lacy. I'll hasten, Peggy, to make short return.—
But please your honour go unto the lodge,
We shall have butter, cheese, and venison;
And yesterday I brought for Margaret
A lusty bottle of neat claret-wine:
Thus can we feast and entertain your grace.

P. Edw. 'Tis cheer, Lord Lacy, for an emperor,
If he respect the person and the place.
Come, let us in; for I will all this night
Ride post until I come to Bacon's cell. [*Exeunt.*

SCENE IX. *Oxford.*

Enter KING HENRY, *the* EMPEROR, *the* KING OF CASTILE, ELINOR, VANDERMAST, *and* BUNGAY.

Emp. Trust me, Plantagenet, these Oxford schools
Are richly seated near the river-side:
The mountains full of fat and fallow deer,
The battling pastures lade with kine and flocks,
The town gorgeous with high-built colleges,
And scholars seemly in their grave attire,
Learnèd in searching principles of art.—
What is thy judgment, Jaques Vandermast?

Van. That lordly are the buildings of the town,
Spacious the rooms, and full of pleasant walks;
But for the doctors, how that they be learnèd,
It may be meanly, for aught I can hear.

Bun. I tell thee, German, Hapsburg holds none such,
None read so deep as Oxenford contains:
There are within our academic state
Men that may lecture it in Germany
To all the doctors of your Belgic schools.

K. Hen. Stand to him, Bungay, charm this Vandermast,
And I will use thee as a royal king.

Van. Wherein dar'st thou dispute with me?

Bun. In what a doctor and a friar can.

Van. Before rich Europe's worthies put thou forth
The doubtful question unto Vandermast.

Bun. Let it be this,—Whether the spirits of pyromancy or geomancy be most predominant in magic?

Van. I say, of pyromancy.

Bun. And I, of geomancy.

Van. The cabalists that write of magic spells,
As Hermes, Melchie, and Pythagoras,
Affirm that, 'mongst the quadruplicity
Of elemental essence, *terra* is but thought

To be a *punctum* squarèd to the rest;
And that the compass of ascending elements
Exceed in bigness as they do in height;
Judging the concave circle of the sun
To hold the rest in his circumference.
If, then, as Hermes says, the fire be greatest,
Purest, and only giveth shape to spirits,
Then must these dæmones that haunt that place
Be every way superior to the rest.
Bun. I reason not of elemental shapes,
Nor tell I of the concave latitudes,
Noting their essence nor their quality,
But of the spirits that pyromancy calls,
And of the vigour of the geomantic fiends.
I tell thee, German, magic haunts the ground,
And those strange necromantic spells,
That work such shows and wondering in the world,
Are acted by those geomantic spirits
That Hermes calleth *terræ filii.*
The fiery spirits are but transparent shades,
That lightly pass as heralds to bear news;
But earthly fiends, clos'd in the lowest deep,
Dissever mountains, if they be but charg'd,
Being more gross and massy in their power.
Van. Rather these earthly geomantic spirits
Are dull and like the place where they remain;
For when proud Lucifer fell from the heavens,
The spirits and angels that did sin with him,
Retain'd their local, essence as their faults,
All subject under Luna's continent:
They which offended less hung in the fire,
And second faults did rest within the air;
But Lucifer and his proud-hearted fiends
Were thrown into the centre of the earth,
Having less understanding than the rest,
As having greater sin and lesser grace.
Therefore such gross and earthly spirits do serve
For jugglers, witches, and vile sorcerers;

Whereas the pyromantic genii
Are mighty, swift, and of far-reaching power.
But grant that geomancy hath most force;
Bungay, to please these mighty potentates,
Prove by some instance what thy art can do.

Bun. I will.

Emp. Now, English Harry, here begins the game;
We shall see sport between these learnèd men.

Van. What wilt thou do?

Bun. Show thee the tree, leav'd with refinèd gold,
Whereon the fearful dragon held his seat,
That watch'd the garden call'd Hesperides,
Subdu'd and won by conquering Hercules.

Here BUNGAY *conjures, and the tree appears with the dragon shooting fire.*

Van. Well done!

K. Hen. What say you, royal lordings, to my friar?
Hath he not done a point of cunning skill?

Van. Each scholar in the necromantic spells
Can do as much as Bungay hath perform'd.
But as Alcmena's bastard raz'd this tree,
So will I raise him up as when he liv'd,
And cause him pull the dragon from his seat,
And tear the branches piecemeal from the root.—
Hercules! *Prodi, prodi,* Hercules!

HERCULES *appears in his lion's skin.*

Her. Quis me vult?

Van. Jove's bastard son, thou Libyan Hercules,
Pull off the sprigs from off th' Hesperian tree,
As once thou didst to win the golden fruit.

Her. Fiat. [*Begins to break the branches.*

Van. Now, Bungay, if thou canst by magic charm
The fiend, appearing like great Hercules,
From pulling down the branches of the tree,
Then art thou worthy to be counted learnèd.

Bun. I cannot.

Van. Cease, Hercules, until I give thee charge.—
Mighty commander of this English isle,
Henry, come from the stout Plantagenets,
Bungay is learn'd enough to be a friar;
But to compare with Jaques Vandermast,
Oxford and Cambridge must go seek their cells
To find a man to match him in his art.
I have given non-plus to the Paduans,
To them of Sien, Florence, and Bologna,
Rheims, Louvain, and fair Rotterdam,
Frankfort, Utrecht, and Orleans:
And now must Henry, if he do me right,
Crown me with laurel, as they all have done.

Enter BACON.

Bacon. All hail to this royal company,
That sit to hear and see this strange dispute!—
Bungay, how stand'st thou as a man amaz'd?
What, hath the German acted more than thou?

Van. What art thou that question'st thus?

Bacon. Men call me Bacon.

Van. Lordly thou look'st, as if that thou wert learn'd;
Thy countenance as if science held her seat
Between the circled arches of thy brows.

K. Hen. Now, monarchs, hath the German found his match.

Emp. Bestir thee, Jaques, take not now the foil,
Lest thou dost lose what foretime thou didst gain.

Van. Bacon, wilt thou dispute?

Bacon. No,
Unless he were more learn'd than Vandermast:
For yet, tell me, what hast thou done?

Van. Rais'd Hercules to ruinate that tree
That Bungay mounted by his magic spells.

Bacon. Set Hercules to work.

Van. Now, Hercules, I charge thee to thy task;
Pull off the golden branches from the root.

Her. I dare not. See'st thou not great Bacon here,
Whose frown doth act more than thy magic can?

Van. By all the thrones, and dominations,
Virtues, powers, and mighty hierarchies,
I charge thee to obey to Vandermast.

Her. Bacon, that bridles headstrong Belcephon,
And rules Asmenoth guider of the north,
Binds me from yielding unto Vandermast.

K. Hen. How now, Vandermast! have you met with your match?

Van. Never before was't known to Vandermast
That men held devils in such obedient awe.
Bacon doth more than art, or else I fail.

Emp. Why, Vandermast, art thou overcome?—
Bacon, dispute with him, and try his skill.

Bacon. I came not, monarchs, for to hold dispute
With such a novice as is Vandermast;
I came to have your royalties to dine
With Friar Bacon here in Brazen-nose;
And, for this German troubles but the place,
And holds this audience with a long suspence,
I'll send him to his acadėmy hence.—
Thou Hercules, whom Vandermast did raise,
Transport the German unto Hapsburg straight,
That he may learn by travail, 'gainst the spring,
More secret dooms and aphorisms of art.
Vanish the tree, and thou away with him!

[*Exit* HERCULES *with* VANDERMAST *and the tree.*

Emp. Why, Bacon, whither dost thou send him?

Bacon. To Hapsburg: there your highness at return
Shall find the German in his study safe.

K. Hen. Bacon, thou hast honour'd England with thy skill,
And made fair Oxford famous by thine art:

I will be English Henry to thyself.
But tell me, shall we dine with thee to-day?

Bacon. With me, my lord; and while I fit my cheer,
See where Prince Edward comes to welcome you,
Gracious as the morning-star of heaven. [*Exit.*

Enter PRINCE EDWARD, LACY, WARREN, ERMSBY.

Emp. Is this Prince Edward, Henry's royal son?
How martial is the figure of his face!
Yet lovely and beset with amorets.

K. Hen. Ned, where hast thou been?

P. Edw. At Framlingham, my lord, to try your bucks
If they could scape the teasers or the toil.
But hearing of these lordly potentates
Landed, and progress'd up to Oxford town,
I posted to give entertain to them:
Chief to the Almain monarch; next to him,
And joint with him, Castile and Saxony
Are welcome as they may be to the English court.
Thus for the men: but see, Venus appears,
Or one
That overmatcheth Venus in her shape!
Sweet Elinor, beauty's high-swelling pride,
Rich nature's glory and her wealth at once,
Fair of all fairs, welcome to Albion;
Welcome to me, and welcome to thine own,
If that thou deign'st the welcome from myself.

Elin. Martial Plantagenet, Henry's high-minded son,
The mark that Elinor did count her aim,
I lik'd thee 'fore I saw thee: now I love,
And so as in so short a time I may;
Yet so as time shall never break that so,
And therefore so accept of Elinor.

K. of Cast. Fear not, my lord, this couple will agree,
If love may creep into their wanton eyes:——
And therefore, Edward, I accept thee here,
Without suspence, as my adopted son.

K. Hen. Let me that joy in these consorting greets,
And glory in these honours done to Ned,
Yield thanks for all these favours to my son,
And rest a true Plantagenet to all.

Enter MILES *with a cloth and trenchers and salt.*

Miles. *Salvete, omnes reges,*
That govern your *greges*
In Saxony and Spain,
In England and in Almain!
For all this frolic rabble
Must I cover the table
With trenchers, salt, and cloth;
And then look for your broth.

Emp. What pleasant fellow is this?

K. Hen. 'Tis, my lord, Doctor Bacon's poor scholar.

Miles [*aside*]. My master hath made me sewer of these great lords; and, God knows, I am as serviceable at a table as a sow is under an apple-tree: 'tis no matter; their cheer shall not be great, and therefore what skills where the salt stand, before or behind? [*Exit.*

K. of Cast. These scholars know more skill in axioms,
How to use quips and sleights of sophistry,
Than for to cover courtly for a king.

Re-enter MILES *with a mess of pottage and broth; and, after him,* BACON.

Miles. Spill, sir? why, do you think I never carried twopenny chop before in my life?——
By your leave, *nobile decus,*
For here comes Doctor Bacon's *pecus,*
Being in his full age
To carry a mess of pottáge.

Bacon. Lordings, admire not if your cheer be this,
For we must keep our academic fare;
No riot where philosophy doth reign:
And therefore, Henry, place these potentates,
And bid them fall unto their frugal cates.

Emp. Presumptuous friar! what, scoff'st thou at a king?
What, dost thou taunt us with thy peasants' fare,
And give us cates fit for country swains?——
Henry, proceeds this jest of thy consent,
To twit us with a pittance of such price?
Tell me, and Frederick will not grieve thee long.

K. Hen. By Henry's honour, and the royal faith
The English monarch beareth to his friend,
I knew not of the friar's feeble fare,
Nor am I pleas'd he entertains you thus.

Bacon. Content thee, Frederick, for I show'd these cates,
To let thee see how scholars use to feed;
How little meat refines our English wits.——
Miles, take away, and let it be thy dinner.

Miles. Marry, sir, I will.
This day shall be a festival-day with me;
For I shall exceed in the highest degree. [*Exit.*

Bacon. I tell thee, monarch, all the German peers
Could not afford thy entertainment such,
So royal and so full of majesty,
As Bacon will present to Frederick.
The basest waiter that attends thy cups
Shall be in honours greater than thyself;
And for thy cates, rich Alexandria drugs,
Fetch'd by carvels from Ægypt's richest streights,
Found in the wealthy strand of Africa,
Shall royalize the table of my king;
Wines richer than th' Ægyptian courtesan
Quaff'd to Augustus' kingly countermatch,
Shall be carous'd in English Henry's feast;
Candy shall yield the richest of her canes;
Persia, down her Volga by canoes,
Send down the secrets of her spicery;
The Afric dates, mirabolans of Spain,
Conserves and suckets from Tiberias,
Cates from Judæa, choicer than the lamp

That firèd Rome with sparks of gluttony,
Shall beautify the board of Frederick:
And therefore grudge not at a friar's feast. [*Exeunt.*

SCENE X. *Fressingfield.*

Enter LAMBERT *and* SERLSBY *with the* Keeper.

Lam. Come, frolic Keeper of our liege's game,
Whose table spread hath ever venison
And jacks of wine to welcome passengers,
Know I'm in love with jolly Margaret,
That overshines our damsels as the moon
Darkeneth the brighest sparkles of the night.
In Laxfield here my land and living lies:
I'll make thy daughter jointer of it all,
So thou consent to give her to my wife;
And I can spend five hundred marks a-year.

Ser. I am the lands-lord, Keeper, of thy holds,
By copy all thy living lies in me;
Laxfield did never see me raise my due:
I will enfeoff fair Margaret in all,
So she will take her to a lusty squire.

Keep. Now, courteous gentles, if the Keeper's girl
Hath pleas'd the liking fancy of you both,
And with her beauty hath subdu'd your thoughts,
'Tis doubtful to decide the question.
It joys me that such men of great esteem
Should lay their liking on this base estate,
And that her state should grow so fortunate
To be a wife to meaner men than you:
But sith such squires will stoop to keeper's fee,
I will, to avoid displeasure of you both,
Call Margaret forth, and she shall make her choice.

Lam. Content, Keeper; send her unto us.
[*Exit* Keeper.
Why, Serlsby, is thy wife so lately dead,

Are all thy loves so lightly passèd over,
As thou canst wed before the year is out?

Serl. I live not, Lambert, to content the dead,
Nor was I wedded but for life to her:
The grave ends and begins a married state.

Enter MARGARET.

Lam. Peggy, the lovely flower of all towns,
Suffolk's fair Helen, and rich England's star,
Whose beauty, temper'd with her huswifery,
Makes England talk of merry Fressingfield!

Ser. I cannot trick it up with poesies,
Nor paint my passions with comparisons,
Nor tell a tale of Phœbus and his loves:
But this believe me,—Laxfield here is mine,
Of ancient rent seven-hundred pounds a-year,
And if thou canst but love a country squire,
I will enfeoff thee, Margaret, in all:
I cannot flatter; try me, if thou please.

Mar. Brave neighbouring squires, the stay of Suffolk's clime,
A keeper's daughter is too base in gree
To match with men accounted of such worth:
But might I not displease, I would reply.

Lam. Say, Peggy; naught shall make us discontent.

Mar. Then, gentles, note that love hath little stay,
Nor can the flames that Venus sets on fire
Be kindled but by fancy's motion:
Then pardon, gentles, if a maid's reply
Be doubtful, while I have debated with myself,
Who, or of whom, love shall constrain me like.

Ser. Let it be me; and trust me, Margaret,
The meads environ'd with the silver streams,
Whose battling pastures fatten all my flocks,
Yielding forth fleeces stapled with such wool
As Lemnster cannot yield more finer stuff,
And forty kine with fair and burnish'd heads,

With strouting dugs that paggle to the ground,
Shall serve thy dairy, if thou wed with me.

Lam. Let pass the country wealth, as flocks and kine,
And lands that wave with Ceres' golden sheaves,
Filling my barns with plenty of the fields;
But, Peggy, if thou wed thyself to me,
Thou shalt have garments of embroider'd silk,
Lawns, and rich net-works for thy head-attire:
Costly shall be thy fair habiliments,
If thou wilt be but Lambert's loving wife.

Mar. Content you, gentles, you have proffer'd fair,
And more than fits a country maid's degree:
But give me leave to counsel me a time,
For fancy blooms not at the first assault;
Give me but ten days' respite, and I will reply,
Which or to whom myself affectionates.

Ser. Lambert, I tell thee, thou'rt importunate;
Such beauty fits not such a base esquire:
It is for Serlsby to have Margaret.

Lam. Think'st thou with wealth to overreach me?
Serlsby, I scorn to brook thy country braves:
I dare thee, coward, to maintain this wrong,
At dint of rapier, single in the field.

Ser. I'll answer, Lambert, what I have avouch'd.—
Margaret, farewell; another time shall serve. [*Exit.*

Lam. I'll follow.—Peggy, farewell to thyself;
Listen how well I'll answer for thy love. [*Exit.*

Mar. How fortune tempers lucky haps with frowns,
And wrongs me with the sweets of my delight!
Love is my bliss, and love is now my bale.
Shall I be Helen in my froward fates,
As I am Helen in my matchless hue,
And set rich Suffolk with my face afire?
If lovely Lacy were but with his Peggy,
The cloudy darkness of his bitter frown
Would check the pride of those aspiring squires.
Before the term of ten days be expir'd,

Whenas they look for answer of their loves,
My lord will come to merry Fressingfield,
And end their fancies and their follies both:
Till when, Peggy, be blithe and of good cheer.

Enter a Post *with a letter and a bag of gold.*

Post. Fair lovely damsel, which way leads this path?
How might I post me unto Fressingfield?
Which footpath leadeth to the Keeper's lodge?

Mar. Your way is ready, and this path is right:
Myself do dwell hereby in Fressingfield;
And if the Keeper be the man you seek,
I am his daughter: may I know the cause?

Post. Lovely, and once belovèd of my lord,—
No marvel if his eye was lodg'd so low,
When brighter beauty is not in the heavens,—
The Lincoln Earl hath sent you letters here,
And, with them, just an hundred pounds in gold.
[*Gives letter and bag.*
Sweet, bonny wench, read them, and make reply.

Mar. The scrolls that Jove sent Danaë,
Wrapt in rich closures of fine burnish'd gold,
Were not more welcome than these lines to me.
Tell me, whilst that I do unrip the seals,
Lives Lacy well? how fares my lovely lord?

Post. Well, if that wealth may make men to live well.

Mar. [*Reads.*] *The blooms of the almond-tree grow in a night, and vanish in a morn; the flies haemerae, fair Peggy, take life with the sun, and die with the dew; fancy that slippeth in with a gaze, goeth out with a wink; and too timely loves have ever the shortest length. I write this as thy grief, and my folly, who at Fressingfield loved that which time hath taught me to be but mean dainties: eyes are dissemblers, and fancy is but queasy; therefore know, Margaret, I have chosen a Spanish lady to be my wife, chief waiting-woman to the Princess Elinor; a lady fair, and no less fair than thyself, honourable and wealthy. In that I forsake thee, I leave thee to thine own liking; and for thy dowry I have sent thee an hundred pounds; and ever assure thee of my favour, which shall avail thee and thine much. Farewell.*

Not thine, nor his own,

EDWARD LACY.

Fond Atè, doomer of bad-boding fates,
That wrapp'st proud fortune in thy snaky locks,
Didst thou enchant my birth-day with such stars
As lighten'd mischief from their infancy?
If heavens had vow'd, if stars had made decree,
To show on me their froward influence,
If Lacy had but lov'd, heavens, hell, and all,
Could not have wrong'd the patience of my mind.

Post. It grieves me, damsel; but the earl is forc'd
To love the lady by the king's command.

Mar. The wealth combin'd within the English shelves,
Europe's commander, nor the English king,
Should not have mov'd the love of Peggy from her lord.

Post. What answer shall I return to my lord?

Mar. First, for thou cam'st from Lacy whom I lov'd,—
Ah, give me leave to sigh at very thought!—
Take thou, my friend, the hundred pounds he sent;
For Margaret's resolution craves no dower:
The world shall be to her as vanity;
Wealth, trash; love, hate; pleasure, despair:
For I will straight to stately Framlingham,
And in the abbey there be shorn a nun,
And yield my loves and liberty to God.
Fellow, I give thee this, not for the news,
For those be hateful unto Margaret,
But for thou'rt Lacy's man, once Margaret's love.

Post. What I have heard, what passions I have seen,
I'll make report of them unto the earl.

Mar. Say that she joys his fancies be at rest,
And prays that his misfortunes may be hers. [*Exeunt.*

SCENE XI. *Friar Bacon's cell.*

FRIAR BACON *is discovered lying on a bed, with a white stick in one hand, a book in the other, and a lamp lighted beside him; and the* Brazen Head, *and* MILES *with weapons by him.*

Bacon. Miles, where are you?

Miles. Here, sir.

Bacon. How chance you tarry so long?

Miles. Think you that the watching of the Brazen Head craves no furniture? I warrant you, sir, I have so armed myself that if all your devils come, I will not fear them an inch.

Bacon. Miles,
Thou know'st that I have divèd into hell,
And sought the darkest palaces of fiends;
That with my magic spells great Belcephon
Hath left his lodge and kneelèd at my cell;
The rafters of the earth rent from the poles,
And three-form'd Luna hid her silver looks,
Trembling upon her concave continent,
When Bacon read upon his magic book.
With seven years' tossing necromantic charms,
Poring upon dark Hecat's principles,
I have fram'd out a monstrous head of brass,
That, by the enchanting forces of the devil,
Shall tell out strange and uncouth aphorisms,
And girt fair England with a wall of brass.
Bungay and I have watch'd these threescore days,
And now our vital spirits crave some rest:
If Argus liv'd, and had his hundred eyes,
They could not over-match Phobetor's night.
Now, Miles, in thee rests Friar Bacon's weal:
The honour and renown of all his life
Hangs in the watching of this Brazen Head;
Therefore I charge thee by the immortal God,
That holds the souls of men within his fist,

This night thou watch; for ere the morning-star
Sends out his glorious glister on the north,
The head will speak: then, Miles, upon thy life,
Wake me; for then by magic art I'll work
To end my seven years' task with excellence.
If that a wink but shut thy watchful eye,
Then farewell Bacon's glory and his fame!
Draw close the curtains, Miles: now, for thy life,
Be watchful, and— [*Falls asleep.*

Miles. So; I thought you would talk yourself asleep anon; and 'tis no marvel, for Bungay on the days, and he on the nights, have watched just these ten and fifty days: now this is the night, and 'tis my task, and no more. Now, Jesus bless me, what a goodly head it is! and a nose! you talk of *nos autem glorificare*; but here 's a nose that I warrant may be called *nos autem populare* for the people of the parish. Well, I am furnished with weapons: now, sir, I will set me down by a post, and make it as good as a watchman to wake me, if I chance to slumber. I thought, Goodman Head, I would call you out of your *memento.* Passion o' God, I have almost broke my pate! [*A great noise.*] Up, Miles, to your task; take your brown-bill in your hand; here 's some of your master's hobgoblins abroad.

The Brazen Head. Time is.

Miles. Time is! Why, Master Brazen-head, you have such a capital nose, and answer you with syllables, 'Time is'? Is this my master's cunning, to spend seven years' study about 'Time is'? Well, sir, it may be we shall have some better orations of it anon: well, I'll watch you as narrowly as ever you were watched, and I'll play with you as the nightingale with the slow-worm; I'll set a prick against my breast. Now rest there, Miles. Lord have mercy upon me, I have almost killed myself. [*A great noise.*] Up, Miles; list how they rumble.

The Brazen Head. Time was.

Miles. Well, Friar Bacon, you have spent your seven-years' study well, that can make your head speak but two words at once, 'Time was.' Yea, marry, time was when my master was a wise man, but that was before he began to make the Brazen Head. You shall lie while you ache, an your head speak no better. Well, I will watch, and walk up and down, and be a peripatetian and a philosopher of Aristotle's stamp. [*A great noise.*] What, a fresh noise? Take thy pistols in hand, Miles.

The Brazen Head. Time is past.

[*A lightning flashes forth, and a hand appears that breaks down the* Head *with a hammer.*

Miles. Master, master, up! hell 's broken loose; your head speaks; and there 's such a thunder and lightning, that I warrant all Oxford is up in arms. Out of your bed, and take a brown-bill in your hand; the latter day is come.

Bacon. Miles, I come. [*Rises and comes forward.*] O, passing warily watch'd!
Bacon will make thee next himself in love.
When spake the head?

Miles. When spake the head! did not you say that he should tell strange principles of philosophy? Why, sir, it speaks but two words at a time.

Bacon. Why, villain, hath it spoken oft?

Miles. Oft! ay, marry, hath it, thrice; but in all those three times it hath uttered but seven words.

Bacon. As how?

Miles. Marry, sir, the first time he said 'Time is,' as if Fabius Commentator should have pronounced a sentence; [the second time] he said, 'Time was'; and the third time, with thunder and lightning, as in great choler, he said, 'Time is past.'

Bacon. 'Tis past indeed. Ah, villain! time is past:
My life, my fame, my glory, are all past.—
Bacon,
The turrets of thy hope are ruin'd down,
Thy seven years' study lieth in the dust:
Thy Brazen Head lies broken through a slave,

That watch'd, and would not when the head did will.—
What said the head first?

Miles. Even, sir, 'Time is.'

Bacon. Villain, if thou had'st called to Bacon then,
If thou hadst watch'd, and wak'd the sleepy friar,
The Brazen Head had utter'd aphorisms,
And England had been circled round with brass:
But proud Asmenoth, ruler of the north,
And Demogorgon, master of the fates,
Grudge that a mortal man should work so much.
Hell trembled at my deep-commanding spells,
Fiends frown'd to see a man their over-match;
Bacon might boast more than a man might boast;
But now the braves of Bacon have an end,
Europe's conceit of Bacon hath an end,
His seven years' practice sorteth to ill end:
And, villain, sith my glory hath an end,
I will appoint thee to some fatal end.
Villain, avoid! get thee from Bacon's sight!
Vagrant, go roam and range about the world,
And perish as a vagabond on earth!

Miles. Why, then, sir, you forbid me your service?

Bacon. My service, villain, with a fatal curse,
That direful plagues and mischief fall on thee.

Miles. 'Tis no matter, I am against you with the old proverb,—The more the fox is cursed, the better he fares. God be with you, sir: I'll take but a book in my hand, a wide-sleeved gown on my back, and a crowned cap on my head, and see if I can want promotion.

Bacon. Some fiend or ghost haunt on thy weary steps,
Until they do transport thee quick to hell:
For Bacon shall have never merry day,
To lose the fame and honour of his head. [*Exeunt.*

SCENE XII. *At Court.*

Enter the EMPEROR, *the* KING OF CASTILE, KING HENRY, ELINOR, PRINCE EDWARD, LACY, *and* RALPH SIMNELL.

Emp. Now, lovely prince, the prime of Albion's wealth,
How fare the Lady Elinor and you?
What, have you courted and found Castile fit
To answer England in equivalence?
Will 't be a match 'twixt bonny Nell and thee?

P. Edw. Should Paris enter in the courts of Greece,
And not lie fetter'd in fair Helen's looks?
Or Phœbus scape those piercing amorets
That Daphne glancèd at his deity?
Can Edward, then, sit by a flame and freeze,
Whose heat puts Helen and fair Daphne down?
Now, monarchs, ask the lady if we gree.

K. Hen. What, madam, hath my son found grace or no?

Elin. Seeing, my lord, his lovely counterfeit,
And hearing how his mind and shape agreed,
I came not, troop'd with all this warlike train,
Doubting of love, but so affectionate,
As Edward hath in England what he won in Spain.

K. of Cast. A match, my lord; these wantons needs must love:
Men must have wives, and women will be wed:
Let's haste the day to honour up the rites.

Ralph. Sirrah Harry, shall Ned marry Nell?

K. Hen. Ay, Ralph; how then?

Ralph. Marry, Harry, follow my counsel: send for Friar Bacon to marry them, for he'll so conjure him and her with his necromancy, that they shall love together like pig and lamb whilst they live.

K. of Cast. But hearest thou, Ralph, art thou content to have Elinor to thy lady?

Ralph. Ay, so she will promise me two things.

K. of Cast. What 's that, Ralph?

Ralph. That she will never scold with Ned, nor fight with me.—Sirrah Harry, I have put her down with a thing unpossible.

K. Hen. What 's that, Ralph?

Ralph. Why, Harry, didst thou ever see that a woman could both hold her tongue and her hands? no: but when egg-pies grow on apple-trees, then will thy grey mare prove a bag-piper.

Emp. What say the Lord of Castile and the Earl of Lincoln, that they are in such earnest and secret talk?

K. of Cast. I stand, my lord, amazèd at his talk,
How he discourseth of the constancy
Of one surnam'd, for beauty's excellence,
The Fair Maid of merry Fressingfield.

K. Hen. 'Tis true, my lord, 'tis wondrous for to hear;
Her beauty passing Mars's paramour,
Her virgin right as rich as Vesta's was.
Lacy and Ned have told me miracles.

K. of Cast. What says Lord Lacy? shall she be his wife?

Lacy. Or else Lord Lacy is unfit to live.—
May it please your highness give me leave to post
To Fressingfield, I'll fetch the bonny girl,
And prove, in true appearance at the court,
What I have vouchèd often with my tongue.

K. Hen. Lacy, go to the 'querry of my stable,
And take such coursers as shall fit thy turn:
Hie thee to Fressingfield, and bring home the lass;
And, for her fame flies through the English coast,
If it may please the Lady Elinor,
One day shall match your excellence and her.

Elin. We Castile ladies are not very coy;
Your highness may command a greater boon:
And glad were I to grace the Lincoln Earl
With being partner of his marriage-day.

P. Edw. Gramercy, Nell, for I do love the lord,
As he that 's second to thyself in love.

Ralph. You love her?—Madam Nell, never believe him you, though he swears he loves you.

Elin. Why, Ralph?

Ralph. Why, his love is like unto a tapster's glass that is broken with every touch; for he loved the fair maid of Fressingfield once out of all ho.—Nay, Ned, never wink upon me; I care not, I.

K. Hen. Ralph tells all; you shall have a good secretary of him.—
But, Lacy, haste thee post to Fressingfield;
For ere thou hast fitted all things for her state,
The solemn marriage-day will be at hand.

Lacy. I go, my Lord. [*Exit.*

Emp. How shall we pass this day, my Lord?

K. Hen. To horse, my lord; the day is passing fair,
We'll fly the partridge, or go rouse the deer.
Follow, my lords; you shall not want for sport. [*Exeunt.*

SCENE XIII. *Friar Bacon's cell.*

Enter to FRIAR BACON, FRIAR BUNGAY.

Bun. What means the friar that frolick'd it of late,
To sit as melancholy in his cell
As if he had neither lost nor won to-day?

Bacon. Ah, Bungay, my Brazen Head is spoil'd,
My glory gone, my seven years' study lost!
The fame of Bacon, bruited through the world,
Shall end and perish with this deep disgrace.

Bun. Bacon hath built foundation of his fame
So surely on the wings of true report,
With acting strange and uncouth miracles,
As this cannot infringe what he deserves.

Bacon. Bungay, sit down, for by prospective skill
I find this day shall fall out ominous:

Some deadly act shall 'tide me ere I sleep;
But what and wherein little can I guess.

Bun. My mind is heavy, whatsoe'er shall hap.

[*Knocking within.*

Bacon. Who 's that knocks?

Bun. Two scholars that desire to speak with you.

Bacon. Bid them come in.

Enter two Scholars.

Now, my youths, what would you have?

First Schol. Sir, we are Suffolk-men and neighbouring friends;
Our fathers in their countries lusty squires;
Their lands adjoin: in Cratfield mine doth dwell,
And his in Laxfield. We are college-mates,
Sworn brothers, as our fathers live as friends.

Bacon. To what end is all this?

Second Schol. Hearing your worship kept within your cell
A glass prospective, wherein men might see
Whatso their thoughts or hearts' desire could wish,
We come to know how that our fathers fare.

Bacon. My glass is free for every honest man.
Sit down, and you shall see ere long, how
Or in what state your friendly fathers live.
Meanwhile, tell me your names.

First Schol. Mine Lambert.

Second Schol. And mine Serlsby.

Bacon. Bungay, I smell there will be a tragedy.

Enter LAMBERT *and* SERLSBY *with rapiers and daggers.*

Lam. Serlsby, thou hast kept thine hour like a man:
Thou'rt worthy of the title of a squire,
That durst, for proof of thy affection
And for thy mistress' favour, prize thy blood.
Thou know'st what words did pass at Fressingfield,
Such shameless braves as manhood cannot brook:
Ay, for I scorn to bear such piercing taunts,
Prepare thee, Serlsby; one of us will die.

Ser. Thou see'st I single [meet] thee [in] the field,
And what I spake, I'll máintain with my sword:
Stand on thy guard, I cannot scold it out.
An if thou kill me, think I have a son,
That lives in Oxford in the Broadgates-hall,
Who will revenge his father's blood with blood.

Lam. And, Serlsby, I have there a lusty boy,
That dares at weapon buckle with thy son,
And lives in Broadgates too, as well as thine:
But draw thy rapier, for we'll have a bout.

Bacon. Now, lusty younkers, look within the glass,
And tell me if you can discern your sires.

First Schol. Serlsby, 'tis hard; thy father offers wrong,
To combat with my father in the field.

Second Schol. Lambert, thou liest, my father's is th' abuse,
And thou shalt find it, if my father harm.

Bun. How goes it, sirs?

First Schol. Our fathers are in combat hard by Fressing-field.

Bacon. Sit still, my friends, and see the event.

Lam. Why stand'st thou, Serlsby? doubt'st thou of thy life?
A veney, man! fair Margaret craves so much.

Ser. Then this for her.

First Schol. Ah, well thrust!

Second Schol. But mark the ward.

[LAMBERT *and* SERLSBY *stab each other.*

Lam. O, I am slain! [*Dies.*

Ser. And I,—Lord have mercy on me! [*Dies.*

First Schol. My father slain!—Serlsby, ward that.

Second Schol. And so is mine!—Lambert, I'll quite thee well. [*The two* Scholars *stab each other, and die.*

Bun. O strange stratagem!

Bacon. See, friar, where the fathers both lie dead!—
Bacon, thy magic doth effect this massacre:

This glass prospective worketh many woes;
And therefore seeing these brave lusty Brutes,
These friendly youths, did perish by thine art,
End all thy magic and thine art at once.
The poniard that did end their fatal lives,
Shall break the cause efficiat of their woes.
So fade the glass, and end with it the shows
That necromancy did infuse the crystal with.
[*Breaks the glass.*

Bun. What means learn'd Bacon thus to break his glass?

Bacon. I tell thee, Bungay, it repents me sore
That ever Bacon meddled in this art.
The hours I have spent in pyromantic spells,
The fearful tossing in the latest night
Of papers full of necromantic charms,
Conjuring and adjuring devils and fiends,
With stole and alb and strong pentageron;
The wresting of the holy name of God,
As Sother, Eloim, and Adonai,
Alpha, Manoth, and Tetragrammaton,
With praying to the five-fold powers of heaven,
Are instances that Bacon must be damn'd
For using devils to countervail his God.—
Yet, Bacon, cheer thee, drown not in despair:
Sins have their salves, repentance can do much:
Think Mercy sits where Justice holds her seat,
And from those wounds those bloody Jews did pierce,
Which by thy magic oft did bleed afresh,
From thence for thee the dew of mercy drops,
To wash the wrath of high Jehovah's ire,
And make thee as a new-born babe from sin.—
Bungay, I'll spend the remnant of my life
In pure devotion, praying to my God
That he would save what Bacon vainly lost. [*Exeunt.*

SCENE XIV. *Fressingfield.*

Enter MARGARET *in nun's apparel, the* Keeper, *and their* Friend.

Keeper. Margaret, be not so headstrong in these vows:
O, bury not such beauty in a cell,
That England hath held famous for the hue!
Thy father's hair, like to the silver blooms
That beautify the shrubs of Africa,
Shall fall before the dated time of death,
Thus to forgo his lovely Margaret.

Mar. Ah, father, when the harmony of heaven
Soundeth the measures of a lively faith,
The vain illusions of this flattering world
Seem odious to the thoughts of Margaret.
I lovèd once,—Lord Lacy was my love;
And now I hate myself for that I lov'd,
And doted more on him than on my God,—
For this I scourge myself with sharp repents.
But now the touch of such aspiring sins
Tells me all love is lust but love of heavens;
That beauty us'd for love is vanity:
The world contains naught but alluring baits,
Pride, flattery, and inconstant thoughts.
To shun the pricks of death, I leave the world,
And vow to meditate on heavenly bliss,
To live in Framlingham a holy nun,
Holy and pure in conscience and in deed;
And for to wish all maids to learn of me
To seek heaven's joy before earth's vanity.

Friend. And will you, then, Margaret, be shorn a nun, and so leave us all?

Mar. Now farewell world, the engine of all woe!
Farewell to friends and father! Welcome Christ!
Adieu to dainty robes! this base attire

Better befits an humble mind to God
Than all the show of rich habiliments.
Farewell, O love! and, with fond love, farewell
Sweet Lacy, whom I lovèd once so dear!
Ever be well, but never in my thoughts,
Lest I offend to think on Lacy's love:
But even to that, as to the rest, farewell.

Enter LACY, WARREN, *and* ERMSBY, *booted and spurred.*

Lacy. Come on, my wags, we 're near the Keeper's lodge.
Here have I oft walk'd in the watery meads,
And chatted with my lovely Margaret.

War. Sirrah Ned, is not this the Keeper?

Lacy. 'Tis the same.
Keeper, how far'st thou? holla, man, what cheer?
How doth Peggy, thy daughter and my love?

Keeper. Ah, good my lord! O, woe is me for Peggy!
See where she stands clad in her nun's attire,
Ready for to be shorn in Framlingham:
She leaves the world because she left your love.
O, good my lord, persuade her if you can!

Lacy. Why, how now, Margaret! what, a malcontent?
A nun? what holy father taught you this,
To task yourself to such a tedious life
As die a maid? 'twere injury to me,
To smother up such beauty in a cell.

Mar. Lord Lacy, thinking of my former 'miss,
How fond the prime of wanton years were spent
In love (O, fie upon that fond conceit,
Whose hap and essence hangeth in the eye!),
I leave both love and love's content at once,
Betaking me to him that is true love,
And leaving all the world for love of him.

Lacy. Whence, Peggy, comes this metamorphosis?
What, shorn a nun, and I have from the court
Posted with coursers to convey thee hence
To Windsor, where our marriage shall be kept!

Thy wedding-robes are in the tailor's hands.
Come, Peggy, leave these peremptory vows.

Mar. Did not my lord resign his interest,
And make divorce 'twixt Margaret and him?

Lacy. 'Twas but to try sweet Peggy's constancy.
But will fair Margaret leave her love and lord?

Mar. Is not heaven's joy before earth's fading bliss,
And life above sweeter than life in love?

Lacy. Why, then, Margaret will be shorn a nun?

Mar. Margaret
Hath made a vow which may not be revok'd.

War. We cannot stay, my lord; an if she be so strict,
Our leisure grants us not to woo afresh.

Erms. Choose you, fair damsel,—yet the choice is yours,—
Either a solemn nunnery or the court,
God or Lord Lacy: which contents you best,
To be a nun or else Lord Lacy's wife?

Lacy. A good motion.—Peggy, your answer must be short.

Mar. The flesh is frail: my lord doth know it well,
That when he comes with his enchanting face,
Whate'er betide, I cannot say him nay.
Off goes the habit of a maiden's heart,
And, seeing fortune will, fair Framlingham,
And all the show of holy nuns, farewell!
Lacy for me, if he will be my lord.

Lacy. Peggy, thy lord, thy love, thy husband.
Trust me, by truth of knighthood, that the king
Stays for to marry matchless Elinor,
Until I bring thee richly to the court,
That one day may both marry her and thee.—
How say'st thou, Keeper? art thou glad of this?

Keep. As if the English king had given
The park and deer of Fressingfield to me.

Erm. I pray thee, my Lord of Sussex, why art thou in a brown study?

War. To see the nature of women; that be they never so near God, yet they love to die in a man's arms.

Lacy. What have you fit for breakfast? We have hied
And posted all this night to Fressingfield.

Mar. Butter and cheese, and umbles of a deer,
Such as poor keepers have within their lodge.

Lacy. And not a bottle of wine?

Mar. We'll find one for my lord.

Lacy. Come, Sussex, let us in: we shall have more,
For she speaks least, to hold her promise sure. [*Exeunt.*

SCENE XV. *Friar Bacon's cell.*

Enter a Devil.

Devil. How restless are the ghosts of hellish sprites,
When every charmer with his magic spells
Calls us from nine-fold-trenchèd Phlegethon,
To scud and over-scour the earth in post
Upon the speedy wings of swiftest winds!
Now Bacon hath rais'd me from the darkest deep,
To search about the world for Miles his man,
For Miles, and to torment his lazy bones
For careless watching of his Brazen Head.
See where he comes: O, he is mine.

Enter MILES *in a gown and a corner-cap.*

Miles. A scholar, quoth you! marry, sir, I would I had been made a bottle-maker when I was made a scholar; for I can get neither to be a deacon, reader, nor schoolmaster, no, not the clerk of a parish. Some call me dunce; another saith, my head is as full of Latin as an egg 's full of oatmeal: thus I am tormented, that the devil and Friar Bacon haunt me.—Good Lord, here 's one of my master's devils! I'll go speak to him.—What, Master Plutus, how cheer you?

Dev. Dost thou know me?

Miles. Know you, sir! why, are not you one of my master's devils, that were wont to come to my master, Doctor Bacon, at Brazen-nose?

Dev. Yes, marry, am I.

Miles. Good Lord, Master Plutus, I have seen you a thousand times at my master's, and yet I had never the manners to make you drink. But, sir, I am glad to see how conformable you are to the statute.—I warrant you, he 's as yeomanly a man as you shall see: mark you, masters, here 's a plain honest man, without welt or guard.—But I pray you, sir, do you come lately from hell?

Dev. Ay, marry: how then?

Miles. Faith, 'tis a place I have desired long to see: have you not good tippling-houses there? may not a man have a lusty fire there, a pot of good ale, a pair of cards, a swinging piece of chalk, and a brown toast that will clap a white waistcoat on a cup of good drink?

Dev. All this you may have there.

Miles. You are for me, friend, and I am for you. But I pray you, may I not have an office there?

Dev. Yes, a thousand: what wouldst thou be?

Miles. By my troth, sir, in a place where I may profit myself. I know hell is a hot place, and men are marvellous dry, and much drink is spent there; I would be a tapster.

Dev. Thou shalt.

Miles. There 's nothing lets me from going with you, but that 'tis a long journey, and I have never a horse.

Dev. Thou shalt ride on my back.

Miles. Now surely here 's a courteous devil, that, for to pleasure his friend, will not stick to make a jade of himself.—But I pray you, goodman friend, let me move a question to you.

Dev. What 's that?

Miles. I pray you, whether is your pace a trot or an amble?

Dev. An amble.

Miles. 'Tis well; but take heed it be not a trot: but 'tis no matter, I'll prevent it. [*Puts on spurs.*

Dev. What dost?

Miles. Marry, friend, I put on my spurs; for if I find your pace either a trot or else uneasy, I'll put you to a false gallop; I'll make you feel the benefit of my spurs.

Dev. Get up upon my back.

[MILES *mounts on the* Devil's *back.*

Miles. O Lord, here 's even a goodly marvel, when a man rides to hell on the devil's back! [*Exeunt, the* Devil *roaring.*

SCENE XVI. *At Court.*

Enter the EMPEROR *with a pointless sword; next the* KING OF CASTILE *carrying a sword with a point;* LACY *carrying the globe;* PRINCE EDWARD; WARREN *carrying a rod of gold with a dove on it;* ERMSBY *with a crown and sceptre;* PRINCESS ELINOR *with* MARGARET *Countess of Lincoln on her left hand;* KING HENRY; BACON; *and* Lords *attending.*

P. Edw. Great potentates, earth's miracles for state,
Think that Prince Edward humbles at your feet,
And, for these favours, on his martial sword
He vows perpetual homage to yourselves,
Yielding these honours unto Elinor.

K. Hen. Gramercies, lordings; old Plantagenet,
That rules and sways the Albion diadem,
With tears discovers these conceivèd joys,
And vows requital, if his men-at-arms,
The wealth of England, or due honours done
To Elinor, may quite his favourites.
But all this while what say you to the dames
That shine like to the crystal lamps of heaven?

Emp. If but a third were added to these two,
They did surpass those gorgeous images
That gloried Ida with rich beauty's wealth.

Mar. 'Tis I, my lords, who humbly on my knee
Must yield her orisons to mighty Jove
For lifting up his handmaid to this state;
Brought from her homely cottage to the court,
And grac'd with kings, princes, and emperors,
To whom (next to the noble Lincoln Earl)
I vow obedience, and such humble love
As may a handmaid to such mighty men.

P. Elin. Thou martial man that wears the Almain crown,
And you the western potentates of might,
The Albion princess, English Edward's wife,
Proud that the lovely star of Fressingfield,
Fair Margaret, Countess to the Lincoln Earl,
Attends on Elinor,—gramercies, lord, for her,—
'Tis I give thanks for Margaret to you all,
And rest for her due bounden to yourselves.

K. Hen. Seeing the marriage is solémnizèd,
Let's march in triumph to the royal feast.—
But why stands Friar Bacon here so mute?

Bacon. Repentant for the follies of my youth,
That magic's secret mysteries misled,
And joyful that this royal marriage
Portends such bliss unto this matchless realm.

K. Hen. Why, Bacon,
What strange event shall happen to this land?
Or what shall grow from Edward and his queen?

Bacon. I find by deep prescience of mine art,
Which once I temper'd in my secret cell,
That here where Brute did build his Troynovant,
From forth the royal garden of a king
Shall flourish out so rich and fair a bud,
Whose brightness shall deface proud Phœbus' flower,
And over-shadow Albion with her leaves.
Till then Mars shall be master of the field,
But then the stormy threats of war shall cease:
The horse shall stamp as careless of the pike,
Drums shall be turn'd to timbrels of delight;

With wealthy favours plenty shall enrich
The strand that gladded wandering Brute to see,
And peace from heaven shall harbour in these leaves
That gorgeous beautify this matchless flower:
Apollo's heliotropion then shall stoop,
And Venus' hyacinth shall vail her top;
Juno shall shut her gilliflowers up,
And Pallas' bay shall 'bash her brightest green;
Ceres' carnation, in consórt with those,
Shall stoop and wonder at Diana's rose.

K. Hen. This prophecy is mystical.—
But, glorious commanders of Europa's love,
That make fair England like that wealthy isle
Circled with Gihon and swift Eúphrates,
In royalizing Henry's Albion
With presence of your princely mightiness,—
Let 's march: the tables all are spread,
And viands, such as England's wealth affords,
Are ready set to furnish out the boards.
You shall have welcome, mighty potentates:
It rests to furnish up this royal feast,
Only your hearts be frolic; for the time
Craves that we taste of naught but jouissance.
Thus glories England over all the west. [*Exeunt omnes.*

Omne tulit punctum qui miscuit utile dulci.

NOTES.

THE TRAGICAL HISTORY OF

DOCTOR FAUSTUS.

DRAMATIS PERSONAE.

The Pope. In the quartos of 1604 and 1609 'the Pope' is not identified with any particular historical Pontiff, but in the scene inserted in the quarto of 1616 he is addressed as 'Pope Adrian,' and is introduced as having overcome the attempt of a rival, 'Saxon Bruno,' who had been 'elected' Pope by the Emperor, and as having in this victory apparently enjoyed the aid of 'lord Raymond, King of Hungary.' All this, of which there is nothing in the old Faustbuch, is without any foundation in fact, whether as referring to the pontificate of Adrian VI (1522–1523), or to any other. The historical 'Saxon Bruno,' a kinsman of the Emperor Otto III, held the Papacy as Gregory V from 996–999, and is therefore out of the question. It is hardly possible that there can be any allusion, as Notter suggests, to Giordano Bruno, who was burnt for heresy at Rome in 1600 (Faustus in the edition of 1616 proposes that Bruno shall suffer the same fate for the same reason); or, as is likewise suggested by Notter, that there should be a reference to Bruno bishop of Toul, a relation of the Emperor Henry III (who was not a 'Saxon'), and elevated to the Papacy in 1049 as Leo IX. This last Bruno appears to have reconciled the Emperor with the King of Hungary; but that king's name was Andrew I, nor was there ever, so far as I am aware, a 'Raymond King of Hungary.'

Cardinal of Lorrain. The reason why Marlowe gave this name to the Cardinal, was simply that the Cardinals of Lorraine—members of the house of Guise—had played so prominent a part in the history of the sixteenth century that the conjunction had a familiar sound for

English ears. The first of these Cardinals, John (the brother of Duke Claude), who would be the 'Cardinal of Lorrain' of the play, died in 1550; the second (the brother of Duke Francis) in 1574; of the third (the brother of Duke Henry) the assassination is introduced into Marlowe's Massacre at Paris.

The Emperor of Germany. Charles V (see Chorus before sc. viii, l. 14), Emperor from 1519-1556. In the Faustbuch the corresponding episode is laid at Innsbruck, whence Charles V had to take flight on the sudden hostile approach of Maurice of Saxony in May 1552.

The Duke of Vanholt. 'Vanholt' is a corruption for 'Anhalt'; and it is just possible that the Dutch form of the name, as well as the allusions to the revolt in the Netherlands, i. 91–95, and the reference to the Low-German town of Emden, v. 23, may point to some Dutch manipulation of the story of Faustus before it was dramatised by Marlowe. Compare Introduction, pp. liii–liv. In this connexion it may be worth noting that in the *Dutch* legend of Faustus, the magician demands grapes from his attendant spirit (there called Jost) in midwinter, just as Faustus does for the Duchess from Mephistophiles in the play. The mis-spelling is the more curious, as the name of the princes of Anhalt ought to have been well known in London from the year 1596, when Lewis Prince of Anhalt and his brother Hans Ernst were in London, and visited the theatres. (See Cohn, Shakespeare in Germany, pp. xiv–xvi.) According to the Faustbuch (see Introduction, p. lxxiii) Faustus's host was 'the Count of Anhalt,' [of the house] 'who are nowadays princes.' This does not agree with history; for the first of the Counts of Anhalt who called himself Prince was Henry, who succeeded in 1212. The various possessions of the house were temporarily united in the middle of the sixteenth century; and from a passage in this episode in the Faustbuch, mentioning a hill near the town, on which the magic of Faustus had built a castle, it has been conjectured that the place may be Aschersleben, near which lay an old ruined castle Ascharien, or Ballenstätt, where there was likewise an ancestral castle of the princes of Anhalt-Zerbst. A little town and a castle are likewise mentioned in the Volksbuch of Eulenspiegel (Owl-glass), in a passage relating how that popular personage took service with the Count of Anhalt; and this, as Kühne conjectures, may be the origin of the introduction of the name of Anhalt into the story of Faustus.—It may be noticed that the Cologne broadsheet-poem on Doctor Faustus states that Faustus was 'born of Anhalt.'

Faustus. See Introduction, pp. xxxiii–xliv.

Valdes. Whether or not, as has been thought probable, 'German' Valdes (i. 63 and 96) be a mere misrepresentation of the name of 'Hermann'—for why should Faustus distinguish Valdes as a German, when he was himself of that nation?—it remains unknown whom Marlowe intended by this personage. Düntzer's fancy that he was thinking of Peter Waldus, 'the founder' (?) of the sect of the Waldenses, who as heretics were likewise accused of a compact with the Evil One, must be rejected; Waldus was born at Lyons in France, and died rather more than three centuries before the birth of Cornelius Agrippa, with whom he is here coupled. I expect no better fate for the supposition, that there may be a reference to Juan de Valdès, the brother of Charles V's secretary Alfonso de Valdès. Juan, who went to Naples as secretary of the Viceroy, was, like his brother, a man of humanistic learning, but having become estranged from the way of thinking of Catholic Spain, held views on Justification which were afterwards condemned by the Inquisition. See Ranke, Die Römischen Päpste (6th ed.), i. 91. He has accordingly come to be reckoned among the Protestants of the sixteenth century. He is said to have been accused of Socinianism; and it may be noticed that a 'Faustus Socinus' (apparently the nephew of Laelius Socinus and a resident in Poland 1579–1604; see Masson's Life of Milton, iv. 42) is mentioned as having been confounded with the real Doctor Faust.

Cornelius. Although, oddly enough, in i. 115–116 'Agrippa' appears to be spoken of as deceased, while 'Cornelius' is on the scene, there can be no doubt but that both are intended for the same historical personage, the famous Henry Cornelius Agrippa von Nettesheim, of whom Delrio states Faust to have been a friend and companion. Agrippa was at and after the time of his death accounted a magician, and his fame at an early date reached England, where a translation, by James Sandford, of one of Agrippa's most celebrated works appeared in 1569 under the title 'Of the Vanitie and Uncertaintie of Artes and Sciences,' and was several times reprinted. He is frequently mentioned in R. Scot's Discovery of Witchcraft (1584). The life of Cornelius Agrippa, of which an account, together with a summary of the contents of his two most famous works, will be found in H. Morley's biography (2 vols. 1856), is one of the most curious and interesting pictures of the labours and struggles of the Humanists of the Renascence. 'He began his life,' says Professor Morley, 'by mastering nearly the whole circle of the sciences and arts as far as books described it, and ended by declaring the uncertainty and vanity' of both. Born at Cologne in 1486, he served the Emperor Maximilian I both as secretary and soldier, and obtained the honour of knighthood in recognition of his gallantry. He was at the same time an eager student, and at the early age of 22 had already composed the three books De Occultâ Philosophiâ which, when published many years later (1531), brought upon his name the infamy long attached to it by monastic and popular superstition. This work was a treatise on Cabbalism, inspired by Reuchlin's Hebrew-Christian method of interpreting the mystic lore of the Jews. Meanwhile the life of Agrippa had been that of a wanderer, divided between military and diplomatic service, university lectures and authorship, and controversy with the monks. Employed in a prominent way at the Council of Pisa, he drew upon himself the excommunication of Pope Julius II, which was removed by the next Pope, Leo X. In 1518 he accepted the post of Advocate and Orator to the Free City of Metz, but two years later was driven from the town as a successful opponent of Dominican intolerance. He then practised medicine in Switzerland, where he came into closer contact with the Reformation movement, without however seceding from the Church of Rome. In 1524 he took service at Lyons as court physician to Louisa of Savoy, and here wrote his work De Incertitudine et Vanitate Scientiarum et Artium, a satirical review of their existing condition. In this book he recanted whatever errors there might be in his juvenile work, and without denying the existence of the Cabbala, discouraged the search for it. But the attacks made in this later work upon the Court and courtiers brought upon him the wrath of the Emperor Charles V, when the book was published in 1531. Three years previously Agrippa had removed to Antwerp, where he had been appointed Councillor of the Archives and Historiographer. Thus, having been involved in difficulties and in a quarrel with the monks of the University of Louvain, he had to fly from the Empire, and died as a homeless wanderer at Grenoble in 1535 on his way to Lyons, where the completest extant edition of his works was published about the year 1550. Superstition and intolerance busied themselves with his mysterious habits of life, and more especially converted a favourite black dog, by which he was attended in his closing days, into a familiar spirit. This legend, which long survived, and which has many parallels (as for instance that of the dog of Doctor Faustus, and that of Friar Bungay), was commemorated in a brutally intolerant inscription over his grave, and was discussed *pro* and *con* by pious writers who, like Bodinus and Lercheimer (1586), believed in the diabolical agency, and by a faithful and intelligent follower, Johannes Wierus (1515-1588), who in vain endeavoured to give a rational explanation of the relation between the man and the dog. Wierus did further service to Agrippa's memory by protesting against the ascription to him, twenty-seven years after his death, of a foolish compilation called the fourth book of the work De Occultâ Philosophiâ (reprinted by Scheible, Kloster, iii. 564 seqq.). Whatever may be thought of the prudence of Agrippa in publishing, in his mature years, juvenile speculations of which he himself confessed the rashness, there can be no doubt that he laboured and suffered much in the twin causes of Truth and Tolerance, and that no noble name has ever undergone more grievous and shameful aspersion than his.

Wagner, servant to Faustus. The name of Faustus's *famulus* (the usual term for students employed as assistants by German professors) is spelt 'Wagner' and 'Wagener' in the Faustbuch, where his Christian name is given as 'Christoph.' Widmann spells the name 'Waïger,' and gives 'Johan' as the Christian name. Goethe used the form 'Wagner;' and the curious circumstance is mentioned by Mr. Hayward, that one of Goethe's early friends—Henry Leopold Wagner—bore that name, who signalised himself by stealing from Faust (which had been confidentially communicated to him before publication) the idea of the tragic portion relating to Margaret, and making it the subject of a tragedy called The Infanticide. But it is clear from Goethe's Autobiography that he did not choose the name by way of revenge.—For the references to Wagner in the Faustbuch see Introduction, pp. lxv, lxxvii, lxxxii. It is noteworthy that Widmann makes Wagner the son of a Catholic priest (at Wasserburg in Bavaria). The requisite data as to the Wagnerbuch, and its English version, have been given in the Introduction, pp. xlvi, xlviii, lvi. In Wagner's adventures a Spirit called 'Auerhan' (woodcock, or 'Attercocke' in the Second Report; compare 'Urian' as a name for the Devil) plays a part corresponding to that of Mephistophiles, and in the Second Report Wagner has a 'boy' in his service called 'Arthur Harmarvan;' just as in Marlowe (ii. 4) one of the scholars calls Wagner Faustus's 'boy,' i.e. servant.

Clown. To this 'Clown' the 'Hans Wurst' (Jack Pudding) of the German puppet-plays on the story of Doctor Faustus (see Introduction, p. xlvii) corresponds. In some of these Hans Wurst takes the still surviving name of 'Caspar' or 'Casperle.' Douce, in his Essay on the Clowns and Fools of Shakspeare (Illustrations of Shakspeare, vol. ii), shows that while the terms 'clown' and 'fool' were used as synonymous by our old writers, the clown was a character of much greater variety. He was occasionally the general domestic fool, but also a mere country booby (like Thomas and Richard in Friar Bacon), or a witty rustic, or a shrewd and witty servant. Thus he constituted an indispensable personage in the old English plays; and it is precisely the full licence to 'gag' allowed to the favourite performers of the character which renders it impossible to say how much, or how little, of the farcical business and dialogue in such a play as ours was 'written down' for him by the author. The English drama was rescued from the supremacy of the Clown at a relatively early period in its history, but in Germany he ruled the stage for the better part of a couple of centuries.

Robin. The familiar abbreviation for Robert, which even Queen Elizabeth did not disdain to apply to her favourite, Leicester, and by which, according to Thomas Heywood, Robert Greene was invariably called.

Vintner, i. e. wine-seller; improperly addressed as 'Drawer,' ix. 7, if there be not some confusion in the passage, which is different in the quarto of 1616.

Horse-courser, i. e. horse-dealer or horse-changer. To 'scorse, scorce or scourse' is an old word of doubtful origin, frequently used in the sense of 'to exchange.' So in the passage quoted in Nares from Harington's Orlando Furioso, xx. 78:

> 'This done, she makes the stately dame to light
> And with the aged woman cloths to scorse;'

and in its special reference to horses: 'Will you scourse with him? you are in Smithfield, you may fit yourself with a fine easy-going street-nag,' etc. Jonson's Bartholomew Fair (iii. 1), in which play one of the characters is 'Dan Jordan Knockem, a horse-courser and a ranger of Turnbull' (Turnmill-street). One of the German translators humorously renders the word by 'Pferdephilister'; the French more literally by 'maquignon.' The Faustbuch has 'Rossteuscher.'

A Knight. Of this unfortunate personage the Faustbuch politely states that the author was desirous not to mention the name, inasmuch as he was a knight and a born baron; but the margin is less generous, adding 'Erat Baro ab Hardeck.' See Introduction, p. lxxii.

An Old Man. The 'Old Man' of the Faustbuch is 'a Christian pious god-fearing physician' (see Introduction, p. lxxv), in Lercheimer we have merely an 'old god-fearing man.' He is called 'a pious pastor' in a late version of the legend; and may be identifiable with the historical Dr. Kling. See Introduction, p. xli. In a late version of the story Faust has a final interview with his old father.

Scholars, i. e. students.

Lucifer. The morning- and evening-star was known in ancient Italy under the name, among others, of 'Lucifer,' which was possibly a translation of the ordinary Greek name for the morning-star, Ἑωσφόρος or Φωσφόρος. The name was applied by Isaiah, xiv. 12, to Nebuchadnezzar King of Babylon, and transferred by Eusebius and subsequent authors to the chief of the angels expelled as rebels from heaven. In the systems of infernal government constructed by later writers, Lucifer was either placed at the head of all the devils, or reckoned as one of the seven chief infernal potentates ('electors') under the supremacy of Belial. In Marlowe's play he holds the supreme position (see iii. 67), though the term 'Prince of the East,' which was probably suggested by his name as the morning-star, and which is used of him v. 104, is in its Latin form applied to Belzebub, iii. 17. According to the Faustbuch (ch. xiii) it is Lucifer who rules 'in *Orient*,' hence he is called 'prince of the east' in our play (v. 104); while Beelzebub, to whom the title 'Orientis princeps' is given in the conjuration of Faustus (iii. 17), rules 'in *Septentrione*.' In Friar Bacon, ix. 144 and xi. 109, the titles of 'guider' and 'ruler of the north' are given to Asmenoth. According to the belief of dæmonology, a division of the quarters of the world among four angels existed before the Fall, and it was the 'Prince of the East' who rebelled, and to whom half of the universe was henceforth closed, so that he became the 'prince of this world,' as in Luther's hymn *Ein' feste Burg*. Compare as to the fall of Lucifer, note to iii. 63; and see Caedmon, 246 seqq., and Cursor Mundi, i. 33 seqq. According to the belief of the Franciscans and others, since the year 1000 A. D. the Devil, after his millenary captivity (Revelations, xx. 2), had been let loose from hell 'to deceive the nations.' See T. Arnold's note, Select English Works of Wyclif, i. 133.

Belzebub. The name Belzebub ('Baal-zebub') signifies 'the god of flies'; 'Baal' ('Lord') being a general name for 'god' among the Semitic nations, which 'designated their different Baals or gods by names compounded of this word and others indicating localities or signifying qualities. . . . This particular deity was worshipped at Ekron in Palestine (2 Kings i. 2, 3), where the plague of flies or insects which afflicts hot countries seems to have been particularly felt; and that he was an important deity of Palestine may be gathered from his being referred to afterwards (St. Matthew, xii. 24) as "Beelzebub, the prince of the devils."' From Masson's note on Milton's Paradise Lost, i. 80, 81.—'With such gentlemen as you,' says Goethe's Faust (Hayward), 'one may generally learn the essence from the name, since it appears but too plainly, if your name be fly-god, destroyer, liar.' Compare the passage in The Faery Queene, i. 1. 38, where Archimago summons spirits like flies.—In the Faustbuch (ch. xxiii) 'Beelzebub' appears as one of the seven principal spirits introduced to Faustus by their chief Belial, and is thus described: 'He had hair of flesh-colour, and an ox's head, with two terrible ears, was also quite covered with bristles and hair, and had two large wings, as sharp as the thistles in the field, half green and yellow, only that over the wings flew streams of fire; he had a cow's tail.' —The spellings of the name in the quarto of 1604 are 'Belsabub,' 'Belzabub,' and 'Belsibub.'

Mephistophilis. Of this name the etymology is very doubtful. It is spelt in the quarto of 1604 'Mephastophilis,' or 'Mephastophilus'—hence a vocative in '*e*,' v. 29—and also 'Mephostophilis'; compare the form 'Mephostophilus' used by Pistol in The Merry Wives, i. 1. 132. The form 'Mephistophiles' adopted by Goethe, is said (by Engel, *u. s.*,

34) first to occur in an old German popular play, Johann Faust, which was printed at Munich in 1775. The form 'Mephistophiel' is used in the Praxis Cabulae nigrae Doctoris Johannis Fausti, etc. (1612). Widmann calls it a Persian name; no Semitic derivation has yet been discovered for it, as it has for most names of Spirits. The original form 'Megastophiles' ('Megistophiles?') is a feeble guess, founded on Dürr's conjecture (1676) 'Megastophilus,' i. e. a lover of greatness and pre-eminence. The conjectured derivations from 'mephitis' with φίλος or ὠφελεῖν, and Düntzer's from 'Mephotophiles' who does not love the light, are more ingenious than probable. Unger has suggested that the last of these derivations was mixed with another—'Mefaustophiles'—'no friend to Faust'! See Scheible's Kloster, xi. 349–350, and v. 135–6 and notes, where the various names taken by the Devils or Familiar Spirits are enumerated. In the systems of the infernal hierarchy constructed by the writers on magic in the seventeenth century this Spirit figures either as one of the seven 'Electors,' or as one of the seven 'Grand-dukes' who hold the next rank to the six chiefs; elsewhere he is described as the vicegerent of Lucifer over all Spirits. In the Dutch legend the attendant Spirit of Faustus bears the name of Jost. The Middle-High German poets called the Devil 'Valant,' 'Foland' or 'Volland' (Goethe's 'Junker,' i.e. squire, 'Voland'), who is identical with the lame god Loki of German mythology; Loki had seven-league-boots, as Mephistophiles can travel with speed whither he likes. More to our purpose is the self-identification of Goethe's Mephistophiles (2 Faust, act ii) with the 'Old Iniquity' (whence 'Old Nick') of the old stage-plays. Compare Loeper, Goethe's Faust, i. 127, ii. 176, 79. Hence the playfulness of this Spirit even in Marlowe. Our poet treats Mephistophiles as the servant of Lucifer (iii. 40; v. 30; ix. 37–39); but as a not ignoble Spirit (xiii. 79–81); this however is not, as it seems to me, a proof of the spuriousness of all the ignoble passages in which he is made to play a part. Of the irony of Mephistophiles, which Thirlwall referring to Goethe's character describes as the darker, and truly diabolical, kind of irony, and of which there are traces in the Faustbuch, there are few or none in Marlowe, whose vein was hardly humorous enough for the developement of this feature, and whose conception of his theme was tragic – though he was willing to introduce comic scenes for the benefit of the groundlings.

Good Angel. Evil Angel. These characters are not introduced in the Faustbuch, where the only direct supernatural warning received by Faustus is that of the inscription on his arm; in the German puppet-play their interposition is far less strongly marked than in Marlowe's tragedy. See Introduction, p. lvi. The belief in the protecting care through life of the Good Angel, of which it is unnecessary to recall the biblical origin, is attested by many mediaeval legends. It is made use of by other dramatists. In Lodge and Greene's A Looking-Glass for London and England an 'Angel' directs the proceedings of 'Jonas,' and an 'Evil Angel' tempts the Usurer to suicide (compare xiii. 52). In Massinger's The Virgin Martyr, which as Hallam observes followed the model of the Spanish 'autos,' Theophilus is followed by an evil spirit called Harpax, in the shape of a secretary (as in the old miracle-play he is attended by the Devil himself), and Dorothea by a good spirit called Angelo, in the shape of a page. Goethe has introduced an 'Evil Spirit' (who is not Mephistophiles) in Margaret's cathedral-scene, and at the close of the First Part of the tragedy a 'voice from above' proclaims her salvation. The warning of 'a Voice' is introduced with considerable effect in the juvenile endeavour of Alfred de Musset to produce a species of Faust-drama (La Coupe et les Lèvres, i. 3).

The Seven Deadly Sins. The Seven Deadly Sins, who do not appear in the Faustbuch (see note on vi. 112), are enumerated (as Pride, Envie, Accidie or Slouthe, Avarice or Coveitise, Glotonie and Lecherie) and discussed at length in The Persone's Tale, the sermon or tractate on penitence translated by Chaucer from a French religious manual, of which he likewise had before him the English version, the Ayenbite of Inwyt. See also The Vision concerning Piers the Plowman, Passus v. 63 seqq., and Skeat's note *in loc.* The Seven Deadly Sins also make their appearance in the old English miracle of Mary Magdalene and in the morality of The Castle of Perseverance. The famous clown Tarlton contrived an extemporal play called The Seven Deadlie Sins, of which the 'platt' (or skeleton sketch fixed on a pasteboard for consultation by the performers) is extant, and reprinted by Collier in his History of English Dramatic Poetry, iii. 394. Compare Introduction, p. lv. The names here correspond to those in our text; of three Sins the effects are severally illustrated by examples (such as Sardanapalus of Sloth), as doubtless the effects of the remaining four were in the First Part of the play. The performance is supposed to take place before King Henry VI, and 'Lidgate' acts as a kind of Chorus. Dekker's The Seven Deadly Sinnes of London (1606, recently reprinted by Mr. Arber) is a tractate directed against some of the favourite vices and malpractices of London life. The scheme of the pamphlet is cleverly assimilated to that of a series of 'triumphs' or processions; 'the names of the actors in this old Enterlude of Iniquite,' which 'seuen may easily play, but not without a Diuell,' being Politike Bankruptisme, Lying, Candle-light, Sloth, Apishnesse, Shauing, and Crueltie. It may be added that seven is for many reasons a favourite classifying number with writers on cabbalism and magic; but the Seven Deadly Sins, together with the Seven Cardinal Virtues and the Seven Spiritual Works of Mercy, reappear in a work of a different kind, Cosin's Book of Devotions, as late as 1627 (see Gardiner's Personal Government of Charles I, i. 23). Cyril Tourneur, in his poem The Transformed Metamorphosis, makes a familiar controversial use of the number of the Deadly Sins, in allusion to the seven hills of Rome:

'On sinne's full number (loe) she is erect;
For why? Great Pluto was her architect.'

Spirits in the shapes of **Alexander the Great**, of his Paramour— The word 'paramour' corresponds to the '*Gemählin*' (consort) of the Faustbuch (see Introduction, p. lxx). The term was formerly used without any disreputable meaning, see for instance Spenser, The Shepheards Kalendar, April, 139. The origin of the word is a French (and Italian) idiom, of which Tyrwhitt (in a note to the passage in The Knightes Tale, 1157, where Arcite says of Emelia 'par amour I loved hire') quotes the following apposite example from Froissart: 'Il aima adonc par amours, et depuis espousa, Madame Ysabelle de Juillers.'— Van der Velde considers that if Marlowe intended the wife of Alexander, he is guilty of an anachronism, inasmuch as the marriage of Alexander with Roxane did not take place till after his final victory over Darius (whose overthrow is represented in the dumbshow in the quarto of 1616, cited in note before x. 67), and that he may therefore possibly after all have had Thais in his mind. But in the dumbshow in question the paramour does not enter till after the fall of Darius.

and of **Helen**. See Introduction, p. lxxiv. The various treatments by Greek and other poets of the story of Helen in its different phases and versions it is impossible to enumerate here; hers is one of the most prominent figures of Classical legend and literature, and from these she passed into those of the Middle Ages, finding a place even in the Third of those 'Sibylline Books' which connected mediaeval beliefs with the traditions of antiquity, as 'a beautiful Fury sprung from Sparta, an undying theme of song, but a fruitful germ of evil to Asia and Europe.' It should however be noticed, in connexion with her introduction as a shade into the story of Faustus, that already in Greek legend her figure is associated with similar traditions. Stesichorus in his Palinodia told how 'the Helen who had been seen in Troy was a mere shadow (*φάσμα, εἴδωλον*); while the true Helen had never embarked from Greece. In Laconia there were popular legends of Helen having appeared as a shade long after her death, like her brothers Castor and Pollux. Others supposed that the marine demigod Proteus formed a false Helen, with whom he deceived Paris; and the Egyptians having converted Proteus into a king of Egypt, said that he took her from

Paris, who carried a mere phantasm to Troy, and kept her there for Menelaus. This was the story Herodotus (ii. 112) heard in Egypt. Euripides adapted this legend in his Helena, in which tragedy the gods form a false Helen whom Paris takes to Troy, the true Helen being carried by Hermes to the Egyptian king Proteus.' (From Müller's History of Greek Literature, i. 267 and note.) According to yet another legend, Achilles after his death quitted the Lower World to rejoin Helen, whom he had loved in life, in the island of Leuce (not in Pherae, as Goethe's Faust says, Part ii. act ii) in the Black Sea. From their union sprang Euphorion. (Pausanias, iii. 19. 11, quoted by Kühne and Loeper.) Already in the Cypria of Stasimus, Aphrodite and Thetis bring about a meeting between Achilles and Helen, the former having desired to see the fairest of all women. (See Welcker, Die Griechischen Tragödien mit Rücksicht auf den epischen Cyclus geordnet, i. 159, to which work the student may be referred for other passages on the treatment of the story and figure of Helen in Greek poetry.) The familiarity of the later Middle Ages with the story of Troy in mediaeval literary versions is well known. It should be added that Marlowe translated a late Greek poem by Coluthus (fl. A.D. 500), The Rape of Helen (Ἑλένης ἁρπαγή), which had been paraphrased by Thomas Watson in Latin verse (1586). Marlowe's translation (1587) is lost; a later English translation, by Fawkes, is printed in vol. xx. of Chalmers' English Poets. The Helena of the Second Part of Goethe's Faust can only be referred to as a subject for separate study, for which full materials will be found in Loeper's admirable edition of Goethe's work (1870).

Chorus. The 'Chorus,' in the language of the Elizabethan stage, is the actor who speaks the prologue, and the passages interspersed in the play to aid its progress by narrative or comment. So in Henry V the First Folio has 'Enter Prologue' for the opening speech, and 'Enter Chorus' for the speeches before the later acts and at the close. Already to the old miracle-plays it was usual to prefix a species of general prologue spoken by a herald; while at times an 'expositor' moralises upon the course of the action. Doctor Faustus is the only play by Marlowe which has a Chorus by that name; Tamburlaine and The Jew of Malta have prologues, that to the latter play being spoken by Machiavel.

Chorus.

1. *fields of Thrasimene* (quarto of 1604 'Thracimene'), the battle of the lacus Trasumennus (now Lago di Perugia), in which Hannibal completely defeated the Romans under G. Flaminius (217 B.C.), and which Livy, xxii. 4, calls one of the most noted routs of the Roman people.

2. *mate*, match, pit himself against. Compare Henry VIII, iii. 2. 274:

'That in the way of royalty and truth
Toward the King, my ever royal master,
Dare mate a sounder man than Surrey can be.'

Dyce explains 'confound, defeat'—a common use of the word; compare 1 Tamburlaine, i. 1:

'How now, my lord! what, mated and amaz'd
To hear the King thus threaten like himself?'

and Friar Bacon, ii. 154; but Marlowe can hardly have so far forgotten his history. Van der Velde translates 'allied himself with;' F. V. Hugo 'espoused warlike Carthage.'

4. *In courts of kings*. 'Neither' or 'nor' should be supplied before these words.

Ib. state, majesty, power. Compare xiii. 118, and Friar Bacon, xvi. 1. Marlowe alludes to such plays as The Misfortunes of Arthur (1587), The Famous Victories of Henry V (before 1588), and his own Tamburlaine, the prologue to which last promises to lead the audience 'to the stately tents of war.' Compare the closing lines of the prologue to Ford's Chronicle Historie of Perkin Warbeck.

6. *vaunt*, the reading of the later quartos for 'daunt.' Compare Friar Bacon, vii. 11.

Ib. his. It is unnecessary to reject this reading of all the quartos, and substitute 'her.' Compare for the use of the word 'Muse' as equivalent to 'poet' Shakespeare's Sonnet xxi. 1–2:

'So is it not with me, as with that Muse
Stirr'd by a painted beauty to his verse';

and Milton's Lycidas, 19–21:

'So may some gentle Muse
With lucky words favour my destined urn;
And, as he passes, turn.'

In Dryden's Absalom and Achitophel, Part I, the Earl of Mulgrave (Buckinghamshire) is introduced as

'Sharp-judging Adriel, the muses' friend,
Himself a muse.'

Ib. heavenly, supremely powerful or beautiful. Compare iii. 27 and xiii. 85.

7, 8. *perform The form*. Marlowe was fond of this kind of jingle. Compare sc. vi. 42, and 2 Tamburlaine, iv. 4:

'But presently be prest to conquer it';

ib. v. 3:

'Plead in vain unpleasing sovereignty';

and in the same scene of the same play:

'Hell and darkness pitch their pitchy tents';

and The Jew of Malta, i. 1:

'Haply some hapless man hath conscience.'

9. *appeal our plaud*, appeal for our applause. Compare Prologue to 1 Tamburlaine:

'And then applaud his fortune as you please';

and the 'Plaudite' at the end of Roman comedies. The phrase however is harsh, and the quarto of 1616 reads for this line:

'And now to patient judgments we appeal.'

11. *his parents base of stock.* For examples of this nom. abs. construction, with an adjective in the place of a participle, see Abbott, § 380.

12. *Rhodes.* See Introduction, p. lvii.

13. *Wittenberg;* quarto of 1604 here and i. 87 Wertenberg; see Introduction, p. lviii.

14. *Whereas*, where. See Abbott, § 135. Compare Dido Queen of Carthage, i. 2:

'When suddenly gloomy Orion rose,
And led our ships into the shallow sands,
Whereas the southern winds with brackish breath
Dispers'd them all among the wreckful rocks.'

15. *profits*, makes progress. Compare The Merry Wives, iv. 1. 16: 'My husband says my son profits nothing in the world at his book.'

16. *The fruitful . . . grac'd*, the fruitful garden of scholarship being adorned by him.

17. *That*, so that. See Abbott, § 283. The antithesis in these two lines is however very feeble, and l. 16 is omitted in the quarto of 1616.

18. *whose sweet delight disputes*, whose sweet delight it is to dispute.

19. *In.* Modern English would here demand 'on'; but the interchanges between Elizabethan and modern usage with regard to the employment of these prepositions are numerous. Compare note to Friar Bacon, ii. 95.

20. *cunning*, knowledge (from *cunnan*, to be able, to know). The word is repeatedly used in this sense in our play, and in Friar Bacon. The adjective 'cunning' is used in the same sense in our play, i. 115. Trench, in Select Glossary, quotes a striking instance of this use of the word from Foxe's Book of Martyrs: 'I believe that all these three Persons [in the Godhead] are even in power and in cunning and in might.' Compare also Psalm cxxxvii. 5; and for the adjective 1 Samuel xvi. 18. The substantive 'craft' and the adjectives 'crafty' and 'artful' may be noticed as examples of a similar degradation of meaning in ordinary usage.

20. *of*, out of. See Abbott, § 169. Compare Friar Bacon, vi. 166; and The Jew of Malta, i. 1:

'Tell not me 'twas done of policy.'

21. *waxen wings*. Icarus, when accompanying his father Daedalus on his flight through the air to escape from the wrath of Minos, approached too near to the sun, which melted the wax by which his wings were attached to his body. He fell into the sea (hence called the Icarian) and was buried on an island (Icarus or Icaria) by Heracles. The myth is thrice alluded to in Henry VI (Part I, iv. 6. 54; ib. iv. 7. 17; and Part III, v. 6. 21). Wagner compares the expression in the Faustbuch (see Introduction, p. lx): 'He took to himself the wings of an eagle; and thought to study all secrets in heaven and earth.'

22. *melting*, i.e. they (the wings) melting. As to this absolute use of the participle without a noun, see Abbott, § 378. Compare i. 25: 'Or, being dead' for 'Or, they being dead'; and 2 Tamburlaine, i. 3:

'Where Amazonians met me in the field,
With whom, being women [i.e. they being women], I vouchsafed a league.'

25. *necromancy* (quarto of 1604 'negromancy'). Necromancy (*νεκρομαντεία*) is defined by the evil spirit Auerhan in the Wagnerbuch (Scheible, Kloster, iii. 115 seqq.) as the art which 'awakeneth the dead, proceedeth to the tombs, useth the ceremonies thereto appertaining, and thus conjureth the spirit of the deceased, that it shall come forth and appear to them, as thou readest of the witch at Endor, who awakened Samuel.' He proceeds to distinguish two sorts of necromancy, viz. necyomancy (*νεκυομαντεία*, the art of which Faustus desires to possess the power, i. 25), 'when one makes the dead bodies alive again, then one of us hath to slip into the corpse, and bring it on its feet again, so that it can walk and stand,' and scyomancy (properly sciomancy, *σκιομαντεία*), 'when one merely reproduces the shadow of a deceased, as Aeneas did in Virgilio,' and as Auerhan at Wagner's request proceeds to do with the shade of Achilles, and as Faustus does with those of Alexander and his paramour in sc. x. of our play. As to the necyomancy of the ancients see Maury, La Magie et l'Astrologie dans l'Antiquité et au Moyen Age, 59-60. 'This word *Necromancie*,' says King James I in his Daemonologie, Bk. I. ch. iii, 'is a Greeke worde compounded of *Νέκρος* and *μαντεία*, which is to say, the prophesie by the dead. This last name is given to this blacke and vnlawfull sinne by the figure *Synecdoche*, because it is a principal part of that art, to serue themselues with dead carcages in their diuinations.' The form 'nigromancy' or 'negromancy' (which is that of the quarto of 1604) was derived from the Latin mediaeval writers, and was translated into the popular English term 'the Black Art' (compare our play, x. 2). 'The

Latin mediaeval writers, whose Greek was either little or none, spelt the word "nigromantia," while at the same time getting round to the original meaning, though by a wrong process, they understood the dead by these "nigri" or blacks, whom they had brought into the word. Thus in a Vocabulary, 1475: Nigromansia dicitur divinatio facta *per nigros.*' Trench, English Past and Present, p. 306. Ariosto wrote a comedy, Il Negromante, and Skelton a morality, The Nigramansir. Compare note on Friar Bacon, i. 98.

27. *prefers before.* A common construction; compare Othello, i. 3. 187:

'Preferring you before her father.'

28. *this,* for 'this is.' Compare King Lear, iv. 6. 187: 'This' a good block'; and other instances of this kind and similar contractions cited by Abbott, § 461. Compare note on Friar Bacon, ix. 34.

Scene I.

Faustus *discovered in his study*—or, as the quarto here and at sc. v. has it, *Enter Faustus in his Study.* 'Most probably the Chorus, before going out, drew a curtain, and discovered Faustus sitting.' (Dyce.) This scene or situation, to which the beginning of sc. xi. of Friar Bacon forms a kind of parody, is 'the only part in which the Faustus of Marlowe bears any similarity to that of Goethe' (Hayward, Goethe's Faust, p. 159). Byron reproduced the situation in his Manfred (ib. p. 162). This opening situation is at the same time so naturally suggested by the subject, that in the extant project of a Doctor Faust by Lessing the first scene was to be of a similar kind, and that it repeats itself in most of the German puppet-plays on the story of Faustus. In the first scene of the most famous of Chinese dramas, the Pi-Pa-Ki, or The Story of the Lute, the hero, a Senior Wrangler in the state examinations, is discovered uttering the following reflexions: 'What is this world? I have studied everything; the books which I have read would make not less than ten thousand volumes.' The situation in which Faustus is here found, contemplating the apparitions in his magical circle, is that in which he is depicted in a famous etching by Rembrandt.

1. *Settle thy studies,* arrive at a definite choice among thy subjects of study. The Act of Settlement is that which establishes the succession to the Crown in a particular line.

2. *profess,* adopt as the subject of public teaching, be a 'professor' of.

3. *Having commenc'd,* being a doctor of theology. 'Inception' is the process originally necessary to the taking of a master's degree in any faculty; nor was there any difference between a 'master' and a 'doctor'

according to old Oxford terminology. (Anstey, Munimenta Academien, Introduction, p. xciv.) The annual opening solemnity of the Faculties is still called the 'Commencement' at Cambridge (the 'Act' at Oxford), though the term 'commencing' is only used in reference to the inferior or bachelor's degree.

4. *level*, aim. Compare Edward II, iii. 3:

'That 's it these barons and the subtle queen
Long levell'd at';

and Greene's Orlando Furioso:

'This happy prize
At which you long have levell'd all your thoughts.'

Ib. the end of every art, viz. metaphysics: see below, 47.

5. *Aristotle's works*. In Lessing's Fragment Faust remembers how a scholar was said to have summoned the devil, while studying the ἐντελέχεια (the real state of action and being) of Aristotle. 'Whence, a number that fetch the articles of their beliefe out of Aristotle, and thinke of heauen and hell as the heathen philosophers, take occasion to deride our ecclesiasticall state, and all ceremonies of diuine worship, as bug-beares and scar-crows.' (Nash, Pierce Penilesse his Supplication.) Marlowe elsewhere bears testimony to the supremacy of Aristotle in academical education; Ramus says, in The Massacre at Paris, i. 8:

'And this for Aristotle will I say,
That he that despiseth him can never
Be good in logic or philosophy.'

Compare also Edward II, iv. 6:

'Thy philosophy
That in our famous nurseries of arts
Thou suck'dst from Plato and from Aristotle.'

In Calderon's El Magico Prodigioso, Cyprian is studying Pliny.

6. *Analytics* (quarto of 1604 'Anulatikes'). 'The "Prior Analytics" of Aristotle were well described in their old title "On the Syllogism"; the "Posterior Analytics" are entitled "On Demonstration," and treat of reasoning in general, whether the result is Opinion or Science; of reasoning, the result of which is Science, Inductive or Deductive; of Dialectical reasoning, the result of which is opinion.' (Donaldson, History of the Literature of Ancient Greece, ii. 287.) 'But this art [of Judgment] hath two several methods of doctrine, the one by way of direction, the other by way of caution: the former frameth and setteth down a true form of consequence, by the variations and deflections from which errors and inconsequences may be exactly judged. Toward the composition and structure of which form, it is incident to handle the parts thereof, which are propositions, and the parts of propositions, which are simple words: and this is that part of Logic which

is comprehended in the Analytics.' (Bacon, Advancement of Learning, ii. 198; Kitchin.) The form 'Analytics' correctly renders the Greek neuter plural (τὰ ἀναλυτικά); but the word is here treated as a singular, as if it were analogous to the forms 'mathematics,' 'metaphysics,' 'poetics,' which are secondary forms of feminine singular adjectives (ἡ ποιητικὴ τέχνη, etc.).

7. *Bene . . . logices.* 'To argue well is the end of logic.' Although this is introduced in connexion with Aristotle, it seems rather to be taken from one of the Anti-Aristotelian works on logic. Ramus defines logic as 'Ars s. Virtus disserendi.' Marlowe was at Cambridge; and it is curious that one of the early and few English Ramists was William Temple at Cambridge, who published an edition of Ramus's Dialectica with notes and a dedication to Sir Philip Sidney (2nd edition, 1591).

12. *Economy* (quarto of 1604 'Oncaymæon': the word seems to have been too much for the old printers; in Skelton's Garlande of Laurell, 328, 'Esiodus' is the 'Icononucar'). Both Xenophon and Aristotle use the term 'œconomics' in its proper sense of the science of domestic management ('economique' is rightly defined in this sense in Gower's Confessio Amantis, bk. vii); nor is there any instance of the general meaning of 'philosophy' being attached to the word 'economy,' as here (where Müller properly translates 'Farewell, Philosophy'). If Marlowe really wrote 'economy,' it doubtless sufficed for him that Aristotle had written (or rather was reputed to have written) two books Οἰκονομικῶν, besides having treated the subject in bk. i. of his Politics.

Ib. Galen. Claudius Galenus, the famous physician and prolific writer on medical and other subjects, was born at Pergamum in Mysia 130 A.D. His essay 'On the Art of Medicine' was 'the text-book and chief subject of examination for medical students in the middle ages, when it was known in barbarous Latin as the Tegnum or Microtegnum (Microtechnum) of Galen.' In Dekker's The Seven Deadly Sinnes of London the term 'Gallenist' is used as equivalent to physician.

13. *Ubi . . . medicus.* Where the philosopher leaves off, there the physician begins.

15. *etérniz'd*, made eternal in fame. This verb, formed from the adjective 'eterne,' which is used by Shakespeare, recurs in 1 Tamburlaine, i. 2; 2 Tamburlaine, v. 1 and v. 2; also in Friar Bacon, ii. 43, and towards the beginning of Greene's Orlando Furioso. Similar formations are 'royalize,' i.e. made royal, in 1 Tamburlaine, ii. 3; Friar Bacon, ix. 264, and xvi. 68; and Peele's Edward I, sc. i. 12; 'enthrónize,' in Edward II, v. 1, and Peele's Edward I, sc. i. 250; 'scandalize,' i.e. turn into dishonour, in Lodge and Greene's A Looking-Glass for London and England; besides 'canónize,' in our scene, 118,

and 'solémnize,' in Peele's Edward I, i. 250. A large collection of similar forms, including 'echoize' and 'chaoize,' is to be found in Cyril Tourneur's poem, The Transformed Metamorphosis.

16. *Summum . . . sanitas.* The supreme good of medicine is health.

19. *found aphorisms* (quartos of 1604 and 1609 'sound'). The term 'aphorisms,' as specially applied to medical science, was derived from the title of a work by the famous physician Hippocrates (b. 460 B.C.), which 'contains more than four hundred short sentences of a practical nature, either culled by Hippocrates himself at a later period of his life from his other works and from the memoranda of his medical practice, or formed by some writer of his school soon after his death,' and in which are to be found 'the germs of all his doctrine.' Donaldson, u. s., ii. 408 (Düntzer notes that the first of the 'aphorisms' of Hippocrates, 'Life is short and art is long,' is put by Goethe into the mouth of Faust's famulus Wagner). The term, employed in the same sense by Galen, came to be applied generally to pithy, pregnant sentences containing the gist of a subject, and is so used and abused to this day. It was in due course applied to the teachings of the science of magic, and repeatedly occurs in this sense in Friar Bacon. This special use long continued; thus the book Arbatel de Magia Veterum, published in Germany in 1686, comprises 49 'aphorismi' furnishing 'a brief instruction in *Magiam.*'

20. *bills.* The word 'bill' (from Middle Latin 'billa,' French 'billet,' properly a small paper with the 'bulla' or documentary seal attached) seems to have been used (as it is now) of formal documents of one kind or another (but the parliamentary term 'bill' has a different derivation). So in the well-known passage in Much Ado about Nothing, i. 1. 32: 'He set up his bills here in Messina and challenged Cupid at the flight.' Thus below, v. 65 and xiv. 40, the deed by which Faustus pledges his soul to Mephistophilis is called a 'bill.' Faustus probably here refers not so much to ordinary prescriptions, as to the advertisements by which, as a migratory physician, he had been in the habit of announcing his advent, and perhaps his system of cure, and which were now 'hung up as monuments' *in perpetuum.* Such a proceeding would be quite in harmony with the proceedings of physicians *in partibus* of all times. Compare the expression 'tooth-drawers' bills' (advertisements, placards) in Fletcher's Wit without Money, iv. 5. Nothing as to his having practised as a physician is narrated of the historical or the legendary Faust; the typical magician-physician was Theophrastus Paracelsus (see Introduction, p. xxviii); possibly, as Düntzer suggests, Goethe took the hint of the scene in which his Faust receives the thanks of the peasantry for the wondrous cures effected by his father and assisted by his own efforts, from the statement that Nostradamus as a young man visited

Provence during the plague which broke out there in 1525, and saved many villagers' lives by his peculiar remedies.

25. *being dead.* See opening Chorus, 22. This power was ascribed to Asclepius (Æsculapius), the mythical father of medicine, whom Zeus struck with lightning for having revived the dead. See Pind. Pyth. iii. 46 seqq.; and compare The Faery Queene, i. 5. 36.

27. *Justinian.* 'Under his reign' (527–565) 'and by his care, the civil jurisprudence was digested in the immortal works of the CODE, the PANDECTS, and the INSTITUTES; the public reason of the Romans has been silently or studiously transfused into the domestic institutions of Europe, and the laws of Justinian still command the respect or obedience of independent nations.' Gibbon, Decline and Fall, c. xliv.

28. *Si una . . . rei, &c.* If one and the same thing is left by will to two persons, one shall [take] the thing, and the other the value of the thing, &c. What the *Institutes* (lib. ii. tit. xx.) say is, that 'si eadem res duobus legata sit,' it is divided between them, in case both take the legacy. But, according to a quotation in the *Digest* (lib. xxx. p. 418, Mommsen) from Paulus, 'si pluribus eadem res legata fuerit,' if this has been done 'separatim,' and if there is no evidence of priority, 'tunc uni pretium, alii ipsa res adsignatur,' the right of choice belonging to the first claimant of the legacy. See also Gaius, lib. ii. § 205.

30. *Exhaereditare . . . nisi, &c.* A father cannot disinherit his son except, &c. This again does not seem a quotation from the Institutes, but with the addition of the word 'nominatim' ('by name') it would express one of the rules of lib. ii. tit. xiii. ('De Exhaeredatione liberorum').

31. *institute.* The 'Institutionum libri iv.' of Justinian, chiefly based on the Institutions of Gaius, were by order of the Emperor compiled by three lawyers (among whom was Tribonian), to the end 'ut sint totius legitimae scientiae prima elementa.' The 'institutions' of law are therefore its principles.

33. *His.* The later quartos have 'this'; but 'his' may be retained as standing for 'its,' a form which only gradually came into use in the Elizabethan age, and is rarely employed by Shakespeare. See Abbott, § 228; and compare x. 30 and also vii. 18, where 'his' and 'her' are used, but where in either case a modern writer would have employed 'its.' In 2 Tamburlaine, v. 3, Marlowe uses 'his' for 'its':

'His subject [i. e. body], not of force enough
To hold the fiery spirit it contains,
Must part, importing *his* impressions,' &c.

34. *external trash,* the outward recompense of money. 'Trash' or 'dross' is the worthless stuff remaining over when the wheat has been

thrashed out; hence 'dross-wheat' for refuse-wheat given to swine. Compare xiii. 97:

'All is dross that is not Helena.'

'Trash' is here used of worthless money, as in Greene's Alphonsus King of Arragon, act iii: 'King Crœsus' trash.' Cassio says, 'Who steals my purse, steals trash'; and compare Friar Bacon, x. 158. In the old play No-Body and Some-Body, l. 1950, the word 'trash' is used of counterfeits of all kinds.

35. *servile and illiberal.* These terms correspond to the Greek *βάναυσος*, which is often rendered in English by 'mechanical,' and thus contrasted with 'liberal,' the term applied to those arts which are not pursued as a trade, as in The Tempest, i. 1. 73:

'For the liberal arts
Without a parallel.'

36. *When all is done*, after all.

37. *Jerome's Bible.* The Vulgate, or Latin translation of the Bible attributed to St. Jerome, by whom the greater part of it was composed (392-404 A. D.). (Goethe's Faust translates the beginning of the Gospel of St. John from the original.) As F. V. Hugo points out, Faustus must be supposed during the whole of this soliloquy to have before him a heap of folios, which he successively takes up and lays down again after having read a few lines in each.

38. *Stipendium peccati mors est*, 'the wages of sin is death.' Romans vi. 23.

42. *there's no truth in us.* A more accurate translation of 1 Epistle of St. John, i. 8, than that in the Authorised Version.

43. *belike*, apparently an abbreviation for 'it may be like,' as is shown by the construction in The Two Gentlemen of Verona, ii. 4. 90:

'Belike that now she hath enfranchised them.'

'May be like' is still a Northamptonshire provincialism.

45. *Che sera, sera.* An older form of the Italian proverb (the motto of the Russell family), 'Che sarà sarà.'

46. *What will be, shall be.* The proper modern English translation of the Italian proverb would be 'What shall be, will be,'—i.e. that which is fixed by fate to happen will happen; or 'what shall be, shall be,'—i. e. that which is fixed by fate to happen will inevitably happen. But the Elizabethan use of 'shall' and 'will' had by no means fixed itself. See Abbott, §§ 315-321, and compare Friar Bacon, xiii. 45, 'one of us will die,' where we should say 'shall.' Faustus' despairing reference to the difficulties of the doctrine of predestination recalls the passage in Chaucer's Troilus and Cresseyde, b. iv, where Troilus repeats the arguments of Boëthius against the freedom of the human will, without reproducing the philosopher's endeavour to solve the problem.

47. *metaphysics of magicians.* Compare the passage in 2 Tamburlaine, iv. 3, describing an ointment distilled by an alchemist:

'In which the essential form of marble stone
Tempered by science metaphysical
And spells of magic from the mouths of spirits,' &c.

49. *Lines . . . characters.* These form the ordinary machinery of conjurations, as described in the spurious fourth Book of the De Occultâ Philosophiâ, of which the first three Books were written by Cornelius Agrippa, and as more briefly enumerated in ch. i. of the Faustbuch; see Introduction, p. lix. The magicians used to draw round themselves 'lines' and 'circles' for protection against the evil spirits—a notion possibly taken from the enclosures which protected courts of justice. 'Scenes' appears to have no special meaning. 'Letters' refers to the magical combinations of letters taken from the several forms of the divine name; see below, sc. iii. 8; 'characters' are here the signs appropriated to good spirits of various kinds, which, according to Pseudo-Agrippa, are used in the formation of '*pentacula*,' the sacred signs which 'are to protect us against evil influence, and tame invidious daemons, and on the other hand to bring beneficent spirits to our aid.'

53. *artizan.* This word, now used only of the handicraftsman or mechanic, was employed as late as the eighteenth century as equivalent to 'artist.' See Johnson's Dictionary.

54. *quiet*, because fixed.

55. *emperors*, a dissyllable.

56. *their several provinces*, the regions of the earth subject to each of them.

58. *his dominion that exceeds in this*, the dominion of him who is paramount in this art, who excels in it. For this use of 'exceed' compare Friar Bacon, ii. 124, and Pericles, ii. 3. 16:

'In framing an artist, art hath thus decreed,
To make some good, but others to exceed;
And you are her labour'd scholar.'

61. *tire.* So the later quartos; quarto of 1604 'trie'; hence Wagner reads 'try.'

Ib. to gain a deity, to gain the divine character belonging to a magician.

63. *The German* (quarto of 1604 'Germaine') *Valdes and Cornelius.* See notes to Dramatis Personae.

66. *conference*, conversation. Compare Chorus before viii, l. 7, x. 82, and xiii. 9.

71. *that*, i.e. the magical book.

74. *Jove.* Here and in iii. 90, and in the Chorus before vii, l. 3, 'Jove' is the God of Christianity. So in Friar Bacon, xvi. 18, Margaret says

that she 'must yield her orisons to mighty Jove'; but she is specially fond of classical phraseology. The use is common in Elizabethan poetry. Compare 2 Tamburlaine, ii. 2, where, to make the confusion complete, it is a Mahometan who says:

'Then, if there be a Christ, as Christians say,
But in their deeds deny him for their Christ,
If he be son to everlasting Jove,' &c.

75. *these elements.* As Dyce points out, 'these' is here and below, v. 117, equivalent to 'the.' 'Not unfrequently in our old writers "these" is little more than redundant,' like the English 'this' formerly, and the French 'ce' still used in the dating of letters and documents, as 'this 27th of March'; compare also the favourite French collocations 'ces dames,' 'ces messieurs,' 'ce 1er Janvier.' 'Those' is similarly used in Friar Bacon, vii. 17.

76. *glutted with conceit of this,* filled with the fancy of attaining to such a power.

78. *Resolve,* satisfy, inform; as again iii. 101 and vi. 64; and Friar Bacon, ii. 46, 'resolve you' = be satisfied or assured. Compare also The Jew of Malta, ii. 2:

'Oh, 'tis the custom, then I am resolved';

and A Pleasant Comedie of Faire Em, iii. 8. 729:

'First, what I am I know you are resolv'd,
For that my friend has let you t' understand,' &c.

81. *orient pearl,* bright, shining pearl. A favourite phrase of both Marlowe (see 2 Tamburlaine, i. 3; The Jew of Malta, i. 1, and iv. 1) and Shakespeare (see A Midsummer Night's Dream, iv. 1. 59, and Antony and Cleopatra, i. 5. 41, and The Passionate Pilgrim, x). In Venus and Adonis, 981, a tear is called 'an orient drop,' and in Hero and Leander, ii. *ad fin.*, from Hero's countenance might be seen

'A kind of twilight break, and through the air,
As from an orient cloud, glimps'd here and there.'

82. *the new-found world,* America.

83. *delicates,* delicacies; so 'knightly delicates' in Faire Em, ii. 2. 119; and 'a prince's delicates' in 3 Henry VI, ii. 5. 51. The abbreviation 'cates' (1 Tamburlaine, iv. 4, and 1 Henry IV, iii. 1. 163) is still used, in this sense; in Friar Bacon it is so used, ix. 261, but also of food which is the reverse of delicate in the same scene, 237 and 248.

86. *I'll have . . . brass,* as Friar Bacon designed to wall England. See as to this line Introduction, p. vi.

87. *And make . . . Wittenberg.* To 'circle' is to 'encircle'; so Friar Bacon, xvi. 67; and constantly in Shakespeare, as in Richard III, iv. 4. 382, of the crown:

'The imperial metal, circling now thy brow.'

Wittenberg (see opening Chorus, 13) is on the Elbe; but it seems idle to enquire whether Marlowe thought it lay on the Rhine, which he correctly designates as 'swift.' (Wagner compares 'the cold, swift-running Rhyn' in Chapman's Alphonsus, Emperor of Germany, act iv. Whether Marlowe and Chapman thus described the Rhine from personal observation, must in either case be left an open question; it seems more probable in the latter case than in the former: in the Netherlands, where Marlowe possibly had been, the Rhine is not swift.) The power of producing artificial torrents of water, and thus deceiving besieging armies, was pretended to by mediaeval magicians; G. v. Loeper, in commenting on a passage in Part ii. of Goethe's Faust, where the notion is made use of, cites a narrative of the siege of Città di Castello in 1474, according to which the commander of the besieged city declined the assistance of the rain-makers as of impious persons. Compare as to the power of magic over the waters of the earth, l. 142, and iii. 39.

88. *the public schools*, the University class-rooms, as the term is still used at the English Universities. In Friar Bacon, ix. 1, the term 'schools' is applied to the buildings of the University of Oxford in general; and, ib. 17, the 'Belgic schools' are the Universities of the Low Countries.

Ib. silk, Dyce's conjecture for 'skill,' the reading of all the quartos. Compare 1 Tamburlaine, iv. 2:

'The townsmen mask in silk and cloth of gold.'

89. *Wherewith . . . bravely clad.* 'Brave' is fine; 'bravery,' fine dress; and 'to brave,' to make fine. See for instance the punning passage in The Taming of the Shrew, iv. 3. 125. Silk was considered a reprehensible luxury in persons not belonging to the upper or wealthier classes, as late as the reign of Philip and Mary (see the sumptuary law cited by Fairholt, Costume in England, p. 200); and in Thynne's Debate between Pride and Lowliness (cited ib. p. 211) these abstractions are typified under the forms, the latter of a pair of cloth breeches 'withouten pride and stitche,' the former of a pair

'Of velvet very fine,
The neather stockes of pure Granada silke,
Such as came never upon legges of myne.'

For students to 'brave it' in silk was particularly heinous. Simplicity of apparel was enjoined in both the English and German Universities; and as for academical dress, the gowns even of fellow-commoners must at Oxford at this day, according to a University statute, be 'ex quovis panno nigro *non serico* confectae.'

91. *chase the Prince of Parma from our land*, i.e. the Empire, of which the Netherlands formed part till the Peace of Westphalia in 1648. Alexander Farnese, Prince (from 1586 Duke) of Parma, arrived in the Netherlands as governor-general in 1579, and remained there

(with the exception of a campaign in France) till his death in 1592. To him was due the re-establishment of the power of Spain in Flanders and in the whole of what afterwards remained the Spanish Netherlands.

92. *our*; the later quartos have 'the'; but the term is not necessarily here used technically of the Provinces of the Netherlands. Compare above, 56.

93. *the brunt of war*, the heat of war. 'Brunt' is another form of burnt; compare German brunst, and the twin A.-S. forms byrnan and brinnan. The word is only now used in the phrase 'to bear' or 'bide the brunt,' i.e. the heat of the fight. The latter form of the phrase occurs in Friar Bacon, iv. 19; 1 Tamburlaine, i. 2; and twice in Peele's Sir Clyomon and Sir Clamydes. In the Promptorium Parvulorum 'brunt' translates 'impetus'; and the word is used in the sense of a blow in the Early English Alliterative Poems edited by Morris (A. 174):

'Baysment gef myn hert a brunt.'

94. *the fiery keel at Antwerp's bridge*, the 'demon fire-ship,' as it was called by the Spaniards, which effected a breach in Parma's famous bridge across the Scheldt during the siege of Antwerp (July 1584–August 1585), by which exploit, but for the incompetency of the Dutch admiral and the prompt energy of Parma, the great work of the latter might have been annihilated. For a full account of Gianibelli's famous 'floating marine volcanos,' and of the course and result of the enterprise, see Motley's History of the United Netherlands, i. 189–203. 'The image of the Antwerp devil-ships,' says Motley, 'imprinted itself indelibly upon the Spanish mind, as of something preternatural, with which human valour could only contend at a disadvantage; and a day was not very far distant—one of the memorable days of the world's history, big with the fate of England, Spain, Holland, and all Christendom—when the sight of a half-dozen blazing vessels, and the cry of "the Antwerp fire-ships" was to decide the issue of a most momentous enterprise.' (As to the indignation excited by the treatment of Antwerp after its reduction, see The Faerie Queene, v. 10. 25 seqq.; the play called A Larum for London, or The Seige of Antwerp, in which, according to a MS. note in Mr. Collier's copy, 'our famous Marloe had a hand,' treats of the 'Spanish Fury' of 1576.)

95. *to invent.* For the insertion of 'to' see Abbott, § 349; and compare xiii. 59.

Ib. Faustus' design to perform great military achievements by the aid of spirits is in accordance with mediaeval, and even later legends. The victory of Charles V at Pavia was said to have been brought about by a conjuror; the Thirty Years' War has many such stories; Oliver Cromwell (according to the title of a tract of 1720) concluded a 'Compact with the Devil for seven years, on the Day in which he gain'd the Battle of Worcester;' and the victories under Lewis XIV of the Duke of Luxemburg were similarly accounted for. 'Dialogues of the Dead' between the last-named and Doctor John Faust were published at Leipzig in 1733.

F. Notter, in a note of extreme length on the whole of this passage, inclines to consider the reference to Parma and the Spanish war in the Netherlands an insertion of later date, possibly the 'adycyons' for which Henslowe in his Diary notes having paid Dekker on December 20th, 1597. In the October preceding Queen Elizabeth had asked subsidies from Parliament to enable her to ward off Philip II of Spain's designs against the religion, liberty, and independence of England. This view Notter supports by the following arguments among others:—In the rest of the play there is no mention of the war, upon influencing the course of which Faustus here shows himself so specially intent. Again, l. 86 is clearly borrowed from Friar Bacon, xi. 22, which was certainly produced *after* Dr. Faustus. And the Faustbuch which Marlowe so closely follows, contains a passage (c. xxvi) narrating how Faustus travelled on Mephistophiles, changed into a winged horse, from Wittenberg to Holland, Zealand, Brabant, and Flanders—so that the writer whom Marlowe had before him was well aware of the fact that Wittenberg was not, as the present passage seems to imply, in the Netherlands.—Though it may be questioned whether so much is actually implied by our text, the juxtaposition is certainly at least suspicious. Wittenberg, as Notter points out, was taken by the Spaniards in the Smalcaldic War (1547); and in an addition to the Faustbuch (in the second edition of 1587; Scheible, Kloster, ii. 1041) it is related that Doctor Faustus distinguished himself as an artilleryman when in a castle 'besieged by the Emperor Charles's Spanish soldiery.' Düntzer's view, that the 'Prince of Parma' is not meant for Alexander Farnese, but for the Duke who was reigning at the time when the passage was written, is a superfluous piece of correctness.

101. *only . . . fantasy.* Dyce conjectures 'alone' for 'only.'

102. *That will receive no object; for my head.* This is clearly the correct interpunctuation, and not that of the quarto of 1604: 'That will receive no object for my head.' The meaning must be, 'that will not receive anything offered from without.' But this and the preceding line are probably corrupt, and are omitted, with that which follows, in the quarto of 1616.

107. This line is also omitted in the later quartos.

Ib. vile, spelt 'vild' in the old editions, which have the same spelling iv. 56; xiii. 42, and Friar Bacon, ix. 70. According to Dyce, in the first folio of Shakespeare we sometimes find 'vild,' and sometimes 'vile.' 'Vild' also occurs in Spenser. The addition of a *d* is more usual in English to an *n* terminating syllables than to other liquids (compare lawnd = lawn, Friar Bacon, i. 3; and bands = bans, *ib.* vi. 127), but it is also made to *r* in afford (O. Fr. afeurrer from M. Lat. aforare, N. Fr. afforer). See Mätzner, Englische Grammatik, i. 178; and compare Morris, English Accidence, 65.

111. *Gravell'd*, puzzled, brought to a stop. Compare As You Like It, iv. 1. 74, and Andromana, or The Merchant's Wife, i. 3, where it clearly means 'stuck fast': 'Yet the prince is so far gravell'd in her affection.'

112. *the flowering pride*, the 'flos juventutis' of the students.

114. *sweet Musaeus when he came to hell.* According to F. V. Hugo, 'Marlowe's classical reminiscences deceive him. It is not Musaeus who descended to the infernal regions, but Orpheus. The error is curious on the part of the translator of Hero and Leander' (of which poem Musaeus, or rather a Pseudo-Musaeus, was the author). It is however the translator who is at fault. Marlowe who, as Miss Lee says, 'knew his Virgil from cover to cover,' had in his mind the passage in the Aeneid, vi. 666, where the Sibyl addresses the crowd in the 'happy fields' of the lower regions:

'Musaeum ante omnis: medium nam plurima turba
Hunc habet, atque humeris exstantem suscipit altis.'

Musaeus was as a poet closely associated with the Eleusinian Mysteries, of which several poems ascribed to him treat; he was sometimes called the son or scholar of Orpheus, with whom he was jointly celebrated by later poets.

115. *Agrippa.* See CORNELIUS in Dramatis Personae.

116. *shadows* (unnecessarily altered to 'shadow' in the later quartos), the shadows raised by Agrippa. In Bk. i. of his work De Occultâ Philosophiâ, Agrippa gives directions for the operations of sciomancy (see note to opening Chorus, 25).

119. *Indian Moors.* In unconscious accordance with the probable etymology of the word, the term 'Moors' (properly applicable to the Saracens of Africa, whence they conquered Spain) was used generally of members of dark-coloured races, and so survives in the popular word 'blackamoor.' Shakespeare makes no distinction between 'moor' and 'negro.' Here the term refers to the dark-coloured races of the New World.

120. *the subjects of every element.* The later quartos read 'spirits' for 'subjects,' which term appears to signify the bodily forms taken by the spirits belonging to the several elements (those belonging to the elements of fire and earth are discussed in Friar Bacon, ix. 45 seqq.). Marlowe uses the word 'subject' to signify 'bodily form' or 'body' in 2 Tamburlaine, v. 3:

'Your soul gives essence to our wretched subjects';

and again in the same scene:

'This subject, not of force enough
To hold the fiery spirit it contains.'

122. *Like lions.* Spirits occasionally made their appearance in the shape of wild animals; compare Burton's Anatomy of Melancholy, I. ii. 1. 2, 'Digression of Spirits,' where reference is made to the text in 1 Epistle of St. Peter, v. 8. So the shape assumed by Belial in the Faustbuch (ch. xxiii) is that of 'a hairy and quite coalblack bear,' while the inferior spirits appear 'in the same shape as unreasoning animals,' including bears, wolves, and buffaloes. 'Tregetoures,' according to Chaucer's The Frankeleine's Tale, 11458, could among other apparitions make 'a grim leoun' 'seme come.' On the other hand, 'lions' is the name given in one of the magical books (Commentary of Psellus on the Magic Oracles of Zoroaster, Scheible, Kloster, iii. 399) to apparitions in the 'circle of Hecate,' connected with the sign of the Lion in the Zodiac.

123. *Like Almain rutters with their horsemen's staves.* Compare the line occurring twice in 1 Tamburlaine, i. 1:

'Sclavonians, Almains, Rutters, Muffs and Danes.'

'Almain' (Allemand) is a common Elizabethan equivalent for 'German'; so in Friar Bacon, vii. 6 and 14, the German Emperor is called 'the Almain monarch' and 'the Almain emperor'; and compare Othello, ii. 3. 86. 'Almain rutters' are German horsemen (Reuter, Reiter, a word which the French corrupted into reître or rêtre). The lance, the distinctive weapon of the 'hommes d'armes' and of the chivalry of the Middle Ages in general, fell into disrepute towards the close of the sixteenth century, and was only partially adopted by the German cavalry-regiments formed already under Charles V on the model of the 'Landsknechte' of Maximilian I—the

'Stout lanciers of Germany,
The strength and sinews of the Imperial host,'

mentioned in 2 Tamburlaine, i. 1. The German horsemen, and afterwards the French cuirassiers or 'reîtres,' soon exchanged their staves for pistols. In England, as we learn from Harrison's Description, ii. 16, travellers sometimes carried 'long staves of 12 or 13 feet with a pike of 12 inches at the end,' but 'a case of dags or pistols' was also found to be desirable. Hence the 'staves' in our passage may be lances, or pikes.

124. *Lapland giants.* Compare 2 Tamburlaine, i. 1:

'From the shortest northern parallel
Vast Grantland' [Greenland], 'compassed with the Frozen Sea,
(Inhabited with tall and sturdy men,
Giants as big as hugy Polypheme).'

Lapland is mentioned as a home of monsters in Jonson's Underwoods, xvi; and Burton, in the chapter cited above, speaks of Lapland as the familiar abode of witches. A 'Finnkona' is equivalent to a witch in Norse tales.

In the Life and Death of Christoph Wagner (c. xxxiii) it is related how he was by the spirit Auerhan conducted into Lapland, a country of which the inhabitants 'are like the Devil himself,' but in which he does not appear to have met with any giants.

126. *Shadowing*. If this was really what Marlowe wrote, it must mean, 'shadowing or imaging forth.' Compare 'shadowing passion,' Othello, iv. 1. 42, in the sense of a passion full of shapes and images.

127. *Than have the*. This is the reading of the quarto of 1616; the earlier quartos have 'than in their,' for which Wagner conjectures 'than's in the.'

128. *argosies*. This favourite Elizabethan word is derived from the M. Lat. 'argis,' a vessel of heavy burden, which again is derived from the name of the famous mythical ship Argo.

129, 130. *And from America . . . Philip's treasury*. The reference is to the annual plate-fleet upon which English patriots so long cast covetous eyes, which nearly fell into the hands of Ralegh and his companions after the raid upon Cadiz in 1596 (see the lines concerning this expedition to 'th' Iberian city' upon which 'golden-finger'd India had bestowed such wealth' in Chapman's Third Sestiad of Hero and Leander), and which at a later date (1628) it was the good fortune of a Dutch mariner actually to capture. Elsewhere, in 2 Tamburlaine, i. 2, Marlowe speaks of

> 'Armados from the coasts of Spain
> Fraughted with gold of rich America'—

and it is well known how vast an income Spain derived from her American possessions during the reign of Philip II, although the close of that reign left her in a condition of national bankruptcy.—The allusions to the 'golden fleece' which Iason brought from Colchos are frequent in our early literature, in which the story had been told by Chaucer, Gower and Lydgate, before Caxton printed his 'boke of the hoole lyf of Jason,' translated from the French of Raoul le Fevre; Marlowe alludes to it in 1 Tamburlaine, iv. 4, and in The Jew of Malta, iv. 4.—Philip II is called 'old Philip' with no special reference to his age, but because his name was so familiar to English ears; compare 'old Nick.'

133. *object it not*, do not suggest the objection 'if I will be resolute.'

137. *Enrich'd with tongues*. 'The Latin tongue was, in the Middle Ages, accounted the language of spirits and ghosts. A certain degree of preliminary instruction was indispensable for intercourse with the spiritual world; accordingly in Hamlet (i. 1. 42) when the Ghost appears, Marcellus says to Horatio:

"Thou art a scholar; speak to it, Horatio."

Compare also Fletcher and Shirley's The Night-Walker (ii. 2), where on beholding a supposed apparition, Toby proposes to

"Call the butler up, for he speaks Latin,
And that will daunt the devil."

Thus it is in Latin that Faustus summons Mephistophiles.' (From a note by F. V. Hugo.)

Ib. well seen in minerals, well versed in the knowledge of minerals (for chemical purposes). The 'Opus naturarum' of Albertus Magnus contains books on minerals, a subject not treated by Aristotle, of the commentaries on whom the work forms part.—'Well seen' (compare A Taming of the Shrew, i. 2. 135: 'a schoolmaster well seen in music') would seem to have the same meaning as the Latin 'spectatus,'—of proved capacity, of a high reputation.

138. *principles*, rudiments ('principia'), that which lies at the root of magic. Compare 'principles of art,' Friar Bacon, ix. 7. Not here used in the technical sense in which the word was employed in 'Zoroastrian' magic.

139. *renown'd* (Fr. renommé). The word is frequently thus spelt in the old editions of Marlowe's Tamburlaine, and also in other old plays.

140. *the Delphian oracle*, also referred to in Friar Bacon, ii. 18.

142. *they can dry the sea.* The redemption of a large tract of land from the sea is the great work the coming results of which Goethe's Faust (Part ii. act v) contemplates with joyful pride at the moment when his end is approaching.

143. *the treasure of all foreign wrecks.* Wagner points out that 'in those days Venetian, Portuguese and Spanish ships used to carry greater treasures and freights of higher value than the English.'

144. *all the wealth.* The power of discovering treasures hidden in the earth was naturally ascribed to magicians (see Dousterswivel in The Antiquary); and in the Faustbuch (ch. lix) it is related how Faustus found in an ancient ruined chapel near Wittenberg (which has been identified with a chapel pulled down by the Elector John Frederick the Magnanimous in 1542), 'guarded by an ugly big worm,' a heap of coals which in his house turned to silver and gold, 'valued at some thousand florins.' Teutonic mythology abounds in legends of treasures guarded by serpents and dragons; hence gold was poetically called 'Wurmbett' (worm- or snake's-bed) or 'Wurmbettsfeuer' (fire). Compare the A.-S. 'wyrmhord' for 'treasure.'

145. *massy.* Shakespeare uses this word of metals; hence it is here used of the metal-bearing earth. It is a favourite adjective of Marlowe's; compare 1 Tamburlaine, ii. 7; 2 Tamburlaine, i. 1; iv. 3; v. 3; it also

occurs in Friar Bacon, ix. 56. For similar formations from nouns with the suffix *y* see Abbott, § 450. In our play we have 'pitchy,' iii. 4, which also occurs in 2 Tamburlaine, v. 3; and 'yoky,' Chorus before sc. vii. l. 6. The old play of Edward III, ii. 2, has 'helly.' From adjectives, Marlowe has the formations 'steepy' in 'The Passionate Shepherd to his Love,' 'hugy' 1 Tamburlaine, iii. 3; from a verb, 'jetty' 1 Tamburlaine, iv. 1.

149. *lusty*. This epithet, which means 'pleasant,' is exchanged in the quarto of 1609 for 'little,' and in that of 1616 for 'bushy.' Wagner unnecessarily conjectures 'hidden.'

150. *possession*, should be pronounced as a word of four syllables, like 'companions' in Chorus before viii. line 5. Compare 'exhalátións,' 1 Tamburlaine, i. 2; 'satisfáctión,' *ib.* ii. 3.

152. *wise Bacon*. See Introduction, pp. xviii. seqq.

Ib. Albanus. So all the quartos; but following the correction of 'I. M.' in the Gentleman's Magazine for Jan. 1841, Dyce and all subsequent editors read 'Albertus.' It is at the same time open to question whether Marlowe did not, as Düntzer suggests, refer to Pietro d'Abano (Petrus de Apono), an Italian physician and alchemist who narrowly escaped burning by the Inquisition. He was born about 1250 and died about 1316, and wrote a work called Conciliator Differentiarum Philosophorum et Medicorum. Of a 'Heptameron, or Elements of Magic' ascribed to him a translation is printed in Schieble, Kloster, iii. 591 seqq.

If, on the other hand, Marlowe wrote or meant 'Albertus,' the conjunction of this name with that of Bacon may have suggested itself from the circumstance, that both Albertus Magnus and Roger Bacon were credited with the inventions of brazen heads which could speak. (See Introduction, pp. xxiv. seqq.) 'Albertus Magnus' (Albrecht von Bollstädt) was born in 1193 of knightly parents at Lauingen in Suabia. After studying for several years at Padua, he entered the Dominican Order, in whose service he taught monastic schools at Cologne (where Thomas Aquinas was his pupil) and in other German towns. His reputation as a teacher however reached its greatest height at Paris, whence he afterwards returned to Germany. After being elected Provincial of his Order for Germany in 1254 he for a time held the see of Ratisbon: and after an active life as a teacher, writer, and ecclesiastical politician, died at Cologne in 1280. Two years before his death he had ceased to teach, his memory having failed him; and from this circumstance arose the legend that the Blessed Virgin had promised shortly before his death to take from him all secular learning, so that his last hour might find him restored to childlike faith. He was afterwards canonised, and remains a special saint of the Dominicans. His works, which in the Lyons edition fill

21 folios, comprise voluminous commentaries on Aristotle and on the Old and New Testament; he was equally eminent as a theologian and as a scientific enquirer, in which latter capacity he acquired the title of 'doctor universalis.' The fame of his genuine works was however far surpassed by that of the writings falsely ascribed to him in subsequent centuries, such as the 'Liber aggregationis s. liber secretorum Alberti Magni de virtutibus herbarum lapidum et animalium quorundam,' and the treatise 'de mirabilibus mundi.' It was on the basis of these that the popular notion of Albertus Magnus in the later Middle Ages was built up. (Abridged from v. Hertling.)

153. *the Hebrew Psalter.* 'To cite Bealphares (proved the noblest carrier that ever did serve any man upon earth) you must read the 22. and 51. Psalms all over; or else rehearse them by heart; for these are accounted necessary,' &c. Scot's Discovery of Witchcraft, bk. xv. ch. 14. Conjuration by the use of the Psalms of David was one of the mysteries, upon which whole volumes were written, of the Hebrew Cabbalah. See H. Morley, Life of Cornelius Agrippa, i. 80.

Ib. and New Testament. The use of the first verses of the Gospel of St. John in conjurations is constantly recommended in the handbooks of magic; in the Life of Wagner, c. xxv, the spirit Auerhan complains that in conjurations for molesting such spirits as himself, for finding treasures, and for expelling spirits, the Gospel of St. John and the Psalms are wont to be 'misused.'

154. *whatsoever else.* Loose construction for 'of whatsoever else.' For similar omissions of prepositions see Abbott, § 200.

156. *the words of art,* with which to conjure.

157. *all . . . learn'd,* nominative absolute; see Abbott, § 376.

160. *perfecter.* This comparative occurs in Coriolanus, ii. 1. 90, and the superlative 'perfectest' in Macbeth, i. 5. 2. For other examples of the use of these inflexions where we now generally use 'more' and 'most' see Abbott, §§ 7 and 9. Compare 'beautifulest,' 'admirablest,' xiii. 10 and 12.

161. *after meat.* 'Meat' is used in the sense of dinner or food generally (compare vii. 69, xii. 11); as in the common phrase 'grace before meat.'

162. *canvass.* 'To canvass a matter is a metaphor taken from sifting a substance through canvass' (Fr. canevas, Lat. cannabis, cannabus, hemp), 'and the verb "sift" itself is used in like manner for examining a matter thoroughly to the very grounds.' Wedgwood.

Ib. quiddity, a scholastic term like quantity, quality. It was used for the predicables (genus and species) which answer to the question 'quid est'; and was equivalent to 'essentia,' a translation of the Aristotelian τὸ τί ἦν εἶναι. Compare The Massacre at Paris, i. 8:

'Excepting against doctors' actions
And *ipse dixi* with this quiddity:
Argumentum testimonii est inartificiale.'

Shakespeare uses both the forms *quiddities* and *quiddits*, the latter of which is also applied to lawyers' quibbles in Dekker's The Seven Deadly Sinnes of London. The passage in Hudibras, Part i. canto i, is well known:

'He could reduce all things to acts,
And knew their natures and abstracts,
Where entity and quiddity
The ghost of defunct bodies fly.'

164. *therefore*, for it. So in A Midsummer Night's Dream, iii. 2. 78:

'An if I could, what should I get therefore?'

Scene II.

2. *sic probo*, doubtless an expression usual in scholastic disputations.

4. *his boy*, servant; compare Morris, English Accidence, 84. See WAGNER in Dramatis Personae.

5. *sirrah*. As to the derivation of this form see Abbott, § 378. 'The *er final* seems to have been sometimes pronounced with a kind of "burr," which produced the effect of an additional syllable; just as "sirrah" is another and more vehement form of "sir."' The suggested derivation of the form from a compound 'sir-ha!' or 'sir-ho!' is accordingly unnecessary; while that from the Irish sirreach (poor, sorry, lean) may be rejected.

8. *that follows not*, as a logical consequence or conclusion; see l. 11 below. Compare The Jew of Malta, ii. 2: 'This follows well'; and Richard III, i. 1. 59:

'And, for my name of George begins with G,
It follows in his thought that I am he.'

12. *licentiates*. 'The Degree of a Licentiate is not in use in either of our two Universities, so called from the word *Licentia*, which is given to a person of this degree to ascend to a Doctor's or Master's at his pleasure; wherefore a very strict and rigorous examination is requir'd for the same, since the highest Degree in Learning follows thereupon.' Ayliffe, The Antient and Present State of the University of Oxford (1723), ii. 195. The grade of 'lic. theol.' is I believe still granted in Germany.

Ib. stand upon 't, insist upon it. Compare 2 Henry VI, iii. 1. 261:

'And do not stand on quillets how to slay him.'

15. *on 't*. 'On' is frequently used for 'of,' see Abbott, § 181, and compare v. 111; or for 'out of,' compare xi. 32; xii. 15. On the other hand, 'of' is used where we should use 'on' in vi. 34, 112, in the

stage-direction after vii. 82, and in the Chorus before sc. viii, ll. 7 and 9; and where we should use 'in,' in the Chorus before sc. vii, l. 10. The free interchange between 'on' and 'of' is well exemplified by the following passage in Faire Em, sc. xvii. (1388–1390):

'*Mount.* And I say *this:* and thereof will I lay an hundred pound.
Val. And I say *this:* whereon I'll lay as much.'

17. *Ask my fellow if I be a thief.* His evidence is worthless, for he is no better than I am.

21. *corpus naturale . . mobile.* This seems to be a reminiscence of Ramist logic (compare note on i. 7). 'Mobile' is commonly used as the 'proprium' of 'corpus' in the 'Tree' of Porphyry.

24. *forty foot.* Some words expressive of quality, mass or weight, are used in the same form in the singular as in the plural. Many of these were originally neuter and flexionless in the plural. See Morris, English Accidence, §§ 81 and 82; and compare, among other examples, The Tempest, i. 2. 396:

'Full fathom five they father lies';

and *ib.* 53:

'Twelve year since
Thy father was the Duke of Milan.'

Compare also the singular use of 'million,' Friar Bacon, i. 160.

Ib. the place of execution, viz. the dining-room of Faustus, 'where execution is done upon meat and drink,' the word being immediately afterwards interpreted in its more common sense. (From Wagner's note.)

26. *set my countenance like a precisian.* A 'precisian' is an old term for a Puritan; compare a passage cited by R. Simpson from A Merry Knack to know a Knave, one of the series of plays against the Puritans and Martinists which began in the year 1589:

'Thus preach we still unto our breth-e-ren,
Though in our heart we never mean the thing,
Thus do we blind the world with holiness,
And so by that are termed pure Precisians.'

In The Jew of Malta, i. 2, Barabas when sending his daughter into a nunnery, bids her be

'So precise
As they may think it done of holiness.'

Compare 1 Henry VI, v. 4. 67:

'Is all your strict preciseness come to this?'

The term was afterwards in constant use; see the passages in Nares, and especially Sir Thomas Overbury's 'character' of 'a Precisian' there referred to; compare also a passage cited in the New Shakspere Society's Transactions, 1875-6, p. 458, from R. Bernard's 'Terence in English,' ed. 1607 (first edition 1598): '*P. dignus es cum tua religione odio; nodum in scirpo quaeris.* You are well worthie to be hated for your peevish preciseness: you make a doubt, where all is as plaine as a pike staffe, you seeke a knot in a bulrush, in which is never any at all;' and Field's Amends for Ladies, iii. 3: 'Precise and learned Princox, dost not thou go to Blackfriars?' Marlowe speaks of 'a bashful Puritan' in Edward II, v. 4, and the French Protestants are called 'Puritans' in The Massacre at Paris, ii. 4 and 6. I see no reason for supposing from this allusion that the present scene is a later 'addition.'

29. *this wine.* Wagner must be supposed to be carrying wine in his hands.

Ib. it would. So in the quarto of 1604. As to such insertions of the pronoun (more usual after proper than after common nouns) see Abbott, §§ 242, 243.

31. *my dear brethren, my dear brethren!* The later quartos omit this repetition, which is however quite in character.

33. *they two.* This use of the personal pronoun for the demonstrative 'those' (compare the vulgarism 'them two') is most common in constructions 'where the relative is omitted between pronominal antecedent and a prepositional phrase, especially where locality is predicated,' as 'they in France,' 'he at the gate.' Abbott, § 245; compare also St. Matthew's Gospel, xix. 5 and xxi. 31, for the phrases 'they twain' and 'them twain'; and 'hie þry' (they three) in the A.-S. version of Daniel, 361.

35. *allied to me,* connected with me as a friend or acquaintance. So Hen. VIII, i. 1. 61:

'Neither allied
To eminent assistants.'

37. *the Rector,* of the University: the title still used in Germany and Scotland.

39. *I fear me.* Compare below, x. 25; and so in Friar Bacon, x. 75, 'counsel me' = take counsel with myself. For examples of words now used intransitively used reflexively by Shakespeare see Abbott, § 296.

Scene III.

Compare with this scene the extracts from the Faustbuch, Introduction, pp. lx-lxiii.—Goethe and Byron may be said to have written the corresponding scenes of their tragedies independently. Ticknor, History of Spanish Literature, ii. 108, considers that a to some extent analogous scene in act ii. of the Numancia of Cervantes surpasses the incantations of Marlowe's Faustus in dignity.

2. *Orion's drizzling look.* Compare σθένος ὄμβριμον Ὠρίωνος, Hesiod, Op. Di., 619; 'nimbosus O.,' Verg. Æn. i. 535; 'aquosus O.,' *ib.* iv. 52; see also *ib.* x. 763–766, and Hor. Od., i. 28. 21–22 and *ib.* iii. 27. 17–18. In Dido Queen of Carthage, i. 2, Marlowe speaks of 'gloomy O.'; see also Paradise Lost, i. 305–306. Orion, says Preller, is 'the Wild Huntsman' of the Greek heavens, a conception no doubt suggested by the appearance of this constellation at the beginning of winter, when it rises in the evening and does not set till early morning.

3. *th' antarctic world.* 'Antarctic' (quarto of 1604: 'antartike') means 'opposed to the north,' 'southern.' Compare 1 Tamburlaine, iv. 4:

'We mean to travel to the Antarctick pole';

and 2 Tamburlaine, v. 3:

'From the Antartic Pole eastward behold
As much more land, which never was described.'

See also Paradise Lost, ix. 79. Brazil was called 'Antarctic France' by Protestant emigrants sent out by Coligny to that colony.—In Hom. Od. v. 274 Arctos 'looks at' or 'observes' Orion.

4. *the welkin,* the sky, lit. the clouds (A.-S. wolcn, O. E. wolcen, welkin). Compare 1 Tamburlaine, iv. 2:

'As when a fiery exhalation,
Wrapt in the bowels of a freezing cloud,
Fighting for passage, makes the welkin crack.'

Ib. pitchy, dark as pitch. See i. 145.

6. *hest,* behest. A.-S. hæs, a command, and hætan, to command; and compare German heissen, Geheiss.

8, 9. *Within this . . . anagrammatiz'd* (quarto of 1604: 'and Agramithist'). An 'anagram' is defined by Johnson as 'a conceit arising from the letters of a name transposed.' This exercise of ingenuity, which has long sunk into a harmless amusement ('mild anagram,' as Dryden calls what Ben Jonson termed 'hard trifles') played a most significant part in the labyrinthine mysteries of the Hebrew Cabbalah, of which the principles but not the details were accepted by Christian scholars such as Reuchten and Agrippa. Here, 'of all names by which wonders can be wrought, the Mirific Word of Words, the concealed name of God, —the Schem-hammaphorash' or Semiphoras, was the chief. See Morley, *u. s.*, i. 78. This mystic name of seventy-two letters was formed by an 'extracted' collection of seventy-two names of God and the angels, 'springing as branches from a tree' from the name Jehovah, of which the true pronunciation was itself accounted a holy secret concealed from men. Of the seventy-two names we read that 'denotant semper Nomen Dei, sive legantur a principio, fine' [seu fine?] 'vel a dextris aut sinistris, suntque ingentis virtutis.' See tractates and diagrams giving more details on the subject than it is easy to follow in Scheible, Kloster, iii.

289 seqq. Compare Friar Bacon, sc. xiii. 93 seqq., where some of the forms of the Divine Name used in the magic charms are mentioned.

10. *The breviated names of holy saints* (later quartos, 'th' abbreviated,' but the form 'breviated' is quite in Marlowe's fashion). R. Scot, in his Discourse of Divels and Spirits, c. xxiv, has some caustic remarks on the exorcising and other gifts ascribed to the saints of the Roman calendar. The 'elect souls of the blest' formed part of one of the 'hierarchies' of the heavenly system to which appeal was made in magic.

11. *every adjunct to the heavens*, every star joined to, or suspended in the heavens.

12. *characters of signs and erring stars*, symbols (conventional in magic, astrology, and astronomy) of the signs of the Zodiac and the planets (πλανήτης, from πλανᾶσθαι, to wander). So in Hamlet ghosts are spoken of, i. 1. 154, as 'extravagant and erring' spirits. Compare v. 167 and vi. 44; and Tomkis's Albumazar, i. 1:

> 'Your patron Mercury, in his mysterious character,
> Holds all the marks of the other wanderers.'

See R. Scot's Discovery of Witchcraft, bk. xv. ch. 6: 'The names of the Planets, their characters, together with the twelve signs of the Zodiake, their dispositions, aspects, and government,' &c.; and in Arbatel de Magia Veterum (Scheible, Kloster, iii. 232) the characters, with the corresponding magical names, of the twelve 'signa' and of the seven planets, the latter of whom represent the seven angels standing before the throne of God, but likewise appear to correspond to the seven ruling spirits of the firmament (whose names and 'characters' are given *ib.* pp. 243 seqq.).

16–24. *Sint mihi . . . Mephistophilis!* 'May the gods of Acheron' (the infernal powers) 'be propitious to me! May the threefold deity of Jehovah prevail! Spirits of the fire, the air and the water, hail! Belzebub prince of the East, monarch of burning hell, and Demogorgon, we propitiate ye, that Mephistophiles may appear and arise . . . .: by Jehovah, Gehenna, and the consecrated water which I now pour, and by the sign of the cross which I now make, and by our prayers, may Mephistophilis whom we summon now arise!'

In this passage the words 'quod tumeraris' (an impossible form) are an apparently hopeless corruption. The later quartos have: 'surgat Mephistophilis Dragon, quod tumeraris.' Mr. J. Crossley proposed (rejecting the word 'Dragon') to read 'quod tu mandares' (as a clause governing the previous one; but, as Dyce points out, the 'tu' does not agree with the preceding 'vos'); Mitford suggested 'surgat Mephistophiles, per Dragon (or Dagon), quod numen est aëris'; Wagner, 'Mephistophiles qui arbiter est aëris;' Düntzer (I think) 'quod nominaris.' Further on, the first two quartos read 'dicatis,' which Wagner seems not quite willing to consider impossible as joined with 'nobis'; and F. V. Hugo boldly corrects 'nostris dictatis.' 'Dicatus' is the reading of two of the later quartos. As to the earlier *crux*, I can suggest no solution, and would rather take refuge in the saying of Bodinus (quoted by v. Loepell) that 'it is a principle of magic for unintelligible words to have more force than intelligible.'

17. *Orientis princeps Belzebub.* See LUCIFER in Dramatis Personae.

18. *Demogorgon.* This evil spirit has an extensive literary reputation. He is thought to be alluded to by Lucan (Pharsal. vi. 744) and by Statius. The first writer who is said to have distinctly named him is Lactantius, a Christian writer of the fourth century. He is stated to be mentioned by Boccaccio, Bojardo, Tasso and Ariosto (Orlando Furioso, xlvii. 4). Marlowe speaks of 'Gorgon prince of hell' in 1 Tamburlaine, iv. 1; Greene of 'Demogorgon, master of the fates,' in Friar Bacon, xi. 110, and of 'Demogorgon ruler of the fates' in Orlando Furioso. Spenser, in the Faerie Queene, i. 1. 37, describes Archimago as

> 'A bold bad man! that dar'd to call by name
> Great Gorgon, prince of darkness and dead night,
> At which Cocytus quakes, and Styx is put to flight';

and Milton, Paradise Lost, ii. 964, introduces 'the dreaded name of Demogorgon,' together with 'Orcus and Ades,' by the side of Chaos and Night. See Mr. Masson's note on the passage. Though the name was associated with the myth of the Gorgon's head, fatal of aspect, it is thought to have been originally a corruption of δημιουργός, this power being regarded as the evil creator of all things in Arcadian mythology.

Enter MEPHISTOPHILIS. The stage-direction in the first and second quartos is here: 'Enter a Diuell.' As to the name MEPHISTOPHILIS, see Dramatis Personae.

25. *an old Franciscan friar.* See Introduction, p. lxi; the Franciscans (Minorites) were called Grey Friars from their habit.

26. *That . . . best.* This is a sentiment which need not be ascribed to Marlowe himself, although both in our play, vii. 52, and elsewhere (compare The Massacre at Paris, i. 3, and the characters of Jacomo and Bernardino in The Jew of Malta) he gladly seizes an opportunity for a stroke against the monks. Already in Gammer Gurton's Needle, iii. 2, it is observed from another point of comparison:

> 'Look, even what face Friar Rush had, the devil had such another.'

The notion of bringing the devil and the monks into so close a connexion may originally have been suggested by the ancient appellation of the former in German popular legend as Graumann (grey man) or Graumännlein, noted by Jacob Grimm, but it was of course cherished in consequence of the later unpopularity of the monastic orders. For notices of legends in which devils or evil spirits appear as monks, see Düntzer, Sage von Faust, 126–129; in the Faustbuch the Devil is called *simpliciter* 'D. Fausti Monk.' Luther tells a story of the Evil One taking service in a kitchen of a monastery, and the pious Widmann (compare Introduction, p. xiv) has much to say about evil spirits in the shape of monks, and in his commentary on the apparition in such a shape of the evil spirit of Doctor Faustus. dwells on the appropriateness of the assumption. He observes that the Devil when he appeared to our Lord, very possibly came in the shape of a Pharisee or a monk, but while inveighing against the 'fratres ignorantiae' who contributed so largely to the darkness of the 'Bapsthumb,' allows that 'D. Fausti Frater ignorantiae' was not one of so simple a sort, but a regular of experience. (See Scheible, Kloster, ii. 345 seqq.) Yet it was a Franciscan who, according to an old chronicle, sought to convert the real Faust at Erfurt. See An Old Man in Dramatis Personae.

27. *virtue*, power. So in As You Like It, v. 4. 108: 'much virtue in If.' For the same use of the word, compare 2 Tamburlaine, v. 3:

'Now, eyes. enjoy your latest benefit,
And when my soul hath virtue of your sight
Pierce through the coffin,' &c.

The phrase 'by virtue of' for 'by the force of' is still in use.

Ib. heavenly words; compare opening Chorus, 6.

32. *conjuror laureat*, a conjuror of acknowledged distinction, one who has 'taken his degree' as a conjuror. The poet-laureateship was, according to the more ancient use of the term. 'a degree in grammar, including rhetoric and versification, taken at the university, on which occasion the graduate was presented with a wreath of laurel.' Dyce, Introd. to the Poetical Works of Skelton, i. xii. (The Bacca-laureateship is symbolical by its name of a hopeful preliminary stage of academical progress.) Compare notes to Friar Bacon, iv. 64 and ix. 116.

34. *Quin . . . imagine.* 'For indeed thou hast dominion in the image of thy brother Mephistophiles,' a blasphemous allusion to the words of Gen. i. 26. Probably, as Wagner suggests, the word 'frater' specially alludes to the habit of a Franciscan friar in which Mephistophiles appears.

Re-enter . . . friar. This stage-direction in the quarto of 1604 is merely, 'Enter Mephostophilis.'

36. *I charge thee wait.* As to the continued use of infinitives without 'to,' after the infinitive suffix 'en' had been dropped, see Abbott, § 349. Compare Friar Bacon, iv. 40; vii. 2; viii. 48; x. 56.

38. *to make the moon drop from her sphere.* In the Life of Wagner, c. 15 (Scheible, Kloster, iii. 72), a 'very learned' student, 'who was

taken to be Paracelsus,' cites certain passages in point from the ancients on the powers of magicians; viz. the statement of Apuleius (Metam. s. de Asin. Aur. bk. i, where see the commentary of Beroaldus), 'magico susurramine . . Solem inhiberi, Lunam despumari' (is drawn down with a rush), &c.; Tibullus' (i. 2. 43) description of a sorceress whom he saw 'de coelo ducentem sidera' (compare also i. 8. 21); and Medea's recital of her magical performances, Ov. Metam. vii. 192 seqq., ending with

'Te quoque Luna traho.'

Compare also Verg. Ecl. viii. 69:

'Carmina vel caelo possunt deducere lunam';

and Hor. Epod. v. 45-46; xvii. 57-58; Lucan. Phars. vi. 499-506.—R. Plot, in his Natural History of Oxfordshire (1677), 215, when discussing Bacon's glasses, cites and translates from his Book of Perspective a passage which explains the origin of this supposed effect: 'Greater things are performed if the *vision* be *refracted*, for [by *refraction*] 'tis easily made appear that the *greatest things* may be represented *less*; and *little things* as the *greatest*; and that things *afar off* may be represented *near*. Thus we can make the *Sun*, and *Moon*, and *Stars*, to all appearance, to come down to us here below,' etc. Compare Friar Bacon, ii. 48 and xi. 14-15, where Bacon more modestly ascribes to himself the power to 'dim fair Luna to a dark eclipse,' and to make her 'hide her silver looks.' It was to relieve or aid in her struggle, the moon when labouring under an eclipse, that it was customary at Rome to make a noise with metal instruments of various kinds; see Liv. xxvi. 5; Tacit. Annal. i. 28; Juvenal, vi. 443. As to similar superstitions among the Indians and other peoples, see Jacob Grimm, Deutsche Mythologie (4th edit.), ii. 589.

39. *Or th' ocean.* This word is to be scanned as a trisyllable, as in The Merchant of Venice, i. 1. 8:

'Your mind is tossing on the ocean.'

The power of magical incantations over the water of sea and rivers is asserted in the classical passages referred to in the last note; compare note to i. 87.

46. *per accidens*, (quarto, 'accident.') 'Per accidens' is a technical term in logic; but the meaning here is plain: 'not because of your conjuring, but because of something it happened to contain.'

47. *rack*, torture. The reference is to the anagrammatising of the Divine name in the conjurations. Compare Friar Bacon, xiii. 93:

'The wresting of the holy name of God.'

51. *Whereby.* As to the construction of 'such' and 'so' with 'where,' see Abbott, § 279.

55, 56, printed as one line in the quarto of 1604.

57. *but only.* For examples of this and similar redundancies compare Abbott, § 130.

60. *For he . . . Elysium,* he makes no distinction between them. R. Simpson (New Shakspere Society's Transactions, 1875-6, p. 168 note) suggests that this passage is perhaps glanced at in Nash's Epistle prefixed to Greene's Menaphon: 'for what can be hoped of them that thrust Elysium into hell,' &c.

61. *His ghost,* spirit (A.-S. gast). Compare The Debate of the Body and Soul, 6:

> 'A body on a bere lay,
> * * * * * * *
> The gost was oute, and scholde away.'

We still say: 'to give up the ghost.'

Ib. with the old philosophers. Hardly, as Van der Velde explains, because as they are in hell (compare Dante's Inferno, c. iv), it will be an endurable place of sojourn; but because they, according to Faustus, likewise did not believe in states of eternal reward and punishment after death.

63. *that Lucifer thy lord.* See Dramatis Personae (LUCIFER) and Introduction, p. lxii; and compare Widmann, chapters 18 and 19, and R. Scot's Discourse of Divels and Spirits (1584), chapters 8, 9, and 10, 'on Lucifer and his fall.' The fall of Lucifer is referred to by Gower in the Confessio Amantis, bk. i:

> 'For Lucifer with hem that felle
> Bar pride with him into helle.
> There was pride of to grete cost
> Whan he for pride hath heven lost.'

It supplied Shakespeare with the magnificent image in Henry VIII, iii. 2. 371, and it is referred to in Friar Bacon, ix. 59 seqq.

64. *Arch-regent.* Lucifer is therefore here Satan himself—

> 'The arch-enemy,
> And thence in heaven called Satan.'

Milton, Paradise Lost, i. 81-82.

66. *lov'd of God.* For examples of 'of' placed before an agent (from whom the action is proceeding), where modern usage demands 'by,' see Abbott, § 170. 'Of' is used to express agency in A.-S., but 'by' never.

68. *Aspiring,* a favourite word with Marlowe. Compare vii. 18; and also 1 Tamburlaine, ii. 7 (bis); Edward II, i. 1; iii. 3; v. 6; The Massacre at Paris, i. 1; i. 2. It is also frequently used by Greene; see Friar Bacon, x. 98; xiv. 16; and James IV, act iv. and act v. Compare Paradise Lost, i. 38, and Pope's Essay on Man, i. 127-128:

'Aspiring to be Gods, if Angels fell,
Aspiring to be Angels, Men rebel.'

76. *Why, this . . out of it.* The idea recurs below, v. 119. Dyce compares Paradise Lost, iv. 75:

'Which way I fly is hell; myself am hell.'

A similar thought occurs in Quevedo's Visions (L'Estrange's Translation, 224). C. E. Turner (Studies in Russian Literature, in Fraser's Magazine for June 1877, p. 700) cites from Sumarokoff's Demetrius the Pretender: 'Flee! but whither? thou bearest thy hell about with thee.' Compare also Dante's Inferno, c. xiv.

84. *passionate*, agitated by strong feeling. Compare xi. 42, and note on Friar Bacon, i. 20.

85. *being.* This word, and below, l. 89, 'seeing,' are, as Wagner points out, to be pronounced as monosyllables.

90. *Jove's deity.* See note on i. 74.

92. *So*, provided that; compare v. 32; xii. 14; xiv. 94.

Ib. four and twenty years. Quarto of 1604: '24 yeares.'

94. *on me.* Observe the awkward change of pronoun. Compare Introduction, p. ix. note 2.

100. *midnight*, to be accentuated on the ultimate, as again v. 28. Marlowe uses both accents for this word.

101. *resolve.* See note on i. 78.

106. *thorough*, for 'through,' as again below, vii. 15; and in 1 Tamburlaine, i. 2; ii. 3, and iii. 2. See note to Friar Bacon, vii. 131. On the other hand, below, vi. 172, 'throughly' is used for 'thoroughly.' The two forms are used promiscuously (compare 'burgh' and 'borough'). 'Both' (Laud and Wentworth) 'were advocates of that which in the jargon of their confidential correspondence they called *Thorough*, of the resolute determination of going *through* with it, as it might nowadays be expressed.' Gardiner, Personal Government of Charles I, i. 160.

108. *bind*, surround, enclose. So Shakespeare uses to 'bind in' Richard II, ii. 1. 61:

'England, bound in with the triumphant sea.'

109. *continent to*, adjoining; a confusion between 'continent' and 'contingent,' or 'forming a whole with.'

114. *speculation*, study, especially by means of contemplation. Compare C. Tourneur, The Atheist's Tragedie, v. 1:

'Behold, thou ignorant Astronomer,
Whose wand'ring speculation seekes among
The planets for men's fortunes, with amazement
Behold thine errour and be planet strucke.'

In the Faustbuch, c. vi, Faustus declares that he resolved to 'speculate the elements' (' die *elementa* zu speculieren'). 'Specularii' was properly the name of those who enquired into the future with the aid of a magical mirror (speculum). See Maury, La Magie et l'Astrologie, etc., 438; and compare Introduction, p. xxiv.

Scene IV.

This scene, which Dyce thinks most probably plays in a street, while F. V. Hugo heads it 'a room in the house of Faustus,' varies considerably in the quarto of 1616. Both versions may be regarded as in all probability later additions; they correspond, as Wagner has pointed out, to the scene in the German popular play in which 'Hans Wurst' is engaged by Wagner (sc. 5 of 'Das Volks Schauspiel Doctor Johann Faust' in Engel's edition). Wagner likewise notes that the first three lines of the dialogue of our scene recur with little variation in the old Taming of a Shrew (compare the scene between Polidor's Boy and Sander in 'Six Old Plays on which Shakespeare founded his Taming of the Shrew,' &c., i. 184); which suggests the likelihood 'that such stale jests as we find in this passage belonged to the stock requisites of the acting companies.' Compare Introduction, p. l.

2. *swowns*, a vulgar oath (spelt 'sounes' in the old play cited in previous note) which long survived in the form 'zounds.'. These and similar French and German mutilations of the Divine name, combined with attributes of the Passion, may have been originally due to a feeling of reverence forbidding the use of the name in full.

3. *pickadevaunts* (French 'pic-à-devant,' from pic a point; so a perpendicularly formed mountain is said to be 'coupé à pic), beards cut to a point, like that of Charles I in Vandyck's portraits. These beards were also called 'stiletto beards.' See Fairholt, Costume in England, 230. Harrison in his Description of England, ii. 7, professes to decline to 'meddle with our varietie of beards, of which some are shauen from the chin like those of Turks, not a few cut short like to the beard of marques Otto, some made round like a rubbing brush, other with a *pique de vant* (O fine fashion!), or now and then suffered to grow long, the barbers being grown to be so cunning in this behalf as the tailors.' See also Lyly's Midas, v. 2.

3. *quotha*, as again below, xi. 45. As to this change of *he* into *'a*, due to the rapidity of Elizabethan pronunciation, see Abbott, § 402. Compare Friar Bacon, iii. 61.

12. *by'r Lady* (quarto of 1604: 'burladie'), by our Lady (the Blessed Virgin).

15. *Qui mihi discipulus*. The first words, according to Dyce, of W. Lily's 'Ad discipulos carmen de moribus':

'Qui mihi discipulus, pace, es, cupis atque doceri,
Huc ades,' &c.

These words, as Müller cleverly suggests, are scanned by Wagner's hand on the Clown's back. Hence the phrases 'beaten silk' and 'staves-acre' are puns.

17. *beaten silk.* I cannot explain this epithet.

Ib. staves-acre, 'a species of larkspur (corrupted from the Greek name σταφὶς ἀγρία) . . . Coles, in his Dictionary, calls it "herba pedicularis."' Cunningham.

18. *knaves-acre.* Knave's Acre (Poultney Street) is described by Strype, vi. 84, quoted in P. Cunningham's Handbook for London, Past and Present, as 'but narrow, and chiefly inhabited by those that deal in old goods and glass bottles.' (It ran into Glasshouse Street.)

25. *bind yourself,* as a servant.

27. *familiars,* attendant-demons. Dyce. Compare 2 Henry VI, iv. 7. 112: 'Away with him! he has a familiar under his tongue; he speaks not o' God's name.'

30. *their.* Quarto of 1604, 'my.'

32. *take these guilders,* as hiring-money. Guilders are Dutch florins. The Clown wilfully misunderstands the name, which, as Douce notes, Shakespeare anachronistically, in the Comedy of Errors, introduces with 'ducats' and 'marks' into the ancient city of Ephesus. 'Guilders' are not mentioned by Harrison in the passage quoted in the next note but one, but he speaks of 'dalders' (Thaler, dollars) 'and such, often times brought over.'

36. *Mass,* by the Mass.

Ib. French crowns. 'Of forren coines we have . . . finallie the French and Flemish crownes, onlie currant anong vs, so long as they hold weight [. . . the franke makes two shillings, and three franks the French crowne].' Harrison's Description of England, bk. ii. ch. 25. See as to this passage, Introduction, p. lxxxvi. note 1.

47. *Baliol and Belcher.* Doubtless facetiously invented names; 'Baliol' *quasi* a Scotch form of Belial, and 'Belcher' = Spitfire.

52. *the round slop.* 'Slops' are breeches, though the word was also used in early English, as it is in modern sailors' language, of other clothing. 'Round slops' were large trunkhose, worn very short and very wide, a fashion reprobated in Chaucer's The Persone's Tale. and afterwards regarded as boorish, till it again became fashionable in the early part of Elizabeth's reign. In Euphues' Golden Legacie (1592) a countryman's dress is described as comprising 'a large slop barred all across the pocket-holes with three fair guards, stitched on either side with red thread.' As a clown's article of dress, they were worn by the

famous Tarlton, as appears from an epigram by Rowland, and a passage from Wright's Passions of the Minde, quoted by Fairholt, Costume in England, p. 217. The clown of the modern pantomime wears, and puts to the purposes of his calling, a similar habiliment.

74. *diametarily*, of course for 'diametrically.'

75. *vestigias nostras*. So all the quartos. Dyce. The editors all read 'vestigiis nostris,' being at the pains to correct Wagner's Latin, but not his English.

76. *fustian*. 'Fustian' (cotton cloth used for jackets and doublets) is metaphorically used for high-sounding nonsense, or nonsensical jargon, probably because fustian often sought in vain to imitate velvet. So in Othello. ii. 3. 281: 'squabble? swagger? swear? and discourse fustian with one's own shadow'; and 'fustian Latin' in Webster's The White Devil, iii. 1, cited by Wagner. See also Ford's The Broken Heart, iv. 1:

'Blunt and rough-spoken,
Vouchsafing not the fustian of civility.'

Compare the metaphorical use of the term 'bombast.' Below, xi. 11, the word 'fustian' is introduced as a punning misnomer for 'Faustus.'

Scene V.

2. These lines are printed as arranged by Dyce: the quarto of 1604 reads,

'Now Faustus must thou needes be damnd,
And canst thou not be saved.'

7. *O, something . . . ears*. Compare the passage in Goethe's Faust, where, as Faust raises the cup of poison to his lips, the sound of the ringing of the bells and of the singing of the Easter hymn draws it irresistibly away.

14. *offer . . . babes*. The immolation of human beings was a charge which, having been brought against the early Christians by the pagans, was afterwards brought against the pagans by the Christian world. It became an ordinary accusation against magicians. In the legend of St. Cyprian the converted magician confesses to having engaged in the practices of his fraternity, which included the massacre of children at the breast. See Maury, *u. s.*, 147. Compare Macbeth, iv. 1. 30. Examples of the loathsome accusation brought against the Jews of drinking the blood of children murdered by them are cited by the credulous Widmann in his commentary (Scheible, Kloster, ii. 339 seqq.). Hondorff, Promptuarium Exemplorum (1572; *ib.* 237), speaks of a similar crime as having been committed by two sorceresses at Berlin in 1553. The belief in the crucifying of children

by Jews is alluded to by Marlowe in The Jew of Malta, iii. 5. It was a fixed popular belief, particulary since the spread of the story of the crucifixion of Hugh of Lincoln (dated 1255 by Matthew Paris), to whose prayers Chaucer makes his Prioresse appeal after reciting her Tale on a similar theme. Mr. Lecky (History of England in the Eighteenth Century, i. 264) notes that the story of the crucifixion of Christian children by Jews was revived in the debates on the Jews' Naturalisation Bill in 1753.

19. *makes.* For numerous examples in Shakespeare of the third person plural in *s* (which probably arose from the Northern E. E. third person plural in *s*, A.-S. *ath*) see Abbott, § 333. Compare iv. 58, though the singular there may be a mere vulgarism. In our passage it may possibly be the result of the singular noun 'lunacy' in line 18.

23. *the signiory of Embden.* Emden near the mouth of the Ems, the chief town of the ancient principality of East-Friesland (after many vicissitudes now re-incorporated in Prussia), at the present day, having all but lost its water, retains a mere shadow of its ancient maritime trade. But the dignified buildings which front its quay, above all the stately Rathhaus, erected in 1573 and containing interesting historical memorials, recall the times when under its native East-Frisian lords (created Counts of the Empire in 1454 and Princes in 1654) Emden was a flourishing commercial port. In 1563 Count John of East-Friesland concluded a species of treaty of alliance with Queen Elizabeth, which was followed by an attempt to open relations of trade with England. In 1564 Emden was for the first time visited by an English fleet, received by the citizens with great pomp and solemnity. Thus the town was well known to Englishmen of the Elizabethan age. The glories of this once prosperous city, which is remarkable as having been a warm adherent of the Reformation and the real cradle of Anabaptism, were celebrated by the humanist Gnaphaeus in a series of Latin poems, including an 'Encomium civitatis Emdanae' (1557), translated and published with a memoir of its author by H. Babucke (Emden, 1875).

25. *What god.* Quarto of 1616, 'What power.' See Introduction, p. lxxxvii.

26. *Cast no more doubts*, reckon up or consider no more doubts.

29. *Mephistophile.* See Dramatis Personae as to this vocative form.

30. *tell me what says.* Quarto of 1604: 'tel, what sayes.'

38, 39. I follow Wagner in separating these lines, as clearly intended for verse.

42. *Solamen . . . doloris.* The source of this line, which is also quoted in Dekker's Seven Deadly Sinnes of London, is unknown. Wagner, who remarks that it is usually cited as ending with the word 'malorum,' suggests that its purport may have been originally derived from Seneca,

de Consolatione ad Polybium, xii. 2: 'est autem hoc ipsum solatii loco, inter multos dolorem suum dividere,' and adds that 'Mr. Jerram aptly compares Paradise Regained, i. 398:

'Envy they say excites me, thus to gain
Companions of my misery and woe.'

For a similar idea compare Cædmon, 403 seqq. Cowper, in his last original poem, The Cast-away, so touching by its reference to the poet's own misery, has a similar idea:

'Misery still delights to trace
Its semblance in another's case.'

It is remarked by v. Loepell, that in the Faustbuch also Mephistophiles shows a fondness for proverbial phrases. See c. lvi: 'how the Evil Spirit vexes the sorrowful Faustus with strange mocking jests and proverbs.'

43. *Why.* This word is not in the first two quartos, but is added in the third.

Ib. torture. Quarto of 1604, 'tortures,' which spoils the sense.

50. *bind thy soul.* The term 'bind' is here used in the same sense as above, iv. 8. The blood with which the bond is signed represents the earnest-money of the future full payment—the soul of the man who signs it. Of such compacts signed with blood the history of magicians has many examples—from Theophilus in the sixth century down to a Paris lawyer, who, as Bodinus relates, was hanged in 1571 for having thus signed a bond with the Devil. For the passage in the Faustbuch see Introduction, p. lxiv.

55. *Assure,* pledge, solemnly promise; so in Twelfth Night, iv. 3. 26:

'Plight me the full assurance of your faith.'

59, 60. These two lines, and again 61, 62, are respectively printed as single lines in the quarto of 1604.

63. *fire,* a dissyllable. 'Monosyllables ending in *r* or *re,* preceded by a long vowel or diphthong, are frequently pronounced as dissyllables.' Abbott, § 480. Compare 2 Tamburlaine, ii. 3:

'And kills us süre as it swiftly flies';

and *ib.*:

'Thy words assüre me of kind success.'

So in Friar Bacon, xii. 45:

'The Faïr Maid of merry Fressingfield';

and *ib.* xiii. 38:

'Serlsby, thou hast [pronounce = Thou'st] kept thine höur like a man.'

See note to Friar Bacon, vii. 131.

64. *staying,* standing still; see below, 67. So in King John, iii. 1. 78:

'The glorious sun
Stays in his course.'

For a transitive use of the verb 'to stay,' see Chorus before sc. viii. l. 3.

65. *bill*. See note to i. 20.

Re-enter (quarto '*Enter*') MEPHISTOPHILIS *with a chafer of coals*. A 'chafer' (Fr. chauffier) is a pan or brazier for heating coals, from 'chafe' (chauffer), to heat. In Heywood's Mery Play between Johan Johan the Husbonde &c., the Husband is obliged to 'chafe wax' at the fire; and we still use the phrase 'to chafe the hands.' Hence 'to chafe,' intransitive, is to become heated or angry, as below, viii. 6.

70. *set it on*, viz. the hand on the chafer. See Introduction, p. lxiv.

74. *Consummatum est*, 'it is finished,' a blasphemous allusion to the last words on the Cross, St. John's Gospel, xix. 30.

76, *this inscription*. See Introduction, p. lxiv; and Widmann's version, c. 10 (Scheible, Kloster, ii. 329). In the puppet-play Dr. Johannes Faust, edited by Simrock, ii. 1, Faustus sees the letters 'H. F.,' which he first interprets as the warning 'Homo Fuge!' but on second thoughts thinks may mean—'F.' 'Faustus,' and 'H.' 'Herrlichkeit' (lordly prosperity).

77. *whither should I fly?* Doubtless a reminiscence of Psalm cxxxix. 6-9. Compare xiv. 86-87.

79. *writ*, written. For other such forms compare Abbott, § 343.

82. *somewhat*, something. Compare Morris, English Accidence, § 217.

83. *show*, pageant, procession, as in the term dumbshow (the gist of the action of a play conveyed by pantomime). Compare vi. 111.

86, 87. Observe the rhyming of these lines, and of 89, 90 below, where the quartos of 1624 and 1631 omit the words 'this scroll.'

86. *may I*, have I power to (A.-S. mæg).

95 *seqq*. See Introduction, p. lxiv. In the English 'History of Doctor Faustus' (ed. of 1648, cited by Dyce) the 'third Article' stands thus: 'That Mephistophiles should bring him anything, and doe for him whatsoever'—a later edition adding 'he desireth': which are the words of our play. F. V. Hugo well observes that while 'for Goethe the contract with the Devil is only a symbol, for Marlowe it is a real act. Hence in Marlowe a precision, a logic, a truth which is wanting in Goethe. Hence also with the former a far more telling effect than with the latter. In Marlowe, his very prosaism augments the impression, while Goethe's scepticism diminishes it. This accent of truth, which we find in the English drama, we also find in the old German legend. And why? For the same reason: the legend, like the drama, was written in an epoch of superstitious belief and not in a time of philosophic enquiry.'

103. *these presents*. This term properly means a letter or mandate exhibited *per praesentes*.

106. *the articles . . . inviolate*, to be construed as a nom. abs., with or without the repetition of the participle 'being.'

111. *on't.* Compare note on ii. 15.

113. *question with thee*, put questions to thee. Compare Friar Bacon, ix. 23. Such questionings are those in the A.-S. Dialogue of Salomon and Saturn, and its wide-spread later developements. (See Ælfric Society's Publications, i. ii. and Kemble's Introduction.)—As to Faustus' disputation about hell with Mephistophiles see Introduction, p. lxvi, and compare Widmann, c. 24 (Kloster, ii. 432 seqq.).

117. *these elements.* See note on i. 75.

120. *In one self place*, in one and the same place. 'Self' in A.-S. was an adjective, agreeing in gender, number and case with the noun or pronoun with which it was joined. This use maintained itself, even after 'self' had begun to be regarded as a noun; compare Richard II, i. 2. 22: 'that self mould.' See Morris, English Accidence, 162-169; and Abbott, § 20. According to Cunningham, among archers at the present day 'a self bow' means a bow made of one piece of wood.

Ib. where we are is hell. Compare iii. 77.

121. *there.* This word is not in the quarto of 1604, but is added in the later quartos.

123. *shall be purified*, shall have been purified, in other words, when purgatory shall have come to an end. For the whole of this passage Marlowe may have had in mind 2 Epistle of St. Peter, iii. 10-14.

124. *that are not.* Quarto of 1604, 'that is not.'

131, 132. These lines are thus printed in the quarto of 1604:

'Thinkst thou that Faustus is so fond
To imagine, that after this life there is any paine.

131. *fond*, foolish.

133. *mere old wives' tales.* For this familiar expression compare 1 Epistle to Timothy, iv. 7: 'old wives' fables.' So Milton, hardly with reference to either of Peele's plays, in his Animadversions upon the Remonstrants Defence against Smectymnus (1641), speaks of 'that old wives' tale of a certain Queene of England that sunk at Charing-Crosse, and rose up at Queen-hithe' (see Dyce, Works of R. Greene and G. Peele, p. 342 note). The title of Peele's comedy, The Old Wives' Tale, means a story told to make the night pass; 'so I am content,' says gammer Madge, 'to drive away the time with an old wives' winter's tale.' The term is similarly used in Lyly's Sapho and Phao, ii. 1. Compare the phrase 'a winter's tale' in Dido Queen of Carthage, iii. 3; and in The Jew of Malta, ii. 1:

'Now I remember those old women's words,
Who in my wealth would tell me winter's tales.'

137. *an*, if; as in x. 64 and Friar Bacon, i. 95. 'And' (both in this

full form and abbreviated into 'an' (as it often was even in its ordinary sense already in Early English) was used as equivalent to 'if' by Early English as well as by Elizabethan writers. For emphasis, and in the sense of 'even if' or of 'if indeed,' the latter employed the combination 'and if' or 'an if'; compare Friar Bacon, xiv. 78. See Abbott, §§ 101–105.

139. *let me have a wife.* See Introduction, p. lxvi; and Widmann, c. 25 (Kloster, ii. 636 seqq.). In Widmann's version of the legend, one of the articles of the compact provides that Faustus is not to marry, which gives rise to a long commentary from the Lutheran moralist.

147. *me*, omitted in the quarto of 1604.

148, 149. These lines are printed as prose in the quarto of 1604.

151. *no*, omitted in the quarto of 1604.

152. *She*, for 'her.' See Abbott, § 211; and compare as to the use of 'he' for 'him,' *ib.* § 206.

154. *Saba*, the Queen of Sheba (1 Kings x. 1–13). So 'sage Saba' in Peele's Sir Clyomon and Sir Clamydes. The geographical position of Saba (which is mentioned as an Eastern land below, xii. 22) is strangely moved from its real locality (Arabia Felix) in lines occurring both in Peele's Old Wives' Tale and Greene's Orlando Furioso:

> 'Saba, whose inhaunsing streams
> Cut twixt the Tartars and the Russians.'

156. *take this book.* See Introduction, p. lxvi.

Ib. peruse, examine throughout, (pervisere); so that the 'thoroughly' here and the 'throughly,' vi. 172, are redundant.

157. *iterating*, repeating.

159. *thunder and lightning.* 'Thunder' should be pronounced as a monosyllable, and 'light-e-ning' as a trisyllable.

161. *men in armour.* See i. 123; and compare 'the Three Mighty Ones' summoned by Mephistophiles in act iv. of the Second Part of Goethe's Faust.

163–173. Wagner has attempted, by interpolating words here and there, to arrange these lines as verse, in which form they were undoubtedly originally written.

166. The stage-direction here and in 170, 176 is, according to the imperative fashion of the old play-books, printed '*turne to them.*'

168. *characters and planets*, probably a hendiadys for 'characters of planets.' See iii. 12.

176. *I warrant thee*, viz. that the book contains what I say.

Scene VI.

I have begun a new scene here, though neither the quarto of 1604 nor that of 1609 indicate a break in the dialogue. In the quarto of

1616 however there follow upon v. 176 the lines assigned to the Chorus at a later part of the play (at the close of the present scene) in the first two quartos, but in the third given to Wagner; after which the third quarto has. 'Enter Faustus in his Study, and Mephistophilis.' It is possible that the dialogue originally continued unbroken; but it is more probable, as Dyce observes, that something was intended to intervene here between the 'exit' of Faust and Mephistophiles and their re-appearance on the stage. Possibly, there was a dumbshow introducing apparitions from classical mythology; for to some such, as produced by Mephistophiles, Faustus, as van der Velde suggests, appears to allude in lines 26-30 of the present scene. Moreover, as Prof. Wagner points out, Faustus's expression 'long ere this' (l. 24) would seem to imply that some considerable time had elapsed since Faustus had consigned himself to the Evil One.

12. *repent; yet.* The quarto of 1604 interpunctuates 'repent yet;' but the change adopted by both Dyce and Wagner seems preferable. Yet = even now.

15. *Be I*, even if I am; or rather 'even if I were.'

Ib. may, can. See l. 13, and compare v. 86.

21. *then swords and knives*, &c. These imaginary temptations to suicide, which are merely the delusions (compare Macbeth's dagger) of Faustus' own self-tortured mind, are to be distinguished from his temptation to suicide by Mephistophiles, xiii. 52. According to Düntzer, Lessing's first scheme of his Doctor Faust was probably to end by Faustus committing suicide in despair.

26. *blind Homer.* The tradition of Homer's blindness was as old as the Homeric Hymn to Apollo. See line 172 of the Hymn, and compare Thucydides, iii. 104.

27. *Alexander*, Paris the son of Priam. The double name has been variously explained; according to some, Paris was called Ἀλέξανδρος as the 'protector of men,' i. e. of the shepherds.

Ib. Oenon's death. Oenone (whose name is here melodiously abbreviated into 'Oenon'—'Enon' in the quarto of 1604—as in Friar Bacon, iii. 70; compare 'Iphigene' for 'Iphigenia' in the Jew of Malta, i. 1; 'Adon' for 'Adonis' in Orlando Furioso and elsewhere; 'Aeol' for 'Aeolus' in Greene's Never too late) was the nymph of Ida beloved by Paris in his youthful days among the shepherds before the three goddesses had appeared to him. He then abandoned her (see Ovid, Heroid., Ep. v), nor (according to the later poets and artists) did she behold him again till towards the close of the siege of Troy he had been mortally wounded by the poisoned arrow of Philoctetes. When they met, she refused to heal him, and afterwards died of grief and remorse.—Compare the passage in Friar Bacon; Oenone appears in Peele's Arraignment of Paris.

28. *he that built the walls of Thebes*, Amphion, who, while his twin-brother Zethos was dragging heavy stones to build the walls of Thebes, moved rocks of twice their size by the sounds of his lyre. Compare the references in Pausanias, ix. 8. 4, and Plutarch, de Musica, 3. Wagner also cites the references to the tradition in Hor. Od. iii. 11. 2 and Ov. Metam. xv. 427. Preller notices the parallel myth of Poseidon and Apollo co-operating in the building of the walls of Troy—mechanical strength moving the blocks, and harmony fitting them into their proper places.

34. *argue of divine astrology.* For 'of' in the sense of 'about,' 'concerning,' compare Friar Bacon, i. 158; ii. 100; The Tempest, ii. 1. 81, 'You make me study of that;' and other passages cited by Abbott, § 147.—As to the disputation on astrology, compare Introduction, p. lxvii; but Marlowe has no particular obligation in this passage to the Faustbuch.

37. *this centric earth.* Compare Troilus and Cressida, i. 3. 85:

> 'The heavens themselves, the planets and their centre
> Observe degree, priority and place.'

The Ptolemaic or pre-Copernican system of astronomy regarded the earth as the centre of the heavenly system; hence it is here termed 'centric,' that which is placed in the centre. See Mr. Masson's note (Milton's Poetical Works, iii. 221–223) concerning the ideas of astronomy entertained by Milton, who adopted the Ptolemaic system, without feeling able entirely to abandon belief in the Copernican; especially with reference to Raphael's ironical allusion (Paradise Lost, viii. 84) to the words 'centric' and 'eccentric' as technical terms of the Ptolemaists applied to the centric and non-concentric motions of the planetary bodies. Compare also the reference in Bacon's Essay of Seditions and Troubles to 'the old opinion'; 'which is, That every of them [the Planets], is carried swiftly, by the Highest Motion, and softly in their owne Motion'; and see Mr. Aldis Wright's note, p. 305 of his edition of the Essays.

40, 41. Printed as one line in the quarto of 1604.

42. *terminine*, a form apparently invented by Marlowe, equivalent to 'terminus' or 'term.' Compare the form 'convertite' for convert, Jew of Malta, i. 2, which is still occasionally employed. As to the antithetical jingle of this line compare note to opening Chorus, 7, 8.

44. *erring stars.* See iii. 12. The meaning I suppose is that they are actual bodies moving through the firmament.

45, 46. *both situ et tempore*, as to both the direction of, and the time occupied by, their revolutions.

58. *freshmen's suppositions*, elementary statements fit for a student in his first year.

59. *dominion or intelligentia.* 'Every individual person or thing may possess peculiar properties, because, from the beginning, it contracts, together with its essence, a certain wonderful aptitude both for doing and for suffering after a particular manner, partly through the influences of the celestial bodies streaming down from particular configurations, partly . . . . But from a Divine Providence these influences proceed as their first cause, and by it they are distributed and brought into a peculiar harmonious consent. The seal of the ideas is given to the governing intelligences, who, as faithful officers, sign all things entrusted to them with ideal virtue.' From H. Morley's sketch of Cornelius Agrippa's First Book 'Of Occult Philosophy' in 'Life of Agrippa,' i. 125. Compare for the idea, Dante's Inferno, vii. 72 seqq.

63. *the empyreal heaven*, the highest and most refined region of heaven, supposed to be formed of the element of fire (ἔμπυρος). The phrase recurs in 1 Tamburlaine, ii. 7, and 2 Tamburlaine, ii. 4; compare 2 Tamburlaine, iii. 4, 'the empyreal orb.'

65. *conjunctions, oppositions, aspects.* Terms of astrology, implying the friendly or hostile relations towards one another of particular stars. See Morley, *u. s.*, i. 128. Compare 2 Tamburlaine, iii. 5:

'The shepherd's issue (at whose birth
Heaven did afford a gracious aspéct
And joined those stars that shall be opposite,
Even till the dissolution of the world).'

See also Lodge and Greene's A Looking-Glass for London and England:

'Retrograde conjunctions of the stars
Or oppositions of the greater lights';

and Greene's James IV, i. 1:

'Dread king, thy vassal is a man of art,
Who knows, by constellation of the stars,
By oppositions and by dry aspécts,
The things are past and those that are to come.'

In the same scene King James, striking Ateukin on the ear, bids him tell

'What star was opposite when that was thought.'

67. *Per inaequalem motum respectu totius*, 'on account of their unequal motion with regard to the whole,' i. e. I suppose, because of the several motions which the stars have within the general system of the universe.

72. *Move me not*, do not exasperate me. So in Romeo and Juliet, iv. 5. 95:

'Move them no more by crossing their high will.'

75. *against our kingdom*, i.e. against the laws of the infernal monarchy. Compare Titus Andronicus, v. 2. 30:

'Revenge, sent from the infernal kingdom';

and Richard III, i. 4. 47:

'The kingdom of perpetual night.'

76. *on*, for 'of,' but more emphatic. See note on ii. 15.

78. *Think, Faustus . . . the world.* I have ventured to adopt Wagner's suggestion and to assign these words, given to Faustus in the quartos, to the Good Angel. In the quartos, the Good and the Evil Angel are not made to re-enter till after line 81.

79. *ugly*, frightful in the literal sense of the word (O. N. uggligr, terrible, from ugga, to fear). Compare 1 Tamburlaine, v. 2: 'ugly darkness with her rusty coach.' The phrase 'ugly hell' recurs below, xiv. 120.

85. *raze thy skin*, touch the mere surface of thy skin (from French raser, Latin radere).—The stage-direction following these words is not in the quarto of 1604.

87. *Seek to save.* Perhaps Marlowe wrote 'Seek thou to save'; but on the other hand this may be one of the lines defective in their first syllable, which as Dyce observes, commenting on 1 Tamburlaine, ii. 7. 1,

'Barbarous and bloody Tamburlaine,'

and *ib.* 3,

'Treacherous and false Theridamas,'

we occasionally find in our early dramatists; 'and in some of these instances at least it would seem that nothing has been omitted by the transcriber or printer.' Compare x. 29; xiv. 65.

91, 92. These lines are printed without a break between them in the quarto of 1604.

92. *my companion-prince in hell.* Compare Paradise Lost, i. 79-81.

95. *contrary.* The same accentuation occurs in Hamlet, iii. 2. 221:

'Our wills and fates do so contrary run.'

97. *And of his dam too.* Cunningham and Wagner refuse to accept these words as Marlowe's, and regard them as a piece of actor's 'gag.' It is certainly an inappropriate suggestion for Mephistophiles to make in so serious a passage. The devil and his dam (i.e. his mother, or according to the more popular fancy, his grandmother; in the quarto of 1604 the word is spelt 'dame' in accordance with its derivation) are frequently combined in Shakespeare; compare also C. Tourneur, The Atheist's Tragedie, iv. 3:

'Coniure up
The Diuell and his Dam.'

See on the 'Teufels muoter' Grimm's Deutsche Mythologie, 959-960.

100, 101, 102. These lines are omitted in the quarto of 1616; see Introduction, p. lxxxvii.

Enter the Seven Deadly Sins. As to the Seven Deadly Sins see Dramatis Personae, and compare Introduction, p. lv. The scene which follows is justly described by Düntzer as one of the happiest of the additions made by the drama to the legend; in the Faustbuch (c. xxiii) we have instead Belial introducing 'all the spirits of hell to Doctor Faustus, among them seven of the highest rank named by name.'

112. *of*, for 'on'; see note on ii. 15.

116. *Ovid's flea.* The 'Carmen de pulice,' formerly supposed to be by Ovid, is described by Bernhardy as 'a farcical toy and production of the later Middle Ages.'

117. *perriwig.* This word is a corruption of the French *perruque*, (Müller compares Italian *perrucca*, Spanish *peluca*, Sardinian and Sicilian *pilucca*, derived like the verb *piluccare*, French *éplucher*, from the Latin *pilus*, hair), and spelt 'periwinke' in Hall's Satires. According to Fairholt, 'the earliest notice of perriwigs occurs in the privy purse expenses of Henry VIII, where we find under December, 1529, an entry of twenty shillings "for a perwyke for Sexton the king's fool." By the middle of this century their use had become frequent. They are noticed as worn by ladies in Middleton's A Mad World, my Masters, 1608' (iv. 4).

120. *cloth of arras*, so called from Arras in Artois, where the principal manufacture of such stuffs was. See Nares, where reference is made to 1 Henry IV, ii. 4. 549, and Hamlet, iii. 4. In both these scenes the walls are hung with arras, and so Harrison, in his Description of England (bk. ii. ch. 12), mentions 'hangings of tapistrie, arras work or painted cloths,' but says nothing of floor-carpets or floor-cloths. Of course arras would be a preposterously ostentatious covering for the floor, which (as Wagner observes) was not carpeted in olden times, but merely strewed with rushes; and Pride, like Clytaemnestra in the Agamemnon, exceeds all bounds in her wish

'The soil o' the road to strew with carpet-spreadings.'

130. *case*, couple. So Harrison speaks of a 'case of dags' or daggers. The expression in Henry V, iii. 2. 5, 'I have not a case of lives,' is explained by Delius to mean 'I have not a couple of lives.'

132. *some of you shall be my father*, i.e. one of you (the devils) is doubtless my father.

134. *Envy.* Compare the description of Envy in the Faerie Queen, v. 12. 29:

'Thereto her hew
Was wan and leane, that all her teeth arew
And all her bones might through her cheekes be red.'

140. *with a vengeance.* Compare for this still common expression,

Coriolanus, iii. 1. 261: 'What the vengeance!' In R. Bernard's 'Terence in English,' ed. of 1607 (1st ed. 1598), the Latin words 'Quid (malum) me tandem censes velle' are translated with 'What (a vengeance), thinke you, desire I to have.' See New Shakspere Society's Transactions, 1875–6, p. 460.

144. *bevers* (from O. Fr. *bevre* or *boivre*, to drink; whence beverage), a refreshment between breakfast and dinner. In Nares an amusing passage from Beaumont and Fletcher's The Woman-Hater, i. 3, is cited, mentioning 'ord'nary eaters, that will devour three breakfasts, and as many dinners, without prejudice to their bevers, drinkings or suppers' —an improvement on the 'quatre repas par jour' which French writers are in the habit of considering the proof of a good digestion waiting upon a comfortably supplied appetite. Harrison, bk. ii. ch. 16, observes that 'heretofore there hath beene much more time spent in eating and drinking than commonlie is in these daies, for whereas of old we had breakefasts in the forenoone, beuerages, or nuntions after dinner, and thereto reare suppers generallie when it was time to go to rest (a toie brought into England by hardie *Canutus* . . . .). Now these od repasts—thanked be God—are verie well left.'

148. *Peter Pickle-herring.* Such alliterative names as this, and Margery March-beer below, were common in the old moralities, and in the early comedies; see for instance the 'dramatis personae' of Ralph Roister Doister. Pickle-herring was the Dutch Hans Wurst, who had many similar aliases according to the nationality he was intended to represent.

Ib. Martlemas-beef. It is stated in Nares, that 'Martlemas (a corruption of Martin-mass, the feast of St. Martin, Nov. 11th)'—(compare Christmas, Michaelmas)—'was the customary time for hanging up provisions to dry, which had been salted for the winter;' see George-a-Greene, the Pinner of Wakefield, where the passage, slightly varied, occurs twice:

> 'You shall have wafer-cakes your fill,
> A piece of beef, hung up since Martlemas,
> Mutton, and veal.'

151. *March-beer*, or march-ale, is, according to the same authority, citing the Ballad of Robin Hood and Clorinda, 'a choice kind of ale, made generally in the month of March, and not fit to drink till it was two years old.'

157. *Sloth.* 'Sloth' is one of the 'Seven Deadly Sinnes of London' in Dekker's pamphlet (see Dramatis Personae), where the entry of Sloth at Bishopsgate is described with some humour, '*Sleepe* and Plenty leade the Fore-Asse,' and among the suite are 'an *Irish Beggar* on the one side, and *One that sayes he has been a Soldier* on the other.'

162. *Minx*, probably from minikin; a diminutive of minion (French mignon). 'Mistris Minx, a marchant's wife,' is a type in Nash's Pierce Pennilesse.

165. As this line is not assigned to any fresh speaker in the quarto of 1604, I have given it to Lucifer, as the manager of the show, rather than to Faustus (as Dyce does), especially as it hardly accords with his subsequent declaration that what he has seen 'feeds his soul.'

170, 171. These lines, and again 172–174, and 175–176, are printed as continuous prose in the quarto of 1604.

171. *Thou shalt.* As to Faustus' descent into hell see Introduction, p. lxvii.

172. *take this book.* The book after reading which Faustus may assume whatever shape he chooses is not mentioned in the Faustbuch.

Ib. throughly, for 'thoroughly.' See note to iii. 106.

173. *thyself.* This word should probably be omitted as redundant to the metre.

175. *chary*, carefully. 'Chary' is the A.-S. cearig, anxious; compare care, cark. So in the Ormulum, 1274: 'turrtle ledeþþ chariȝ lif.' Wagner compares Shakespeare's Sonnet xxii. 11–12:

'Bearing thy heart, which I will keep so chary
As tender nurse her babe from faring ill.'

177. *Exeunt omnes.* This is the stage-direction of the quarto of 1604.

Chorus.

These lines are in the quartos of 1604 and 1609 given to Wagner ('Enter Wagner solus'), but in the quarto of 1616 to the Chorus, to whom they evidently belong. As Dyce observes, 'The parts of Wagner and of the Chorus were most probably played by the same actor; and hence the error.' Before these lines a comic scene between 'Robin' and 'Dick' is added in the quarto of 1616, which is doubtless a later addition.

1. *Learnèd Faustus*, &c. As to the ascent of Faustus into the heavens see Introduction, p. lxvii.

3. *Jove's.* See note to i. 74.

6. *Drawn by the strength of yoky dragons' necks.* Wagner directs attention to the entry in Henslowe's Diary (p. 273 Collier) in his 'Enventary tacken of all the properties for my Lord Admeralles men, the 10 of Marche 1598,' 'j dragon in fostes;' and suggests that 'possibly Faustus alighted in his chariot drawn by dragons,' or at least one dragon, at the beginning of the scene following; or, even more likely,' (?) 'we may suppose Henslowe's note to refer to the performance

indicated by the lines added' in the quarto of 1616 between lines 5 and 6 of our text, which are worth transcribing:

'He views the clouds, the planets, and the stars,
The tropic zones, and quarters of the sky,
From the bright circle of the hornèd moon
Even to the height of Primum Mobile;
And, whirling round with this circumference,
Within the concave compass of the pole,
From east to west his dragons swiftly glide,
And in eight days did bring him home again.
Not long he stayed within his quiet house,
To rest his bones after his weary toil;
But new exploits do hale him out again:
And, mounted then upon a dragon's back,
That with his wings did part the subtle air'—

Ib. yoky. Compare note to i. 145.

7. *to prove cosmography*, to essay or study the science which, as a line added in the quarto of 1616 explains, 'measures coasts and kingdoms of the earth.'

8. *as I guess.* This phrase, now considered an Americanism, occurs several times in Shakespeare,

10. *of*, where we should say 'in.' See note to ii. 15.

Ib. holy Peter's feast, St. Peter's day (June 29th).

11. *to this day*, to-day (O. E. tô-dæge; compare O. E. to-yere, this year, to-eve, yesterday evening).

Scene VII.

1. *Having now*, &c. As to the journeys of Faustus, see Introduction, pp. lxvii seqq.

2. *the stately town of Trier.* The use of the German form of the name is noteworthy, as indicating that Marlowe followed the German Faustbuch. In his translation of Lucan's Pharsalia he uses the form 'Trevier' as an equivalent for the Latin 'Trevir' (Lucan, i. 441) as the appellation of the members of the tribe. The attention which the antiquities of Treves (Augusta Trevirorum) commanded in Marlowe's days is illustrated by the admiration expressed by Abraham Ortelius in his 'Itinerarium per nonnullas Galliae Belgicae partes' (Antwerp, 1584), cited by Wyttenbach, concerning the famous 'Porta Martis' ('Porta Nigra').

3. *airy mountain-tops.* Wagner compares the Latin 'aërii montes.' This is not a Shakespearian use of the epithet.

4. *With walls of flint.* The 'Porta Nigra' at Treves was used as a fortification in the later Middle Ages in the petty wars between the clergy and the citizens.

Ib. lakes, ditches.

6. *coasting*, passing along the side or frontier of. Compare French côte, side.

7. *We saw*, at Mainz.

11. *straight forth*, in straight lines. (like the streets of Thurii designed by Hippodamus). Compare 'forth-rights' = straight paths, in The Tempest, iii. 3. 3.

12. *equivalents*, equal parts, quarters. The quartos of 1604 and 1609 print 'equivalence.'

13. *learnèd Maro's golden tomb.* In Vergil, as reputed a magician in the Middle Ages (see Wright's Narratives of Sorcery and Magic, i. 99 *seqq.*, on 'Virgil the Enchanter') Faustus would naturally take special interest. Vergil, says Prof. Sellar, who cites a reference to 'Maronis mausoleum' from a mass sung in honour of St. Paul at the end of the fifteenth century, 'was buried at Naples, where his tomb was long regarded with religious veneration and visited as a temple; and tradition long associated his name, as that of a magician, with the construction of the great tunnel of Posilippo in the immediate neighbourhood.'

14. *The way he cut.* See preceding note Dyce quotes a passage from Petrarch's Itinerarium Syriacum, describing the famous 'crypt' or tunnel, 'quod vulgus insulsum a Virgilio magicis cantaminibus factum putant: ita clarorum fama hominum, non veris contenta laudibus, saepe etiam fabulis viam facit.' According to Wright, Vergil was also said to have made a contrivance 'by which no man could be hurt in the miraculous vault.'

15. *Thorough.* See note to iii. 106.

17. *In one of which.* This is the reading of the quarto of 1616; those of 1604 and of 1609 have 'in midst of which.' The corresponding passages in the Faustbuch (see Introduction, p. lxviii) leave some doubt as to which church was here intended. The expression 'a sumptuous temple' points to St. Mark's at Venice, and this was so understood by the author of the additional lines in the quarto of 1616,

> 'Whose frame is pav'd with sundry-colour'd stones,
> And roof'd aloft with curious work in gold'—

referring of course to the wonderful mosaic-work of St. Mark's. On the other hand, the line

> 'That threats the stars with her aspiring top'

would seem rather to indicate the church of St. Antonio at Padua; for the description is inapplicable to St. Mark's, while in the Faustbuch (*n. s.*) Padua is mentioned as possessing a beautiful 'church with a tower' (Thumbkirch), and it is stated that there (at Padua) is a church 'called S. Anthonii, the like of which is not found in all Italy.' Of course, supposing Marlowe not to have merely copied the Faustbuch, he might have had some other Italian church with a lofty tower in his mind's eye,—not however the Duomo at Milan, which would at the present day occur as the readiest example of an Italian church with an 'aspiring top,' for its central tower and spire had not been completed in Marlowe's day.

18. *threats*, threatens. For similar verbal forms see Abbott, § 290.

Ib. with her aspiring top. See note to i. 33. Though 'his' ordinarily represented the genitive of 'it,' 'her' might be used where personification, or association with the notion of female sex, or the gender of the corresponding Latin substantive caused the noun represented by the pronoun to be treated as of the feminine gender. See Abbott, § 229. The last is the case here; 'temple' is used as a synonym for 'church,' the Latin and Greek words for which are feminines.

33, 34. These lines, which are wanting in the quartos of 1604 and 1609, are inserted from that of 1616 by Dyce 'as being absolutely necessary to the sense.'

35. *four stately bridges.* This is the reading of the two first quartos; the third has 'two.' The Faustbuch does not help us here; but the actual number of bridges at Rome in the fifteenth century appears to have been four (the Ponte Angelo, the two bridges of the Insula, and the Bridge of the Senators). See the account of Poggio (1431) in Gregorovius, Geschichte der Stadt Rom, vi. 709.

37. *Ponte* (all the quartos 'Ponto') *Angelo.* The Ælian bridge, built by the Emperor Hadrian as an approach to his tomb, was called the 'Bridge of St. Peter' in the days of Gregory I; it was not till the eleventh century that the locality began to be called the 'Mons S. Angeli,' whence the same name afterwards came to be used of both castle and bridge.

39. *store of ordnance are.* For the construction of 'store' (signifying 'abundance') as a collective noun with a plural compare Richard II, 1. 4. 5:

'And say, what store of parting tears were shed?'

40. *double cannons.* This probably means cannons with double bores. Two cannons with *triple* bores were taken from the French at Malplaquet, and are now in the Woolwich Museum.

41. *cómplete.* For the accent compare Hamlet, i. 4. 52:

'That thou, dead corse, again in cómplete steel.'

42. *pyramides.* Marlowe frequently uses this plural; so 1 Tamburlaine,

iv. 2; The Massacre at Paris, i. 2; and Dido Queen of Carthage, iii. 1. The singular occurs in Beaumont and Fletcher's Philaster, iv. 4:

'Place me, some god, upon a Piramis
Higher than earth.'

43. *Which Julius Caesar brought from Africa*, i. e. from Egypt. But this it would have been rather beyond Julius Caesar's power to do; perhaps Marlowe was thinking of the obelisk, brought to Rome from Thebes in Egypt by the Emperor Constantius about A.D. 353.

45, 46. *Of Styx .... Phlegethon.* As F. V. Hugo observes, Faustus, in accordance with the fashion of the Renascence, identifies the heathen with the Christian lower world. The Styx, by which even the gods swore (Hesiod, Theogon. 400), was the most ancient, and probably originally the only stream of which the Greeks conceived the existence in the lower world; the Acheron (the river of wailing) and the Pyriphlegethon (the river of fire) are first mentioned in the Odyssey, x. 513.

48. *bright-splendent.* See as to such compounds of two adjectives ('deep-contemplative,' 'strange-suspicious,' &c.) of which the first has an adverbial force and qualifies the second, Abbott, § 2.

56, 57. These two lines are clearly corrupt.

58. *Unseen by any.* This power of suddenly vanishing or making to vanish was ascribed to the gods of pagan antiquity, and afterwards to the evil spirits into which the popular belief of the Middle Ages had converted them. The power of rendering invisible was attributed to the hat of Fortunatus in the old Teutonic and Breton legend, treated by Dekker in a play (Olde Fortunatus) which has a certain affinity with Doctor Faustus. Compare as to this kind of beliefs, Grimm's Deutsche Mythologie, i. 431–432.

Sound a Sonnet. This word, which is spelt in various ways (the spelling 'Signate' shows its origin), is of frequent occurrence in the stage-directions of old plays. It means 'a particular set of notes on the trumpet or cornet, different from a flourish'; for in Nares is cited the following direction from Dekker's Satiromastix: 'Trumpets sound a florish, and then a sennate.'

The Cardinal of Lorrain. See Dramatis Personae.

61. For what follows, whether it was written by Marlowe or not, compare Introduction, p. lxix.

62. *Fall to.* This colloquialism explains itself by a comparison of Friar Bacon, ix. 237:

'And bid them fall into' [i. e. upon] 'their frugal cates.'

Compare 'go to,' i. e. go on.

67. *Milan*, spelt 'Millaine' in the quarto of 1604.

72. *ha't*, have it.

76. *a pardon*, or indulgence, shortening his stay in Purgatory.

77. *a dirge*, a funeral service; according to Wedgwood, from the words of Psalm v. 8, 'dirige Domine Deus meus in conspectu tuo vitam meam,' repeated in the anthem used by the Church of Rome on such occasions. The form 'dirige' is used by Skelton in Colyn Cloute, 427; and in The Boke of Phyllyp Sparowe, 562:

'The sacre with them shall say
Dirige for Phyllyppes soule';

whence the sneer of Barklay towards the close of The Ship of Fooles:

'It longeth not to my science nor cunninge
For Philip the Sparow the dirige to singe.'

79. *crossing of yourself.* Compare 1 Tamburlaine. iii. 3:

'Why stay we thus prolonging of their lives?'

and The Jew of Malta, iv. 2: 'He stands as if he were begging of bacon.' These apparent participles are explained by Abbott, § 178, as verbal nouns, before which the prepositional 'a,' 'in,' or 'on' has been omitted; so that the present passage is equivalent to 'are you a-crossing of yourself?' On the other hand, in such passages as xiv. 79, Friar Bacon, ii. 20, and Edward II, i. 4. 272,

'And in the chronicle enrol his name
For purging of the realm of such a plague,'

the substantive use of 'naming' and 'purging' is evident from the preposition 'for' before these words.

81. *Aware*, (ywar in Chaucer), beware. Compare Love's Labour 's Lost, v. 2. 43:

''ware pencils, ho!'

So afore=before, ix. 20.

84. *with bell, book, and candle.* 'In the solemn form of excommunication used in the Romish Church, the bell was tolled, the book of offices for the purpose used, and three candles extinguished.' Nares, where reference is made to King John, iii. 3. 12. Compare also Fletcher's The Spanish Curate, v. 2:

'Out with your beads, curate,—
The devil's in the dish,—bell, book and candle!'

88, 89. These lines are printed without a break between them in the quarto of 1604.

96. *took.* Wagner suggests 'strook'; but compare Measure for Measure, ii. 1. 189: 'If he took you a box o' the ear'; and other passages in Shakespeare. The verb 'to take' is frequently employed in O. E. in the sense of 'to give'; see for instance The Vision of Piers the Plowman, iii. 45:

'Mede . . . .
Tolde hym a tale and toke hym a noble,
Forto ben hire bedeman.'

Chorus.

3. *stay'd*, stopped. See note on v. 64.

5. *companions*. A quadrisyllable. Compare i. 150.

6. *gratulate his safety*, congratulate him on his safety, testify their pleasure in it. Compare Greene's Orlando Furioso:

'But friendly gratulate these favours found';

and Peele's Edward I, v. 58:

'Friends, gratulate to me my joyous hopes';

and Titus Andronicus, i. 1. 221:

'And gratulate his safe return to Rome.'

7. *conference of*, conversation on. Compare i. 65, and see note on ii. 15.

9. *of astrology*. See the same note.

11. *As*. Compare x. 23, and Friar Bacon, x. 30 and 61; xii. 18; and see Abbott, § 109, for other examples of the Elizabethan use of 'as' for 'that' with the antecedents 'so' and 'such.'

16. *in trial*, by way of experiment or testimony.

17. *'t*, added by Dyce.

Scene VIII.

6. *chafing*. See note to v. 69.

7. *look thee out*, find thee out.

9. *keep out*, keep off. Compare the modern vulgarism 'get out.'

11. *roaring*. 'Roaring' is a favourite slang term of our old writers; one of the characters in Jonson's Bartholomew Fair is 'Val. Cutting, a roarer or bully'; the heroine (a real personage) and title of one of Middleton's comedies is 'The Roaring Girl'; Sir Thomas Overbury draws the character of a 'Roaring Boy'—a cant term for bully; and in Middleton and Rowley's A Faire Quarrel the whole art of town bullying is taught at a 'roaring academy.'

21. *ippocras* (quarto of 1604, ''ipocrase') or hippocras is defined by Dyce as 'a medicated drink composed of wine (usually red) with spices and sugar. It is generally supposed to have been so called from Hippocrates (contracted by our earliest writers to "Hippocras" [so in Skelton's Garlande of Laurell, v. 1426: 'Ipocras']), perhaps because it was strained,—the woollen bag used by apothecaries to strain syrups and decoctions for clarification being termed "Hippocrates' sleeve."'

Ib. tabern, tavern (*taberna*).

23. *Master Parson*. Compare Master Doctor Faustus, x. 1; and the abbreviation 'Mas doctor' in Friar Bacon, vii. 26.

27. *horse-bread*, or horse-loaves, described in Nares as a peculiar sort of bread, made for feeding horses. 'It appears to have been formerly much more common than at present to give bread to horses.' The receipts for making 'horse-loaves are given in various books of hunting'; and reference is made to Fletcher and Shirley's The Night-Walker, v. 1:

> 'Oh, that I were in my oat-tub with a horse-loaf,
> Something to hearten me.'

28. *of free cost*, at no expense. Compare 2 Henry VI, iv. 6. 3 (cited by Abbott, § 168): 'Of the city's cost, the conduit shall run nothing but claret wine.'

Scene IX.

A scene, as Dyce points out, is evidently wanting between the 'exeunt' and 'enter' of Ralph and Robin.

2. *ecce, signum!* The same phrase is used by Falstaff, 1 Henry IV, ii. 4. 187.

3. *a simple purchase*, a clear gain or acquisition. So 1 Tamburlaine, ii. 5 (of the acquisition of the crown):

> 'I judge the purchase more important far.'

The word purchase, says Trench in his Select Glossary, is 'properly to hunt, "pourchasser," "procacciare"; and then to take in hunting; then to acquire; and then, as the commonest way of acquiring is by giving money in exchange, to buy. The word occurs six times in our Version of the New Testament . . . in none of these is the notion of buying involved.'—'Purchase' was hence used of the booty of thieves, and became a cant term among them. See Nares, *s. v.*

6. *gull.* Both substantive and verb are favourite slang terms for 'dupe,' still in use, in allusion to the ease with which the bird so called can be caught, and the flutter of its movements. See the lines 'Of a Gull' by J. D. (John Davies), one of the epigrams printed together with Marlowe's 'Ovid's Elegies.'

7. *Drawer.* 'There is an inconsistency here; the Vintner cannot properly be addressed as "Drawer."' Dyce. (See Dramatis Personae; the Vintner is the publican who sells the wine, the Drawer the servant who draws it for the customers.)

9. *Soft.* Compare Othello, v. 2. 338:

> 'Soft you, a word or two before you go.'

10. *from you*, by you.

12. *etc.* This 'etc.,' which recurs l. 30 below, shows that room was left for *extempore* additions by the clowns.

18. *a matter of truth*, a charge affecting their credit for honesty.

Compare The Merry Wives, i. 1. 125: 'what matter have you against me?'

19. *tone*, the one. As the forms 'tone' and 'tother' (Scoticè tane, tither) where they occur in O. E. have the article 'the' prefixed to them, Mätzner is inclined to explain the initial *t* as part of 'that,' used as the definite article and frequently prefixed in O. E. to 'one' and 'other.'

20. *afore*, before. Compare 'aware' for 'beware,' vii. 81.

22. *scour*, a slang term for 'chastise.' So Nym says to Pistol, Henry V, ii. 1. 60: 'I'll scour you with my rapier.'

ib. you had best. This seems equivalent to 'you would be or were best,' as to which phrase see Abbott, § 352.

36. After this line the quartos of 1604 and 1609 make Mephistophiles say: 'Vanish villaines, th' one like an Ape, an other like a Beare, the third an Asse, for doing this enterprise.' These words, to which there is nothing equivalent in the corresponding passage in the later quartos, are omitted by Dyce, as what follows (46-47) shews that they ought to have no place in the text.

38. *awful*, full of awe or fear. For the double (active and passive) meaning of such adjectives, see Abbott, § 3.

40. *villains*, low fellows. Compare x. 80.

48. *fine sport with the boys*. Compare Love's Labour 's Lost, iv. 3. 169:

'And Nestor play at push-pin with the boys.'

Scene X.

Before this scene another, between Martino, Frederick, and Benvolio, gentlemen of the Imperial Court, is added. For the passage in the Faustbuch to which sc. x. corresponds, see Introduction, pp. lxx. seqq.

2. *thy knowledge*. Throughout this scene the Emperor addresses Faustus with 'thou' and Faustus replies with 'you.' Compare as to the use of 'thou' and 'you,' Abbott, §§ 231 seqq.

Ib. the black art. See note on opening Chorus, 25.

4. *for*, in the sense of 'as regards.' See Abbott, § 149. Compare sc. xiii. 14, 22, 27; and Friar Bacon, xvi. 1.

Ib. rare effects, wonderful achievements or manifestations.

Ib. familiar, attendant.

5. *list*, a contraction for 'listest.' So Tempest, iii. 2. 138: 'If thou beest a devil, take 't as thou list.' Compare the A.-S. form 'berst,' second person singular from 'berstan,' to burst.

10. *endamaged*, harmed; an obsolete word frequently used by Shake-

speare and other Elizabethan writers, and also occurring in Milton and South.

14. *nothing*, in no respect. For this adverbial use of 'nothing,' see Abbott, § 55; and for the corresponding adverbial use of 'something,' *ib.* § 68.

Ib. answerable to, in keeping with. Compare The Taming of the Shrew, ii. 1. 361:

> 'I have a hundred milch-kine to the pail,
> Six score fat oxen standing in my stalls,
> And all things answerable to this portion.'

'Adjectives, especially those ending in *ful, less, ble*, and *ive*, have both an active and a passive meaning—so "unmeritable," "medicinable."' Abbott, § 3.

15. *for that.* For the use of 'that' as an affix to prepositions giving them a conjunctival meaning ('for that,' 'in that,' 'after that') see Abbott, § 287. Compare 'for that' xiii. 18, and Friar Bacon, ii. 105; and ''fore that' (before) *ib.* viii. 35. For the general use of 'that' as a conjunctional affix compare 'if that,' xiii. 3, and Friar Bacon, i. 157; and 'how that,' Friar Bacon, viii. 21.

17–28. These lines are printed as prose in the quarto of 1604, the rest of the Emperor's speech being printed as verse.

18. *sometime*, once; here used as a mere indefinite adverb of time, as in 1 Henry VI, v. 1. 31:

> 'Henry the Fifth did sometime prophesy,' &c.

In the concluding Chorus of our play, l. 3, 'sometime' means 'formerly.'

Ib. solitary, an adverb. Compare 'lively,' l. 51; and 'chary,' vi. 175.

Ib. set, seated. Compare The Jew of Malta, v. 4:

> 'When thou seest he comes
> And with his bassoes shall be blithely set,'

i. e. comfortably seated; and 3 Henry VI, iv. 3. 2:

> 'The king by this is set him down to sleep.'

The O. E. 'sette' (to place; A.-S. settan) has the participles 'seted' and 'set.' Compare A.-S. sendan, past participle 'sended' and 'send.'

19. *closet*, private room. Compare the Gospel of St. Luke, xii. 3 (A. V.), where Tyndale has 'secret places.'

21. *won.* 'May be right; but query "done"?' Dyce. The A.-S. winnan was used in the sense of 'to labour.'

Ib. prowess, O. Fr. proese (N. Fr. prouesse), from O. Fr. prou, preu, pro (N. Fr. preux), probably derived from the Latin probus, though the derivatives of prudens (prude, whence prud'homme, preud'homme) may have influenced the meaning.

22. *riches.* If the line be not corrupt (which, as Wagner suggests, the feminine ending alone suggests as probable), the question is whether 'riches' can here be accentuated on the last syllable. Chaucer still spells and accentuates this word according to its original French singular form 'richesse'; Shakespeare uses it both as a singular and as a plural, but never accentuates it on the ultimate.

23, 24. 'A corrupted passage (not found in the later quartos).' Dyce.

23. *As.* Compare note on Chorus before viii, l. 11.

28. *the world's pre-eminence*, the pre-eminent men of the world.

29. *The bright . . . acts.* Dyce regards this line as one of the lines defective in the first syllable, adverted to in note on vi. 87.

30. *his*, for 'its.' See note to i. 33. The pronoun refers to the verbal noun 'shining,' but it would almost seem as if Marlowe had had the supposed antecedent 'sun' in his mind.

31. *As*, for 'so as,' which is frequently used for 'so that' (Abbott, § 109).

Ib. motion, mention. More usual in the sense of 'proposal'; compare Friar Bacon, v. 16.

33. *cunning*, knowledge. See note on opening Chorus, l. 20.

36. *paramour.* See Dramatis Personae.

42. *so far forth*, to such an extent. Compare Chaucer, The Man of Lawes Prologue, 19: 'as far forth as ye may.'

44. *that's just nothing at all*, that is a very easy feat. Compare xii. 12.

45. *if it like your grace*, if it please your grace. Compare Friar Bacon, iv. 55, and Henry V, iv. 3. 77:

> 'Why, now thou hast unwish'd five thousand men;
> Which likes me better than to wish us one.'

The form of address 'your grace' is made use of in Shakespeare to kings and queens, as well as to persons of princely, ducal, and high ecclesiastical rank. In 2 Henry VI, i. 2. 71, it is however contrasted with 'majesty,' the royal or imperial style introduced under Henry VIII, in place of the formerly usual 'highness.' In Friar Bacon, i. 170 and viii. 19, the Prince of Wales is addressed as 'your honour'; in viii. 160 as 'your grace.'

49. *marry*, the common interjection, a corruption of 'Mary' (the Blessed Virgin).

50. *grace*, in the sense of goodness or virtue, the effect of the grace (mercy) of Heaven. Compare xiii. 56, 66.

51. *lively*, in a lifelike manner. See note on l. 18 above; and compare The Winter's Tale, v. 3. 19:

> 'Prepare
> To see the life as lively mocked as ever
> Still sleep mock'd death.'

56. *Go to.* The adverbial use of 'to' in this phrase must be explained as indicating a forward motion; 'go on to your business.' Compare 'fall to,' vii. 62.

Ib. presently, at once.

60. *as true as*, as true as that.

Ib. Diana. The story of Diana's punishment of Actaeon is in Ovid's Metamorphoses, iii. 138 seqq. Compare Edward II, i. 1 (in Gaveston's description of the 'Italian masks' proposed by him):

'One, like Actaeon peeping through the grove,
Shall by the angry goddess be transform'd,
And running in the likeness of a hart,
By yelping hounds pull'd down, shall seem to die.'

64. *an*, if. See note on v. 137.

65. *I'll meet with you*, I'll come across you (and settle with you). See l. 83 below.

Ib. anon, immediately (A.-S. on ân, in one, at once).

Re-enter Mephistophiles with Spirits in the shapes of Alexander and his Paramour. The quarto of 1616, in which the dialogue of this scene is much fuller, has the following stage-direction for a dumb show at this point: '*Sennet. Enter, at one door, the* Emperor Alexander, *at the other*, Darius. *They meet.* Darius *is thrown down;* Alexander *kills him, takes off his crown, and, offering to go out, his* Paramour *meets him. He embraceth her, and sets* Darius' *crown upon her head; and, coming back, both salute the* Emperor, *who, leaving his state, offers to embrace them; which* Faustus *seeing, suddenly stays him. Then trumpets cease, and music sounds.*' As to these exhibitions of the 'sciomantic' art, see note to opening Chorus, l. 25; and compare the story of the summoning of Hector and Achilles by a necromant at the court of the Emperor Maximilian narrated by Wier in his work De Praestigiis, &c. (Scheible, Kloster, ii. 188).

68. *had a wart or mole.* See for this incident, Introduction, p. lxxi. Kühne quotes a similar story with reference to the shade of Mary of Burgundy, summoned by Tritheim in the presence of her widower, Maximilian I, who recognised a black mark on the neck of the apparition; and a parallel touch in the Indian 'Somaveda.'

Re-enter the Knight *with a pair of horns on his head.* Tricks of the same kind were related of the Bohemian conjuror Zyto; see Scheible, Kloster, xi. 282.

80. *Villain*, low fellow (peasant, villanus), in antithesis to gentleman (i.e. man of rank, compare 'an honourable gentleman' of the Duke of Vanholt, xi. 93). Compare ix. 46.

81. *good.* This adjective (like 'dear' and 'sweet' in modern usage) is frequently used in the vocative, both by itself, and in the combinations

'good thou,' and more especially 'good now.' Compare The Tempest, i. 1. 3; Romeo and Juliet, i. 5. 8; and Hamlet, i. 1. 70. 'Lovely' is used without a substantive in Friar Bacon, x. 111; but with a participial vocative conjoined. See also note on Friar Bacon, ix. 192.

82. *are you remembered*, do you remember. So frequently in Shakespeare, e. g. in As You Like It, iv. 5. 131:

'He said mine eyes were black and my hair black;
And, now I am remembered, scorned at me.'

As to the use of 'to be' with intransitive verbs, and the consequent indefinite and apparently not passive use of passive participles, see Abbott, §§ 295, 374; and compare xi. 51, xiii. 74.

Ib. conference. Compare i. 66.

83. *met with you.* Compare l. 65.

88. *injurious*, insolent, offensive. Compare Friar Bacon, viii. 24, and 'injurious villain' in Richard II, i. 1. 91, and see Clark and Wright's note, *l. c.*

91. *transform him straight.* In the quarto of 1616, Benvolio (as the Knight is there called) seeks to revenge himself upon Faustus by setting an ambush against him, but only to the worse confounding of himself and his friends. This 'addition' corresponds to ch. 35 of the Faustbuch. The stage-direction '*Mephistophilis removes the horns*' is not in the quarto of 1604.

Scene XI.

Here evidently begins a new scene, which plays first on 'the fair and pleasant green' mentioned by Faustus (l. 8), and afterwards (from l. 10) in the house of Faustus at Wittenberg, where he falls asleep in his chair (l. 44). The representation of Faustus's journey on the stage recalls the ambulatory scenes of the Indian drama.

Enter a Horse-courser. See Dramatis Personae. For the trick played by Faustus upon the horse-courser compare Introduction, p. lxxii. A similar trick is played by Wagner upon a dealer in mules at Florence in 'Christoph Wagner's Leben,' ch. xxii (Scheible, Kloster, ii. 107). Kühne has collected a host of similar stories, beginning with the famous exploit of the Egyptian thief in Herodotus, ii. 121, and including a trick of Eulenspiegel (Owl-glass), and a Bohemian story of the conjuror Zyto, who changed a handful of grass into thirty pigs, which he sold to a baker called Michael. The baker was afterwards got rid of by the same device as that in our scene; and the story gave rise to the Bohemian proverb, 'A profit, like Michael's from his pigs.' Compare also Scheible, Kloster, xi. 278.

11. *Fustian*, a punning misnomer for Faustus. See iv. 76.

Ib. mass. Compare iv. 36.

25. *at any hand*, in any case, any way. Shakespeare uses the phrases 'at any hand,' 'in any hand,' and 'of all hands' in the same sense. So in The Taming of the Shrew, i. 2. 147:

'All books of love, see that at any hand.'

30. *am I made man.* We should say, I am a made man. 'Made' is 'finished, complete'; so Fluellen, Henry V, iv. 7. 45, protests against the tales being taken out of his mouth, 'ere it' (the tales) 'is made and finished.'

31. *for forty.* 'Twice forty' and 'forty more' have been here suggested as emendations by Dyce and Wagner.

Ib. the quality of hey-ding-ding, hey-ding-ding. Of this no explanation has been suggested; the reference is apparently to the refrain of some song.

33. *slick*, sleek; an epithet used, as Johnson points out, by Chapman of horses, Iliads, ii. 680:

'Whom silver-bow'd Apollo bred in the Pierian mead,
Both slicke and daintie, yet were both in warre of wondrous dread.'

Compare the verb 'to slick,' i. e. make smooth, *ib.* xxiii. 259.

Ib. God b'wi'ye (quartos of 1604 and 1602 'god buy'), God be with ye, the origin of our 'good bye.'

40. *Thy fatal time*, the time allotted to thee by fate. In Friar Bacon, xiii. 81, 'fatal' signifies 'doomed.'

Ib. final end. As to this omission of the article (indefinite or definite), see Introduction, p. ix. For the tautology compare 'vital life,' l. 3, above.

41. *into.* Quarto of 1604 'unto.'

42. *Confound these passions with a quiet sleep*, Faustus, lull this agitation in a quiet sleep. Compare Friar Bacon, i. 20; and for the adjective 'passionate,' iv. 84. See also Paradise Lost, i. 165 (of Satan):

'Cruel his eye, but cast
Signs of remorse and passion.'

43. *call*, mercifully address, offer salvation to. 'Many be called, but few chosen,' St. Matthew xx. 16. Faustus may have had in mind the lines in the 'Dies irae':

'Et latronem exaudisti,
Mihi quoque spem dedisti';

and

'Voca me cum benedictis.'

44. *in conceit*, in thy thoughts, in mind. So Marlowe uses the word as equivalent to fancy or imagination, 1 Tamburlaine, i. 2:

'That in conceit bear empires on our spears.'

and *ib.* v. 2:

'Behold her wounded, in conceit, for thee.'

45. *quoth a.* See note on iv. 3.

46. *Doctor Lopus.* An allusion to Roderigo Lopez, the Spanish private physician to Queen Elizabeth, who entered into a plot to poison the Queen. Of this plot, which was brought to light by the activity of Essex, and in which King Philip of Spain was implicated, several narratives were drawn up, among the rest one by Bacon, who had been present at the trial of Lopez on February 28th, 1594, when he was found guilty. Bacon's True Report of the Detestable Treason intended by Dr. Roderigo Lopez appears not to have been printed till 1657, and will be found in Spedding's edition of the Letters and Life, vol. i. A fuller report, thought by Mr. Spedding to be by Coke, was printed in the year of Lopez' condemnation to death. The plot is referred to in Middleton's A Game at Chess, iv. 2, cited by Dyce.

Ib. has, for 'he has,' modern 'he 's.'

51. *known of.* So in quarto of 1604; and there seems no reason to alter the reading. Compare Othello, iii. 3. 319, where the folios read 'Be not acknown on 't,' and the first and third quartos 'Be not you known on 't,' i. e. be not you aware of it. See note on x. 82.

52. *rid*, a preterite used by Shakespeare as well as 'rode.'

54. *bottle of hay*, a truss of hay. So in Mucedorus, Mouse, carrying home his bottle of hay, tumbles over the bear; compare also A Midsummer Night's Dream, iv. 1. 37, and Field's A Woman is a Weathercock, where the saying in which the term is still used occurs: 'Methinks he and his lady should show like a needle in a bottle of hay.' The word 'bottle,' used in this sense of bundle, has a different derivation from the word as now ordinarily employed. The former is from the French botel, a diminutive of botte, a bundle, itself a word probably of Germanic origin (compare N. H. G. bosse, a bundle of flax, O. H. G. pozô, a blade of flax), and used in modern French in such phrases as botte de paille, de foin. The latter is from the French bouteille (Italian bottiglia, M. Lat. buticula, a diminutive of butta; compare Greek πίθος, Gaelic bôt, A.-S. butte, N. H. G. butte, bütte, a large vessel or boot).

56. *the dearest horse*, viz. to him, he shall have to pay most dearly for it.

57. *snipper-snapper*, a comic contemptuous expression for the serving-man (Mephistophiles), from the reduplication 'snip-snap,' which occurs in a song in the old interlude 'Like will to Like' &c., and in Love's Labour 's Lost, v. 1. 63. 'Schnippschnapp' is, I think used in German for idle talk; and the term 'whippersnapper,' in the sense of a contemptible little fellow, is still in use.

58. *hey-pass*, juggler, from the phrase 'hey-pass' employed by jugglers, as 'hey-presto' continues to be, at the critical point of their tricks.

Compare in Pierce Pennilesse's Supplication: 'there are a thousand iugling trickes to be vsed at *Hey, passe,* come aloft!' and L. Barry's Ram-Alley or Merry Tricks, ii. 1:

'*Taf.* There's no offence;
My mind is changed.
Adri. I told you as much before.
Con. With a hey-pass—with a repass.'

63. *glass-windows.* Very probably Faustus was supposed to be sitting at the window of his house. Glass-windows were still not universal in these times, although already largely in use. See Harrison's Description of England, bk. ii. ch. 12. We can hardly suppose that the Horse-courser alludes to spectacles worn by Faust—which is an ingenious alternative suggestion of Professor Wagner's, but would have been more appropriate in the case of Friar Bacon, who was credited with the invention of spectacles.

73. *So-ho,* the sportsman's cry on finding the hare in her form.

75. *away,* i.e. out or off.

82. *Where be they?* For the use of 'be' in questions where doubt is suggested, see Abbott, § 299. Compare xii. 24.

83. *ostry,* inn or lodging (compare hostelry). In A Looking-Glass for London and England the term 'ostry-faggot' signifies a faggot in an inn.

91. *the Duke of Vanholt.* See Dramatis Personae.

93. *gentleman,* nobleman or prince. Compare x. 79.

Scene XII.

Before this scene the quarto of 1616 inserts another, in which the Horse-courser merely repeats in a narrative form the excellent jest played upon him.—For Faustus's visit to the court of the 'Duke of Vanholt,' see Introduction, p. lxxiii, and compare Widmann's narrative, Part ii. ch. 17 (Scheible, Kloster, ii. 615). For similar instances of magicians conjuring up fruit, dishes of food, &c., see Görres' notes (*ib.* 31; and compare *ib.* xi. 273). The best-known example is the exploit of Faust in Auerbach's cellar at Leipzig. See Introduction, p. xxxvii.

4. *madam,* quarto of 1604 'Madame' (and so throughout the scene).

11. *meat,* food. See note on i. 161.

12. *that's nothing.* Compare x. 44.

14. *so,* provided that. Compare iii. 92.

15. *on them,* of them. See note on ii. 15.

18. *how.* This word, or the preceding '*that,*' is redundant to the construction, which is anacoluthic.

22. *Saba.* See note on v. 154.

24. *be they.* See note on xi. 82.

33. *beholding*, for beholden. Compare xiii. 15; and see Abbott, § 372, as to the use of the affix 'ing' as if equivalent to the old affix 'en' of the passive participle. For the converse use of 'known' for 'knowing,' see xi. 51.—This line and the next are printed as verse in the quarto of 1604.

Scene XIII.

In the quarto of 1616 the stage-direction runs as follows: 'Thunder and lightning. Enter Devils with covered dishes. Mephistophiles leads them into Faustus' study; then enter Wagner.' As to Faustus' will, see Introduction, p. lxxvii; and compare Widmann's narrative, Part iii. ch. 1 (Scheible, Kloster, p. 646). Wagner's speech is printed as prose in the quarto of 1604.

1. *I think . . . shortly.* Very probably, as Wagner suggests, this line should read:

'I think my master shortly means to die.'

2. *goods.* After this the quarto of 1616 adds:

'His house, his goods, and store of golden plate,
Besides two thousand ducats ready-coined.'

3. *methinketh.* I follow Wagner in reading thus for 'methinks,' for the sake of the metre.

Ib. if that. See note to x. 15.

5. *even now*, at this very moment. See Abbott, § 38.

8. *belike.* See note to i. 43.

9. *conference.* Compare i. 66.

11. *we have determined with ourselves*, we have agreed with one another. The English language possessing no reciprocal pronouns, the simple personal pronoun, with or without the adjective self, sufficed in A.-S. to express reciprocity. This usage survived; so in the Authorised Version, St. Luke's Gospel, xxii. 23: 'And they began to enquire among themselves.'

Ib. Helen. See Dramatis Personae. For the summoning of Helen, compare Introduction, p. lxxiv; and as to these summonings in general, compare notes to opening Chorus, line 25, and to x. 68. Moehsen (1771; see Scheible's Kloster, ii. 256) relates how the real Dr. Faust summoned 'the heroes of Homerus' before the students at Erfurt; compare ch. liii. of the Faustbuch of 1590 (Kühne, p. 140).

10, 12. *beautifulest, admirablest.* See note on i. 160.

13. *that favour, as to*, such a favour as to. 'Such' being frequently used with 'which,' naturally 'that' was also used with 'as' ('in which way') used for 'which.' See Abbott, § 280.

14, 15. *whom . . . for majesty.* This line recurs below, l. 27. For the use of 'for,' compare x. 4.

15. *beholding.* See note to xii. 33.

18. *For that.* See note to x. 15.

22. *otherways*, or 'othergates' (Twelfth Night, v. 198), equivalent to 'otherwise,' which is the reading of the quarto of 1616.

Ib. for. Compare x. 4.

23. *Sir Paris.* 'Sir' is the chivalrous prefix of mediaeval romance; so Pistol in The Merry Wives of Windsor, i. 2. 83, speaks of 'Sir Pandarus of Troy,' and *ib.*, ii. 1. 122, of 'Sir Actaeon.'

24. *the spoils.* Wagner understands 'the spoils' to refer to Helen herself; nor would this be impossible. Compare the use of 'trophe' in the sense of 'victim of Love' (as a translation of Boccaccio's name 'Filostrato,' explained by him to signify 'uomo vinto ed abbattuto da Amore') in Lydgate's Prologue to his Fall of Princes. But Paris, as is repeatedly indicated in the Iliad, robbed Menelaus not only of his wife, but also of other things that were his.

Ib. Dardania, Troy (properly the more ancient city on Mount Ida founded by Dardanus).

25. *Be silent . . . words*, a happy reminiscence of the Greek *εὐφημεῖτε* and Latin 'favete linguis,' the formulae pronounced before religious solemnities such as sacrifices. Apparitions, as the story of Tam o' Shanter teaches, will not always bear being spoken to. For the description of the apparition of Helen in the Faustbuch, see Introduction, pp. lxxiv–lxxv.

27. *Whom . . . majesty.* See ll. 14, 15, above.

28. *pursu'd.* To 'pursue' is to follow with a desire to inflict punishment or vengeance, to prosecute; hence the legal term 'pursuer' used for 'prosecutor' in Scotland. Compare King Lear, ii. 1. 91:

'If it be true, all vengeance comes too short
Which can pursue the offender.'

Hence it means to seek to inflict punishment or wreak vengeance for an offence, as in our passage, and in Measure for Measure, v. 1. 109:

'It imports no reason
That with such vehemency he should pursue
Faults proper to himself.'

30. *passeth all compare*, exceeds all comparison. Shakespeare frequently uses 'compare' for 'comparison;' so Romeo and Juliet, iii. 5. 238:

'That same tongue
Which she hath praised him with above compare.'

See also Friar Bacon, i. 84. As to this use of verbal infinitives ('nearly all of French origin') as substantives see Abbott, § 451. So Marlowe,

1 Tamburlaine, iii. 2, uses 'arise' for 'rising'; Greene, Friar Bacon, i. 2, 'shine' for 'shining'; *ib.* vii. 2, 'repair' for 'arrival'; *ib.* ix. 183, 'entertain' for 'entertainment'; *ib.* ix. 205, 'greets' for 'greetings'; and *ib.* xiv. 15, 'repents' for 'penances'; in Orlando Furioso, 'this bad agree' signifies 'this bad agreement'; in A Looking-Glass for London and England we have

'Venus in the brightness of her shine';

and

'to give attend' [i. e. attendance] 'on Rasni's excellence';

and in Peele's Sir Clyomon and Sir Clamydes:

'The which propound' [i. e. proposition] 'within my mind doth oftentimes resolve.'

32. *paragon*, model, example. The word is derived through the French from the Spanish 'paragon' or 'parangon,' which is explained from the common combination of the Spanish prepositions 'para' and 'con,' meaning 'compared with.' That however a derivation from the Greek (παρ' ἀγῶνα) was thought of, seems clear from the use of the word in the sense of 'supremely excellent, or incomparable model'; the English 'over-match' (compare Friar Bacon, i. 63) being evidently intended as an equivalent. So in A Looking-Glass for London and England:

'Come, lovely minion, paragon for fair,'

i. e. incomparable as to beauty.

Enter an Old Man. This stage-direction is not given in the quarto of 1604. The Old Man's speech is longer in the quarto of 1616.—Compare as to the Old Man's endeavour, as related in the Faustbuch, Introduction, pp. lxxv–lxxvi; and see AN OLD MAN in Dramatis Personae.

41, 42. *repentant . . . filthiness,* heaviness repentant of, etc. Compare as to the transposition, Abbott, § 419 a.

42. *vile.* The quarto of 1604 has 'vilde.' See note to i. 107.

44. *sin.* The quarto of 1604 has 'sinnes.'

50. *calls for.* The quarto of 1616 reads 'claims his.'

Ib. roaring. Compare 1 Epistle of St. Peter, v. 8.

51. *almost.* This word is wanting in the quartos of 1604 and 1609.

52. *now.* This word is likewise wanting in the first two quartos.

Ib. to do thee right, to pay thee thy due.

Mephistophilis gives him a dagger. Wagner doubts whether Marlowe himself 'could have resorted to the clumsy trick of letting Mephistophilis present a dagger to Faustus,' and thinks this passage merely 'a clumsy imitation' of that above, vi. 21–24. There is however a difference between the two situations (see note to vi. 21). It is worthy of note that in Widmann (Part iii. c. 14) Mephistophilis prevents

Faustus from the act of suicide, to which he in our text tempts him. Düntzer refers to several passages in the Acta Sanctorum, in which the Devil tempts to suicide those who have entered into a connexion with him. A novel and effective turn is given to the idea of this passage in Lenau's semi-dramatic poem Faust, in which Faust actually commits suicide, but thereby delivers himself only the more surely into the clutches of the Devil.—In A Looking-Glass for London and England, the Evil Angel 'tempts' the Usurer, 'offering the knife and rope.'

54. *I see an angel hovers.* Wagner rightly explains 'an angel which hovers.' For this omission of the relative, compare Friar Bacon, i. 17, and see Abbott, § 244.—Faustus has not been deserted by his Good Angel.

55. *a vial full of heavenly grace.* The idea is of course taken from that of Unction, especially Extreme Unction.

58, 59. *I feel Thy words to comfort.* 'Thy words' is joined to l. 59 in the quarto of 1604.—There is no reason for substituting 'do' for 'to,' as is suggested by Wagner, who considers the construction of the passage 'in every way irregular.' As to the frequent insertion of 'to' after verbs of perceiving, such as 'feel,' 'see,' 'hear,' see Abbott, § 349, who cites, among other passages, Twelfth Night, i. 5. 315-317:

'Methinks I feel this youth's perfections
. . . .
To creep in at mine eyes.'

61. *with heavy cheer*, in a heavy frame of mind. 'Cheer' properly means countenance (Fr. chère, O. Fr. chière, Spanish and Provençal cara, face, which Diez derives with some hesitation from the M. Lat. cara, Greek κάρα; another derivation has been suggested from Lat. quadra, square, table, in connexion with which may be compared Friar Bacon, i. 59:

'Her front is beauty's table').

Compare The Faerie Queene, i. 1. 2. 8:

'But of his cheere did seeme too solemne sad';

and the passages quoted by Trench from Wiclif's version of Genesis, iii. 19, 'In swoot of thi cheer thou schalt ete thi breed,' and *ib.* iv. 5, 'And Cayn was wroth greetli, and his cheer felde doun.'

62. *hopeless*, for the salvation of which there is no hope. Adjectives with the termination 'less' have both an active and a passive meaning; see Abbott, § 4. Compare note to l. 92 of this scene.

65. *grace*, the divine mercy, as above, l. 55.

69. *in piece-meal.* Compare 1 Tamburlaine, iv. 2:

'That may command thee piece-meal to be torn';

and again 2 Tamburlaine, iii. 5. 'Inchmeal' and limbmeal (O. E. limmæl-um, which shows the suffix to have been originally dative and instrumental) are likewise Shakespearean terms. The suffix 'meal' is the German 'mal' (times), as in 'einmal' (once).

74. *unfeignèd*, for 'unfeigning.' See note to x. 82.

75. *drift*, intention, desire (to repent). Compare 2 Tamburlaine, v. 2:

'The victories
Wherewith he hath so soon dismayed the world
Are greatest to discourage all thy drift.'

Faustus stabs his arm, &c. A stage-direction suggested by Dyce. See as to Faustus's second contract with the Devil, Introduction, p. lxxvi.

76. *age*, old man. 'Age,' says Autolycus, addressing the Old Shepherd (The Winter's Tale, v. 1. 787), 'thou hast lost thy labour.'

80. *I cannot touch his soul.* Compare Book of Job, ch. ii, for the idea. There is a passage not altogether dissimilar to ours in The Witch of Edmonton, ii. 1 (Dyce's Ford, i i. 203).

82. *One thing, good servant.* Compare Introduction, p. lxxvii.

84. *have unto my paramour.* 'Unto' is here used, like 'to' (compare 'unto' for 'to' or 'into,' xiv. 107), to indicate apposition. See Abbott, § 109, where the Latin use of the dative with 'habere' is compared. Compare Friar Bacon, xii. 29.

85. *heavenly.* Compare opening Chorus, l. 6.

87. *These.* I see no reason for altering this reading of the quarto.

88. *keep*, preserve unbroken.

90. *twinkling.* As to the omission of the article see Introduction, p. ix.

Re-enter Helen, according to the quarto of 1616, 'passing over the stage between two Cupids.'

91. *Was this the face that launch'd*, &c. Compare 2 Tamburlaine, ii. 4:

'Helen, whose beauty summoned Greece to arms,
And drew a thousand ships on Tenedos.'

This beautiful passage, which Marlowe has nowhere equalled (perhaps the nearest approach is Tamburlaine's speech on Zenocrate in 1 Tamburlaine, v. 2), was no doubt originally suggested by the passage in the Iliad, iii. 156, where the old men of Troy, on seeing Helen appear in her beauty on the walls, say that she was worth the war caused by her—a tribute to beauty of which the conception is extolled by Lessing in his Laocoon. The outburst of Faust on beholding the real Helena (whom he had previously seen as a magical apparition), at the close of act ii. of part ii. of Goethe's tragedy, should be compared; nor is it possible, in dwelling on this passage, to forget one of the noblest creations of modern English art, Mr. Leighton's Helen on the Walls.

92. *the topless towers*, i. e. the towers which are not (over) topped by any others. Compare Dido Queen of Carthage, iii. 3:

'and cut a passage through his topless hill';

and A Looking-Glass for London and England:

'Six hundred towers that topless touch the clouds.'

Marlowe is very fond of this suffix 'less,' which often has the force of 'not able to be' (see Abbott, § 446); so Dido Queen of Carthage, ii. 1, 'quenchless fire'; Edward II, i. 2, 'their timeless sepulchre'; and 2 Tamburlaine, v. 3, 'his timeless death,' i.e. of which time cannot destroy the memory; 1 Tamburlaine, v. 2, 'our expressless bann'd inflictions'; and *ib.* the 'resistless powers of the gods.' Compare also Greene's James IV, ii. 2:

''Tis foolish to bewail recureless things.'

93. *make me immortal with a kiss.* Compare Dido Queen of Carthage, iv. 4:

'For in his looks I see eternity,
And he'll make me immortal with a kiss.'

94. *Her lips suck forth my soul.* Diluted in Greene's James IV, act iv:

'Methinks I see her blushing steal a kiss,
Uniting both your souls by such a sweet,
And you, my king, suck nectar from her lips.'

I dare not retain the reading 'suckes' of the quarto of 1604.

96. *is.* Quarto of 1604, 'be.'

97. *dross.* See note to i. 34.

100. *Menelaus.* This is the reading of the quarto of 1604; but I doubt whether Marlowe did not write 'Menelas.'

101. *wear thy colours on my plumèd crest.* This is quite in the way of the mediaeval versions of the tale of Troy; see for instance the tournaments in Lydgate's Troy-Booke.

102. *wound Achilles in the heel.* The death of Achilles by an arrow shot by Paris and directed by Apollo was an incident in the Aethiopis of Arctinus, reproduced by Ovid (Metamorphoses, x. 605) and mentioned by Horace and Vergil. That the arrow wounded the invulnerable heel of Achilles is related by Hyginus, but not stated by the Latin poets. In the Iliad (xxi. 166) Achilles is wounded in the right arm. See Preller, Griechische Mythologie, ii. 438 (note).

107. *hapless Semele,* who perished in the flames in which Zeus had appeared to her in answer to her wish, that he should come in his divine majesty.

109. *wanton Arethusa's azur'd arms.* Arethusa being nowhere mentioned as the beloved of the 'monarch of the sky,' whether the phrase be intended to signify Jove or Apollo, Wagner points out that Marlowe's mythology is at fault here, and even suggests a doubt whether there may be 'any corruption' in 'Arethusa.' It would be a sorry attempt to seek to spoil this lovely line by any crude conjecture. Van der

Velde thinks that 'the monarch of the sky' means the sky itself, which is mirrored in the spring Arethusa and thus lends it an azure hue. Arethusa was a general name given by the Greeks to springs; and Marlowe may therefore be excused for using the name to signify 'water-nymph' in general. F. V. Hugo has not improved the probable meaning of the passage by translating 'the monarch of the sky' 'le roi des mers.'—If Marlowe was thinking of the reflexion of the sky, or of the character of Arethusa as a sea-nymph, the epithet 'azur'd' has a special significance here; compare The Tempest, v. 43:

"'Twixt the green sea and the azured vault';

but the word may be merely used as an epithet of the veins of the skin; as in The Rape of Lucrece, 419; and in Friar Bacon, i. 83. Skelton in his 'Dyties Solacyons' addresses a lady as a 'Saphyre of Sadnes, enuayned wyth indy blew.' Compare in the same author's Magnyfycence, l. 1597,

'the streynes of her vaynes as asure inde blewe';

and 'azur'd silk' in Peele's Edward I, vi. 21. Shakespeare uses both the forms 'azure' and 'azured' as adjectives.

110. *none but thou shalt be my paramour.* I have followed Dyce in retaining the ungrammatical 'shalt' of the quartos.

Enter the Old Man. It seems unnecessary here to begin a new scene, as Dyce suggests, though in the corresponding passage of the Faustbuch (see Introduction, p. lxxvi) the Old Man's repulse of the Devils occurs two days after Faustus's second contract with Mephistophiles.

114. *sift.* Wagner compares the Authorised Version of St. Luke's Gospel, xxii. 31: 'Satan hath desired to have you, that he may sift you as wheat.' The word here signifies to test or prove; Shakespeare employs it in the sense 'to examine closely,' as in Hamlet, ii. 2. 58: 'Well, we shall sift him.'

115. *furnace*, an allusion to the furnace from which Shadrach, Meshach, and Abed-nego were delivered, Daniel ch. iii. See also 1 Epistle of St. Peter, i. 7.

118. *state*, power. Compare opening Chorus, l. 4.

Scene XIV.

This scene, which has been described (by Mr. Fleay) as the only dramatic death-bed scene which can be compared in horror to 2 Henry VI, iii. 3, has received important additions in the quarto of 1616, which Wagner has admitted into his text. They consist especially of an opening dialogue between Lucifer, Belzebub and Mephistophilis, and a passage in which the Good and the Evil Angel severally display before the eyes of Faustus the bliss of heaven and the horrors of hell. The latter passage, with a short preliminary dialogue between Faustus and Mephistophilis, is interpolated after the *exeunt* of the Scholars before l. 64.

3. *chamber-fellow.* It was long customary at the universities for two, if not more, students to occupy the same room together. See Masson's Life of Milton, i. 109. This seems to be the sense of 'college-mates' in Friar Bacon, xiii. 24.

5. *comes he not?* This is explained by l. 75 below.

7. *Belike.* See note on i. 43.

Ib. is grown into, has gradually fallen into. So we say 'to grow faint.'

10. *surfeit*, a sickness of the stomach, properly an indigestion caused by excess of eating or drinking. 'Soft, sir,' says Tamburlaine to Bajazet (1 Tamburlaine, iv. 4), 'you must be dieted; too much eating will make you surfeit.' This was the common sickness of the grossly-feeding Elizabethan age. So in Meres' Palladis Tamia, Greene is said to have 'died of a surfet taken at pickeld herrings and Rhenish wine.'

15, 16. These lines are printed as verse in the quarto of 1604.

17. *Ah, gentlemen*, &c. For the speech of Faustus compare Introduction, pp. lxxviii-lxxx; and Widmann's version, part iii. ch. 16 (Scheible, Kloster, ii. 730).

19. *a student*, as we should say, a resident.

31. *yea life and soul*— (quarto of 1604, yea life and soul,). As van der Velde observes, Mephistophilis prevents Faustus from finishing the sentence.

36. *cunning.* Compare opening Chorus, l. 20.

40. *bill.* See note on i. 20.

43. *Why did not*, &c. Compare Introduction, p. lxxx.

50. *save.* This word is wanting in the quartos of 1604 and 1609.

54. *let us*, let us go.

56, 57. *and what noise*, &c. Compare Introduction, p. lxxx.

The clock strikes eleven. In the German popular play reprinted by Engel (p. 45), when the clock strikes eleven, a voice is heard: 'Fauste! Judicatus es!'—when it strikes twelve, a voice says: Fauste! Fauste! in aeternum damnatus es!'

65. *Now hast . . . live.* Probably an incomplete line (compare note to vi. 87), which seems a preferable supposition to that of 'hour' being a dissyllable here. (The instances cited in note to v. 63 are not analogous, as in our passage the accent would lie on the inserted sound.)

69. *Nature's eye.* So Shakespeare frequently calls the sun 'heaven's eye.'

71. *a natural day*, the common length of a day. Compare Richard III, i. 3. 213:

'God, I pray him,
That none of you may live your natural age,'

i. e. the ordinary length of a man's life.

73. *O lente, lente currite, noctis equi.* From Ovid's Amores, i. 13. 40:

'Clamares, "Lente currite, noctis equi";'

translated by Marlowe in his Ovid's Elegies. Faustus's wish is the exact converse of that of the King in Edward II, iv. 3. 33:

'Gallop apace, bright Phoebus, through the sky,
And dusky night, in rusty iron car,
Between you both shorten the time, I pray,
That I may see that most desired day'—

a passage which doubtless suggested to Shakespeare Juliet's

'Gallop apace, you fiery-footed steeds,' &c.

in Romeo and Juliet, iii. 2. 1.—Marlowe occasionally indulges in Latin quotations; see e. g. his Edward II, i. 4. 13; iv. 6. 53-54; v. 4. 67.

74. *still*, constantly, unceasingly. Compare l. 110.

79. *naming of.* For the construction compare note on vii. 79.

80. *Yet will . . . Lucifer.* Though a characteristic feature of 'Marlowe's mighty line' is its masculine or one-syllable ending, yet he occasionally permits himself double endings (see the table of their proportionate numbers in Fleay's edition of Edward II, Introduction, p. 45), especially in proper names, in which he even uses triple endings. So in our passages; and in 1 Tamburlaine, i. 1:

'Your grace hath taken order by Therídamas';

ib. i. 2:

'I must be pleased perforce. Wretched Zenócrate!'

ib. ii. 8:

'Then thou for Parthia; they for Scythia and Média.'

Ib. ii. 4, there is a triple ending not in a proper name:

'Ay, marry am I; have you any suit to me?'

81, 82. *Where is it now . . . brows.* These two lines are printed as three in the quarto of 1604.

82. *ireful.* This adjective (which also occurs in the old interlude Calisto and Meliboea) is coined like 'fiendful' in the closing Chorus, line 5; and 'wreckful' in Dido Queen of Carthage, i. 2.

83. Compare Revelations, vi. 16: 'And said to the mountains and rocks, Fall on us, and hide us from the face of him that sitteth on the throne, and from the wrath of the Lamb.'

84. *God.* Here the quarto of 1616 substitutes 'heaven.' See Introduction, p. lxxxvii.

86. *Then will I . . . earth.* Compare note on v. 77

88. *nativity*, birth. Compare 1 Tamburlaine, iv. 2:

'Smile stars, that reigned at my nativity.'

Hence to 'cast a nativity' was to find out the position of the planets at the time of a person's birth.

91. *labouring clouds.* I have adopted Dyce's suggestion 'clouds' for 'cloud.' Milton has the phrase 'the labouring clouds' in his L'Allegro, 74 (cited by Wagner).

92. *you.* Dyce has suggested (though doubtfully, as 'it is certain that awkward changes of person are sometimes found in passages of our early poets') 'they' for 'you,' and 'their' for 'your' in the next line.

94. *So that,* provided that. Compare iii. 92. The quarto of 1616 reads: 'But let my soul mount and ascend.'

95-97. *Ah, half . . . on my soul.* These lines are printed as arranged by Dyce.

96-98. *O God . . . ransom'd me.* For these lines the quarto of 1616 substitutes the single line:

'O, if my soul must suffer for my sin.'

See Introduction, p. lxxxvii.

102. *limited,* fixed as a limit. So Comedy of Errors, i. 1. 151:

'I'll limit thee this day
To fix thy life to beneficial help.'

105. *Pythagoras' metempsychosis* (quarto of 1604, 'metemsuccossis'). Pythagoras of Samos (born probably in the 43rd Olympiad—608-605—was regarded as the author of the doctrine of the transmigration of souls, which possibly he derived from Egypt, where it was an established dogma. As to Pythagoras as one of the fathers of magic, see Friar Bacon, ix. 30, and note.

107. *Unto,* into or to. Compare note to xiii. 84.

108, 109. Printed as one line in the quarto of 1604.

110. *still,* ever; as above, l. 74, and Friar Bacon, viii. 38. So 'the still-vexed Bermoothes' in The Tempest, i. 2. 229.

The clock strikes twelve. For what follows compare Introduction, p. lxxxi.

119. *let me breathe awhile.* This awfully realistic passage recalls a passage in The Debate of the Body and Soul, 411-416:

'An hundred develen on him dongen,
Ner and ther was he hent;
With hote speres thoruȝ was strongen,
And with oules al to-rent;
At ilke a dint the sparkles sprongen,
As of a brond that were for-brent.'

120. *Ugly hell, gape not.* For the epithet compare vi. 79. The representation of the mouth of hell was familiar to the old mysteries; and fire was often displayed in it. Goethe in his Faust has not omitted the

opening of the jaws of hell (see in act v. of Part ii, the passage which, as Loepell says, recalls Dante's Inferno, canto viii).

121. *I'll burn my books*, of magic. Wagner refers to the passage in The Acts of the Apostles, xix. 19, where it is stated of the Ephesians, that 'many of them which used curious arts brought their books together, and burned them before all men.'

Enter Chorus. Before the entrance of the Chorus, there follows in the quarto of 1616 a short scene between the Scholars, on finding the mangled limbs of Faustus.—Goethe's Faust closes with a 'Chorus mysticus,' as Marlowe's does with a Chorus uttering its solemn moral.

1, 2. *Cut is the branch . . . laurel-bough.* These lines are introduced as a comment on Marlowe's own death, in Mr. R. Horne's short but powerful drama The Death of Marlowe. Compare the closing lines of 2 Tamburlaine.

3. *sometime*, formerly. So in Dido Queen of Carthage, ii. 1:

'Sometime I was a Trojan, mighty Queen.'

'Sometimes' was similarly used; see Abbott, § 68 a.

5. *fiendful.* Compare note to l. 82.

6. *Only to wonder at*, i. e. to content themselves with wondering at, and not to essay in their own persons.

Terminat hora . . auctor opus (quartos of 1604 and 1609, 'author'). The source of this line, which has an Ovidian sound, but does not occur in Ovid, remains undiscovered.

THE HONOURABLE HISTORY OF

FRIAR BACON AND FRIAR BUNGAY.

DRAMATIS PERSONAE.

KING HENRY THE THIRD. Of King Henry III (1216–1272) it may be noticed, in connexion with our play, that he was through life a warm friend and patron of the monks, and that his friendly bearing towards Friar Bacon is therefore quite in character. For the University of Oxford his reign is of signal importance; it is indeed the first reign from which any royal charter or other letter relating to the University has ever been produced. His name was accordingly commemorated as that 'bonae memoriae Henrici quondam regis Angliae' in the annual recitement of the benefactors of the University, referred to in a document of the year 1293. See Introduction to Anstey's Munimenta Academica. He is stated to have introduced large numbers of Parisian students into the University of Oxford, whose members in this reign are said to have at one time numbered 15,000, or according to another altogether incredible account, 30,000. The turbulence of the students was very great; and together with the claims of the ecclesiastics gave rise to the most serious town-and-gown conflicts known in the history of the English Universities. Several visits of the King to Oxford are chronicled in Anthony Wood's History and Antiquities of the University, bk. i.—It may be added that Henry III's love of the chase (compare xii. 82) is historical.

EDWARD PRINCE OF WALES, his son. Edward (afterwards King Edward I) was born in 1239, and was married to Eleanor of Castile in 1254, sixteen years *before* he went on the crusade alluded to in our play (iv. 27; viii. 113). On this crusade be did *no* deeds before the walls of Damascus; but after landing at Acre remained there eighteen months; and, in Lingard's words, 'an expedition to Nazareth, the capture of two small castles, and the surprise of a caravan, comprehend the whole of his military labours.' In the first scene of Peele's Famous

Chronicle History of King Edward the First his exploits in Palestine are similarly overcoloured.—The story of Prince Edward's love for the Fair Maid of Fressingfield, and of her preference for his envoy Lacy to himself, is doubtless a fiction invented by Greene. See Introduction, p. xcv.

Emperor of Germany. Frederick II (1212–1250), 'stupor mundi Fredericus,' the last Emperor of the Swabian house of Hohenstaufen, was of course quite innocent of any connexion with 'Hapsburg' (iv. 45). He was the brother-in-law of King Henry III, whose sister Isabel he married in 1235, without however coming in person to England. The friendly relations between the two houses ended with her death. The Emperor's patronage of a magician like Vandermast is not out of character; his age suspected him of far more serious deviations than this from the orthodoxy which he professed.

King of Castile. Ferdinand III, called the Holy, was King in Castile from 1217, and in Leon from 1230, to his death in 1252. This event occurred two years before his daughter's marriage in 1254; he was succeeded by his son Alphonsus X, called the Wise, afterwards one of the Emperors of the Interregnum.

Lacy, Earl of Lincoln ('of Lincolnshire,' vi. 19). The original of this character is Henry de Lacy, Earl of Lincoln, who after being 'the closest counsellor' of Edward I, was one of the 'Ordainers' under his successor.

Warren, Earl of Sussex. I do not know whether this is an altogether fictitious personage. Warenne was the family name and joint title of a famous Earl of *Surrey* in the reign of Edward I; the family name of the Earls of Sussex in the Tudor period was Ratcliffe, their creation dating from 1529.

Ralph Simnell, the King's Fool—not the Prince's, as Dyce points out, with a reference to vii. 130.

Friar Bacon. See Introduction, pp. xviii. seqq.

Miles, Friar Bacon's poor scholar. This designation, which means a poor student attached to Friar Bacon as 'famulus' (see note on Wagner in Dramatis Personae of Doctor Faustus), is given to Miles in the stage-direction before scene ii. in the quarto of 1599. The English name Miles is said in Lower's Patronymica Britannica to be 'from "Milo," a not unusual personal name among the Normans; oftener perhaps a corruption of "Michael." In some rural districts "Michaelmas" is commonly called "Milemas."'

Friar Bungay. This character was taken by Greene from the Elizabethan story-book (see Introduction, pp. xcvi. seqq.). 'Bungy's dog' (compare p. 114) is mentioned in Jonson's A Tale of a Tub, ii. 1. The historical Friar Bungay was a distinguished member of the group of Franciscan schoolmen who studied and taught at Oxford in the thirteenth century (see Introduction, p. xix). 'Frater Thomas Bongaye' is mentioned in the Registrum Fratrum Minorum as one of the Provincial Ministers of the Order in England, and as buried at Northampton. He incepted at Oxford, and lectured both there and at Cambridge. He is also called 'frater Johannes de Bungey.' See Brewer's Monumenta Franciscana.—It might be thought to be in remembrance of the name of Friar Bungay that 'S. mother Bungie' is mentioned by R. Scot in his Discourse of Divels (1584) as a popular witch's name; probably, however, this is only another form of 'mother Bombie,' made famous by Lyly.—Bungay is a Suffolk local name, and harmonises with the other names of Suffolk places in our play.

JACQUES VANDERMAST. This foreign sorcerer, whose name is Dutch, is accordingly associated with the 'Belgic schools,' ix. 17; and is described as a 'Germane' in the stage-direction of scene iv. in the quarto of 1599, and as 'a German of esteem,' vii. 15. This is not incorrect, as the Provinces of the Netherlands formed part of the Empire; but when Vandermast is said, iv. 45, to be 'brought from Hapsburg' (compare ix. 13), this is a mere confusion with later times, when the Emperors were of the house of Habsburg (compare above, note on EMPEROR OF GERMANY).—I have not succeeded in tracing any mention of a Dutch magician or scholar of this name; the interest excited by the art of magic and its professors in the Netherlands is however attested by the Dutch version of the Faust legend, and by other evidence.

BURDEN. This 'Doctor of Oxford' is, ii. 173, called 'Master' of Brasenose. This is of course an anachronism, as Brasenose College (the title of whose Head has always been 'Principal') was not yet in existence. See note on ii. 12.

MASON; CLEMENT. These are of course fictitious personages; the name of Clement may have possibly been suggested to Greene by that of John Clement, an Oxonian of repute in the earlier part of the sixteenth century (see Wood's Athenae, i. 401-402, ed. Bliss).

THOMAS and RICHARD are clowns, i. e. simple rustics. (See note on CLOWN in Dramatis Personae of Doctor Faustus.)

A POST; i. e. a messenger, as constantly in Shakespeare.

ELINOR, daughter to the King of Castile. Eleanor, daughter of Ferdinand III of Castile and Leon, married Edward Prince of Wales in 1254—the marriage being performed in Spain, according to custom, by proxy on the part of the bridegroom. This is the princess whose fair fame was so foully aspersed by Peele in his Chronicle History of Edward I, possibly on the authority of an old ballad supposed to have been written in the days of popular excitement against Spain in the reign of Philip and Mary. She died in 1290 (not 1291; see C. Wykeham-Martin's History and Description of Leeds Castle, which Edward settled upon Queen Eleanor), deeply lamented both by the people and the King, of whose enduring affection the well-known statue on the Queen's tomb in Westminster Abbey, and the crosses, above all Charing ('Chère reine') Cross, which he erected to her memory, are by no means the only proofs.

MARGARET, the Keeper's daughter, the Fair Maid of Fressingfield. I cannot resist from giving her this title, which is appended to her name in the stage-direction before scene iii. in the quarto of 1599. The heroine of Faire Em is similarly called in that play (sc. xvi. l. 1092) 'the fair maid of Manchester.'

HOSTESS OF THE BELL AT HENLEY. Of this hostelry no traditions remain, while the Red Lion at Henley is famous as having inspired Shenstone with the reflexion, that through life he had found 'the warmest welcome at an inn.'

Scene I.

2. *heaven's bright shine.* Compare note on Doctor Faustus, xiii. 30.

3. *Alate.* The prefix '*a*' in this word represents 'of'; see Abbott, § 24. So in King Lear, i. 4. 308, the quartos have, 'Methinks you are much alate i' the frown,'—where the folios read 'of late.' Compare A Looking-Glass for London and England: 'This is the day that I should pay you money that I took up of you alate in a commodity.'

Ib. ran the deer. The hunting phrases 'to run a fox into cover,' 'to run down a fox,' and 'a good run,' are familiar, as well as the expression 'to course a hare.' Compare the French 'courir le cerf'; and the similar phrase to 'fly the partridge,' xii. 83.

Ib. the lawnds. 'Lawnd' or 'laund' is an old form of lawn, used by Chaucer and several of the Elizabethans. Compare Orlando Furioso:

'The shady lawnds
And thickest-shadow'd groves';

and Dido Queen of Carthage, act i:

'That they may trip more lightly o'er the lawnds.'

The original sense of the word, according to Skeat, was 'a clear space in a wood, and it is probably the same word with lane (compare Dutch laan, a lane, valley).' As to the addition of the *d* to the root, compare note to Doctor Faustus i. 107.

4. *Stripp'd*, out-tripped.

Ib. frolic (German fröhlich), a favourite word in our play; compare below, 11, 133, etc. Herrick (Ode for Ben Jonson) has 'the frolick wine'; Milton (L'Allegro, 18), 'the frolic wind.' The verb 'to frolic' (l. 138 below) occurs in Spenser.

5. *teasers* (quarto of 1599, 'teisers'). The meaning of this word (which occurs again, ix. 180) is explained by a passage quoted by Dyce from Fuller's Holy State: 'But these *Tenzers*, rather to rouze then pinch the game, only made Whitaker find his spirits. The fiercest *dog* is behind, even Bellarmine himself.'

6. *Fressingfield.* The village of Fressingfield in Suffolk lies 4½ miles south of Harleston; the parish contains lands which anciently belonged partly to the De la Pole family, and partly to Bury Abbey and Eye Priory. Here (at Ufford Hall) Archbishop Sancroft was born; and hither he retired after sacrificing his see to conscientious scruples. He died at Fressingfield, to which he left munificent bequests; and was buried in the churchyard, where a monument is erected to his memory. See White's History, &c. of Suffolk.

7. *pull'd down;* as we should say, 'brought down.'

Ib. jolly mates, companions.

9. *frankly*, liberally. Compare iii. 11.

Ib. dealt, distributed. A.-S. dælan, to distribute; dæl (German Theil), a part; hence 'dole,' a share in a distribution, a distribution.

12. *a melancholy dump.* The word 'dump' (which recurs iii. 30; v. 102, 104; vi. 66) was used both in the singular and (as it continues to be) in the plural to signify a low state of spirits, like the modern 'vapours' and the French 'vapeurs.' This word, which is connected with 'damp' and the German 'dumpf' (Grimm mentions a substantive 'Dumpf,' signifying a state of bodily indisposition), was the received term for a melancholy strain in music, and is used in this sense already in Ralph Roister Doister, ii. 1:

'Then twang with our sonnets, and twang with our dumps,
And heigho from our heart, as heavy as lead-lumps.'

The significance of 'dump,' which was also apparently used for a kind of dance, was not necessarily comic; Nares recalls the title of a poem by Davies of Hereford, 'A Dump upon the Death of the most noble Henrie, Earl of Pembroke,' where (as elsewhere) the term is equivalent to 'elegy.' In Orlando Furioso Greene has the verbal form 'dumping.' Compare also the adjective 'dumpish' = melancholy in The Faerie Queene, iv. 2. 5. 7.

15. *Tossing off.* Perhaps the reading of the quarto of 1599, 'tossing of,' might be retained, the construction being as in Doctor Faustus, vii. 79. Compare the Shakespearian 'tosspot.'

16. *the country's sweet content*, the sweet feeling of content inspired by the country.

17. *the bonny damsel fill'd*, the bonny damsel who fill'd. See note on Doctor Faustus, xiii. 54.

18. *stammel red.* Stammel was a coarse kind of woollen cloth, of a red colour inferior to scarlet, used for petticoats; so in A Pleasant Comedie of Pasqvil and Katharine, ii. 1. 7: 'Mistress Smiffe . . . hath newly put on her stammell petticoate.' Apparently 'Brystow' (Bristol) 'red' was used in the same sense; see Skelton's Elynour Rumming, 70; where Dyce quotes from Barclay's Fourth Eglogue:

'London hath scarlet, and Bristowe pleasaunt red.'

Dyce believes that the words 'red' and 'stammel' were seldom used together, the former being the understood colour of the latter.

20. *passions*, trouble or excitement. See note on Doctor Faustus, xi. 42.

21. *Sirrah.* See note on Doctor Faustus, ii. 5.

22. *all amort*, properly alamort, French à la mort, dejected. So in The Taming of a Shrew, iv. 3. 36 (cited by Nares):

'How fares my Kate? what, sweeting, all amort?'

32. *my cap and my coat and my dagger.* Douce, On the Clowns and Fools of Shakspeare, in his Illustrations, ii. 317 seqq., thus describes the two kinds of costume worn by the domestic fool in Shakespeare's time: 'In the first of these the coat was motley or parti-coloured, and attached to the body by a girdle, with bells at the skirts and elbows, though not always. . . . A hood resembling a monk's cowl, which, at a very early period, it was certainly designed to imitate, covered the head entirely, and fell down over part of the breast and shoulders. It was sometimes decorated with asses' ears, or terminated in the neck and head of a cock, a fashion as old as the fourteenth century. It often had the comb or crest only of the animal, whence the term *cockscomb* or *coxcomb* was afterwards used to denote any silly upstart.' [Compare v. 51.] . . . 'In some old plays the fool's *dagger* is mentioned, perhaps the same instrument as was carried by the *Vice* or buffoon of the Moralities. . . . The dagger of the latter was made of a thin piece of lath; and the use he generally made of it was to belabour the Devil. It appears that in Queen Elizabeth's time the Archbishop of Canterbury's fool had a wooden dagger and coxcomb. . . . The other dress, and which seems to have been more common in the time of Shakspeare, was the long petticoat. This originally appertained to the idiot or natural fool. . . . It was, like the first, of various colours, the materials often costly, as of velvet, and guarded or fringed with yellow. See Prologue to Hen. VIII; Marston's Malcontent, i. 7 and iii. 1.'

40. *lovely*, Dyce's correction for the 'lively' of the quartos.

Ib. country-weeds, rustic dress. The A.-S. wæd signifies a garment (hence linwæd, a linen garment, compare the German Leinwand); the word 'wede' is used in this sense by Chaucer; so in The Clerke's Tale, Pars V^a:

'My lord, ye wole, that in my fadres place
Ye dide me stripe out of my poure wede,
And richely ye clad me of your grace';

and 'weede' by Spenser; so in The Shepheard's Calender, July, 168:

'Whilome all these were lowe and lief,
And loved their flocks to feede;
They never stroven to be chief,
And simple was theyr weede.'

The word is now, like its paronym weed (A.-S. weód), contracted in meaning; 'as respects the earth, those only are "weeds" which are noxious, or at least self-sown; as regards the person, we speak of no other "weeds" but the widow's.' (Trench, English Past and Present, 142.)

42. *none such*, no one like unto her (A.-S. swy-lic); hence the old compound 'nonsuch' (the name of Henry VIII's palace near Leatherhead) was used as a substantive, a 'nonsuch,' like the French equivalent, a 'nonpareil;' so in A Looking-Glass for London and England: 'beauty nonpareil in excellence.'

48. *the abbot.* I cannot explain this allusion.

51. *by his whole grammar*, viz. I warrant thee.

53, 54. *her sparkling . . . fire.* Compare Richard II, iii. 3. 68–70:

'Yet looks he like a king: behold, his eye
As bright as is the eagle's, lightens forth
Controlling majesty.'

'To lighten' is similarly used x. 142.

59. *Her front is beauty's table.* The 'front' is the forehead. For the singular 'table' in the sense of tablet (Latin tabula) compare 'the table of my memory' in Hamlet, i. 5. 98, and 'a writing-table' in St. Luke's Gospel, i. 63, where Tyndale has 'tables.' See also Ford's The Broken Heart, ii. 3:

'Time can never
On the white table of unguilty faith
Write counterfeit dishonour';

and the same poet's Love's Sacrifice, ii. 1: 'I will have my picture drawn most compposituously in a square table of some two foot long'; where Dyce explains the word to mean 'the board or strained canvas, on which the picture was to be painted.' In the same play, iv. 2, the word is used very much as in our passage:

'Here was my fate engraven on thy brow,
This smooth, fair, polish'd table.'

In Menaphon's Eclogue in Greene's Menaphon,

'Her brows are pretty tables of conceit
Where love his record of delight doth quote,

the word 'tables' means note-book. Compare note on Doctor Faustus. xiii. 61.

61. *margarites*, pearls (Greek μαργαρίτης, Latin margarita). Compare A Looking-Glass for London and England:

'I'll fetch from Albia shelves of margarites';

and Orlando Furioso:

'Whose shores are sprinkled with rich orient pearl,
More bright of hue than were the margarites
That Caesar found in wealthy Albion.'

Dyce, who quotes the latter passage, notes a reference to the same tradition in Greene's prose-tract, Ciceronis Amor. Probably this word contributed to the choice of the French word for the daisy (marguérite), the flower celebrated by allegorising French and English poets, by Chaucer above all. Skelton, in his Garlande of Laurell, 947, addresses a lady of the name of Margaret (Tylney) as

'Of Margarite,
Perle orient,
Lede sterre of lyght,
Moche relucent';

but it is another lady, Mistress Isabell Pennell, whom he afterwards compares to 'the dasy flowre, the fresshest flowre of May.'

62. *cleeves*, cliffs; as again iv. 6. Compare Drayton's Poly-Olbion, xiii. 763:

'Rob Dover's neighbouring cleeves of sampyre.'

63. *beauty's overmatch*, the overmatch or superior of beauty herself. The word 'overmatch,' clearly a supposed translation of 'paragon' (see note on Doctor Faustus, xiii. 32), is used in the sense of a superior, xi. 113, and in Bacon's Essay of Greatnesse of Kingdomes and Estates: '*England* and *France;* whereof *England* though far lesse in Territory and Population, hath been (neverthelesse) an Overmatch.' Shakespeare has 'overmatching' in the sense of superior in power, 3 Henry VI, i. 4. 21:

'And spend her strength with overmatching waves.'

Compare the similar compound 'countermatch,' ix. 266.

64. *her curious imagery*, the exquisite beauty of her image or appearance. 'Curious' means wrought with care; compare viii. 16; and 'the curious girdle of the ephod' in Exodus, xxviii. 8.

67. *quainter*, more graceful. Compare iii. 82; in iii. 40 the word 'quaint' is used in its ordinary modern sense of odd, out of fashion. Trench, Select Glossary, p. 172, quotes several passages illustrating the old use of 'quaint' in the sense of 'elegant, graceful, skilful, subtle.'

The following passage in Chaucer's Romaunt of the Rose, 2247–2255, illustrates the primitive meaning of the word, 'trim,' which accords with its derivation (from Latin comptus through O. Fr. cointe, O. Engl. coint, quoint, though Diez derives these and cognate Italian and Provençal forms from Latin cognitus):

'And he that loveth truely,
Should him conteine jollily,
Without pride in sundrie wise,
And him disguisen in queintise;
For queint array, without drede
Is nothing proude, who taketh hede;
For fresh array, as men may see,
Without pride may ofte bee.'

See also on this word Earle's Philology of the English Tongue, § 409.

68. *honour's taint.* 'Taint,' as Dyce observes, is equivalent to 'tint' (compare French teint, Latin tinctus). The verb 'to taint' is used in the sense of to touch, to imbue, in Melicertus' Eclogue in Greene's Menaphon:

'From forth the crystal heaven when she was made
The purity thereof did taint her brow';

and compare 3 Henry VI, iii. 1. 40:

'And Nero will be tainted with remorse.'

70. *the courts of love.* Compare 'Venus' courts,' viii. 85. In both passages the allusion is to the Courts of Love of the days of chivalry, in the literature of which their technicalities played so prominent a part. In the poem The Court of Love, probably misattributed to Chaucer, the poet speaks of himself as commanded 'the Court of Love to see,'

'Where Citherea goddesse was and queene.'

Tribunals called Courts of Love, in which questions of gallantry were decided, and the claims and arguments of the parties were put into verse by the poets, were instituted as early as 1180 both in Provence and in Picardy. See Warton's History of English Poetry, section iii. Elsewhere Warton mentions a publication of the year 1566, by the Protestant preacher and poet Thomas Brice, apparently a ballad, called 'The Court of Venus moralised.' Of these Courts of Love the remembrance survives in the French romance-literature of the Grand-Cyrus school, and in our dramatic literature; see Ben Jonson's The New Inn, iii. 2, where a Court of Love is held.

72. *the secret beauties of the maid.* Though Prince Edward is merely speaking of the domestic charms of the Maid of Fressingfield, this pleasing passage irresistibly recalls the beautiful lines in Spenser's Epithalamion, 195–198:

'But if ye saw that which no eyes can see,
The inward beauties of her lively spright
Garnisht with heavenly guifts of high degree,
Much more then would ye wonder at that sight.'

73. *foolery*, empty pretence. So in The Shepheard's Calender, February, 111:

'But sike fancies weren foolerie,
And broughten this Oake to this miserye.'

75. *Whenas*, when. Compare viii. 16; x. 100. For the superfluous addition of 'as' as a conjunctional suffix to words that are already conjunctions (whenas, whereas), see Abbott, §§ 116, 135.

77. *Into the milk-house went I with the maid.* With this pretty picture of the 'country Margaret' in her dairy, compare Sir Thomas Overbury's 'Character' of 'A faire and happy Milk-mayd': 'In milking a cow, and straining the teats through her fingers, it seems that so sweet a milk-presse makes the milk the whiter or sweeter; for never came *almond glove* or *aromatique oyntment* on her palm to taint it.'

79. *Pallas 'mongst her princely huswifery.* Pallas Athene was worshipped under the cognomen 'Εργάνη more especially as the patroness of the arts of spinning and weaving; and in Homer ἔργα 'Αθηναίης is a typical expression for female handiwork of supreme excellence, 'princely huswifery.'

81. *to run her cheese.* 'To run' is to force into a form. So Johnson quotes (from Cheyne): 'What is raised in the day, settles in the night; and its cold runs the thin juices into thick sizy substances.'

83. *Checkèd*, chequered. From Fr. échec, M. Lat. scaccus, plural scacci, the game of chess, derived from the Persian schah (the figure of the king in the game). The Court of Exchequer (scaccarium) took its name from the chequered table in the room where it met.

Ib. with lines of azure. Compare Doctor Faustus, xiii. 109.

Ib. her, the antecedent to 'that' in the following line.

84. *compare.* See note on Doctor Faustus, xiii. 30.

88. *Like Lucrece*, whom (to quote the Argument of Shakespeare's Rape of Lucrece) her husband Collatinus found, 'though it were late in the night, spinning among her maids.'

94. *already*, at once.

95. *an learn me that*, if thou learnest (teachest) me that. As to 'an' for 'if' see note on Doctor Faustus, v. 137. For the elliptical construction may perhaps be compared Richard II, i. 1. 59:

'Setting aside his high blood's royalty,
And let him be no kinsman to my liege,
I do defy him and I spit at him'—

where the 'let' is however of course an imperative.—Of the common confusion between the A.-S. verbs læran (German lehren), to teach, and leornan (German lernen), to learn, an instance may be cited from The Chanon Yeman's Tale, 748:

'Thus was I ones lernèd of a clerk.'

98. *necromancer.* Quarto of 1599, 'nigromancer,' which is the usual spelling in this edition of our play, though the forms necromantia, nicromanticke (and negromanticke) also occur. See note on Doctor Faustus, opening Chorus, 25.

99. *costermongers,* properly costard (apple)-mongers or sellers.

103. *prince it out,* play the prince thoroughly. Compare Cymbeline, iii. 3. 85:

'Nature prompts them
In simple and low things to prince it much
Beyond the trick of others.'

Compare 'to lord it out,' v. 120; and 'to scold it out,' xiii. 48; and for other examples of this construction (as to which see Abbott, § 226) to 'lecture it,' ix. 16; to 'revel it,' v. 117; to 'stab it,' viii. 83; to 'frolick it,' xiii. 1. 'Out' is similarly used in the sense of 'thoroughly' or 'plainly,' ii. 18 and viii. 45.

110. *prease* (quarto of 1599, 'presse'), i. e. press, crowd. So constantly in our old writers; in Chaucer, Skelton, Edwards, and Spenser, as in The Faerie Queene, iv. 4. 34:

'Into the thickest of that knightly prease
He thrust.'

In A Looking-Glass for London and England the verbal form 'to prease' occurs for 'to press':

'My prayers did prease before thy mercy-seat.'

In the same play we have the analogous form a 'mease' for a 'mess' of milk.

Ib. for fear of the cutpurse. The cutting of purses, which were worn hanging at the girdle, corresponded to the picking of pockets of later times. See the amusing scene in Jonson's Bartholomew Fair, iii. 1, where Squire Cokes is the victim of the cutpurse or 'pursecutter,' Ezechiel Edgworth. Hence the term 'cutter' for a sharper or bully. Compare note on v. 19.

111. *swap,* sweep or clap.

Ib. plackerd or placket, pocket.

121. *For why,* because. Compare vi. 114, and Peele's Edward I, xxii. 250:

'And henceforth see you call it Charing-Cross;
For why the chariest and the choicest queen
That ever did delight my royal eyes,
There dwells in darkness whilst I die in grief.'

Compare the use of 'for' in the sense of 'because,' vii. 63; x. 153; xii. 59; and of the emphatic 'for because,' as to which see Abbott, § 151.

122. *stands so much upon her honest points.* Compare A Midsummer Night's Dream, v. 118 (in a double sense): 'this fellow doth not stand upon points,'; and 3 Henry VI, iv. 7. 58:

'Why, brother, stand you therefore on nice points?'

127. *horse us*, put ourselves on horseback. An example of the old reflexive use of the personal pronoun, which the addition of 'self' only rendered more emphatic. Compare 'commends him,' below, 148; 'resolve you,' ii. 46; 'content thee,' ix. 248; 'counsel me,' x. 75.

128. *post*, hasten (compare l. 167). See note on ii. 149.

135. *policy*, stratagem. So 1 Henry VI, iii. 3. 12:

'Search not thy wit for secret policies.'

One of the Seven Deadly Sins of London in Dekker's tract is 'Politike Bankruptisme,' i.e. feigned or pretended bankruptcy.

137. *Harleston fair.* Harleston is a small market-town, 4½ miles from Fressingfield. A fair is held there on July 5th; but St. James's day is the 25th of that month.

140. *That come . . . that day.* A reminiscence of Ovid, Ars Amator. i. 99:

'Spectatum veniunt, veniunt, spectentur ut ipsae.'

Compare Faire Em. sc. v. (l. 411):

'Two gentlemen . . . .
Ofttimes resort to see and to be seen,
Walking the street before my father's door.'

141. *Haunt thee.* The word 'to haunt' is here, ii. 107 and xi. 131, used intransitively; compare also Othello, i. 1. 96; its French original hanter is said to be of Norse origin (O. N. heimta, to fetch home), and to have been introduced into French by the Normans.—For this use of the datives me, thee, &c., see Abbott, § 220, and compare especially such passages as 1 Henry IV, ii. 4. 223: 'I made me no more ado,' and *ib.* 240: 'I followed me close.' See for the use in A. S. March's Anglo-Saxon Grammar, 150.

142. *not far from thence*, a native of the neighbourhood.

143. *Espy*, spy. Compare Titus Andronicus, ii 3. 48:

'Now question me no more; we are espied.'

Ib. who. As to this common use of 'who' for 'whom' compare x. 56; and see Abbott, § 274.

144. *Cote him.* Dyce explains this to mean 'keep alongside of him; French côtoyer.' Shakespeare however uses the word in the sense of 'to pass by'; see Hamlet, ii. 2. 330: 'we coted them on the way'; and compare The Returne from Pernassus, ii. 5: 'presently coted and outstripped them.' Possibly therefore the meaning of our passage may

be, 'outstrip, outvie him'; *vulgo*, cut him out.—In Ford's Perkin Warbeck, i. 2, the verb 'to side' is used in the sense of 'to keep pace with.'

148. *Commends him.* See note on l. 127 above.

154. *send how she fares*, send word how she fares. Compare a similar ellipsis in Antony and Cleopatra, v. 2. 29:

> 'I am his fortune's vassal, and I send him
> The greatness he has got';

i. e. I send him an acknowledgment of the greatness he has got.

157. *As if that.* See note on Doctor Faustus, x. 15.

158. *of the news*, concerning the news. See note on Doctor Faustus, vi. 34.

160. *million.* See note on Doctor Faustus, ii. 24. Shakespeare always uses this word, when without an article, in the plural.

165. *morris-dancer*, Dyce's conjecture for 'morris-dance.' The morris-dance, frequently introduced into our old dramas (so in The Two Noble Kinsmen, iii. 5, in Nash's Summer's Last Will and Testament, in Dekker and Ford's The Sun's Darling, ii. 1, and in The Witch of Edmonton. iii. 4) or mentioned in them, is sometimes called a Morisco. The morris-dance is twice noticed in the satire Friar Bakon's Prophesie. The name is probably derived from its having been an imitation of a Moorish dance; but its origin has also been thought traceable to the Salic dance, said to have been instituted by the King of Veii Morrius, a name pointing to Mars, whose priests the Salii were. The morris-dance was specially performed on May-day; compare 'a morris for May-day,' All 's Well that Ends Well, ii. 2. 25. See Skeat's note in his edition of The Two Noble Kinsmen. Douce in his observations On the Ancient English Morris Dance in Illustrations of Shakspeare, ii. 431 seqq. (where see a Flemish print), cites 2 Henry VI, iii. 1. 364–366:

> 'I have seen
> Him caper upright like a wild Morisco,
> Shaking the bloody darts, as he his bells,'

and notes that 'the bells have always been a part of the furniture of the more active characters in the morris, and the use of them is of great antiquity. The tinkling ornaments of the feet among the Jewish women are reprobated in Isaiah. iii. 16, 18 . . . There is good reason for believing that the morris bells were borrowed from the genuine Moorish dance . . . The numbers of bells round the leg of the morris dancers amounted from twenty to forty . . . The bells were occasionally jingled by the hands, or placed on the arms and wrists of the parties.' Hence the Fool (163) offers to 'tie a bell about' the Prince. Compare as to the bells in the morris-dance the passage cited above from The Witch of Edmonton, and *ib.* ii. 1.

169. *Mayst*, a zeugma for may.

170. *your honour*. For this address compare viii. 19, and see note on Doctor Faustus, x. 45.

Ib. your heart's desire. Query 'all your heart's desire' Dyce.

Scene II.

With the merry foolery of Miles in this and subsequent scenes compare that of Slipper in James the Fourth, and of Adam in A Looking-Glass for London and England.

3. *nos.* As Friar Bacon must be supposed to speak grammatical Latin, this is probably a misprint for 'ne' or 'nobis.'

5. *Ecce quam bonum . . . in unum.* A parody of the first verse of Psalm cxxxiii.

6. *our academic state*, the University, a corporate self-governing community. Below, v. 94, 'college-state' seems to mean the estate or property of the college.

11. *stall'd*, installed, established. Compare Richard III, i. 3. 206:

'Deck'd in thy rights as thou art stall'd in mine.'

Ib. Brazen-nose. The King's Hall and College of Brasenose was founded in 1509, by the joint benefaction of William Smith, Bishop of Lincoln, and Sir Richard Sutton, Knt., of Prestbury, in Cheshire, for a Principal and twelve Fellows. (Calendar of the University of Oxford.) In 1508 Sutton had obtained from University College a lease of 'Brasen Nose Hall' and Little University Hall, on the expiration of which 'Brasen Nose' obtained the freehold. Five other halls were afterwards added. 'Brasen Nose Hall, which gave that singular name to the College, is of great antiquity. In the thirteenth century it was known by the same name, which was unquestionably owing to the circumstance of a nose of brass affixed to the gate. The names of others of the ancient halls were derived from circumstances equally trivial.' See Chalmers' History of the University of Oxford. i. 238–239, where is also cited from Wood's Annals the notice of a building at Stamford 'called Brazenose to this day,' which has 'a great gate, and a wicket, upon which wicket is a face or head of old cast brass, with a ring through the nose thereof.' The following is an extract from Miles Windsore's notes copied in Hearne's Diary (MSS. Bodleian), vol. cxxxii. p. 73:

'Coll. Aeneae Nasi antiquitus vocatum Aula philosophorum in vico Scholarium et Universitatis Aula etiam regia.

'Vocat me hic frequens quaerentium percunctatio de nomine loci hujus antiquiori, ut aliquid respondeam: quibus ita satisfactum vellem Polydori verbis Anglicanae historiae lib. 26°. Guil. Smyth episcopus Lyncolniensis Margaritae exempto ductus, Oxonii eorum adolescentium qui bonis disciplinis dediti se in literis exercerent, Collegium collocavit in aula quam vulgo vocant Brasnose hoc est aeneum nasum: quod eo loci imago aenea facie admodum . . . . pro foribus extet.'

It seems probable that the name of the old 'Brasin' (i. e. Brewing; compare French brassin, a tun for beer) 'House,' which was transferred first to the Hall and then to the College, was changed into 'Brazen-nose' in consequence of the nose of brass over the gate; and that the tradition of Friar Bacon's Brazen Head by reason of his supposed connexion with the place helped to confirm the mistaken spelling. Compare Introduction, p. xx.

13. *that*, for 'that which.' See Abbott, § 244.

Ib. suspect, suspected. As to the omission of the participial suffix *-ed* in some verbs ending in *-te*, *-t*, and *-d*, see Abbott, § 342. Among his examples are 'deject' for 'dejected,' Hamlet, iii. 1. 163; and 'infect' for 'infected,' Troilus and Cressida, i. 3. 187.

15. *pyromancy*. This and numerous other '*species* in *Magia*' are explained to Wagner by his familiar spirit Auerhan in a passage in the Life of Christoph Wagner already referred to in note to Doctor Faustus, opening Chorus, 25. They are likewise defined in a treatise On the Species of Ceremonial-Magic, called 'Goetie,' by 'Georg Pictor of Villingen, Dr. Med.' (see Scheible, Kloster, iii. 615–626), and are combined into an Aristophanic polysyllable in Tomkis's Albumazar, ii. 3:

> 'Now then, declining from Theourgia,
> Artenosoria Pharmacia rejecting,
> Necro-puro-geo-hydro-cheiro-coscinomancy,
> With other vain and superstitious sciences,' &c.

'Pyromancy' is explained by Pictor as 'prophesying from fire. The wife of Cicero is said, when after performing sacrifice she saw a flame suddenly leap forth from the ashes, to have prophesied the consulship to her husband for the same year. Others prophesied from the light of a torch of pitch, which was painted with certain colours. When the flame ran together into a point, the prophecy was altogether good; when it was divided, bad; when it mounted up three-tongued, it announced glory; when it divided itself in several directions, it signified death to the sick and sickness to one in health; if it nearly went out, it signified danger; if it hissed, misfortune.'

16. *hydromancy*. The quarto of 1599 has 'thadromaticke'; but I think we should clearly read 'hydromancy.' Below, 147, where Dyce prints 'necromatic,' the same quarto has 'nicromanticke.'—Of 'hydromancy' Auerhan states: 'In this you conjure the spirits into water; there they are constrained to show themselves, as Marcus Varro testifieth, when he writeth, how he had seen a boy in the water, who

announced to him in a hundred and fifty verses the issue of the Mithridatic War. Numa Pompilius likewise had a peculiar way by which he could learn coming events.'—The ancient Italians, says Professor Seeley (in the Introduction to his edition of Livy), attributed to the deities of streams and fountains (lymphae) an influence over the mind, a power of producing both inspiration and insanity. Hence the words 'lymphatus' and 'lymphaticus.' Of these deities the most widely known in Latium were Juturna and Egeria. Egeria was one of the Camenae (or in the older forms Casmenae, Carmenae), Italian water-deities to whom such powers were attributed; and the Muses of the Greeks were likewise originally water-nymphs.

17. *aeromancy*, prophecy from the air. According to Pictor, 'if the wind blew from the east, it signified good fortune; if from the west, evil; calamity, from the south; disclosure of what was secret, from the north; if the wind blew from all quarters at the same time, it signified storm, hail and violent rain.'

18. *To plain out*, to explain, answer clearly. See note on i. 103. Shakespeare uses the verb 'to plain,' Pericles, Prologue to act iii. line 14:

'What's dumb in show I'll plain with speech.'

Ib. as Apollo did. This appears to refer to the answering of questions in general, rather than to aeromancy. Compare v. 86. The earliest Greek oracle, that of Zeus at Dodona, has been well said to have been originally a meteorological observatory; but the Delphic method was a different one.

20, 21. *by rehearsing of these names.* As to this construction, see note on Doctor Faustus, vii. 79; and compare l. 25 below.

21. *the fable of the Fox and the Grapes.* This fable, which is the vth and (slightly altered) the clxx[th] in Furia's edition of the Fables of Aesop, is there said not to be in the Planudine edition, but to be reproduced by both Phædrus and Babrias. It occurs in Roger L'Estrange's collection of Fables of Aesop and other eminent Mythologists, and is the xxxiii[rd] of La Fontaine's Fables, beginning:

'Certain renard gascon, d'autres disent normand.'

25. *a brazen head.* See Introduction, pp. xxiv. seqq.

26. *aphorisms.* See note on Doctor Faustus, i. 19.

30. *To compass England with a wall of brass.* See Introduction, p. vi; and compare Doctor Faustus, i. 86.

34. *Mother Waters' strong ale.* I cannot identify this worthy; perhaps she was a kinswoman of 'S. mother Still,' mentioned by Reginald Scot.

35. *Copper nose.* In the story-book Miles calls the Brazen Head 'Copper-Nose.' In Troilus and Cressida, i. 2. 114, Cressid, in answer

to the statement of Pandarus that Helen had praised the complexion of Trolius above Paris, says, 'I had as lief Helen's tongue had commended Troilus for a copper nose.' 'Copper face' and 'Nose Almighty' were nicknames given to Oliver Cromwell, the former perhaps with an allusion to his brewery.—Compare note on v. 42.

38. *suppos'd,* held, regarded as. Compare 1 Henry VI, v. 3. 110:

'Say, gentle princess, would you not suppose
Your bondage happy, to be made a queen?'

39. *cunning.* See note to Doctor Faustus, opening Chorus, 20.

43. *Etérnize.* See note to Doctor Faustus, i. 15.

46. *Resolve you,* satisfy yourselves, be assured. Compare note on i. 127; and note on Doctor Faustus, i. 78.

47. *Make storming Boreas thunder from his cave.* The 'cave of Boreas' is the rocky island of Aeolus, the father of the winds, described in the beginning of the xth Book of the Odyssey.

48. *dim fair Luna tó a dark eclipse.* Compare xi. 14–15, and see note on Doctor Faustus, iii. 38.

51. *pentageron.* The pentagramma, pentageron or pentalpha is the mystic figure 'produced by prolonging the sides of a regular pentagon till they intersect one another. It can be drawn without a break in the drawing, and viewed from five sides exhibits the form of the Λ (pentalpha). This star-pentagon, according to Lucian, served the Pythagoreans as a salutation and symbol of health (ὑγιεία); afterwards it became a favourite tavern-sign and ale-mark. . . . In German mythology this sign was regarded as the foot-print of swan-footed "Nornen" and beneficent "Druden," till Christian notions changed these beings into evil spirits and witches. Henceforth the *Drudenfuss*, the Pentagramma in question, was by the side of the sign of the Cross placed at the door to avert "Druden" and witches.' From Loeper's note to the passage in Goethe's Faust, where the sight of the pentagramma prevents Mephistophiles from walking out of the room.—In a letter by Cornelius Agrippa (see Morley's Life, i. 245) the 'pentagram in Matthew' is spoken of, apparently (according to Morley's reference to ch. iii) referring to the visible figure of the Holy Spirit descending from the heavens.

54. *necromancy.* See note on Doctor Faustus, opening Chorus, l. 25.

Ib. to the deep, to the bottom or dregs.

56. *Belcephon* (ix. 143 accentuated Bélcephon), so far as I know a name invented by Greene.

59. *that,* for 'so that.' See Abbott, § 283.

62. *The work that Ninus reared at Babylon.* The gates of Ninus are mentioned by Herodotus, iii. 155. But the reference here and in the next line, and again iv. 3–4, is to the walls of which Herodotus, i. 184,

speaks as built by the Assyrian rulers of Babylon, Semiramis among the number, and which Ovid (Metam. iv. 58) calls 'coctiles,' of brick. Compare Gower's Confessio Amantis, bk. iii:

'I rede a tale, and telleth this,
The citee, which Semiramis
Enclosed hath with wall about.'

64. *the portal of the sun*, perhaps with a reference to the description of the palace of Phoebus and its silver gates in Ov. Metam. ii. 1 seqq.

65. *rings*, encircles. Compare iv. 2.

66. *Rye,* connected with the history of the English drama as the birthplace of Fletcher, is now one of the 'dead cities' of Kent, which in the Elizabethan age were still struggling against their inevitable doom of insignificance.

73. *mathematic rules:* compare iv. 53. Mathematics and magic were brought into connexion, as a developement of the Pythagorean doctrine of numbers, of which the significance is 'that numbers contain the elements of all things, and even of the sciences.' It was clearly seen that everything in nature may be reduced to numeral conditions; Pythagoras applied numerals to the spiritual world, and thereby solved questions which are now wholly unknown to arithmetic. See Ennemoser's History of Magic (Howitt's Translation), i. 394 seqq.; and compare the treatment of the subject in Cornelius Agrippa's Second Book of Occult Science, Morley's Life of Agrippa, i. 164 seqq. It is however manifest that in our and similar passages 'mathematics' merely signifies astrology. Compare Confessio Amantis, bk. vii:

'Mathematique above the erth
Of high science above the ferth,
Which speketh upon astronomie
And techeth of the sterres high,
Beginning upward frō the mone';

and Peele's The Honour of the Garter, Ad Maecenatem Prologus:

'. . . Mathesis . . .
That admirable mathematic skill,
Familiar with the stars and zodiac,
To whom the heaven lies open as her book.'

Already the Egyptian astrologers were generally called 'mathematici' by the Greeks. See Maury, La Magie et l'Astrologie, etc., 63.

76. *roves a bow beyond his reach*, tries to shoot with a bow beyond his strength, promises more than he can perform. For this use of 'to rove' in the sense of shooting an arrow with an elevation, see the instances quoted in Nares.

79. *in state of schools*, in the honours the schools can give. In modern phrase: have I not taken as good a degree as he?

83. *This is a fable Aesop had forgot.* Burden is thinking of Miles's reference to a fable supposed to be Aesopic, l. 21 above.

88. *what thou can,* whatever thou mayest be able to ask. 'Can' is the subjunctive.

89. *pick-pack,* explained in Nares as 'the older form of pick-a-back, i.e. carried like a pack over the shoulders.' Miles means: 'he'll be upon you,' or 'at you, at once.'

90. *whether the feminine . . . be most worthy.* This notable distinction is still to be found in at least one well-known modern Latin grammar.

95. *What book studied you thereon.* in what book did you study. Compare l. 152, and xi. 16; and Hamlet, iii. 1. 44: 'Read on this book.' See Abbott, § 180; and compare for the use of 'on' for 'in' xi. 42, and for that of 'in' for 'on' Doctor Faustus, opening Chorus, l. 19.

100. *I pass not of,* I care not for. Compare Alphonsus King of Arragon, act i:

> 'Whoe'er it be, I do not pass a pin;'

and Ford's Love's Sacrifice, i. 1:

> 'If, when I should choose,
> Beauty and virtue were the fee propos'd,
> I should not pass for parentage.'

For the use of 'of' in the sense of 'concerning' see note to Doctor Faustus, vi. 34.

105. *for that.* See note to Doctor Faustus, x. 15.

106. *cabalism,* secret art. Compare ix. 29: 'the cabalists that write of magic spells.' The word 'cabal' is from the Hebrew Rabbinical term Kabbalâ (from the Chaldaean kabbêl, to receive), properly meaning the mysterious interpretation of the Old Testament; hence any mysterious or secret doctrine in general; then any secret league, combination, conspiracy or intrigue. On the connexion between the Cabbalah and the religious and the general philosophy, as well as the notions as to magic of the Middle Ages see Ennemoser's History of Magic (Howitt's Translation), i. 7 seqq., where it is pointed out that the philosophy of Agrippa, Paracelsus, van Helmont, and others closely resembles the Jewish teachings; and that in the Cabbalah are to be found the principal outlines of the later magic, and more especially of witchcraft, which is perfectly represented there. See also for an account of the Cabbalah and the literature of Cabbalism, Morley's Life of Agrippa, i. 69 seqq. Among the Christian writers on Cabbalism the foremost place belongs to Reuchlin, of whose labours the best account will be found in L. Geiger's biography. The term 'Talmud skill' is used as a synonym for Cabbalism in Jonson's The Alchemist, iv. 3.

107. *haunts to Henley.* See note on i. 141. For this use of 'to'

without any sense of motion compare Marlowe's Edward II, ii. 1, 'smelling to a nosegay all the day'; and see Abbott, § 188.

108. *for to*, to. Miss Lee (New Shakspere Society's Transactions, 1875-6, p. 242) points out that Greene uses 'for to' eight times in our play. See as to the probable origin of the phrase, Abbott, § 152.

109. *alchemy*, the Arabic al-Kîmiâ, a word formed with the Arabic article 'al' from the Greek *χημεία*, which is derived from Χημία, the land of Cham or Ham, a name for Egypt. Thus 'chemistry' is the right spelling, not 'chymistry,' which implies a derivation from *χυμός*, sap (*χύω*). 'It was not,' says Trench, English Past and Present, 193, 'with the distillation of herbs, but with the amalgamation of metals, that the chemic art occupied itself at its rise.'

110. *To multiply*, i.e. to multiply gold. Compare All's Well that Ends Well, v. 3. 101-104:

> 'Plutus himself,
> That knows the tinct and multiplying medicine,
> Hath not in nature's mystery more science,
> Than I have in this ring.'

The 'multiplying medicine' of the alchemists was the tincture with which they professed to have the power of making gold. Compare Antony and Cleopatra, i. 5. 36-37:

> 'That great medicine hath
> With his tinct gilded thee';

and see Sir Epicure Mammon's description of the effects of this secret liquid in Jonson's The Alchemist, ii. 1:

> 'When you see th' effects of the Great Medicine
> Of which one part projected in a hundred
> Of Mercury, or Venus, or the Moon,
> Shall turn it to as many of the Sun,
> Nay to a hundred, so *ad infinitum*,
> You will believe me.'

The philosopher's stone was also supposed to have the power of increasing the size of a piece of gold.

111. *private*, privately. Compare 'gorgeous' for 'gorgeously,' xvi. 57; and 'chary' for 'charily,' Doctor Faustus, vi. 175. See Abbott, § 1.

124. *exceed*, be excessively or exceptionally good. Compare note on Doctor Faustus, i. 58.

126. *What art thou?* For this use of 'what' where modern usage would have 'who' compare below, l. 137, vii. 51, and ix. 121; and see Abbott, § 254.

130. *'gainst*. As to this now purely colloquial use of 'against' see Abbott, § 142.

Ib. guess, for 'guests,' a not uncommon slurring; so in Munday and Chettle's The Downfall of Robert Earl of Huntingdon, iii. 2:

'It greatly at my stomach sticks,
That all the day we had no gues,
And have of meat so many a mess.'

Compare the Americanism 'less' for 'let us.'

131. *of door.* As to the omission of the article after prepositions and adverbial phrases see Abbott, § 90.

135. *nor fearèd naught.* For the construction in this line compare viii. 72 and 101, and ix. 44; and see Abbott, § 408. As to the double negative see *ib.* § 406.

149. *in such post*, in such haste. Compare vi. 179 and xv. 4; Shakespeare frequently uses the phrase 'in post' in this sense, so Romeo and Juliet, v. 3. 273:

'And then in post he came from Mantua
To this same place.'

So 'to post' is used for 'to hasten,' i. 128; and in Alphonsus King of Arragon, act iii, occurs the phrase 'posting pace.' The combination 'post-haste' is likewise Elizabethan; the poet Posthaste in the play of Histrio-Mastix is supposed by the late Mr. Simpson to be intended for Shakespeare, at least in the later recension of the play.

154. *mated*, confounded. As to this verb 'mate' or 'amate' (for a different verb 'to mate' see Doctor Faustus, opening Chorus, 2) compare the adjective 'mat' in Chaucer, Old French mat (M. Latin mattus) and mater, from the term 'schach mat' (checkmate) signifying in the Persian game of chess 'the shah (king) is dead.' Diez compares the Hebrew mût, to die; met, dead.—Compare Orlando Furioso:

'Worse than Medusa mateth all our minds';

and Macbeth, v. i. 86:

'My mind she hath mated and amazed my sight.'

156. *'bash*, for 'abash,' look foolish, from the French ébahir; hence the adjective bashful. In xvi. 61, the verb is used in the sense of 'to lower,' as if from the French abaisser.—These omissions of the prefix are very common; the following are among those in our play: ''miss' for 'amiss,' xiv. 56; 'gree' for 'agree,' vi. 130; 'vouch' for 'avouch.' vii. 19; 'foretime' for 'aforetime,' ix. 128; ''tide' for 'betide,' xiii. 14; ''gin' for 'begin,' in our scene, 159; also ''tirèd' for 'attired,' iii. 45; 'treat' for 'entreat,' v. 82; and 'closure' for 'enclosure,' x. 118. Compare also 'gree' for 'degree'; 'file' for 'defile;' 'tice' for 'entice'; 'dain' for 'disdain.'

157. *miss'd*, a punning repetition of the first syllable of 'mistress.'

165. *motion*, proposal. Compare to 'move questions,' l. 87 above.

171. *frame his art by proof*, give evidence of how he manages his art.

Compare King Lear, i. 2. 107: 'Frame the business after your own wisdom.' The A.-S. 'fremman,' O. E. freme, means to perform or manage; so in The Faerie Queene, i. 8. 30:

'That on a staffe his feeble steps did frame.'

173. *he the Master there.* See Burden in Dramatis Personae.

176. *Hecate.* 'Hecat'' is used as a dissyllable, xi. 18. Shakespeare likewise uses the name both as a dissyllable, and, in 1 Henry VI, iii. 2. 64, as a trisyllable.—Hecate (whose name was originally a cognomen of the Moon-goddess meaning 'the far-shooting one') was in Greece as well as in Italy the centre of all magic art and ghost-stories. She appears as a powerful deity already in the Theogony of Hesiod and in the Homeric Hymn to Demeter, and continued to be worshipped to a very late date; thus the Emperor Diocletian established a place of worship for her in a crypt at Antioch. 'She was,' says Preller, 'the favourite figure of superstition and of all obscure practices based on the superstition of women, of the common people, or on the other hand of the weakly and the over-educatad.' Thus she passed into mediæval legend, and plays a prominent part in magic, where her 'circle' was one of those formed by conjurors.

178. *et nunc et semper*, a quotation doubtless from the Liturgy.

Scene III.

2. *good cheap* (quarto of 1599, 'good chape'), at a low price, French à bon marché. Compare 1 Henry IV, iii. 3. 51: 'The sack that thou hast drunk me would have bought me lights as good cheap at the dearest chandler's in Europe'; and see Burton's Anatomy of Melancholy, i. 2. 3. 15: 'the best is alwayes best cheap.'

5. *cope*, purchase or exchange. So Conscience as a broomseller sings in The Three Ladies of London:

'Have you any old boots,
Or any old shoon,
Pouch-rings or buskins,
To cope for new broom.'

The root of the word is the same as that of cheap, cheapen, chapman (see l. 16)—the A.-S. substantive ceáp means a purchase or object of purchase; the A.-S. verb ceapian, to buy and sell; cypan, to sell. Compare German kaufen. A 'chipping' was the old English term for a market-place; hence many English local names, such as Chipping Norton, Chepstow. Cheapside and Eastcheap were the old market-places of London. Copenhagen (Kjöbnhavn) is equivalent to Chipping Haven. See Isaac Taylor, Words and Places, p. 374.

8. *prize it* (quarto of 1599, 'prise it'), price it, put a price upon it. Compare 'to appraise,' another derivative of the Latin pretium. Shakespeare uses both the substantive and the verb 'prize' in the sense of 'price': so xiii. 41; and Antony and Cleopatra, v. 2. 182:

> 'Caesar's no merchant, to make prize with you
> Of things that merchants sold';

and Love's Labour's Lost, v. 2. 224:

> 'Prize you yourselves: what buys your company.'

10. *naughts*, trifles (Latin nugae).

11. *frank*, free, i.e. liberal, bountiful. Compare i. 9. So Shakespeare, Sonnet iv. 4, says of Nature:

> 'Being frank, she lends to all are free.'

13. *Phoebus*. It was Zeus, and not Phœbus, who courted Semele (see Doctor Faustus, xiii. 107); but the mythology of the old dramatists is not always very exact. See Doctor Faustus, xiii. 109; and the scene in Peele's Arraignment of Paris, where Saturn sits peaceably with Jupiter and the other gods.

16. *If that*. See note on Doctor Faustus, x. 15.

Ib. chapmen. Compare note to l. 5 above. Chaucer uses the word in The Shipmanne's Tale:

> 'For of us chapmen all, so God me save
> . . . .
> Scarsly among us twenty ten shul thrive
> Continually, lasting unto oure age.
> . . . .
> For evermore mote we stand in drede
> Of hap and fortune in our chapmanhede.'

22. *soothe me up*, soothe me completely. This is a favourite use of 'up' by Greene; compare 'hamper up,' vi. 136; 'unite it up,' *ib.* 159; 'mumbling up,' *ib.* 150; 'taunt us up,' vii. 108; 'honour up,' xii. 21; 'furnish up,' xvi. 74; and towards the close of Alphonsus King of Arragon:

> 'When I come to finish up his life.'

Marlowe in 1 Tamburlaine, i. 1, uses to 'sound up' in the sense of 'sound loudly.'—It thus appears that precedents are not wanting for the use of the expletive in the phrase 'to open up,' which is so much objected to by purists.

23. *too broad before*, too openly displayed.

30. *in a dump*. See note on i. 12.

38. *Beccles*. This still flourishing little market-town in Suffolk, on the south side of the navigable river Waveney, which separates it from Norfolk, has an interesting local history. It formerly was part of the manor of Bury St. Edmunds monastery. The parish comprises about

1400 acres of marshes and common, which had once belonged wholly to the inhabitants under the name of Beccles Fen, and concerning the tenure and management of which there was a long series of disputes in the Tudor period, ending with the surrender of the fen (previously managed by their own fen-reeves) by the inhabitants to the Crown, and the grant of letters patent to the Corporation of Portreeve, Surveyors and Commonalty of the Fen of Beccles in 1584, confirmed in 1588 and 1605. See White's History of Suffolk.

Ib. by, hard-by. So in Love's Labour's Lost, v. 2. 94:

'I stole into a neighbour thicket by.'

40. *quaint*, here in the sense of strange, shy. (Compare for the other use note on i. 67.) So Bellona, who roughly 'shaked her speare' at Vulcan when after delivering her from her father's head he 'proffered her some cortesie,' is called 'queint Bellona' in The Shepheard's Calender, October, 114 (see the 'Glosse').

45. *Tirèd*, attired. See note to ii. 156.

49. *You forget yourself.* These words are, according to Dyce, assigned to Margaret in the quartos.

52. *little manners.* So we still speak of 'small courtesy,' 'small kindness.'

59. *Goodman Cob.* Goodman and goodwife (goody) were popular terms for the heads of families; compare in the Authorised Version St. Matthew's Gospel, xx. 11, and elsewhere. Miles, xi. 51, addresses the Brazen Head as 'Goodman Head'; and, xv. 50, the Devil as 'goodman friend.'—In Jonson's Every Man in his Humour the name 'Cob' gives rise to another pun.

61. *a'*, he. Compare note on Doctor Faustus, iv. 3.

62. *hilding*, low creature; a term used of both men and women. According to Nares, the word is 'derived by some from "hinderling," a Devonshire word signifying degenerate. . . . . Perhaps after all, no more originally than a corruption of "hireling" or "hindling," diminutive of "hind," which the following passage in Cymbeline, ii. 3. 128, seems to confirm:

"A base slave,
A hilding for a livery, a squire's cloth,
A pantler, not so eminent."'

65. *erst*, formerly, hitherto. Chaucer uses this superlative form as a comparative. See The Knightes Tale, 708 (Morris).

66. *quickened*, enlivened.

69. *in grey*, a phrase frequently used of the homely garb of a shepherd. Mitford, cited by Dyce, quotes from the Shepherd's Ode in Greene's Ciceronis Amor:

'A cloak of grey fencèd the rain,
Thus 'tirèd was this lovely swain;
. . . .
Such was Paris, shepherds say,
When with Œnone he did play;'

and from Peele's Wars of Troy:

'So couth he (Paris) sing . . .
. . . .
And wear his coat of grey and lusty green.'

Dyce adds the following passage from Orlando Furioso:

'As Paris, when Œnone lov'd him well,
Forgat he was a son of Priamus,
All clad in grey, sat piping on a reed.'

Compare also in The Song of a Country Swain at the Return of Philander in Greene's The Mourning Garment:

'Fond pride, avaunt! give me the shepherd's hook,
A coat of grey! I'll be a country clown.'

This description of a shepherd's dress is not adopted by Spenser in The Shepheard's Calender; it is only when his shepherds are in mourning, that

'The blew is black, the greene in gray is tinct.'

See November, 107.—As to Paris and Œnone, and as to the abbreviation 'Œnon.' see note on Doctor Faustus, vi. 27.

72. *Who but*, ellipsis for 'who was admired or sought but.'

74. *Passeth*, surpasseth. Compare vi. 169.

82. *quaint*, trim, pretty, as in i. 67.

87. *store*, plenty, abundance. So constantly in Shakespeare; and compare Doctor Faustus, vii. 39.

88. *gramercies*, or gramercy, many thanks. From the French grand merci or grand mercy, which Chaucer uses in the original form. The phrase recurs v. 112 and xvi. 6. Milton uses the word 'grammercy' for 'great thanks' in the Areopagitica, p. 25 (Hales).

Scene IV.

2. *Ring'd*, encircled. Compare ii. 65.

3. *surge is.* The quartos, according to Dyce, read 'surges.'

4. *That compass'd high-built Babel in*, the walls of Babylon. Compare ii. 63.

6. *promontory-cleeves.* Compare i. 62.

10. *Who dar'd . . seas.* See Elinor in Dramatis Personae.

11. *And venture . . deep.* 'A corrupted line. Query, "And venture as Agenor's damsel did"? (Greene would hardly have written here "through

the deep," when the preceding line ended with "through the seas.").' Dyce.—Europa, the daughter of Agenor King of Sidon (according to Homer the daughter of Phoenix), was carried off by Zeus in the shape of a bull, and borne across the sea into Crete. She is the wandering moon-goddess, and appears on Phoenician coins and in Phoenician legends as identified with Astarte.

12. *wanton*, amorous.

14. *The Pyren Mounts*, the Pyrenees (Pyrenaei montes).

15. *Castile*. This accentuation is in accordance with the derivation of the name. It was given to the country previously called Bardulia' about the ninth century, probably in allusion to the castles (castellae) which the Christians built in this district, so much exposed to the assaults of the foe. See Schäfer, Geschichte Spanien's, ii. 333.

19. *bide the brunt*. Compare note on Doctor Faustus, i. 93.

21. *After that*. See note on Doctor Faustus, x. 15.

22. *counterfeit*, portrait (from French contrefaire, compare German Konterfey); so in The Merchant of Venice, iii. 2. 115: 'Fair Portia's counterfeit!'

25. *the virtuous . . deeds*, the discourse or report of his deeds of virtue (valour).

27. *Done*. Dyce suggests the alteration 'shown.' Or perhaps this and the previous line may have been respectively transposed.

Ib. at the Holy Land, in the Holy Land. For this use of 'at' for 'in' with reference to a country, compare The Winter's Tale, i. 2. 39:

'When at Bohemia
You take my lord.'

In Thackeray's The Virginians the American Miss Lydia van den Bosch speaks of the manners and customs 'at America.'

Ib. Damas' (quarto of 1599, 'Damas'), Damascus. Compare viii. 113:

'Who at Damasco beat the Saracens.'

Edward, however, never fought before Damascus. See Edward Prince of Wales in Dramatis Personae.

29. *like so of*, to conceive or take such a liking for. Compare x. 56. For a possible explanation of this construction as a result of the old impersonal use of the verb 'me liketh,' 'him liketh,' see Abbott, § 177. But compare 'accept of,' ix. 200.

33. *To Suffolk side*, to the border of Suffolk. So 3 Henry VI, iv. 6. 83:

'In secret ambush on the forest side.'

The 'country-side' is a term still used in the sense of 'district.'

Ib. to merry Framlingham (quarto of 1599, 'Fremingham,' which is near the O. E. spelling 'Fremigham'). Framlingham, famed according to Evelyn for its growth of oaks, the tallest and largest perhaps in the world,—one of them furnished the beams of the Royal Sovereign,—is still more famous for its ancient castle, the origin of which is ascribed to Redwald, King of the East Angles from 593. It was here that King Edmund, the saint and martyr, was besieged by the Danes. After the Norman Conquest, the castle remained royal for two reigns, and after being held by the Bigods (afterwards Earls of Norfolk), and reverting to the Crown under Edward II, was granted by him to his brother Thomas Plantagenet, whom he created Earl of Norfolk. It then passed by marriage to the Mowbrays, to whose honours and a great part of whose estates the Howards afterwards succeeded. At Framlingham died the victor of Flodden Field; by the attainder of his son the castle was forfeited to the Crown, till Queen Mary, who had found shelter at Framlingham on the death of Edward VI, reversed the attainder. On the execution of the next duke in 1572 the castle and manor once more passed to the Crown, by whom they were granted to Thomas Lord Howard, Baron of Walden, and his uncle Lord Henry Howard. In 1635 the castle was sold to Sir Robert Hitcham, who in the next year, finding the title to the estate hopelessly perplexed, 'in thankfulness to God for his wonderful success,' settled it for pious uses on Pembroke Hall (now Pembroke College), Cambridge. See White's History of Suffolk, where a special History of Framlingham by Robert Hawes, published at Woodbridge in 1798, is mentioned. The mansion at Framlingham called the 'Guildhall' occupies the site of a hall which belonged to the Guild of the Blessed Virgin Mary, founded here at an early period, and dissolved about 1537. We may fancy that it was here that the Fair Maid of Fressingfield was to be 'shorn a nun' (xiv. 48).

35. *Hampton-house.* This seems to be an anachronism; for Hampton Court was not a royal residence till Cardinal Wolsey, who had built it, exchanged it with Henry VIII for Richmond. (See Cavendish's Life of Wolsey.)

40. *To will him come,* to desire him to come. The word 'to will' here is the A.-S. willian; see Morris, English Accidence, 187. Compare Henry VIII, iii. 1. 18:

'They will'd me say so, Madam';

and Faire Em, sc. xv. (l. 1045):

'Therefore, by me
He willeth thee to send his daughter Blanch.'

As to the omission of 'to' before 'come,' compare note on Doctor Faustus, iii. 36.

45. *From Hapsburg* (quarto of 1599, 'Hasburg'), i. e. from Austria (though the Habsburg of course was in Switzerland), or the Empire in general. Compare ix. 13.

47. *Jaques.* This name is always used as a dissyllable; see James IV; As You Like It; and Fletcher's The Noble Gentleman.

48-50. *Padua . . . Rheims.* All these were university towns. The practice of passing from one university to the others was very common in the Middle Ages and the Renascence period, more especially of course with such 'scholastici vagantes' as Vandermast.

49. *Bologna.* Pronounce Bolognia (Bononia). The quarto of 1599 spells accordingly, 'Bolonia.'

52. *chiefest.* Compare vi. 34, and Orlando Furioso:

'Her love Orlando,
Chiefest of the western peers.'

The form occurs not less than seven times in the Authorised Version.

53. *mathematic rules.* See note on ii. 73.

55. *likes me well.* Compare vi. 139; and see note on Doctor Faustus, x. 45.

58. *wonder Vandermast.* There is no reason to change 'wonder' into 'wondrous,' as Dyce suggests. Compare A.-S. compounds such as 'wundor-werc;' in The Knighte's Tale:

'Ther saw I many another wonder storie';

and in The Man of Lawe's Tale:

'For to see this wonder chance.'

The construction may probably have arisen from the use of these compounds, unless it is to be explained by the ellipsis of the genitival prefix 'of,' as after 'maner' (manner, sort) in Chaucer and Spenser ('all manner wights,' The Faerie Queene, iv. 10. 7). See also note on v. 75.

61. *Set him but nonplus.* Compare ix. 111. 'To be non-plussed' is a vulgarism current at the present day.

64. *a poet's garland made of bays.* The reference here seems to be, not to the laureateship as a university degree, as in Doctor Faustus, iii. 32, but to the special compliment of the bestowal of a laurel wreath upon poets or literary men, of which usage common in the days of the Renascence the example of Petrarch, who was laureated as both poet and historian, is the most famous. The English poet-laureateship as a Court office seems to have arisen out of the engrafting of this custom upon the ancient office of the King's Versifier. Compare note on ix. 116.

66. *Whilst,* i. e. until. Compare x. 55. See for this use Abbott, § 137, where he cites, with other passages, Macbeth, iii. 1. 44:

'We will keep ourself
Till supper-time alone. While then, God be with you!'

In Masson's Life of Milton, v. 94, is cited a sentence upon a blasphemer in Scotland (1656), who was condemned 'to be hanged on a gibbet while he be dead.'

Ib. we set (quarto of 1594, according to Dyce, 'fit'), i. e. we set forth. Compare Henry V, Chorus before act ii, line 34:

'The King is set from London.'

Ib. with our troops, i. e. our trains or suites; see above, line 56.

Scene V.

3. *at an inch*, to the nicest point of time. Compare 2 Henry VI, i. 4. 45:

'We watched you at an inch.'

5. *post-horse'*. As to the elision compare note on opening Chorus of Doctor Faustus, l. 28.

6. *fetch*, trick. So in Hamlet, ii. 1. 38: 'a fetch of wit.' A 'fetch' was a common expression as late as the eighteenth century for a practical joke.

8. *the Isle of Ely*. Ralph may possibly be thinking of the popular fancy embodied in the rhyme:

'Saddle your goat or your green cock
And make his bridle a bottom of thread
To roll up how many miles you have rid.'

'Of the green cock,' says Ben Jonson, cited by Wright, Sorcery and Magic, i. 290, 'we have no other ground (to confess ingenuously) than a vulgar fable of a witch, that with a cock of green colour, and a bottom of blue thread, would transport herself through the air, and so escaped (at the time of her being brought to execution) from the hand of justice. It was a tale when I went to school.' The green cock recalls Wagner's Auerhan, who transported him through the air, as Faustus was transported by dragons (see Doctor Faustus, Chorus before sc. vii. l. 6), and as in the Faustbuch (ch. xxvi) he is carried by Mephistophilis in the shape of a horse with wings 'like a dromedary.' The stories of the flights of magicians and witches through the air are infinite in number and variety. Ralph's proposed exploit is one in later times accomplished by Baron Münchausen.—The Isle of Ely was still essentially an undrained fen in the Tudor times; so that it is appropriately mentioned as a home of geese.

19. *cutting*, cheating, cozening, bullying. The term is probably originally derived from the practice of 'cutting purses,' see note to i. 110. The expression 'cutter' for 'bully' is very common; so in Dekker's Seuen Deadly Sinnes of London the author says of 'Shauing,' one of the Sins: 'Wee haue beene quicke (you see) in *Trimming* this *Cutter* of *Queene Hith*, because 'tis his propertie to handle others so.' In Jonson's

Bartholomew Fair one of the characters is 'Val. Cutting, a roarer or bully'; and as late as the Restoration period Cowley reproduced a comedy under the title of 'Cutter of Coleman Street,' of which a disreputable swaggerer is the chief character.

22. *swords and bucklers.* Hence the term 'swash-buckler,' a swaggerer who tries to frighten people by clashing his sword against his buckler.

28. *subsizer.* Sizars (called at Oxford 'servitors') is the Cambridge name for poor scholars, who in addition to a pecuniary exhibition, receive their commons or food free. A 'size' is a term still used at Cambridge for a small portion of food, or for a gill of ale. Subsizars, or under-sizars, is a term still used at Trinity College, Cambridge.

33. *Tully's phrase,* Ciceronian Latin. The fashion of calling Cicero by his gentile name, Tully, which was followed by our old writers such as Chaucer and Skelton, obtained with English scholars to a very late date. Of one of Greene's prose-tracts, 'Ciceronis Amor,' the name is rendered into English as 'Tully's Love.'

37. *I can be heard, felt, and understood.* A humorous condensation of the definition of a noun substantive.

42. *Coppersmith's Hall.* There is a Cooper's Hall in London belonging to a company incorporated in 1501; but I cannot discover a Coppersmith's Hall. It is comically mentioned in A Looking-Glass for London and England, where Adam says, 'his nose was in the highest degree of noses, it was nose *autem glorificam,* so set with rubies, that after his death it should have been nailed up in Coppersmith's hall for a monument.' Compare note on ii. 35.

49. *reparrel,* a blunder for 'apparel.'

51. *coxcombs.* See as to this kind of fool's cap, note on i. 32; and compare King Lear, i. 4. 114.

52. *spring,* start, make to fly off. Compare to 'fly the partridge,' xii. 83.

54. *be.* For this use of be after a verb of thinking, see Abbott, § 299.

56. *swones,* a further mutilation of the oath in 53.

62. *fast,* immoveable. Compare 'fast-fancied,' l. 79 below; and the German 'fest,' used of the effects of magic both as a simple word and in the compound 'bannfest.'

65. *light-fingered.* This expression, still applied to cutpurses and pickpockets, occurs already in the old Interlude of Nice Wanton, where Eulalia says to Xantippe:

> 'Your son is suspect light-fingered to be;
> Your daughter hath nice tricks three or four.'

75. *Thy fool disguis'd,* thy disguise as a fool. Perhaps we might read

'thy fool disguise' as equivalent to 'thy foolish disguise'; for 'fool' is used adjectivally (like 'wonder' and 'manner'; see note on iv. 58); so in The Merchant of Venice, i. 1. 102, 'this fool gudgeon, this opinion'; and *ib.*, ii. 9. 26, 'the fool multitude, that choose by show.'

79. *Fast-fancied*, tied by fancy; compare 62. 'Fancy' is here used for love, as viii. 7, and elsewhere. Compare 'fancy-free' in A Midsummer Night's Dream, ii. 1. 164.

82. *treat*, entreat. See note on ii. 156.

86. *Apollo*, the Delphic Apollo. Compare ii. 18.

94. *strength*, strengthen. As to the discarding of the suffix *en* in the conversion of nouns and adjectives into verbs, see Abbott, § 290, and compare note on vi. 8.

Ib. thy college-state, the state or estate of thy college. Compare 1 Henry IV, iv. 1. 46:

'Were it good
To set the exact wealth of all our states
All at one cast?'

107. *'fore that*, afore or before that. As to this use of 'that,' see note on Doctor Faustus, x. 15.

99. *your manhood and your sword is.* For this use of a singular verb with two singular nouns as subject, see Abbott, § 336.

110. *in a glass prospective.* As to Bacon's magical glass, see Introduction, p. xxiii. 'Prospective' is that which looks forward,—whether into the future, or the distance, or that which is hidden from the bodily eye,—hence equivalent to 'divining'; so 'prospective skill,' xiii. 12. Compare R. Armin's A Nest of Ninnies, p. 4 (Old Shakespeare Society's Publications, 1842): 'a philosopher's cell, who, because he was alwayes poking at Fortune with his forefinger, the wise wittily namde him Sotto, as one besotted—a grumbling sir; one that was wise enough, and fond enough, and solde all for a glass prospective, because he would wisely see into all men but himselfe, a fault generall in most.'

112. *Gramercies.* See note to iii. 88.

Ib. quite, i. e. requite, as again vi. 29, 180; viii. 35; xiii. 73. From the Old French quiter (from the adjective quite, cuite, Latin quietus).

118. *Till . . . awhile*, till I and Friar Bacon shall have talked awhile.

121. *black-pots.* According to Nares, a 'black-pot' is a Somersetshire term for a black-pudding; and the word is used by Thomas Heywood for a jug (as 'black-jack' is frequently used; see note on x. 3). Ralph may therefore be referring to the exploits which he contemplates in the taverns; but it is more likely that he is alluding to the black caps of the masters and scholars. He afterwards (vii. 82) irreverently refers to the 'doting night-caps' of the doctors.

Scene VI.

2. *tempers*, fashions by or after heating. So in Orlando Furioso:

'Where sits Tisiphone, tempering in flames
Those torches that do set on fire avenge.'

Hence the word comes to mean 'to manage,' as in xvi. 44; and compare Alphonsus King of Arragon, act iii:

'Long since dame Fortune temper'd so her wheel,
As that there was no vantage to be seen
On any side, but equal was the gain';

and 'to mix,' as x. 36.

Ib. toys, trifles; the German Zeug, compare Spielzeug (play-things).

3. *his consistory-court.* The consistory-court in England is that of the diocesan-bishop, held by the bishop's chancellor or his commissary, acting as judge.

4. *plead homage*, acknowledge the supreme authority of.

7. *the Lincoln earl.* For this adjectival use of local names, compare 'the Lincoln Countess,' l. 126 below; 'the Sussex Earl,' v. 76; 'the Castile Elinor,' iv. 23; and 'the Albion diadem,' viii. 131.

8. *glad'st*, gladdenst. So frequently in Shakespeare. For this use of adjectives as verbs, see Abbott, § 290, and compare 'to short,' viii. 103; and 'to rich,' *ib.* 131. As to the discarding of the suffix *en*, compare note to v. 94.

9. *How Lacy meaneth to*, how Lacy is disposed towards,—whether he intends or not to deal fairly by.

Enter Margaret and Friar Bungay. 'Perhaps the curtain which concealed the upper stage (i. e. the balcony at the back of the stage) was withdrawn, discovering Margaret and Bungay standing there, and when the representation in the glass was supposed to be over, the curtain was drawn back again.' Dyce.

12. *brightsome.* The quartos, 'bright-sunne.' Dyce.

Ib. the paramour of Mars, Venus.

17. *That . . . swain.* 'Query: "That this fair, witty, courteous," &c. See Margaret's first speech (iii. 64 seqq.) and her speech in the present scene, 31 seqq.' Dyce.

19. *Earl of Lincolnshire.* See LACY in Dramatis Personae.

21. *cunning.* See note on Doctor Faustus, opening Chorus, l. 20.

22. *procure*, bring about the success of, as an intermediary. Compare 'proctor' from 'procurator.'

23. *holp*, an old preterite of 'help,' of which the A.-S. form was 'healp.' Even the past participle 'holpen' used in the Authorised Version is now archaic. Shakespeare uses the form 'holp.'

29. *quite*, requite. See note on v. 112.

32. *avouch*, avow, maintain, be sufficient for, undertake. Compare x. 86; and 'vouch,' vii. 19.

Ib. to shadow, to cover with an excuse.

Ib. rape. The quartos, 'cape.' Dyce.

37. *England's paramour.* Query, did Greene write 'paragon'? The consonance with the preceding line is unpleasing.

50. *Daphne.* The story of Daphne, who flying from Apollo was changed into a laurel-tree, is told in Ovid's Metamorphoses, i. 452 seqq.

54. *Recant thee*, retract thy course. 'Thee' is here probably to be construed as an accusative; though it might be a dative following a neuter verb; compare i. 141.

56. *secret*, confidential.

58. *exception.* The quarto of 1594, 'acception.' Dyce.

65. *For better die.* The quarto of 1599, 'for dye.' Malone conjectures, 'For sooner dye.'

68. *You're . . . near.* 'An allusion to the proverb, "Early up, and never the nearer."

"In you, ysfaith, the proverb's verified,—
Y'are earely up, and yet are nere the neare."

Munday and Chettle's The Death of Robert Earl of Huntington' [iii. 2]. Dyce. 'Near' is the old comparative of nigh (A.-S. neah). Abbott, § 478, cites, with other passages, Richard II, v. 1. 88:

'Better far off than near, be ne'er the near.'

So Chaucer has 'dere' for 'dearer.'

69. *in a morn*, in the morning.

76. *I marvel . . himself.* 'Brought love is better than sent love' is still current as a proverbial saying.

81. *the idea.* Pronounce 'th' idéa.' The 'idea' is the 'image,' as in the original use of the Greek word *ἰδέα*. Compare Richard III, iii. 7. 13:

'I did infer your lineaments,
Being the right idea of your father,
Both in your form and nobleness of mind.'

87. *timely*, early. Compare x. 126. '*Timely*, adv. early. Macbeth, ii. 3. 51:

"He did command me to call timely on him."—

Molto a buon-hora, very timely, verie early.—1598; Florio.' (New Shakspere Society's Translations, 1875-6, p. 459.)

Ib. too-too. Compare Alphonsus King of Arragon, act iv:

'*Cari.* What, hear you nothing of them all this while?
Duke. Yes, too-too much, the Milan Duke may say';

and *ib.*, act v:

'Then for that love, if any love you had,
Revoke this sentence, which is too-too bad';

and see 'Observations on the correct method of punctuating a line in Hamlet, i. 2. 129,'

['O! that this too-too solid flesh would melt!']

'with reference to the exact force of the word too-too,' by J. O. Halliwell (The Shakespeare Society's Papers, part i. pp. 39-43. in the Shakespeare Society's Publications, 1844), where it is shown that 'too-too' is not a mere reduplication of 'too' ('too, too'), but a provincial word, which became a recognised archaism and signified 'exceeding.' The word is used by Cromwell in a letter from Linlithgow (Carlyle, ch. xxvii): 'The Enemy is at his old lock, and lieth in or near Stirling; where we cannot come to fight him, except he please, or we go upon too-too manifest hazards.'

88. *Deus hic.* These words are from the Vulgate translation of Genesis xxviii. 16 ('Surely the Lord is in this place'); unless they are a transposition of the words in a verse of the Roman liturgy for 'Holy Saturday': 'Hic Deus meus,' &c., Exodus xv. 2.

91. *No . . news?* The quartos, according to Dyce, assign these words to 'Mar.'

92. *pursuivants,* the officers attached to the heralds.

104. *some other.* This use of 'other' as a substantival pronoun is explained by its derivation ('on—ther,' one of two); 'other some' was however a frequent combination.

108. *once,* on this occasion.

114. *For why,* because. See note on i. 121.

118. *I not deny.* As to this omission of the auxiliary 'do' before 'not,' see Abbott, § 305.

121. *mean.* The earlier quartos, 'meant.' Dyce.

127. *bands,* bans. See note on Doctor Faustus, i. 107.

130. *gree,* agree. See note to ii. 156.

132. *'Twere . . between.* I have followed Dyce in printing this and the next line as (corrupted) verse.

135. *that.* For this insertion of 'that' in the second coordinate clause after its omission in the first, see Abbott, § 285.

136. *hamper up.* See note on iii. 22.

137. *portace.* This word, of which the spelling varies as 'portos' (Chaucer), 'portass,' 'portasse,' 'portise,' 'portesse' (Spenser), 'porteous,' and 'porthose,' and which is the same as 'portal' in a statute of James I, is an equivalent of the Latin 'portorium,' i. e. portable breviary or prayer-book. It is of constant occurrence in our old writers.

140. *Then hand-fast hand.* To 'hand-fast' is to betroth. Betrothal by means of a form called 'hand-fasting,' in which a double ring, constructed with hoops so as to enclose the fingers of the betrothed pair (a symbol used already in early English and Scottish times, and said to

have been practised by the Danes), was employed, customarily preceded the marriage ceremony. The following is extracted from Charles Knight's William Shakspere, a Biography (Pictorial Shakspere), p. 214: 'In a work published in 1543, "The Christian State of Matrimony," we find this passage:—"Yet in this thing also, must I warn every reasonable and honest person to beware, that in the contracting of marriage they dissemble not, nor set forth any lie. Every man likewise must esteem the person to whom he is hand-fasted, none otherwise than for his own spouse; though as yet it be not done in the church, nor in the street. After the hand-fasting, and making of the contract, the church-going and wedding should not be deferred too long."' See also, as illustrating the custom of free-contract or trothplight, Measure for Measure, iv. 1. 72-75; Twelfth Night, v. 154-164; The Winter's Tale, i. 2. 278; The Tempest, iv. 1. 13 seqq.—The above particulars have been collected in a pamphlet published (1873) by Mr. J. C. Hodgson for Mr. J. Malam, the owner of a curious picture considered by him to be an authentic representation of the hand-fasting between Shakespeare and Ann Hathaway, 'which preceded actual marriage at church nearly five months, without bringing any stigma on either.'

146. *Help, Bacon .. now.* 'Some word, or words, wanting here.' Dyce.

150. *mumbling up*, so as to prevent his mumbling through. Compare note on iii. 22.

151. *Why speak'st not.* Compare vii. 115 and viii. 13; and see as to such ellipses, Abbott, § 401, where it is observed that while the nominative in the second person plural (or first person) is less commonly omitted, 'the inflexion of the second person singular allows the nominative to be readily understood, and therefore justifies its omission.'

Ib. Hud, hud. I do not know the particular force of this interjection of the 'mute' Bungay. 'Hout, hout' is however cited by Mätzner from Otway's Venice Preserved, iii. 1, as an interjection used for sending a dog to kennel; and perchance the Friar is attempting to exorcise 'the devils' who have 'enchanted' him (see lines 155-6). The devil usually announced his appearance with some such exclamation in the old mysteries.

154. *passions.* According to Dyce, the quarto of 1594 reads 'passions,' which I have ventured to leave unchanged. For 'passions,' compare i. 20, and Doctor Faustus, xi. 42; and as to the third person plural in 'th, see Abbott, § 334.

158. *what*, equivalent to 'which,' as the neuter of 'who.' See Abbott, § 252; as also for the use of 'what .. it' in the present passage.

159. *unite it up.* See note to iii. 22.

160. *miscreant*, literally misbeliever (O. French mescreant, N. French

mécréant). Margaret here seems to be thinking of the death of heretics, and thus to be using the word in its literal sense. In 1 Henry VI Shakespeare seems to use the word both in this sense (v. 3. 44) and in the ordinary modern sense of 'villain' (iii. 4. 44), so that Trench's observations (English Past and Present, pp. 129-130) on Talbot's application of the term to the Maid of Orleans (iii. 2) lose much of their point.

161. *Bungay.* The quartos, 'Bacon.' Dyce.

163. *straight.* Dyce's suggestion for 'straightway.'

166. *Of courtesy.* Compare note on Doctor Faustus, opening Chorus, l. 20.

169. *we were passing unkind.* Query, 'passing unkind we were.' Dyce.—'Passing' is here equivalent to 'surpassingly.' Compare iii. 74; and 'passing the love of women,' 2 Samuel i. 26.

176. *for fear.* 'Some word or words wanting here.' Dyce.

179. *in post.* See note on ii. 149.

180. *quite,* requite. See note on v. 112.

Scene VII.

1. *the Regent-house,* the house where the Regents meet, the house of Congregation. Regency is an academical term which has very little significance at the present day, and of which the origin is not very clear. 'Regent Masters' appear originally to have been those who for about two years after their degree held a school in Grammar or any other Faculty at Oxford ('regere scholas Oxoniæ') or at any other 'studium generale'; non-Regents, those who had passed this period of probation and were not necessarily engaged in lecturing. 'Regents' are still distinguished as 'necessario Regentes' or 'Regentes ad placitum.' The former comprise all Doctors of every Faculty and all Masters of Arts for two years from their degrees; the latter Professors, Heads of Houses, certain University and College officers, and Doctors of every Faculty if resident in the University. See Oxford Calendar, and Anstey's Introduction to Munimenta Academica.

2. *It fits us talk,* it befits us to talk. For the use of the infinitive without 'to' compare note on Doctor Faustus, iii. 36.

Ib. the king's repair (quarto of 1599, 'the long repaire'), the King's repairing or coming to this place. Compare Hamlet, v. 2. 228, 'I will forestal their repair hither'; and see as to this use of infinitives as substantive nouns, note on Doctor Faustus, xiii. 30.

3. *troop'd with,* attended by; as again xii. 16. For this use of 'with' for 'by,' see Abbott, § 193. 'Troops' is used in the sense of 'trains' or 'suites,' iv. 66.

4. *alongst,* along. 'Along,' 'amid' and 'among,' being all derived from adjectives or substantives, had genitive forms (alonges, amiddes, amonges), the *s* in which was changed in usage into *st.* The *st* in 'against' and 'whilst' has the same origin.

Ib. by east, to the east. Compare in the Prologue to the Canterbury Tales, 388, 'woning fer by weste,' with Morris's note, *l. c.*; and the nautical expression, 'north-east-by-east.' 'The Dantzic seas' are the Baltic, for which the German name is the Eastern Sea (Ostsee).

6. *Almain,* German. Compare note on Doctor Faustus, i. 123.

Ib. Saxon. The quartos, 'Scoccon.' Dyce.

8. *resolv'd for,* resolved to come or go to. Compare 2 Henry IV, ii. 3. 67:

'I will resolve for Scotland.'

9. *plots of stately tragedies.* 'Plots,' 'plats' or 'platforms' of plays were properly outlines or schemes of performances, like that of The Seven Deadlie Sinns mentioned in note on Dramatis Personae of Doctor Faustus.—It need hardly be observed that the exhibition of plays as a part of the entertainments offered to sovereigns when visiting the universities, though common in the reigns of Elizabeth and of her successors, is an anachronism as applied to that of Henry III.

10. *proud Roscius.* The famous Roman actor Q. Roscius did not perform before 'Roman emperors,' for he died in B.C. 62.

11. *Vaunted,* proudly displayed. Compare Doctor Faustus, opening Chorus, l. 6.

12. *To welcome . . . potentates.* In the quartos this line is given to Clement. Dyce.

15. *of esteem,* of repute. Compare l. 109 below.

16. *Don Jaques Vandermast.* See Dramatis Personae.

17. *those,* for 'the.' See note to Doctor Faustus, i. 75.

19. *vouch this task,* answer for, sustain, undertake it. (Latin vocare, O. Fr. voucher, a law-term used when a person whose possession was attacked *called upon* a third person to stand in his shoes and defend his right. In a secondary sense 'to vouch for me' is to answer to the call, to give your own guarantee for the matter in dispute. Wedgwood; and see *ib., s. v. advocatus.*) Compare xii. 55, and 'avouch,' vi. 32.

20. *countervail,* match. Compare Romeo and Juliet, iii. 6. 4:

'Come what sorrow can,
It cannot countervail the exchange of joy
That one short minute gives me in her sight.'

To 'vail' or 'avail' is to be of use or value (French valoir, Latin valere). Compare xiii. 98.

23. *hold the German play,* match himself against the German. Compare the phrases cited by Schmidt, to 'hold a wager,' 'hold a penny';

and perhaps to 'hold hand,' in King John, ii. 494: (she) 'holds hand with any princess.' The passage in Henry VIII, v. 4. 90,

'I 'll find
A Marshalsea shall hold ye play these two months,'

seems correctly explained by Schmidt 'a prison which shall keep you under,' and wrongly by Delius 'where you shall play (i. e. have hard labour) as a punishment.'

26. *Mas doctor.* In Nares several instances are quoted of this colloquial abbreviation of 'Master,' among them Jonson's Staple of News, ii. 1,

'And you, mas broker,
Shall have a feeling';

and Greene's Quip for an Upstart Courtier, where the plural 'masse' occurs in the phrase 'masse shoemakers.' The term 'mashyp' was similarly used as an abbreviation for 'mastership.' Compare 'Master Doctor Faustus' in Doctor Faustus, x. 1, and 'Master Parson,' *ib.* viii. 23.

32. *rumour,* noise (Latin rumor, French rumeur).

33. *hurly-burly.* Of this word, which, according to Henry Peacham, in The Garden of Eloquence (1577), is an example of 'onomatopoeia, when we invent, devise, fayne and make a name intimating the sound of that it signifyeth, as hurlyburly, for an uprore and tumultuous stirre,' an early use has been pointed out in a large number of instances. See the note in Furness's Variorum edition on Macbeth, i. 1. 3, 'When the hurly-burly 's done.' A still earlier instance of the use of the expression 'Hurlee Burlee' than any of these has recently been pointed out in N. Udall's translation of the Apophthegms of Erasmus, of which translation the first edition was in 1542. (See an article on a reprint of the 1554 edition of Udall's translation in The Saturday Review, November 24th, 1877.) Shakespeare uses the compound as an adjective in 1 Henry IV, v. 1. 78. 'Hurly' seems to come from the French 'hurler,' to howl or yell; Littré gives the French 'hurlu-burlu' as of unknown derivation.

35. *before the doctors.* See note to l. 1.

37. *rufflers.* A 'ruffler' is, according to Nares, the term used for a cheating bully in several Acts of Parliament, particularly in one of 27 Henry VIII, and is constantly used to signify any lawless or violent person. Compare the German 'Raufbold' for a brawling bully; and our 'ruffian.' To 'ruffle' is to be turbulent; and a 'ruffle' is used in the sense of a bustle or scene of plunder in a passage quoted in Nares from The Lover's Complaint, 58:

'A reverend man that grazed his cattle nigh—
Sometime a blusterer, that the ruffle knew
Of court, of city.'

40. *Salve, Doctor Burden!* The form of verse in which Miles has the audacity to talk before the Dons is the 'Skeltonical,' so called from its employment by John Skelton, poet-laureate to Henry VIII, in several of his satires, notably in Phyllyp Sparowe, Colyn Cloute, and Why come ye nat to Courte? It is mentioned with great contempt by Puttenham in his Arte of English Poesie, and belongs to the kind of verse of which, as King James I says, 'the maist part be out of ordour, and keipis na kynde nor reule of flowing, and for that cause are callit *tumbling verse.*' It is well described as follows in Disraeli's Curiosities of Literature: 'The Skeltonical short verse, contracted into five or six, and even four, syllables, is wild and airy. In the quick-returning rhymes, the playfulness of the diction, and the pungency of new words, usually ludicrous, often expressive, and sometimes felicitous, there is a stirring spirit which will be best felt in an audible reading. The velocity of his verse has a carol of its own. The chimes ring in the ear, and the thoughts are flung about like coruscations.' Skelton has the further peculiarity of borrowing in his free way the device of 'macaronic' poetry, which properly consists of the addition to half-lines in one language of half-lines in another (generally Latin), but which in a wider use of the term means the insertion of foreign fragments, quotations, proverbs, and phrases of all kind, by way of varying and enlivening the diction. Skelton himself justly says of his verse, Colyn Cloute, 53-58:

'For though my ryme be ragged,
Tattered and iagged,
Rudely rayne beaten,
Rusty and moughte' [moth] 'eaten,
If ye take well therwith,
It hath in it some pyth.'

Skeltonical verse is introduced in Munday's The Downfall of Robert Earl of Huntingdon in the mouth of Skelton himself, who in this play appears as a kind of Prologue and Chorus, and performs the part of Friar Tuck, in which he likewise often falls into (iv. 2)

'the vein
Of ribble-rabble rhymes Skeltonical.'

For other examples of the use of this metre see Dyce's Introduction to his edition of Skelton's Poetical Works, pp. cvii-cxxx.

41. *lurden* (from Old French lourdin, Modern lourdaud, from lourd, heavy; compare in Gower's Confessio Amantis, bk. v, 'so lourd a wight'), a lumpish, lazy fellow. This word is frequently used by Skelton, so in Magnyfycence, 1848:

'I sawe a losell lede a lurden, and they were bothe blynde';

and also spelt by him 'lurdayne' and 'lurdeyne.' It likewise occurs in the forms 'lourd' and 'lourden,' and was at one time supposed to be derived from 'lord Dane,' in hatred and derision of the Danes. See the references to this etymology, cited in Nares, in Lambarde's Perambulation of Kent, The Mirror for Magistrates, and Warner's Albion's England.

63. *For they say*, because they say. See note to i. 121.

67. *lovely*. This word, which has become obsolete as a general epithet of praise except in America, is a favourite with both Greene and Marlowe. In 2 Tamburlaine, i. 3, the hero calls his sanguinary sons 'lovely boys.'

68. *sugar'd*. One of the many examples of the use of a participial form with a merely adjectival force; see Abbott, § 294, and compare 'azur'd' in Doctor Faustus, xiii. 109. 'Sugar'd' merely means 'sweet as sugar,' and was so used metaphorically, as in Alphonsus King of Arragon, Prologue, 5, 'Homer's sugar'd Muse,' and in the well-known passage in Meres's Palladis Tamia, Wit's Treasury mentioning Shakespeare's 'sugred Sonnets among his private friends.'

69. *Bewrays*, discovers or betrays. So in Orlando Furioso,

'These words bewray thou art no base-born Moor';

in Edward II, i. 2. 34,

'His countenance bewrays he is displeased';

and frequently in Shakespeare. Compare 'thy speech bewrayeth thee' in St. Matthew xxvi. 73. The dialect form 'wree' still recalls the A.-S. wrêgean, wrêgan, to accuse (German rügen).

71. *a proctor*, a person who speaks with irresistible authority as the executive officer of the University.

73. *veriment*, truly. Chaucer has the form 'verament' in the Rime of Sir Thopas, 2:

'Listeneth, lordings, in good entent,
And I wol tell you *verament*
Of mirth and of solas.'

74. *cease of*. 'Of' is here used in its original sense of 'from,' as the form 'off' is in 'to leave off.'

76. *talis*, tales, what I tell you.

77. *Walis*, Wales. So Skelton in Ware the Hauke, 315-318, rhymes:

'From Granado to Galis [Calais],
From Wynchelsee to Walys,
Non est braynsycke *talis*,' &c.

78. *gregis*, congregation. Miles compliments the doctors by using a quasi-academical term.

81. *Henry's white son*. Compare A Looking-Glass for London and England: 'Therefore that I may do my duty to you, good master, and to make a white son of you, I will so beswinge jealousy out of you as you shall love me the better while you live'; where Dyce has the following note: '"white" is an epithet of endearment, common in our old writers:

so Heywood and Broome in their Late Lancashire Witches, 1634' [act i], "A merry song now, mother, and thou shalt be my white girle"; and Whiting in his Albino and Bellama, 1638 (or 1637):

"A votary, Albino cal'd by name
Nor Fortune's white boy, yet of Abby-blond."'

In 1644 was printed a small 4to. tract entitled 'The Devill's *White* Boyes, a mixture of malicious malignants,' &c. See also Nares, *s. v.* 'White Boy,' where T. Warton's illustration is given, that Dr. Busby used to call his favourite scholars his 'white boys.'

82. *doting night-caps.* Ralph may specially refer to the caps of Doctors of Law and Physic, which are soft to the touch and comfortable of aspect.

Ib. capable of, equal to understanding, recognising.

83. *ingenious*, intellectual (from ingenium).

84. *a ship.* See below, line 101.

85. *niniversity.* A ninny (derived by Johnson from the Spanish nino, a child; the fuller form 'ninnyhammer' is apparently post-Elizabethan, as is 'nincompoop' from non compos) is a fool; compare 'a pied ninny' in The Tempest, iii. 2. 71; R. Armin's A Nest of Ninnies (1608) is a collection of anecdotes of more or less celebrated fools and jesters.

86. *the Bankside in Southwark*, a part of the borough of Southwark, near St. Saviour's Church, so called from its situation on the river-side, where several theatres were successively built, among them the Globe in 1599; and which from the reign of Henry II downwards had a bad reputation.

89. *pantofles*, slippers. The 'pantoffles' worn by ladies in the Elizabethan age and the early Stuart period were richly coloured and ornamented; see the passages quoted in Fairholt's Costume in England, p. 545. In Peele's Edward I, vi. 1, Queen Elinor calls for her 'pantables' or 'pantaphels.'

90. *with the cork.* Fairholt gives an account of a cork shoe of the age of Elizabeth found in the Thames, which proves that 'between the upper leather and the sole was placed a pad of cork rising considerably towards the heel'; and cites from Wily Beguiled the exclamation of one of the female characters: 'How finely could I foot it in a pair of new cork'd shoes I had bought.'

Ib. pinnace (French pinnasse, Italian pinnacia, Spanish pinaça), properly a small sloop or bark attending a larger vessel (Johnson); hence the word is here used perversely.

92. *pioners.* This is according to Dyce the usual, if not the invariable spelling in our old writers of this word, which should here be accentuated on the penultimate; compare Peele's The Old Wives' Tale:

'Well said; thou playest these pióners well.'

The word (for the use of which in our passage compare Hamlet, i. 5. 163) is from the French pionnier, Old French peonier, which properly signifies a foot-soldier like the French pion, Old French peon, from the Italian pedone (pes); hence the 'pawn' in chess.

99. *utrum horum mavis*, doubtless a common form of offering a dilemma in academical disputations.

101. *Like Barclay's ship.* The quartos, according to Dyce, have 'Bartlets ship.' Miles, says Dyce, alludes to 'The Shyp of Folys of the Worlde, translated out of Laten Frenche and Doche into Englysshe Tongue, by Alexander Barclay Preste. London by Richard Pynson. 1509, folio.' For a full account of Barclay and his famous translation see the Introduction to Jamieson's admirable edition, which preserves the indispensable woodcuts (Edinburgh, 1874). Concerning its original (of which a prose translation by Watson was printed by Wynkyn de Worde) —the Narrenschiff of Sebastian Brant, which appeared in 1494 and which Gervinus calls the centre of the whole didactive poetry of the age —the necessary information will be found in Goedeke's recent edition (Leipzig, 1872). Inasmuch as the very first section of Barclay's poem treats of 'inprofytable bokes' and addresses itself to 'worthy doctours and Clerkes curious,' Miles's allusion is specially apt.

106. *Domine Dawcock.* This expression is, as Dyce observes, borrowed from Skelton himself. See his Ware the Hauke (where the last two lines of the quotation serve as a refrain):

'*Construas hoc!*
Domine Dawcocke!
Ware the hawke!'

Compare also The Bowge of Courte, 303; and Howe the Douty Duke of Albany, &c., 380. Hence the term 'daw' was frequently employed as equivalent to 'simpleton'; so in Jonson's Epicoene Sir John Daw is a foolish knight.

107. *hare-brain'd.* Compare the popular expression 'as mad as a March hare.'

108. *taunt us up.* Compare note on iii. 22.

111. *beadles*, or bedels, the officers attached to the person of the Vice-Chancellor and the Proctors of the University. The office is said to be of great antiquity; at the present day there are at Oxford an Esquire Bedel and two Yeoman Bedels (distinguished according to the Faculties), with a Sub-Bedel.

112. *Bocardo*, 'i.e. the old north gate of Oxford, which was used as a prison; so called, we may certainly presume, from some allusion to the Aristotelian syllogism in *Bocardo*. It was taken down in 1771.' Dyce.—'*Bocardo*' is the technical name for one of the moods of the third syllogistic figure. From the extreme difficulty of reducing it to

the first figure, '*Bocardo*' was a bye-word among logic-students; and the gaol at Oxford was called by this name, as being hard to get out of.

Ib. roister, roisterer, rioter. 'Ralph Roister Doister' is the title of the earliest extant English comedy, and the name of its hero, a vain-glorious blockhead, copied from the Pyrgopolinices in the Miles Gloriosus of Plautus. The name recurs in other early English plays. The verb to 'roist' is also used in the sense of to 'riot.' Douce connects 'roister' (and perhaps 'row') with rouse and carouse. See note to ix. 267.

113. *bolts*, irons to fasten a prisoner's legs. Compare Measure for Measure, v. 350: 'Away with him to prison; lay bolts enough upon him.'

115. *What sayest*. See note on vi. 151.

119. *flurt*, explained in Nares as 'a satirical gesture,' with a reference to Quarles's Emblems:

> 'And must these smiling roses entertain
> The blows of scorn, and flurts of base disdain?'

120. *revel-dash*. Skelton, in The Bowge of Courte, 368, has the similar compound 'reuell route.'

131. *Sussex*. The quartos, 'Essex.' Dyce.

Ib. Ermsby, 'a trisyllable here, I believe.' Dyce. There can be no doubt that this is correct. As to the influence of the letter *r* in introducing an extra syllable see the examples discussed in Abbott, § 478, of which the following from Richard II, ii. 3. 21, may be cited as specially in point:

> 'It ís | my són | , young Hár | ry Pé | rcý.'

Such passages as this and that in the text show the addition of a syllable between the *r* and the following consonant; and this further explains the spelling of the O. E. 'thurh' by early writers as 'thorugh' (compare note to Doctor Faustus, iii. 106). A different effect of the burr following the *r* was the form 'sirrah' for 'sir' (compare note to Doctor Faustus, ii. 5). Again a different, but a cognate, practice is the sounding of an additional syllable in such words as 'fire' (compare note to Doctor Faustus, v. 63); and yet a different usage, frequently adopted by Marlowe, is that of sounding a syllable between the *r* and the consonant preceding it, as in 2 Tamburlaine, iv. 4:

> 'And blow the morning from his nost-e-rils.'

The burr upon the *r* is the cause of all these peculiarities of pronunciation.

130. *only*, singularly, specially. See Abbott, § 258, and compare The Faerie Queene, ii. 1. 2. 4:

> 'His onely hart-sore, and his onely foe.'

The A.-S. 'ænlic' signifies singular, excellent.

132. *One of the privy-chamber*, a chamberlain. Compare the phrase 'of the King's chamber'; as in Macbeth, i. 7. 76:

'those sleepy two
Of his own chamber';

and Pericles, i. 1. 152:

'You are of our chamber, and our mind partakes
Her private actions to your secrecy.'

136. *make greater scapes*, commit greater extravagances, improprieties of conduct. A 'scape' is an 'escape' or deviation from rule.

142. *upon that*, on that condition.

Scene VIII.

2. *as did Cassius*. The reference is to the artfulness with which Cassius conducted the conspiracy against Cæsar, as is related in Plutarch's Life of Brutus.

Ib. thy. The quartos, 'his.' Dyce.

4. *Lynceus*. The name of Lynceus (doubtless originally given in allusion to the eyes of the lynx), the steersman of the Argo, became proverbial for one who keeps a keen look-out. Accordingly, in Goethe's Faust, Part ii. Act iii, Lynceus appears as the keeper of the watch-tower.

Ib. from the shores of Graecia. A watch-tower was built in Peloponnesus already in the eighth century by Leo III. Loeper, in a note on the above passage in Goethe's Faust.

7. *fancies*, loves. Compare note on l. 39 below; and v. 79.

8. *portace*. See note on vi. 137.

13. *what answer'st*. See note on vi. 151.

16. *Whenas*. See note on i. 75.

Ib. curious, exquisite. Compare note on i. 64.

19. *your honour*. Compare i. 170; and see note on Doctor Faustus, x. 45.

21. *How that*. See note on Doctor Faustus, x. 15.

24. *Injurious*. Compare note on Doctor Faustus, x. 88.

25. *Hephaestion*, the favourite on the occasion of whose death Alexander the Great displayed so extravagant a grief, as is narrated in Plutarch's Life of Alexander.

26. *passions*. The quarto of 1594, 'passion.' Dyce.

33. *corrival*, rival. Both words are used in the sense of 'companion'; compare 1 Henry IV, i. 3. 207:

'So he that doth redeem her thence might wear
Without corrival all her dignities:
But out upon this half-faced fellowship';

and Jonson's Sejanus, iii. 1:

'And may they know no rivals but themselves.'

Shakespeare uses 'competitor' in the same way, Antony and Cleopatra, v. 1. 42. So Greene uses 'coequal' for 'equal' in Orlando Furioso:

'With a sweet applause
Make me in terms coequal with the gods.'

Compare also 'copartner' for 'partner.'

35. *quite*, requite. See note on v. 112.

Ib. *'fore that*, afore or before that. See note on Doctor Faustus, x. 15.

36. *awry*. The prefix *a* in this word is the O. E. 'an,' modern 'on,' as in 'amid,' 'anew.'

38. *still*, ever. Compare Doctor Faustus, xiv. 110.

39. *fancy*, love, as again 109 and 120, and x. 76; and compare above 7, and v. 79. So in Orlando Furioso:

'Damsel be gone; fancy' [i. e. love] 'hath taken leave.'

Ib. *but over-fond*, only too foolish.

45. *cipher out*, express clearly. For a similar use of the word 'to cipher' see the passage from Gough's Strange Discovery cited in Nares.

48. *force men fall*. See note on Doctor Faustus, iii. 36.

53. *Sethin planks*. I cannot explain 'Sethin,' unless it be a mis-spelling for 'Scythian,' though one would rather have expected 'Syrian.' 'Setine' from Setia would be pointless. Query 'satin,' i.e. of satin-wood, or 'shittim' (the Ark of the Covenant was made of 'shittim-wood,' Exodus xxv. 10).

57. *Like Thetis shalt thou wanton*, i. e. sport. Thetis, the consort of Peleus and mother of Achilles, was a Nereid.

59. *lavoltas*. The 'lavolta' or 'lavolt' is described in Nares as 'a kind of dance for two persons, consisting a good deal in high and active bounds. By its own name it should be of Italian origin; but Florio, in "Volta," calls it a French dance, and so Shakespeare seems to make it, Henry V, iii. 5. 33 [Bourbon *loquitur*]:

"They bid us to the English dancing schools,
And teach lavoltas high, and swift corantos."

See however Dekker and Ford's The Sun's Darling, ii. 1:

"*Folly*. . . . He's an Italian dancer, his name—
Dancer. Signor Lavolta, messer mio."

Compare also Troilus and Cressida, iv. 4. 88, and the description of this dance by Sir John Davies in Orchestra, or A Poem on Dancing, stanza 70:

"Yet is there one the most delightful kind,
A lofty jumping, or a leaping round," &c.'

62. *their.* The quartos, 'her.' Dyce.

68. *Danaë*, whom Jove visited as a shower of gold.

69. *tir'd*, attired. Dyce's conjecture for the readings 'tied' and 'try' of the quartos.

Ib. in Latona's webs, as if the rays of the sun were a garment fashioned for the sun-god by his mother Latona.

70. *lodge*, for 'lodging' or 'dwelling,' as xi. 12. Dyce compares Romeo and Juliet, iii. 2. 2 (according to the First Folio):

'Gallop apace, you fiery-footed steeds,
Towards Phoebus' lodging.'

71. *the dulcet tones of frolic Mercury.* According to the Homeric Hymn to Hermes, the god on the day of his birth saw a tortoise in the path, and after killing the animal and clearing out the shell, converted it into a stringed instrument to which he sang joyous songs. Hence he is often depicted with the attribute of the tortoise, or as the inventor of the lyre.

74. *this point of schools*, this important argument in the disputations of the schools. Compare 'a point of cunning skill' for 'a test-experiment of learned skill,' ix. 86. A 'point of war' is used differently, in the sense of a signal of war on the trumpet.

75. *Ablata . . effectus.* 'If the cause is removed, the result disappears.' A logical formula.

78. *him.* For this insertion of a redundant pronoun when a proper name is separated by an intervening clause from its verb, see Abbott, § 242.

81. *miss*, lose. Compare in 1 Henry IV, v. 4. 105, 'a heavy miss' for 'a heavy loss.'

83. *stab it.* Compare note on i. 103.

85. *Venus' courts.* See note to i. 70.

86. *conquest.* The quarto of 1594, 'conquests.' Dyce.

88. *cease*, cause to cease. Compare l. 133 below, and see Abbott, § 291.

90. *act it well*, execute the sentence thoroughly, carry it out to the end. To 'act' is used transitively in the sense of to 'perform' or 'accomplish,' ix. 50, 120, 139.

97. *vaunt him*, proudly display himself. Compare note on i. 127.

102. *over-live*, survive. Compare German 'überleben.'

103. *short*, shorten. Compare note on vi. 8.

Ib. her. Query 'our'? Dyce.

104. *Rid me*, get rid of me. For this transitive use of 'to rid' compare Peele's Arraignment of Paris, iii. 4:

'I thank you, Sir, my game is quick, and rids' [i.e. clears] 'a length of ground';

ib. iv. 4:

'And rid the man that he may know his pain';

and *ib.*:

'Apollo hath found out the only mean
'To rid the blame from us and trouble clean';

and Sir Clyomon and Sir Clamydes:

'Ah death, no longer do delay, but rid the lives of twain.'

107. *abide*, undergo, suffer. Compare the A.-S. abidan, to suffer, and the phrase 'to bide the brunt.'

113. *Damasco*. See note to iv. 27.

117. *To part . . loves.* This line is not in the later quartos. Dyce.

120, 121. *So in subduing . . . the richest spoil.* Compare the magnificent passage in Edward III, ii. 2:

'Shall the large limit of fair Britany
By me be overthrown, and shall I not
Master this little mansion of myself?
Give me an armour of eternal steel;
I go to conquer kings; and shall I then
Subdue myself, and be my enemy's friend?
It must not be';

and see also the dialogue between Alexander and Hephaestion in Lilly's Campaspe, v. 4:

'*Alex.* How now, Hephestion, is Alexander able to resist love as he list?

Heph. The conquering of Thebes was not so honourable as the subduing of these thoughts.

Alex. It were a shame Alexander should desire to command the world, if he could not command himselfe.'

130. *As if that.* See note on Doctor Faustus, x. 15.

131. *rich'd*, enriched. Compare note on vi. 8.

132. *And doth . . . true?* Query, 'And doth the English prince indeed mean true?' Dyce.

134. *the title of*, his title or claim to.

140. *Aspasia.* The real name of Aspasia of Phocæa, the favourite of Cyrus the younger, was Milto, but it was changed by her lover in memory of the famous Aspasia beloved by Pericles. After the death of Cyrus his favourite passed into the power of his brother King Artaxerxes, who gave her up to his son and heir Darius, but shortly afterwards made her a priestess at Ecbatana. See Plutarch's Lives of Pericles and of Artaxerxes.

144. *revolt*, overthrown. As to this literal use of words now used metaphorically, see Abbott, p. 12. As to the omission of the *èd* after verbs ending in *t*, see note on ii. 13.

149. *I pray God I like her as I lov'd thee.* Dyce adopts Walker's counsel to 'read for harmony's sake, "'Pray God," and pronounce "lovèd."' But the emphasis seems better, because placing the antithesis where the sense demands it, if we accentuate:

'I pray God I like *her* as I loved *thee*';

moreover, the other way of reading the line creates an antithesis between 'like' and 'lovèd' hardly intended by Greene.

153. *looks.* Dyce doubts whether this can be the right word. Perhaps the word 'looks' may here be used in the sense of rapid, i.e. eager or hasty, glances. Below, xi. 14, the word is used of the glancing rays of the moon.

159. *neat,* pure. Compare Peele's The Old Wives' Tale:

'*Del.* Is this the best wine in France?

Sac. Yes.

Del. What wine is it?

Sac. A cup of neat wine of Orleans, that never came near the brewers in England.'—Hence 'neat' is also used of wine not mixed with water.

160. *your grace.* See note on Doctor Faustus, x. 45.

162. *respect,* consider, take into account. Compare 2 Henry VI, iii. 1. 24:

'Me seemeth then it is no policy,
Respecting' [i. e. considering] 'what a rancorous mind he bears
And his advantage following your decease,
That he should come about your royal person.'

Compare the phrase 'with respect to.'

Scene IX.

This scene may, as Wright remarks in his Sorcery and Magic, i. 128, though referring to an earlier episode in the story-book of Friar Bacon, 'be taken as a sort of exemplification of the class of exhibitions which were probably the result of a superior knowledge of natural science, and which were exaggerated by popular imagination. They had been made, to a certain degree, familiar by the performances of the skilful jugglers who came from the East, and who were scattered throughout Europe; and we read not unfrequently of such magical feats in old writers. When the Emperor Charles IV was married in the middle of the fourteenth century to the Bavarian princess Sophia in the city of Prague, the father of the princess brought a waggonload of magicians to assist in the festivities. Two of the chief proficients in the art, Zytho the great Bohemian sorcerer and Gouin the Bavarian, were pitted against each other, and we are told that after a desperate trial of skill, Zytho, opening his jaws from ear to ear, ate up his rival without stopping till he came to his shoes, which he spit out, because, as he said, they had not been cleaned. After having performed this strange feat, he restored the unhappy sorcerer to life again. The idea of contests like this seems to have been taken from the scriptural narrative of the Egyptian magicians against Moses.'

3. *mountains.* This is a poetical licence in topography. The German traveller Hentzner, writing in 1598, mentions 'the hills shaded with wood' encompassing the plain in which Oxford lies. See the Introduction to Harrison's Description of England (in the New Shakspere Society's Publications), p. lxxxvii, and compare Harrison's own account, p. 71.

4. *battling.* The word to 'battle' is another form of 'batten,' and signifies to feed, both transitive and intransitive, to make or grow fat. Compare x. 59; and the passage cited in Nares from the Faerie Queene, vi. 8. 38:

> 'The best advizement was, if bad, to let her
> Sleepe out her fill without encomberment;
> For sleepe, they sayd, would make her battill better.'

At Oxford the terms 'battels' (College provisions) and 'to battel' (to take out provisions from College) are still in use. Diez gives the cognate English words 'batful,' very fertile, 'battable,' capable of tillage, and 'batner,' a fatted ox. The derivation seems to be from the Teutonic root 'bat,' which appears in the forms 'better' and 'best.'

Ib. lade, laden. For other examples of curtailed forms of past participles common in Early English, and used by Elizabethan authors, owing to the tendency to drop the participial inflexion *en*, see Abbott, § 343. So Chaucer uses 'take' for 'taken,' &c.

5. *The town . . . colleges.* It is needless to observe that this spirited description of Oxford applies rather to the age of Greene than to that of Friar Bacon. Speaking of the fifteenth century, Anstey remarks (Introduction to Munimenta Academica, p. lx), that 'of the buildings now at Oxford and which would strike the eye of the stranger, there were few. He would not see at his entrance the tower of Magdalen College (built about 1473); the old Hospital of S. John's was then standing, and used for some years by the new College which displaced its tenants. He would, however, see the spires of S. Mary's and of old All Saints', and the tower of S. John's (Merton) churches. These, with the tower of New College, and the spire of S. Frideswide, alone remain.'

7. *principles of art,* that which lies at the root of the liberal arts. Compare Doctor Faustus, i. 138.

10. *full of pleasant walks.* The College gardens have always been one of the chief charms of the Universities, with their lordly trees and

'level lawns' (Gray). Hentzner notes of the Oxford of 1598 that after meals every student is at liberty 'either to retire to his own chambers, or to walk in the College garden, there being none that hath not a delightful one.'

11. *But for the doctors . . . learnèd.* It is hardly to be supposed that Greene here intended to insinuate as his own the sneer which he puts into the mouth of the 'Hapsburg' doctor. A famous foreign scholar, however, who visited Oxford about the time when this play was written, takes very much the same view of the Oxford doctors as that suggested by Vandermast. Giordano Bruno (who was in England from near the end of 1583 to about the end of 1585), gives the following account of the Oxford professors in a passage referred to by W. König (Shakespeare und Giordano Bruno, in Jahrbuch der deutschen Shakespeare-Gesellschaft, xi. 104), which seems worth extracting from his dialogue 'La Cena de le Ceneri,' no. iv (Opere, Wagner's edition, 1830, i. 179):

'*Frulla.* Questi son i frutti d' Inghilterra; e cercatene pur quanti volete, che li trovarete tutti dottori in grammatica, in queste nostri giorni, ne' quali in la felice patria regna una costellazione di pedantesca ostinatissima, ignoranza e presunzione mista con una rustica inciviltà, che farebbe prevaricar la pazienza di Giobbe. E se non il credete, andate in Oxonia e fatevi raccontar le cose intravenute al Nolano' [Bruno himself], 'quando pubblicamente disputò con que' dottori in teologia in presenza del principe Alasco Polacco, et altri de la nobilità inglese. Fatevi dire, come si sapea rispondere a gli argomenti, come restò per quindici sillogismi quindici volti, qual pulcino entro la stoppa, quel povero dottor, che come il corifeo de l'academia ne puosero avanti in questa grave occasione! Fatevi dire, con quanta inciviltà e discortesia procedea quel porco, e con quanta pazienza e umanità quell'altro, che in fatto mostrava esser Napoletano nato, et allevato sotto più benigno cielo! Informatevi, come gli han fatte finire le sue pubbliche letture, e quelle de immortalitate animae, e quelle de quintuplice sphaera.

Smitho. Chi dona perle a' porci, non si de' lamentar, se gli son calpestate.'

'There is indeed,' writes Milton of Oxford in 1656, 'as you write, plenty of amenity and salubrity in the place where you are; there are books enough for the needs of a University: if only the amenity of the spot contributed so much to the genius of the inhabitants as it does to pleasant living, nothing would seem wanting to the happiness of the place.' See Milton's letter to Richard Jones, translated in Masson's Life of Milton, v. 267.

13. *I tell thee, German,* &c. This assertion resembles that of Harrison,

who observes (*u. s.*, p. 81): 'Finallie, this will I saie that the professors of either of those faculties' [Law and Medicine] 'come to such perfection in both' [the English] 'vniversities, as the best students beyond the sea doo in their owne or else where.'

Ib. Hapsburg (quarto of 1599, 'Haspurge'). Compare iv. 45.

14. *Oxenford.* The old spelling of 'Oxford'; compare the first line of The Millere's Tale:

'Whilom ther was dwelling in Oxenforde,' &c.

17. *Belgic*, as Vandermast is a Netherlander.

18. *charm*, overcome by thy magic.

22. *worthies.* 'Worthies' are representative personages of note; so the Nine Worthies of the world were the chief heroes of history, and London had nine municipal Worthies of her own. Compare Fuller's 'History of the Worthies of England.'

23. *The doubtful question*, the puzzling question, that which he will prove unable to answer satisfactorily. Compare note on Doctor Faustus, v. 113.

24. *pyromancy*. See note on ii. 15.

25. *geomancy.* According to the spirit Auerhan, geomancy is 'especially performed with a die of sixteen angles; this the artists cast on the ground, utter certain conjurationes, psalms and other fictitious words taught by them or us' [the spirits], 'or they use a tetragonal die, in which case they must cast sixteen times. And after this has been done, figures are formed which they call "mother," of these others are formed which they call "*filias*," and then out of these eight they form four figures more; thus there are twelve altogether, like unto the twelve signs of heaven; so afterwards they construct a "thema geomanticum," and therefrom prognosticate all that they desire to know. They ask questions concerning all manner of things: as to how long a man shall live; whether he shall grow rich or not; and whether one who has journeyed away shall return,' &c. See Scheible's Kloster, iii. 120-122, where there is more of this.

29. *cabalists*, writers on magic. See note on ii. 106.

30. *Hermes.* 'The numerous writings (said by Clemens Alexandrinus to fill forty-two books) which bear the mythological name of Hermes Trismegistus, are productions of Egyptian Platonists. Some belonged to the school of Philo, and were known to Plutarch; others were of a much later date and not unaffected by Christianity. . . . These writings, which have borrowed their name from the god *Thoth*, . . . are only so far interesting as showing the extent to which the adoption and incorporation of existing beliefs and traditions were carried in the age of Ammonins (170 to after 243 A.D.) as the founder of the eclectic school of comprehension.' Donaldson, History of the Litera-

ture of Ancient Greece, iii. 186. Compare Gower's Confessio Amantis, bk. iv:

> 'Of whom if I the names calle,
> Hermes was one the first of alle,
> To whom this art is most applied'—

viz. 'alconomie' (alchemy); and 'thrice-great Hermes' in Milton's Il Penseroso, 88. As to the lectures of Cornelius Agrippa on 'Hermes Trismegistus,' see Morley's Life of Agrippa, i. 284 seqq. There is a Dutch translation of Hermes Trismegistus, with 'ene schoone Voorrede' proving that the 'grote Philosooph heeft gebloeyt voor Moyses'; its date is 1652, but it indicates that the fame of Hermes was spread in Vandermast's country.—The choice of the name 'Hermes' was due to the magical (magnetic) powers ascribed to that god; already an old gloss translated 'caduceus' by 'Wunsciligerta' (wishing-rod). See on this subject Ennemoser's History of Magic, ii. 43 seqq. (Howitt's Translation).

30. *Melchie.* 'Meant, I suppose, for Malchus (Melech), i.e. Porphyrius.' Dyce. 'Porphyry owes the name by which he is so well known to the fashion of translating foreign designations which was common in that age. He was born A.D. 233 at Batanea (Bashan), and his native name was Malchus (i.e. Melek, "a king"). His friend Amelius converted the Semitic name into "Basileus," and Longinus, it seems, subsequently changed this substantive into the adjective Porphyrius (*πορφύριος*, "clad in purple or royal robes"), which was intended as a synonym. He was a pupil of Origen at Caesarea, and afterwards at Athens was instructed by Longinus in that form of Neo-Platonism which the great critic still maintained. He ultimately at Rome became one of the most zealous adherents of Plotinus, whose works he published and whose biography he wrote. He died some time after 302 A.D. Among his works are a Life of Pythagoras, a fragment probably belonging to his general history of the philosophers, and "The Epistle to Anebo," an effort of scepticism directed against opinions which Porphyrius himself entertained at one period of his life. He raises doubts as to the truth of dualism and daemonology, and as to the efficacy of theurgic arts, incantations and animal sacrifice. The work provoked a reply generally attributed to his scholar Iamblichus.' Donaldson, *u. s.*, iii. 198 seqq.—As to the significance of Porphyry for the history of magic, see Ennemoser, *u. s.*, i. 443 seqq.

Ib. Pythagoras. Compare notes on ii. 73 and on Doctor Faustus, xiv. 105. As to Pythagoras's 'theory of magic,' see Ennemoser, *u. s.*, i. 126; and compare ib. 393.

33. *a punctum squarèd to the rest,* I suppose equivalent to 'a mere point, when measured by or compared with the rest.'

34. *compass*, for the plural 'compasses,' i.e. sizes. Compare 'post-horse' for 'post-horses,' v. 5, and 'mightiness' for 'mightinesses,' xvi. 69; and see as to the omission of the plural or possessive syllable in writing, and still more frequently in pronunciation, with nouns in which the singular ends in s, se, ss, ce and ge, Abbott, § 471. Compare also note on Doctor Faustus, opening Chorus, l. 28.

39. *only*, i. e. it alone.

40. *that place*, i. e. the fire of the sun.

43. *concave latitudes.* See ll. 34–37 above,

45, 46. *the spirits . . . geomantic fiends.* These are the 'subjects of the elements' referred to in Doctor Faustus, i. 120. 'Spirits' is here a monosyllable.

47. *ground.* The quartos, 'grounds.' Dyce.

48. *strange necromantic.* As Dyce observes, something has dropt out between these two words.

50. *acted*, performed. Compare note on viii. 90.

51. *terrae filii.* See note to l. 25 above.

55. *if they be but charg'd* (quarto of 1599, 'char'd'), i. e. commissioned to do so. Compare below, 104 and 136.

56. *massy.* See note on Doctor Faustus, i. 145.

59. *when proud Lucifer fell.* Compare Doctor Faustus, iii. 70 seqq.

61. *as*, i. e. as they retained.

62. *All subject under Luna's continent.* This I suppose merely means, 'all being in a subject condition under the sky.' The 'continent' is that which covers; compare King Lear, iii. 2. 58:

'Close pent-up guilts,
Rive your concealing continents';

so that which covers the moon is the vault or 'concave continent' of the heavens. Compare xi. 15.—As to this notion of 'sublunary devils,' and in general illustration of this part of the disputation, see Burton's Anatomy of Melancholy, i. 2. 1. 2. The locality of the fallen angels is described as in ll. 63 seqq. in the Dialogue of Salomon and Saturn, *u. s.*, ii. 173, and in the Cursor Mundi, *u. s.*, i. 36.

63. *hung.* The quartos, 'hang.' Dyce.

64. *second faults*, i. e. less faults.

67. *understanding*, intelligence or capacity (for performing works of higher magic).

69, 70. *serve for*, equivalent to 'serve.'

70. *vile.* The quartos, 'vild.' Dyce. Compare note to Doctor Faustus, i. 107.

75. *instance*, experiment. Royal, as well as popular, audiences often prefer the experimental to the expository part of a scientific lecture.

77. *English Harry.* See note to line 178 below.

82. *the garden call'd Hesperides:* Compare Dekker and Ford's The Sun's Darling, iii. 3:

'My garden of th' Hesperides';

Edward III, iv. 4:

'The orchard of the Hesperides';

and Orlando Furioso, sc. 1:

'And richer than the plot Hesperides';

on which latter passage Dyce has the following note: 'Most of our writers, strangely enough, use "Hesperides" as the name of a place. So Shakespeare in Love's Labour 's Lost, iv. 3. 341:

"Still climbing trees in the Hesperides."

And Greene again' [in the passage in the text]: 'Nay, even the very learned and very pedantic Gabriel Harvey has: "the watchfull and dreadfull dragon, which kept the goodly golden apples, in the Occidentall Islands of the Ocean, called Hesperides, one of the renowned prizes of douty Hercules, was a West Indian asse," &c. Pierce's Supererogation, &c., 1593, p. 167.'—The 'Hesperides' were no doubt originally conceived of as nymphs (the daughters of Night), to whom, together with the dragon Ladon, Hera had committed the custody of the golden apples on the Oceanic Isle. But the locality of Atlas and the Hesperides was shifted by later writers, as well as the route taken by Heracles to them. Strabo uses Ἑσπερίδες repeatedly as a geographical expression; and Dionysius (ὁ περιηγητής) in his poetical geography identified these islands with the Cassiterides.

The tree appears. Such magical creations were frequently attributed to conjurors; already in Indian legend Divine power through the hand of a Brahman creates a garden, and Indian conjurors are to this day celebrated for producing flowering trees by their art. 'Virgil' conjured up a garden for the use of Pope Benedict; a similar performance was attributed to Albertus Magnus, and from him transferred to Faustus in the Faustbuch (ch. lvi). See Kühne's note on this passage of the Faustbuch, and his reference to the description of 'tregetoures' performances in Chaucer's The Frankeleine's Tale, vv. 11454 seqq.

85. *lordings* (quarto of 1599, 'lordlings'); as again xvi. 6. Compare for this word (used already by Robert of Brunne) 2 Henry VI, i. 1. 145, and The Passionate Pilgrim, xvi. 1. In The Winter's Tale, i. 2. 63,

'Come, I'll question you
Of my lord's tricks and yours when you were boys:
You were pretty lordings then?'

the word appears to be used in a diminutive sense, such as the termination *ing* occasionally possesses. See Morris, English Accidence, p. 214.

Morris distinguishes between (1) the patronymic termination *ing*, (2) the *ing* which is an ending of substantives originally adjectival in their meaning (such as 'atheling,' 'lording'), and the diminutive *ing*.

86. *a point*. Compare note on viii. 74.

87. *Each*, equivalent to 'every' or 'any.' The A.-S. ælc was thus used.

Ib. scholar, mere student or beginner.

89. *Alcmena's bastard*, Hercules.

Ib. raz'd, i.e. tore from the ground. The word is employed for the sake of the pun which follows.

106. *come*, descended. Compare Orlando Furioso:

'If thou be'st come of Lancelot's worthy line.'

111. *I have given non-plus*. Compare iv. 61.

112. *Sien*, Siena, the foundation of whose university is dated 1380.

114. *Frankfort, Utrecht, and Orleans*. 'The quartos, "Lutrech." This line is certainly mutilated; and so perhaps is the preceding line: from the Emperor's speech, iv. 41 seqq., it would seem that "Paris" ought to be one of the places mentioned here.' Dyce.—'Frankfort' is the Silesian Frankfort-on-the-Oder, where a university was founded in 1560; for all the towns mentioned are university towns.

116. *Crown me with laurel, as they all have done*. Vandermast asks that the King may bestow on him a wreath of laurel as a special compliment (compare note on iv. 64), as the universities mentioned by him have bestowed upon him the laurel wreath which accompanied the university degree of laureate (compare note on Doctor Faustus, iii. 32). This degree might be taken by the same person at several universities. See the entry in the Cambridge University Register on Skelton's admission *ad eundem* in 1493 (cited by Dyce in his Introduction to Skelton's Poetical Works, p. xiii): 'Conceditur Johī Skelton Poete in partibus transmarinis atque Oxon. Laurea ornato, ut apud nos eadem decoraretur.'

117. *to*. Query 'unto'?

120. *acted*. Compare note on viii. 90.

127. *take not now the foil*, do not suffer thyself to be foiled now. Compare the converse phrase to 'give the foil' in 1 Henry VI, v. 3. 23:

'Then take my soul, my body, soul and all,
Before that England give the French the foil.'

To 'foil' is from the Old French 'affoler,' Italian 'affollare,' to press hard; the French 'feuler' and Italian 'follare' are said to be derived from the Latin 'fullo,' a fuller. There is another French 'affoler,' to make a fool of, derived from the M. Latin 'follus,' said to come from 'follĕre,' to move hither and thither, from 'follis,' bellows.

128. *foretime*, for 'aforetime' or 'beforetime.' Compare note on ii. 156.

131. *he*, i.e. he with whom I disputed.

133. *ruinate*, ruin. Compare 3 Henry VI, v. 1. 83:

'I will not ruinate my father's house.'

This is an example of one of the least pleasing kinds of new formations in Elizabethan English. Compare to 'affectionate' for to 'love,' x. 78.

140, 141. *By all the thrones . . . hierarchies.* Compare 1 Epistle to the Colossians, i. 16, 'thrones, or dominions, or principalities, or powers,' and Paradise Lost, ii. 310-313:

'Thrones and Imperial Powers, Offspring of Heaven,
Ethereal Virtues; or these titles now
Must we renounce, and, changing style, be called
Princes of hell?'

See Faustbuch, ch. xiii, in which the system of government (*Regiment und Principat*) of the devils is briefly expounded by Mephistophilis. The later treatises on magic variously developed the system of infernal government, which was regarded as forming part of that of the celestial government. Thus we read in the Semiphoras Salomonis Regis (Scheible's Kloster, iii. 293) that 'there be four parts of the world; the most subtle light of the spiritual world contains 4 *Hierarchias, Cherubin et Seraphin, Potestates et Virtutes, Archangelos et Angelos, Spiritus et Animas Hominum.*' And again (*ib.* p. 311): 'In the middle Hierarchia be Dominationes, Potestates, Virtutes, as spirits of intelligence, for governing the Universe: the first of these order what the others execute. The second oppose that which God's law can prevent. The third administer the Heavens, at times they procure the doing of miracles.' Agrippa's doctrine of Virtues, as sequels of the species and forms of the elements, may be gathered from the statement of it in Morley's Life of Agrippa, i. 121 seqq.; the use of the term in the technical books is, I suppose, more or less indefinite.

142. *obey to Vandermast.* For the construction compare Troilus and Cressida, iii. 1. 165:

'His stubborn buckles,
With these your white enchanting fingers touch'd,
Shall more obey than to the force of steel
Or force of Greekish sinews.'

Compare French 'obéir à.'

143. *Belcephon.* Compare ii. 56.

144. *Asmenoth guider of the north.* So again, xi. 109: 'proud Asmenoth, ruler of the north.' See as to the phrase 'Prince of the East' LUCIFER in Dramatis Personae of Doctor Faustus.

150. *doth more than art*, practises something beyond ordinary magic.

Ib. or else I fail, or I mistake.

153. *came*. 'The quartos, "come;" (but see what follows).' Dyce.

157. *for*, since, because. Compare vii. 63.

162. *'gainst the spring*. 'The quartos, "springs."' Dyce. As to this use of 'against' compare note on ii. 130.

163. *dooms*, sentences, decrees. Compare 'doomer,' x. 139.

Ib. aphorisms. See note on Doctor Faustus, i. 19.

170. *I will be . . . thyself*. Dyce thinks 'something wanting here'; but the line gives very good sense: 'I will reward thee as an English King should reward one who has done credit to England.'

172. *fit my cheer*, prepare my entertainment.

174. *as*. Query, 'as is'?

177. *amorets*. Compare the use of the word xii. 8, 'whence,' as Dyce observes, 'it is plain that Greene uses the word as equivalent to love-kindling looks. (Cotgrave has "*Amourettes*, Loue-tricks," etc.).' Thomas Heywood uses the word to signify a love-sonnet; Chaucer, in the Romaunt of the Rose, 4758, for a loving woman.

178. *Ned*. This familiar style of address is common with our old dramatists, even towards royal personages. Queen Eleanor is 'Nell' to King Edward (as in our play), and he is 'Ned' to her in Peele's Edward I, and in Greene's James IV the King of England calls his daughter, the King of Scotland's bride, 'my Doll,' 'lovely Doll,' 'fair Doll,' etc. Of course Ralph the fool takes the same liberty, and calls his prince 'Ned,' as Falstaff calls his 'Hal.' Even the German Emperor, above l. 77, addresses the King as 'English Harry.'

180. *teasers*. Compare note on i. 5.

Ib. the toil, the net.

182. *progress'd*. 'Progress' was the term usually applied to a royal journey. Compare e. g. Nichols' Progresses and Public Processions of Queen Elizabeth and King James I.

183. *entertain*, entertainment. See note on Doctor Faustus, xiii. 30.

185. *joint*, conjointly.

186. *welcome as*, as welcome as.

192. *Fair of all fairs*, fairest of all fair women. For the use of adjectives as substantives see Abbott, § 5; compare 'gentles,' x. 51; 'lovely,' *ib.* 111; and see note on Doctor Faustus, x. 81.

199. *so as*, in such a way that. See Abbott, § 109. Compare note on Doctor Faustus, Chorus before viii, line 11.

200. *accept of*. Compare iv. 29.

205. *consorting greets*, harmonious greetings. 'Consórt' is company, as xvi. 62, and 'to consórt' to associate with. As to 'greets' for 'greetings' compare note on Doctor Faustus, xiii. 30.

209. *Salvete*, etc. The quarto of 1599 prints this Skeltonical verse as prose.

219. *sewer*. The 'sewer' was the officer who set on the dishes at a feast; the derivation of the word is not (as suggested in Nares) from O. F. 'escuyer' (esquire); see Tyrwhitt's note to The Squiere's Tale, 59:

'And eke it nedeth not for to devise
At every cours the order of hir service.
I wol not tellen of hir strange sewes,
Ne of hir swannes, ne hir heronsewes;'—

where he mentions the word 'sawer' and the Old French 'asseour' from 'asseoir' to place; adding: 'the word "sewes" here signifies dishes, from the same original, as "assiette" in French still signifies "a little dish," or "plate."' The nature of the 'sewer's' office is illustrated by a stage-direction in Macbeth, i. 7, and by the following in Histrio-Mastix, or The Player Whipt, ii. 186-192:

'Bid them come in and sing. The meat 's going up.
Usher. Gentlemen and yeomen, attend upon the Sewer.
. . . .
Enter Sewer *with service, in side livery coates*.'

222. *what skills*, what difference does it make (from O. N. skilja, to separate, divide, to make a difference). Compare Sir Clyomon and Sir Clamydes:

'Whither I go it skills not, for Knowledge is my name;'

and 2 Henry VI, iii. 1. 281:

'It skills not greatly who impugns our doom.'

Ib. where the salt . . . behind. For the well-known custom, according to which, as Dyce says, 'the seats at table above the salt-cellar (which used to be placed about the middle) were assigned to the more distinguished guests; the seats below it, to those of inferior rank,' compare the passage cited in Nares from Jonson's Cynthia's Revels, ii. 2: 'His fashion is not to take knowledge of him that is beneath him in clothes. He never drinks below the salt.'

226. *cover*, viz. the table (see l. 214 above). So in The Merchant of Venice, iii. 5. 62-66, Lorenzo says: 'Bid them cover the table, serve in the meat.' 'For the table, sir,' says Lancelot, 'it shall be served in; for the meat, sir, it shall be covered.' We still speak of 'covers' (Fr. couverts) being laid for dinner.

228. *chop*, where we should say 'hash.'

233. *Lordings* (quarto of 1599, 'Lordlings'). See note on 85 above.

Ib. admire, wonder (as in 'Nil admirari'). Compare Orlando Furioso:

'Heaven admires to see my slumbering dreams';

'wonder not, nor admire not in thy mind,' in Sir Andrew Aguecheek's letter, Twelfth Night, iii. 4. 165; and 'most admired disorder' in Macbeth, iii. 4. 110.

236. *place these potentates.* The Friar leaves it to the King to settle the places according to order of precedence among the imperial, royal and princely guests.

237. *cates.* See note on Doctor Faustus, i. 83.

241. *of thy consent*, from thy consent. Compare xi. 60. 'To proceed of' is a construction used in our Liturgy.

242. *with a.* 'The quarto of 1594, "with such a."' Dyce.

Ib. pittance. This word (French 'pitance,' M. Latin 'pitantia,' most probably derived from the old Romance 'pite,' a trifle, M. Latin 'picta,' small coin, with a reminiscence of 'pietas,' pity or charity) is used of a portion of food in The Taming of a Shrew, iv. 4. 61:

> 'You are like to have a thin and slender pittance';

which is explained, as Schmidt points out, by v. 70:

> 'One mess is like to be your cheer.'

248. *Content thee.* Compare note to i. 127.

Ib. these. 'The quartos, "thee."' Dyce.

250. *How little . . . wits*, how plain a living goes to our high thinking at the English Universities.

260. *in honours*, i. e. in outward show.

261. *drugs*, spices.

262. *carvels.* A carvel, caravel, or carveil (French caravelle) is a kind of ship, thus defined by Kersey in Nares: 'A kind of light round ship, with a square poop, rigg'd and fitted out like a galley, holding about six score or seven score tun.' According to Littré, the term would seem to be Portuguese.

Ib. richest. 'An error. (In the preceding line we have had "rich," and just after this we have "richer" and "richest").' Dyce.

Ib. streights, straits.

264. *royalize*, make royal, do royal honour to. Compare note to Doctor Faustus, i. 15.

265. *th' Ægyptian courtesan.* Cleopatra, who dissolved a pearl in wine.

266. *countermatch*, rival. Compare the form 'over-match,' i. 63.—Mark Antony.

267. *carous'd.* This verb is used both transitively and intransitively by Shakespeare. The word 'carouse' is the Old French 'carrous,' from the German adverb 'garaus,' quite out, i. e. to the bottom of the cup. 'Carousal' cannot have anything to do with the French carrousel, Italian carosello (supposed to be derived from the Latin carrus or currus, festive waggon); perhaps the English 'rouse' (compare

German 'Rausch' and cognate Norse words), though not derived from 'carouse,' was thought to be an abbreviation of it.

268. *Candy.* This place, which still gives its name to an infantile sweetmeat, is in Ceylon.

269. *Persia, down her Volga.* '"This," observes my friend Mr. W. N. Lettsom, 'is much as if France were to send claret and burgundy down her Thames."' Dyce. Dekker, in The Seuen Deadly Sinnes of London, writes: '*Volga*, that hath fifty streames falling one into another, never ranne with so swift and vnresistable a current.'

270. *spicery*, like the German 'Specerey,' which Frisch explains as 'aromata omnium specierum,' is from the Italian 'spezieria,' a collection of drugs and spices—the name given to the magazines of apothecaries' and confectioners' wares in the Italian convents. Compare as to these words M. Müller, Lectures on the Science of Language, i. 303.

271. *mirabolans.* 'The quartos, "mirabiles." Mirabolans are dried plums; compare in Greene's Notable Discovery of Cosenage, 1591: "I have eaten Spanish mirabolanes, and yet am nothing the more metamorphosed."' Dyce. Compare also Jonson's The Alchemist, iv. 1:

'She melts
Like a myrobolane.'—

Goethe has a poem to Marianne von Willemer (Suleika) returning a box in which she had sent him 'Mirabellen.'

272. *suckets*, sugar-plums. The word is of frequent occurrence; so in Cyril Tourneur's The Atheist's Tragedie, ii. 5, 'candied suckets'; and in Lady Alimony (a play wrongly attributed to Lodge and Greene, for it mentions 'crop-eared histriomastixes'):

'For she accounts it as a fruitless toil
To browse on suckets in a barren soil';—

margined: 'Saltibus hirsutis haud spatiantur apes.'

275, 276. *Cates . . . gluttony.* 'A corrupted, or rather (as I think) a mutilated passage. The Rev. J. Mitford (in The Gentleman's Magazine for March 1833, p. 217) alters "lamp" to "balm." . . . "Balm," he says, "or the exudation of the Balsamum, was the *only export* of Judæa to Rome; and the balm was peculiar to Judæa." But the correction "balm" does not suit what immediately follows.' Dyce. The passage is in all probability mutilated, as Dyce thinks. There seems to be some allusion to Nero's setting Rome on fire, and the passage is like the remains of a fine climax to Friar Bacon's bombast.

276. *grudge not*, grumble not. Compare among other passages The Tempest, i. 2. 249; and see below, xi. 111.

Ib. a friar's feast. Compare the preceding burst of culinary enthusiasm with Sir Epicure Mammon's in Jonson's The Alchemist, ii. 1.

Scene X.

3. *jacks of wine*, pitchers or jugs of wine. 'Black-jacks' are mentioned in Nares as a term formerly in use for a kind of pitchers made of leather. Compare Mucedorus: 'Then to the butterie hatch, to Thomas the butler for a jack of beer;' and Greene's James IV, ii. 1: 'The butler comes with a black-jack and says, Welcome, friend! here 's a cup of the best for you.' According to a note in the Index to R. Simpson's School of Shakspere, 'the use of the vessel gave rise to the Frenchman's report, that "the English drink out of their boots."'

7. *Laxfield.* 'A large and pleasant village, near the source of the river Blythe, six miles N. by E. of Framlingham.' White, *u. s.*, p. 463.

Ib. living, income; as still used of ecclesiastical benefices. Compare a passage in George-a-Greene, from which a line has probably dropt out after the first line:

'To mend thy living take thou Middleham-castle,
The hold of both; and if thou want living, complain,
Thou shalt have more to maintain thy estate.'

8 *jointer*, the person on whom the jointure is settled. It is curious that Greene should not use the feminine form 'jointress,' which occurs in Hamlet, i. 2. 9:

'Our queen,
Imperial jointress to this warlike state.'

9. *So*, provided that. Compare l. 15; and Doctor Faustus, iii. 92.

10. *five-hundred marks.* The mark is 13*s.* 4*d.*, so that, reckoning the value of silver at six times the sum stated, Lambert 'could spend' what was equivalent to an income of about £2000 a year at the present day.

11. *lands-lord of thy holds*, landlord of thy tenements or farms.

12. *By copy all thy living lies in me*, i. e. all thy income is derived from land or farms lent out to thee by me on copyhold. Compare above, l. 7. 'Copyhold tenure' is properly that for which the tenant has to show nothing but the copy of the roll—a tenure which grew up out of encroachments by villains on their lords, by which a customary right was established.

13. *raise my due*, raise or increase my rents.

14. *enfeoff.* To 'enfeoff' is to grant out as a 'feoff,' fief or estate. Serlsby, I take it, means absolutely to make over his property to Margaret, while Lambert merely purposes to settle his on her after his death.

15. *take her*, betake herself. Compare Titus Andronicus, iv. 3. 6:

'Sirs, take you to your tools.'

16. *gentles*, gentlemen.

17. *liking*, an adjective.

20. *It joys me.* Compare Richard III, i. 2. 220:

'Much it joys me too,
To see you are become so penitent.'

Dyce observes that if this passage 'be what the author wrote, it is at least very obscurely expressed.' The meaning is: the Keeper is pleased that men of such repute should condescend to take a fancy to a person so lowly as his daughter, and he would think her lucky to be married to even a less man than they are. But the construction is certainly loose. The verb 'to joy' is used personally below, l. 167.

22, 23. *so fortunate to be.* For the omission of 'as' compare Abbott, § 281.

24. *fee* (A.-S. feoh), income, property, condition. Compare the passages cited in Nares: Hamlet, ii. 2. 73:

'Whereon old Norway, overcome with joy,
Gives him three thousand crowns in annual fief';

i.e. 'in annual income'; George-a-Greene:

'Two liveries will I give thee every year,
And forty crowns shall be thy fee';

i.e. 'fixed salary or income.' Compare also Romaunt of the Rose, 6047:

'That certes if they trowed be,
Shall never leave her land ne fee';

and The Faerie Queene, iv. 9. 13, and iv. 1. 35.

30. *As*, that. Compare note on Doctor Faustus, Chorus before viii, line 11.

33. *grave.* 'The quarto of 1594, "graves."' Dyce.

36. *temper'd*, mixed. Compare note on vi. 2.

38. *poesies*, poetical composition. Compare the form 'posy,' as in Orlando Furioso:

'Hardby, I'll have some roundelays hung up,
Wherein shall be some posies of their loves';

especially used of a verse cut on a ring, as in The Merchant of Venice, v. 148.

39. *comparisons*, similes, the staple of the love-poetry of the earlier Elizabethan and Marian age.

48. *gree*, for 'degree.' Compare note to ii. 156.

51. *stay*, steadiness. Compare the adjective staid.

55. *while*, until. Compare note on ii. 156.

56. *Who . . . like.* A comparison with l. 78 below seems to show that 'of whom' is merely a repetition for the sake of emphasis. As to the construction 'to like of,' compare iv. 29. As to the use of 'who' for 'whom,' compare i. 144. As to the infinitive without 'to,' see note on Doctor Faustus, iii. 36.

59. *battling.* See note on ix. 4.

Ib. fatten. 'The quarto of 1594 "fatneth."' Dyce. This was perhaps what Greene wrote.

60. *stapled,* dressed for sale at the staple. 'Staple' (A.-S. stapul, compare Modern German 'stapeln,' to warehouse) originally signified not, as now, the established merchandise of a place, but the established mart of an article. (See in Trench, Glossary, p. 198, the quotation from Phillips's New World of Words: 'Staple; a city or town, where merchants jointly lay up their commodities for the better uttering of them by the great; a public storehouse.') Hence the great free cities in Flanders were the 'staples' of English goods for sale abroad, and the merchants who traded in them were called the 'merchants of the staple,' till Edward III unwisely named nine towns in England to be the exclusive places for sale of the English 'staple' commodities (of which wool was the chief).

61. *As.* Compare note on Doctor Faustus, Chorus before viii, line 11.

Ib. Lemnster, Leominster in Herefordshire, formerly known for its manufactories of woollen cloth, hats, and gloves. Compare Drayton's Poly-Olbion, vii. 145-150:

'*Lemster,* for whose wool whose staple doth excell,
And seems to overmatch the golden *Phrygian* fell.
Had this our Colchos been unto the Ancients known,
When Honor was herself, and in her glory shown,
He then that did command the Infantry of *Greece,*
Had only to our Isle adventur'd for this Fleece.'

Ib. more finer. Compare Alphonsus King of Arragon:

'We should have you more calmer out of hand.'

For other examples of the double comparative and superlative see Abbott, § 11.

63. *strouting,* swelling. The word is used accordingly like the modern 'to strut.'

Ib. paggle (quarto of 1599, I think, 'puggle'). The word seems formed out of reminiscences of 'paddle' and 'bag'; compare The Shepheard's Calender, Februarie, 81:

'Thy ewes, that wont to have blowen bags.'

70. *thy head-attire.* Ladies' head-dresses in the Tudor age, though no longer so wonderfully constructed as in the Plantagenet period, when 'the younger and more beautiful the ladies were, the higher were the *chimneys* which they carried,' still admitted of much finery. See Fairholt, *u. s., s. v.* 'Head-dress' in Glossary.

75. *to counsel me,* to advise, or take counsel with, myself. Compare i. 127.

76. *fancy,* love. Compare viii. 39.

77. *Give me.* 'Query: ought these words to be omitted?' Dyce.

78. *Which or to whom.* Compare l. 56 above.

Ib. myself affectionates. 'Self' is here used as a substantive, as in the first line of the passage noted by Abbott, § 20 (where the reading of the folios may, as he says, be correct), 2 Henry VI, iii. 1. 217–219:

'Even so myself bewails good Gloucester's case,
With sad unhelpful tears and with dimm'd eyes,
Look after him and cannot do him good,' etc.

'To affectionate' is formed like 'to ruinate,' ix. 133, but is not, like it, a Shakespearean word.

80. *such a base esquire.* Notice that below, xiii. 39, the other of the rivals mentions this rank respectfully.

82. *overreach me,* outdo me. Compare overshine, i. 139 and l. 5 above; over-match, i. 63; and over-watch, xi. 26.

83. *thy country braves,* thy rustic boasts. Compare xi. 115 and xiii. 43; and Peele's Edward I, xii. 75:

'And wend with this as resolutely back
As thou to England brought'st thy Scottish braves.'

85. *dint,* blow, stroke.

86. *avouch'd.* Compare vi. 32.

91. *wrongs.* 'Query "wrings."' Dyce.

100. *Whenas.* Compare note on i. 75.

115. *just,* exactly.

118. *closures,* enclosures. Compare ix. 54.

122. *if that.* Compare note on Doctor Faustus, x. 15.

123. *blooms,* blossoms, as xiv. 4.

124. *the flies hæmeræ,* the ephemera, or day-flies.

126. *timely.* Compare vi. 87.

130. *queasy,* fastidious. Compare Much Ado about Nothing, ii. 1. 399: 'In spite of his quick wit and his queasy stomach, he shall fall in love with Beatrice.'

139. *Fond Atè.* The goddess of Mischief, who 'fondly,' i.e. playfully, destroys the happiness of human beings.

Ib. doomer, who doomest or decreest. Compare ix. 163.

142. *lighten'd,* shone forth. Compare i. 54.

149. *shelves,* the sandbanks of the coasts, i.e. the coasts generally. Compare 3 Henry VI, v. 4. 23:

'Shelves and rocks that threaten us with wreck.'

151. *from her lord.* 'Query "from him"? But the earlier part of the speech is also evidently corrupt.' Dyce.

153. *for,* because. Compare vii. 64.

154. *at very thought.* 'The quartos, "euery."' Dyce. Compare as to these omissions of the article, Introduction, p. ix.

158. *Wealth, trash.* 'Query "Wealth shall be trash"?' Dyce.

Scene XI.

I have given Dyce's stage-direction; but the beginning of that of the quarto of 1599 may be quoted as characteristic of the simplicity of Elizabethan stage-arrangements: '*Enter Fryer* Bacon *drawing the courtaines with a white sticke, a booke in his hand, and a lampe lighted by him,*' etc. The 'white stick' is the magic wand, winged staff, or serpent-staff, used by conjurors, the origin of which is traceable to the wishing-rod of German mythology and the sleep-bringing magic wand of the god Hermes. Compare note on ix. 30, and see on this subject Ennemoser, *u. s.*, ii. 45–47. As to the Brazen Head, see Introduction, pp. xxiv-xxvi.

3. *How chance*, how chances it that. Compare Comedy of Errors, i. 2. 42, cited by Abbott, § 37.

5. *furniture*, weapons, equipment. So of a horse in The Faerie Queene, iii. 1. 11:

'His page,
That had his furnitures not firmly tyde.'

12. *lodge*, abode. Compare viii. 70.

14. *three-form'd Luna.* Diana is by Ovid, Metamorphoses, vii. 94 and 177, called 'dea' and 'diva triformis,' as being at once Diana, Luna, and Hecate.

Ib. hid her silver looks. 'Looks' means glances or rays. As to the supposed effects of magic upon the moon, compare note on Doctor Faustus, iii. 38.

15. *her concave continent*, the vault of the sky. Compare note on ix. 62.

16. *read upon.* Compare ii. 95.

17. *tossing*, turning over. Compare xiii. 89.

18. *Hecat'.* Compare note on ii. 176.

21. *aphorisms.* See note on Doctor Faustus, i. 19.

25. *Argus* (quarto of 1599, 'Argos'), the guardian of Io, whom Mercury killed by order of Jupiter, whereupon Juno transferred his hundred eyes to the tail of her bird, the peacock. See Ovid's Metamorphoses, i. 624 seqq.

26. *over-watch*, outwatch, watch through. [Misprinted 'over-match' in the text.]

Ib. Phobetor's (quarto of 1599, 'Phobeter's') *night.* The name Phobetor is formed from the Greek *φόβος*, fear; *νηπίων φόβητρα* are infants' bugbears.

29. *Hangs.* This singular is probably explained by the two substantives 'honour and renown' forming a single idea.

31. *within his fist*, probably with allusion to the Scriptural phrase,

'within the hollow of His hand.' The word 'fist' is used as a dignified one in 3 Henry VI, ii. 1. 154:

> 'Thou shalt know this strong right hand of mine
> Can pluck the diadem from faint Henry's head,
> And wring the awful sceptre from his fist';

and in Orlando Furioso:

> 'Those silver doves
> That wanton Venus mann'th [makes tractable, a falconry term] upon her fist.'

Pistol however uses the word in a way which suggests that it had already acquired a comical sound, in Henry V, ii. 1. 71:

> 'Give me thy fist, thy fore-foot to me give.'

37. *If that.* Compare note to Doctor Faustus, x. 15.

41. *So.* This use of 'so' to express acquiescence like 'well,' is of constant occurrence in Shakespeare.

42, 43. *on the days, on the nights,* for 'in the days, in the nights.' Compare note on ii. 95.

43. *ten and fifty.* The negro Gumbo, in Thackeray's Virginians, adopts a similar method of numeration, stating that at Castlewood in Virginia 'there were twenty forty gentlemen in livery, besides women-servants.'

46. *nos autem glorificare.* Dyce refers to a parallel facetious passage in A Looking-Glass for London and England, already quoted in note on v. 42. 'Nos autem gloriari oportet' are the opening words of an 'Introit' in the Roman liturgy, founded partly on the Epistle to the Galatians, vi. 14.

47. *nos autem popolare.* Quarto of 1599, 'popelares.'

51. *Goodman.* Compare note to iii. 59.

52. *your memento.* Miles refers to the custom of having a Death's head with the inscription 'memento mori' placed for contemplation in a sleeping-chamber. Compare R. Southwell's poem Vpon the Image of Death, stanzas 2 and 3:

> 'I often looke upon a face,
> Most vgly, grisly, bare and thinne;
> I often view the hollow place
> Where eyes and nose had sometimes bin:
> I see the bones across that lie,
> Yet little think that I must die.
>
> I read the labell vnderneath,
> That telleth me whereto I must;
> I see the sentence eake that saith,
> Remember, man, that thou art dust:
> But yet, alas! but seldome I
> Doe thinke indeede that I must die.'

Compare also 1 Henry IV, iii. 3. 31–35:

'*Bard.* Why, sir John, my face does you no harm.

'*Fal.* No, I'll be sworn; I make as good use of it as many a man doth of a death's head, or a memento mori,' etc.

53. *brown-bill.* 'A weapon formerly borne by our foot-soldiers, and afterwards by watchmen: it was a sort of pike or halbert, with a hooked point.' Dyce. In 2 Henry VI, iv. 10. 12, Cade says, 'Many a time, but for a sallet, my brain-pan had been cleft with a brown bill.' 'Brown' is an epithet applied to the 'bill' or 'sword' in A.-S. poetry; so in the Battle of Maldon, 162:

> 'þa Byrhtnoð bræd bill of sceðe (drew sword from sheath)
> brad and brun-ecg' (brown-edged).

54. *hobgoblins.* This familiar word is said in Nares originally to signify 'clown-goblin or bumpkin-goblin, "Hob" having in old times been a frequent name among the common people, particularly in the country' [compare James IV, v. 4].—See a fragment Of spirits called Hobgoblins, or Robin Goodfellows (described as a kind of spirits 'more familiar and domestical than the others') in Halliwell's Illustrations of the Fairy Mythology of A Midsummer Night's Dream (Shakespeare Society's Publications, 1845).—'Hob' is also used as a substitute for the compound.

58. *cunning.* Compare note on Doctor Faustus, opening Chorus, line 20.

Ib. of it, equivalent to 'from it.' Compare ix. 241.

62. *the slow-worm,* a moth. Compare Herrick's The Night-piece, to Julia:

> 'No Will-o'-the-wispe mislight thee
> Nor snake or slow-worme bite thee.'

Chaucer, in The Romaunt of the Rose, v. 4755, has 'a slowe.'

62. *I'll set a prick against my breast.* Sir Thomas Browne, in Pseudodoxia Epidemica, Vulgar Errors, bk. ii. ch. xxviii, questions, among other things, 'whether the nightingale's sitting with her breast against a thorn, be any more than that she placeth some prickles on the outside of her nest, or roosteth in thorny prickly places, where serpents may least approach her?' The fancy is repeatedly mentioned in our old poets; so in Edward III, i. 1:

> 'Fervent desire, that sits against my heart,
> Is far more thorny-pricking than this blade;
> That, with the nightingale, I shall be scar'd,
> As oft as I dispose myself to rest.'

See also The Passionate Pilgrim, xxi. 9–14:

> 'Every thing did banish moan,
> Save the nightingale alone:

She, poor bird, as all forlorn,
Lean'd her breast up-till a thorn,
And there sung the dolefull'st ditty,
That to hear it was great pity';

and Sir Philip Sidney's song, The Nightingale:

'The nightingale, as soon as April bringeth
Vnto her rested sense a perfect waking,
While late bare earth, proud of new clothing, springeth,
Sings out her woes, a thorne her song-book making.
. . . .
O Philomela faire, O take some gladnesse,
That here is iuster cause of plaintfull sadnesse:
Thine earth now springs, mine fadeth;
Thy thorne without, my thorne my heart inuadeth.'

73. *a peripatetian.* The name of the Peripatetics was given to the philosophical school of Aristotle, because he used to teach while walking about under the portico of the Lyceum at Athens.—Miles puns on the meaning of the name in saying that he will be 'a philosopher of Aristotle's *stamp.*'

80. *the latter day*, the last day. Shakespeare constantly uses 'latter' where we should use 'last'; so in 1 Henry VI, ii. 5. 38:

'And in his bosom spend my latter gasp';

and in 3 Henry VI, iv. 6. 43:

'And in devotion spend my latter days.'

Compare Job, xix. 25.

92. *Commentator*, for 'Cunctator.'

99. *ruin'd down*, fallen down. Compare Italian rovinare, to fall down with a rush.

107. *aphorisms.* See note on Doctor Faustus, i. 19.

109. *Asmenoth.* See note to ix. 144.

110. *Demogorgon.* See note on Doctor Faustus, iii. 18.

113. *over-match.* Compare i. 63.

115. *braves.* Compare x. 83.

Ib. end. The re-iteration of the same word or couple of words at the close of several successive lines is a common device in our dramatists; compare that of the name 'Angelica' in Orlando Furioso; Rasni's repetition of the words 'my world' in A Looking-Glass for London and England; that of the words 'my queen' in James the Fourth; and that of the word 'ring' in The Merchant of Venice, v. 192-202.

117. *sorteth to ill end*, comes to an ill end, has an ill ending. Compare 2 Hen. VI, i. 2. 107:

'Sort how it will, I shall have gold for all.'

120. *avoid!* equivalent to 'avaunt!' 'away!' So in 2 Henry VI, i. 4. 43:

'False fiend, avoid!'

and elsewhere in Shakespeare.

126. *the old proverb.* I cannot say what this proverb is.

129. *a crowned cap*, the magician's cap, derived from the wishing-cap of Northern mythology, and perhaps from the cap or helmet (κυνέη) of Hermes. Or perhaps the reference is to the college cap which Miles actually assumes in sc. xv, where it is more appropriately called a 'corner-cap.'

131. *haunt*, intransitive. Compare note to i. 141.

134. *To lo e . . . head.* As to this indefinite use of 'to' with the infinitive in a gerundive sense, see Abbott, § 357. 'To lose' here signifies much the same thing as 'by' or 'after losing or having lost.' Compare xiii. 2, where 'What means the friar to sit?' is equivalent to 'What means the friar by sitting?'

Scene XII.

1. *prime.* 'The quartos, "prince."' Dyce.

4 *To answer England in equivalence.* This is merely a grand way of expressing 'to be a match for England;' just as 'in four equivalents' in Doctor Faustus, vii. 12, merely means 'in four equal parts' or 'in four parts.'

8. *amorets.* Compare note on ix. 177.

12. *gree*, agree. Compare note on ii. 156.

14. *counterfeit*, portrait. Compare note on iv. 22.

16. *troop'd with.* Compare vii. 3.

18. *As.* Compare note on Doctor Faustus, Chorus before viii, l. 11. Dyce considers this line 'corrupted.'

21. *honour up*, celebrate to the end. Compare note on iii. 22.

29. *to thy lady.* Compare Doctor Faustus, xiii. 84.

34. *unpossible.* For adjectives in Shakespeare compounded with *un*, where we use *in*, see Abbott, § 442. In Orlando Furioso Greene has 'unconstant;' in The Arraignment of Paris Peele has 'unpartial.' On the other hand, Green and Lodge in A Looking-Glass for London and England have 'inspeakable.'

37-39. *when egg-pies . . . bag-piper.* For this burlesque suggestion of an impossible contingency (which seems suggested by visions of the 'Land of Cokayne') compare in the Prologue to Alphonsus King of Arragon:

'*Erato.* But pray now, tell me when your painful pen
Will rest enough.
Melpom. When husbandmen shear hogs.'

45. *The Fair.* Here fair is a dissyllable, as Dyce, citing Walker, points out. Compare note to Doctor Faustus, v. 63.

49. *Her virgin's right . . . was.* This line is obscure; but it should be observed that 'rich' is a favourite epithet of Greene's, repeatedly employed by him in our play as a general term of praise; compare iv. 13, x. 95. The meaning seems to be: 'Her right to the name of Virgin is as good as that belonging to Vesta—or to her priestesses, the Vestal Virgins.'

55. *vouchèd*, avowed, declared. Compare vii. 19.

56. *'querry* (quarto of 1599, 'Quiry'), equerry.

59. *for*, because. Compare note on i. 121.

67. *thyself.* This is Dyce's polite emendation for the 'myselfe' of the quartos; xi. 82, however, Bacon had used almost the same expression.

73. *out of all ho.* In Nares this phrase is explained as equivalent to that of 'out of all cry'—from the notion of calling in or restraining a sporting dog, or perhaps a hawk, with a call, or 'ho.' The phrase, as stated in Nares, is used by Swift in his Journal to Stella: 'When your tongue runs, there 's no hoe with you, pray.' 'Out of all cry.'—Compare 'out of all hooping' in As You Like It, iii. 2. 203.

75. *secretary*, person entrusted with secrets.

83. *fly the partridge.* Compare note on v. 52.

Scene XIII.

1. *frolick'd it.* Compare note on i. 103.

2. *To sit.* Compare note to xi. 134.

4. *Ah, Bungay, ah.* Query, 'Ah, Bungay, ah my.' Dyce.

6. *bruited*, noised, (From French bruit, noise.)

11. *As.* Compare note on Doctor Faustus, Chorus before viii, l. 11.

Ib. infringe what he deserves, impair the reputation which is his due.

12. *by prospective skill*, by the art of divination. Compare the 'glass prospective,' v. 110, and below, 28.

14. *'tide*, betide.

23. *Cratfield*, a village nine miles from Framlingham, mentioned in Domesday Book. White, *u. s.*, p. 363.

24. *college-mates*, companions at College. This may imply that as students they shared the same room. See note on Doctor Faustus, xiv. 3.

30. *how that.* Compare note to Doctor Faustus, x. 15.

32. *ere long, how.* 'Query, "ere long, sirs, how."' Dyce.

33. *fathers live.* 'The quarto of 1594, "father liues."' Dyce.

Enter Lambert *and* Serlsby. Compare note from Dyce on the stage-direction before vi. 11.

40. *durst.* The past indicative is here used for the present indicative 'darest.'

41. *prize,* set a price upon (compare note on iii. 8); hence risk or venture in combat.

43. *braves.* Compare note on x. 83.

44. *for,* because. See note on i. 121.

45. *will die.* Modern usage would require 'shall die.' See note on Doctor Faustus, i. 46.

48. *scold it out.* Compare note on i. 103.

49. *An if,* if. See note on Doctor Faustus, v. 137.

50. *the Broadgates-hall.* Segrim or, corruptly, Segreve Hall at Oxford was a very ancient seminary for students of the Civil and Canon Law, existing already in the twelfth century. It was afterwards called Broadgates Hall from the wide form of its entrance, 'aula cum latea porta,' or 'aula late portensis.' In 1624 Pembroke College was founded within this Hall, and new buildings were soon erected, the Hall however being preserved, though it received additions. See A. Chalmers' History of the Colleges, etc. of Oxford.

55. *a bout,* the same as 'a veney' below, 66; literally a thrust at arms (from the French verb bouter, whence botte, a term for a fencing-thrust, Italian bottare, derived from the M. High German bôzen, which is the same as A.-S. beâtan, to beat).

60. *my father's is th' abuse,* he is the aggrieved party.

61. *harm,* take harm.

63. *the event,* the issue.

66. *A veney.* '*Venie,* or as it is sometimes spelt, Venu or Venny, was a very common fencing-term, meaning the onset, from the French venir. [Compare our 'come on!'] See Love's Labour 's Lost, v. 1. 62: 'a sweet touch, a quick venue of wit; where the word, as in most instances of its use, is figuratively employed.' Collier, note to R. Armin's Nest of Ninnies, *u. s.*, p. 67. In Nares it is noted that the term was also used in matches at cudgels; and that in fencing the Italian term 'stoccata' supplanted it, as more fashionable; see Jonson's Every Man in his Humour, i. 5:

> 'Venu, fie, most gross denomination as I ever heard;
> O, the stoccata, while you live, sir, not that!'

69. *mark the ward,* observe how my father guards the thrust.

73. *quite,* requite. Compare note on v. 112.

75. *fathers.* 'Query, "scholars?"' Dyce.

78. *these brave lusty Brutes.* A 'brute' or 'bruit of fame' is a report

of fame (compare 'to bruit,' above, 6), or a famous personage; so in Sir Clyomon and Sir Clamydes:

'And doth Neronis love indeed? to whom doth love she yield?
Even to that noble bruit of fame, the Knight of the Golden Shield';

and *ib.*:

'Since I have given my faith and troth to such a bruit of fame
As is the Knight of the Golden Shield.'

Very probably the name of the mythical Brute or Brut (see note on xvi. 45) may have helped to bring about this personal use of the word. So in Peele's Edward I, ii. 373, Lluellen hopes to be 'chiefest Brute of western Wales,' after previously (in l. 5) having boasted of his descent from 'Trojan Brute.'

81. *their.* 'The quartos, "the."' Dyce.

Ib. fatal, doomed; so in Henry V, ii. 4. 13:

'Late examples
Left by the fatal and neglected English
Upon our fields.'

82. *cause efficiat.* Query, 'cause efficient'?

89. *tossing.* Compare xi. 17.

92. *stole and alb*, sacred vestments which, like holy water, the devils cannot abide.

Ib. strong pentageron. Strong is Dyce's conjecture for strange, in view of ii. 51, where see note on 'pentageron.'

93. *the wresting of the holy name.* Compare Doctor Faustus, iii. 47; and see note on l. 9 of the same scene. The names mentioned in the following lines are equivalents of the Divine Name: 'Soter' is σωτήρ, the Saviour; 'Messiah' and 'J H S' are both mentioned in the 'Semiphoras,' as are 'Eloha,' 'Elohim,' 'Adonay,' 'Melech,' and 'Maniah.' The 'Tetragrammaton' consists of the four letters which form the name 'Jehovah,' for which name 'Adonay' is said to be employed as a substitute. 'Alpha' is one of these letters. See Scheible's Kloster, iii. 293 seqq.

96. *five-fold.* I rather think this should be 'fourfold;' see as to the 'four hierarchies,' note on ix. 140; but perhaps Greene had the virtues of the pentagramma in his mind, and in any case it is impossible to bring order into his loose references to magical lore.

98. *countervail*, be valid against (compare vii. 20); hence seek to equal, usurp the powers of.

100. *repentance can do much*, a text on which Greene preached in his posthumous tract, A Groatsworth of Wit bought with a Million of Repentance.

103. *Which . . . afresh*; apparently a double reference to a kind of miracle related in many legends, and to the superstition that wounds

could be inflicted on the absent by magical charms. Possibly there may be here a reminiscence of Hebrews vi. 6.

106. *from sin.* Either this is a zeugma, the idea of 'wash' having been transferred to 'make'; or 'from' is here used in the sense of 'away from,' 'without.' See Abbott, § 158, for this use of 'from,' in such passages as Cymbeline, v. 5. 431:

'This label on my bosom, whose containing
Is so from sense in hardness.'

109. *what Bacon vainly*, i. e. foolishly, *lost*, viz. his soul.

Scene XIV.

3. *for the hue.* 'Hue' is used by Greene in the sense of 'beauty' in Alphonsus King of Arragon, act iii: 'Alcumena's hue'; compare also in the Hexametra Alexis in laudem Rosamundae in The Mourning Garment:

'did grieve that a creature
Should exceed in hue, compar'd both a god and a goddess.'

4. *blooms*, blossoms. Compare x. 123.

6. *the dated time of death*, the time appointed for his death.

13. *for that.* Compare note to Dr. Faustus, x. 15.

15. *repents*, penances. Compare note on Doctor Faustus, xiii. 30.

16. *aspiring.* Compare note to Dr. Faustus, iii. 68.

20. *Pride . . . thoughts.* 'A slightly mutilated line.' Dyce.

29. *engine*, instrument. So in Venus and Adonis, 367, the tongue of Venus is called 'the engine of her thoughts.'

32. *an humble mind to God;* an inversion for 'a mind humble to, or before, God.'

34. *Farewell, O love!* 'The quartos, "Loue, O Loue."' Dyce.

46. *Peggy.* Quarto of 1859, 'Pegge.'

54. *As die*, as to die. See as to the omission of 'to' after conjunctions, Abbott, § 353.

56. *'miss*, for 'amiss'; compare note to ii. 156. ''Miss' or 'amiss' is used as here in the sense of 'fault' in Orlando Furioso:

'Soldier, let me die for the 'miss of all';

in A Looking-Glass for London and England:

'Then cast we lots, to throw by whose amiss
The mischief came, according to the guise;
And lo! the lot did unto Jonas fall';

and *ib.*:

'But pray amends, and mend thy own amiss';

and in Peele's Arraignment of Paris:

'That I, a man, must plead before the gods,
Gracious forbearers of the world's amiss.'

57. *fond*, 'fondly,—foolishly, vainly.' Dyce.

68. *peremptory*, absolute, positive. Compare Henry V, v. 2. 82:

'We will suddenly
Pass our accept and peremptory answer.'

69. *his interest*, i.e. his claim upon me. Compare viii. 134.

78. *my lord*. 'Most probably an addition by some transcriber; which not only injures the metre, but is out of place in the mouth of Warren, who is himself a "lord," and who, when he last addressed Lacy, called him "Sirrah Ned."' Dyce.

Ib. an if. Compare note to Dr. Faustus, v. 137.

80. *yet*, as yet, still.

87. *Whate'er.* 'The quartos, "Whatsoe'er."' Dyce.

88. *the habit of a maiden's heart*, i.e. the reserve customary to a maiden's heart.

92. *thy husband*. 'Query, thy husband, I"?' Dyce. But I think the line as it stands, with a pause on the first syllable of 'husband,' is musically expressive.

98. *As if.* 'Query, "as glad as if"?' Dyce.

100. *in a brown study*. This phrase, the origin of which is obscure, is used by Adam in A Looking-Glass for London and England: 'Truly, sir, I was in a brown study about my mistress.' Compare also Faire Em, sc. iii. (l. 233): 'How now, Sir Robert, in a study, man?' Other passages are quoted in Nares.

106. *umbles*. From a passage in Holinshed quoted in Nares it appears that the 'umbles,' i.e. the liver, kidneys, and other inward parts of a deer, were among the keeper's perquisites: 'The keeper hath the skin, head, umbles, chine and shoulders.' It is added in Nares that 'the old books of cookery give receipts for making "umble-pies"; and on this was founded a very flat proverbial witticism, "making persons eat umble-pye," meaning "to humble them."'

109. *And not a bottle of wine.* Lacy appears to have a particular objection to a repast unaccompanied by a glass of wine; see viii. 158–159.

112. *she speaks least*, i.e. she promises as little as possible.

Scene XV.

The stage direction of the quarto of 1599 is explicit: '*Enter a* Deuill *to seek* Miles.'

1. *sprites*. 'The quarto of 1594, "spirits."' Dyce.

3. *nine-fold-trenchèd Phlegethon*. Phlegethon, one of the rivers of Hades is so called because fire flows in it instead of water

(φλεγέθειν, to flame; hence the stream is also called Pyriphlegethon); compare Statius' Thebais, iv. 523:

'Fumidus atra vadis Phlegethon incendia volvit';

but the epithet 'nine-fold-trenchèd' seems borrowed from the description 'novies interfusa' (winding nine times round Erebus), twice applied to the river Styx in Vergil (Georgics, iv. 480; Æneid, vi. 439).—In A Looking-Glass for London and England occurs the phrase, 'the nine-fold orbs of heaven.'

4. *scud*, hurry, A.-S. scûdan. Compare in Orlando Furioso:

'The thief of Thessaly,
Which scuds abroad and searcheth for his prey.'

Ib. over-scour, pass over. So in A Looking-Glass for London and England:

'The proud leviathan that scours the sea.'

The word to 'scour' seems to be derived through the O. F. escurer from the Latin excurare, used in the sense 'to sweep clean.' We use the word 'to sweep' and the Germans the word 'fegen' in the same sense of 'to hurry over.'

Ib. in post, in haste. Compare note to ii. 149.

5. *Upon . . . winds.* A reminiscence of Psalm xviii. 10: 'He rode upon the cherubims, and did fly: he came flying upon the wings of the wind.'

8. *lazy bones.* The word 'bones' is constantly used in Shakespeare for the whole body; but 'lazy-bones' as a comic compound does not seem to be Elizabethan.

Enter Miles *in a gown and a corner-cap*, i. e. in his academicals.

15. *as an egg's full of oatmeal.* A Milesian version of the phrase 'as an egg is full of meat,' which Mercutio uses in Romeo and Juliet, iii. 1. 24.

18. *Master Plutus.* Miles confounds Plutus, the god of wealth, with Pluto, the god of the lower regions.—(Of course the names are the same in origin; Plutos the son of Demeter signifies the mineral wealth in the bowels of the earth.)

27. *the statute.* Several sumptuary laws were passed in the Tudor reigns; among them those of 33 Henry VIII, regulating the apparel of the different classes of the community, of 1 and 2 Philip and Mary, against wearing of silk by persons under the degree of a knight's son and heir, and Elizabeth's of 1579 against excessive long cloaks and ruffs. See Fairholt, *u. s.*, pp. 196–197, 200, 206.—Hence the expression 'statute-lace' in A Looking-Glass for London and England.

29. *without welt or guard.* A 'welt' (apparently from the Celtic gwald, border) or 'guard' is a facing to a gown; the terms are used

synonymously. These facings were made of gold or silver lace for both sexes. Both terms and the adjectives 'guarded' and 'welted' occur in other passages; so 'guarded' in The Merchant of Venice, ii. 2. 164, and 'guarded with yellow' of the fool's dress in the Prologue to Henry VIII, line 16; and in Greene's Quip for an Upstart Courtier: 'a black cloth gown welted and faced.' See Fairholt, *u. s.*, in Glossary.

31. *how then?* what then?

32. *Faith, 'tis a place.* Compare Adam's account of his visit to the same place in A Looking-Glass for London and England.

34. *a pair of cards*, a pack of cards. Dyce cites from Greene's Notable Discovery of Cosenage: 'Out commeth an old paire of cardes, whereat the Barnard teaches the Verser a new game,' etc. For other passages see Nares.

Ib. swinging, very big; an epithet still used in modern slang. The original meaning seems to be 'lashing, beating down with a swing of the arm'; the words 'swinger' and 'to beswinge' are used in the same way, as in Orlando Furioso: 'You had best to use your sword better, lest I beswinge you'; and 'swinge-buckler' (used in 2 Henry IV, iii. 2. 24) is an intensification of 'swash-buckler.'

35, 36. *a white waistcoat*, in the language of the modern tap-room a 'head'; but there is an allusion to a garment which was considered disreputable when worn without a gown.

38. *you are . . . you*, i. e. then we shall suit one another. Compare in A Looking-Glass for London and England: 'I am your man; I am for you, sir.'

45. *lets*, prevents; A.-S. lettan.

47. *Thou shalt ride on my back.* This is a favourite piece of horseplay in the old miracles and morals, when the Vice belabours the Devil. Compare Adam's 'bombasting' of the Devil in A Looking-Glass for London and England, and 'Iniquity's' carrying off 'Satan' in Jonson's The Devil is an Ass, v. 4.

50. *goodman.* Compare note to iii. 59.

60. *a false gallop*, i. e. a jolting one.

Scene XVI.

The 'properties' in the stage-direction to this scene may be identified by a reference to a description of the English regalia, kept in the Jewel House in the Tower of London. The 'pointless sword' borne by the Emperor is the curtana or curtein, the sword of King Edward the Confessor, which in the coronations of English kings was borne by the Earl of Chester. It was blunted in both point and blade, in token of the mercy to be shown by the king to the people—hence its name.

See Ducange, s. v. curtana, who cites Matthew Paris's notice of the Earl of Chester bearing the 'curtein' at the wedding festivities of King Henry III. The 'sword with a point' is one of the two swords of Justice, temporal and spiritual. These, like the 'orb' or 'globe,' were originally the symbols of imperial authority, and assumed by kings in imitation of the emperors. The 'rod of gold with a dove on it' is the 'Rod of Equity'; already Charles the Great used such a sceptre of gold, though the dove, signifying the sanctifying power of the Holy Ghost, seems to have been a later addition.

1. *for state*, in, or as to, power and majesty. Compare as to this use of 'for,' note to Dr. Faustus, x. 4; and for the word 'state' in this sense, Dr. Faustus, opening Chorus, 4.

2. *humbles*, humiliates or prostrates himself. Compare All's Well that Ends Well, i. 2. 45:

'In their poor praise he humbled';

(where it seems unnecessary to explain this, with Schmidt, as an absolute construction, or, with Staunton, to read 'be-humbled').

6. *Gramercies*. Compare iii. 88.

Ib. lordings. See note on ix. 85.

7. *That rules . . . diadem*. Compare in Orlando Furioso:

'It fits me not to sway the diadem.'

8. *these conceivèd joys*, these joys conceived by him.

11. *quite*, requite. Compare note on v. 112.

Ib. favourites. 'Query, "favourers"?' Dyce.

15. *They did*, i. e. they would.

Ib. images, figures—of the three goddesses who appeared before Paris.

18. *Jove*. See note on Doctor Faustus, i. 74.

21. *grac'd with*, honoured by. Compare 'troopèd with,' vii. 3; and 'circled with,' below, 67.

25. *wears*, a confusion of construction for 'wearest.'

43. *I find*, &c. These lines form one of those compliments to Queen Elizabeth which, as Dyce observes, frequently occur at the conclusion of dramas acted during her lifetime. Compare Cranmer's prophecy at the close of Henry VIII, which so far as it refers to Elizabeth's reign, I cannot believe to have been written for recitation before her death.—Another complimentary passage of this kind is at the close of Peele's Arraignment of Paris, where 'Diana describeth the nymph Eliza, a figure of the queen'; even in A Looking-Glass for London and England Jonas contrives a tribute to the saving virtues of Elizabeth.

Ib. prescience, accented on the second syllable.

44. *temper'd*. Compare vi. 2.

45. *That here . . . Troynovant*. This is one of the many allusions in

our writers to the legend taken from 'Nennius' by Geoffrey of Monmouth, according to which the first inhabitants of Britain were Trojans led to Italy by Æneas, the wife of whose grandson Silvius bore a son named Brut. Geoffrey of Monmouth, at the end of the First Book of his Historia Britonum, brings Brut to the foundation of Troynovant—New Troy—afterwards London. See H. Morley, English Writers, i. 2. 499–500. Layamon's 'Brut' is an enlarged English version of Wace's Norman-French metrical translation of Geoffrey's History.—Compare 'wandering Brute,' below, 55; and see also note on xiii. 78, and the passage there cited from Peele's Edward I. Compare also Peele's Anglorum Feriae, England's Holidays:

'Those quiet days that Englishmen enjoy
Under our Queen, fair Queen of Brute's New Troy';

and Dekker's The Seuen Deadly Sinnes of London, where London is called 'This fairest facde daughter of *Brute*,' and afterwards 'faire *Troynouant*.'

46. ***From forth.*** For this prepositional use of forth, by itself or with of and from, see Abbott, § 156.

48. ***deface***, obliterate, i.e. outvie.

Ib. ***Phoebus' flower***, the sun-flower.

56. ***these.*** 'Query, "those"? but our early writers did not always make the distinction between "these" and "those" which is made at the present day.' Dyce.

57. ***gorgeous***, gorgeously.

58. ***Apollo's heliotropion.*** The name heliotropium (turnsole) is applied by the old botanical writers to so many distinct plants, that it is needless to suppose Greene in our passage to have had any particular one of these in view.

59. ***Venus' hyacinth.*** According to the legend in Ovid's Metamorphoses, x. 184–215, the hyacinth was sacred, not to Venus, but to Apollo. The Hyacinthia were a Lacedaemonian festival in honour of Apollo's favourite Hyacinthus, with Apolline processions and games. The identification of the hyacinth of the Greeks and Romans has been much disputed; see Bostock and Riley's note to Plin. Hist. Nat., bk. xxi. c. 38.

Ib. ***vail***, lower, a shortened form of avale or avail, from the French avaller (à val, Latin ad vallem).—Compare The Merchant of Venice, i. 1. 26:

'And see my wealthy Andrew dock'd in sand,
Vailing her high-top lower than her ribs
To kiss her burial';

and in George-a-Greene, the Pinner of Wakefield:

'Proud dapper Jack, vail bonnet to the bench
That represents the person of the king.'

60. *Juno . . . up.* Flowers—though not the gilliflower in particular—were associated with Hera, round whose couch they spring in abundance in Homer. The name 'gilliflower' or 'gillyvor' (the form used in The Winter's Tale, iv. 3. 82 and 98) is applied by our old botanists both to the stock (cheiranthus) and to the clove-pink (dianthus). The former is probably the flower intended by Greene; as the clove-pink is a kind of carnation, the flower mentioned l. 62 below.

61. *'bash*, abash or abase. Compare note to ii. 156.

62. *Ceres' carnation.* There seems again no reason why this flower should be connected with Ceres. If any flower is specially associated with her (Demeter) it is the narcissus, which Proserpine (Persephone) was gathering when Pluto carried her off. In the worship of Demeter herself corn was associated with her; and it is in allusion to the golden corn that Pindar calls her *φοινικόπεζα*, purple-footed.

Ib. consórt, company. Compare 'consorting,' ix. 205; and Two Gentlemen of Verona, iv. 1. 64:

'What sayst thou? wilt thou be of our consort?'

With the accent on the first syllable, the word in Shakespeare signifies a band of music; and is probably a mis-spelling of concert (French concert, Italian concerto, from concertare, to discuss; hence an understanding or agreement for a common performance).

63. *Diana's rose*, the rose of England's Virgin Queen. Diana and Cynthia are poetical names constantly applied to Queen Elizabeth. According to Mr. Halpin's Illustrations of the Fairy Mythology of A Midsummer Night's Dream, (old) Shakespeare Society's Publications, 1845, Shakespeare borrowed the phrase 'Diana's bud' (iv. 1. 78) from our passage. See H. P. Stokes, The Chronological Order of Shakespeare's Plays, 51.

64. *is mystical*, is allegorical, has a deeper meaning beneath it.

65. *But, glorious.* 'Some corruption here. Query, "But, glorious comrades of" &c.?' Dyce.

66. *that wealthy isle*, Paradise.

67. *Circled with*, encircled by. Compare 21; and Doctor Faustus, i. 87.

Ib. Gihon. See Genesis ii. 13.

Ib. swift Euphrates. 'The quartos, "first Euphrates."—That I have rightly corrected the text, is proved by the following line of our author's Orlando Furioso:

"From whence floweth Gihon and swift Euphrates."'

Dyce; who in a note to the latter passage points out that 'Euphrătes' is the usual quantity in our early writers.—Compare Marlowe, 1 Tamburlaine, v. 2:

'As vast and deep as Euphrates and Nile.'

Greene is not very particular about his quantities; so in James IV, act v, he has 'Pactŏlus'; *ib.* in the Prologue, 'Erāto'; and *ib.* act i, 'Ixīon.'

68. *royalizing.* Compare ix. 264, and note on Dr. Faustus, i. 15.

69. *mightiness*, for 'mightinesses.' Compare note on ix. 34. King Rasni, in A Looking-Glass for London and England, paraphrases himself as 'Rasni's royal mightiness.'

70. *Let 's march.* 'Query, "Let us march hence"?' Dyce.

74. *It rests*, it remains; French rester.

Ib. furnish up. Compare note on iii. 22.

75. *Only*, for 'if only.'

76. *jouissance.* Compare Peele's Arraignment of Paris, i. 4:

'They make such cheer your presence to behold,
Such jouissance, such mirth, such merriment,
As nothing else their mind might more unbent';

and Spenser's The Shepheard's Calender, May 25:

'To see those folkes make such jovysaunce,
Made any heart after the pype to daunce.'

Omne tulit . . . dulci. From Horace, de Arte Poetica, 343.—This, as Dyce points out, is Greene's favourite motto; it is appended to the titles of eight prose-works by him, including Pandosto, the Triumph of Time.

Erratum.

p. 93 (Friar Bacon, sc. xi. l. 26), *for* 'over-match' *read* 'over-watch.'

September, 1884.

BOOKS

PRINTED AT

The Clarendon Press, Oxford,

AND PUBLISHED FOR THE UNIVERSITY BY

HENRY FROWDE,

AT THE OXFORD UNIVERSITY PRESS WAREHOUSE,

AMEN CORNER, LONDON.

LEXICONS, GRAMMARS, &c.

A Greek-English Lexicon, by Henry George Liddell, D.D., and Robert Scott, D.D. *Seventh Edition.* 1883. 4to. *cloth,* 1*l.* 16*s.*

A Greek-English Lexicon, abridged from the above, chiefly for the use of Schools. 1883. square 12mo. *cloth,* 7*s.* 6*d.*

A copious Greek-English Vocabulary, compiled from the best authorities. 1850. 24mo. *bound,* 3*s.*

Graecae Grammaticae Rudimenta in usum Scholarum. Auctore Carolo Wordsworth, D.C.L. *Nineteenth Edition,* 1882. 12mo. *cloth,* 4*s.*

Scheller's Lexicon of the Latin Tongue, with the German explanations translated into English by J. E. Riddle, M.A. fol. *cloth,* 1*l.* 1*s.*

A Latin Dictionary, founded on Andrews' Edition of Freund's Latin Dictionary. Revised, enlarged, and in great part re-written, by Charlton T. Lewis, Ph.D., and Charles Short, LL.D. 4to. *cloth,* 1*l.* 5*s.*

A Practical Grammar of the Sanskrit Language, arranged with reference to the Classical Languages of Europe, for the use of English Students. By Monier Williams, M.A. *Fourth Edition.* 8vo. *cloth,* 15*s.*

A Sanskrit English Dictionary, Etymologically and Philologically arranged. By Monier Williams, M.A. 1872. 4to. *cloth,* 4*l.* 14*s.* 6*d.*

An Icelandic-English Dictionary, based on the M . collections of the late R. Cleasby. Enlarged and completed by G. Vigfusson. 4to *cloth,* 3*l.* 7*s.*

An Anglo-Saxon Dictionary, based on the MS. collections of the late Joseph Bosworth, D.D. Edited and enlarged by Professor T. N. Toller, M.A., Owens College, Manchester. Parts I and II, each 15*s.* *To be completed in four Parts.*

An Etymological Dictionary of the English Language, arranged on an Historical basis. By W. W. Skeat, M.A. *Second Edition.* 4to. *cloth,* 2*l.* 4*s.*

A Supplement to the First Edition of the above. 4to. 2*s.* 6*d.* *Just Published.*

A Concise Etymological Dictionary of the English Language. By W. W. Skeat, M.A. Crown 8vo. *cloth,* 5*s.* 6*d.*

GREEK CLASSICS.

Aeschylus: Tragoediae et Fragmenta, ex recensione Guil. Dindorfii. *Second Edition*, 1851. 8vo. *cloth*, 5*s*. 6*d*.

Sophocles: Tragoediae et Fragmenta, ex recensione et cum commentariis Guil. Dindorfii. *Third Edition*, 2 vols. fcap. 8vo. *cloth*, 1*l*. 1*s*.

Each Play separately, *limp*, 2*s*. 6*d*.

The Text alone, printed on writing paper, with large margin. royal 16mo. *cloth*, 8*s*.

The Text alone, square 16mo. *cloth*, 3*s*. 6*d*.

Each Play separately, *limp*, 6*d*. (See also page 11.)

Sophocles: Tragoediae et Fragmenta, cum Annotatt. Guil. Dindorfii. Tomi II. 1849. 8vo. *cloth*, 10*s*.

The Text, Vol. I. 5*s*. 6*d*. The Notes, Vol. II. 4*s*. 6*d*.

Euripides: Tragoediae et Fragmenta, ex recensione Guil. Dindorfii. Tomi II. 1834. 8vo. *cloth*, 10*s*.

Aristophanes: Comoediae et Fragmenta, ex recensione Guil. Dindorfii. Tomi II. 1835. 8vo. *cloth*, 11*s*.

Aristoteles; ex recensione Immanuelis Bekkeri. Accedunt Indices Sylburgiani. Tomi XI. 1837. 8vo. *cloth*, 2*l*. 10*s*.

The volumes may be had separately (except Vol. IX.), 5*s*. 6*d*. *each*.

Aristotelis Ethica Nicomachea, ex recensione Immanuelis Bekkeri. Crown 8vo. *cloth*, 5*s*.

Demosthenes: ex recensione Guil. Dindorfii. Tomi IV. 1846. 8vo. *cloth*, 1*l*. 1*s*.

Homerus: Ilias, ex rec. Guil. Dindorfii. 8vo. *cloth*, 5*s*. 6*d*.

Homerus: Odyssea, ex rec. Guil. Dindorfii. 1855. 8vo. *cloth*, 5*s*. 6*d*.

Plato: The Apology, with a revised Text and English Notes, and a Digest of Platonic Idioms, by James Riddell, M.A. 1878. 8vo. *cloth*, 8*s*. 6*d*.

Plato: Philebus, with a revised Text and English Notes, by Edward Poste, M.A. 1860. 8vo. *cloth*, 7*s*. 6*d*.

Plato: Sophistes and Politicus, with a revised Text and English Notes, by L. Campbell, M.A. 1867. 8vo. *cloth*, 18*s*.

Plato: Theaetetus, with a revised Text and English Notes, by L. Campbell, M.A. *Second Edition* 8vo. *cloth*. 10*s* 6*d*.

Plato: The Dialogues, translated into English, with Analyses and Introductions. By B. Jowett, M.A. *A new Edition in five volumes*. 1875. Medium 8vo. *cloth*, 3*l*. 10*s*.

Plato: The Republic, translated into English, with an Analysis and Introduction By B. Jowett, M.A. Medium 8vo *cloth*, 12*s*. 6*d*.

Thucydides: translated into English, with Introduction, Marginal Analysis, Notes and Indices. By the same. 2 vols. 1881. Medium 8vo. *cloth*, 1*l*. 12*s*.

THE HOLY SCRIPTURES.

The Holy Bible in the Earliest English Versions, made from the Latin Vulgate by John Wycliffe and his followers: edited by the Rev. J. Forshall and Sir F. Madden. 4 vols. 1850. royal 4to. *cloth*, 3*l.* 3*s.*

Also reprinted from the above, with Introduction and Glossary by W. W. Skeat, M.A.

(1) **The New Testament in English, according to the Ver-**sion by John Wycliffe, about A.D. 1380, and Revised by John Purvey, about A.D. 1388. 1879. Extra fcap. 8vo. *cloth*, 6*s.*

(2) **The Book of Job, Psalms, Proverbs, Ecclesiastes,** and Solomon's Song, according to the Version by John Wycliffe. Revised by John Purvey. Extra fcap. 8vo. *cloth*, 3*s.* 6*d.*

The Holy Bible: an exact reprint, page for page, of the Authorized Version published in the year 1611. Demy 4to. *half bound*, 1*l.* 1*s.*

Novum Testamentum Graece. Edidit Carolus Lloyd, S.T.P.R., necnon Episcopus Oxoniensis. 18mo. *cloth*, 3*s.*

The same on writing paper, small 4to. *cloth*, 10*s.* 6*d.*

Novum Testamentum Graece juxta Exemplar Millianum. 18mo. *cloth*, 2*s.* 6*d.*

The same on writing paper, small 4to. *cloth*, 9*s.*

The Greek Testament, with the Readings adopted by the Revisers of the Authorised Version:—

(1) Pica type. *Second Edition, with Marginal References.* Demy 8vo. *cloth*, 10*s.* 6*d.*

(2) Long Primer type. Fcap. 8vo. *cloth*, 4*s.* 6*d.*

(3) The same, on writing paper, with wide margin, *cloth*, 15*s.*

Evangelia Sacra Graece. fcap. 8vo. *limp*, 1*s.* 6*d.*

Vetus Testamentum ex Versione Septuaginta Interpretum secundum exemplar Vaticanum Romae editum. Accedit potior varietas Codicis Alexandrini. *Editio Altera.* Tomi III. 1875. 18mo. *cloth*, 18*s.*

The Oxford Bible for Teachers, containing supplementary HELPS TO THE STUDY OF THE BIBLE, including summaries of the several Books, with copious explanatory notes; and Tables illustrative of Scripture History and the characteristics of Bible Lands with a complete Index of Subjects, a Concordance, a Dictionary of Proper Names, and a series of Maps. Prices in various sizes and bindings from 3*s.* to 2*l.* 5*s.*

Helps to the Study of the Bible, taken from the OXFORD BIBLE FOR TEACHERS, comprising summaries of the several Books with copious explanatory Notes and Tables illustrative of Scripture History and the characteristics of Bible Lands; with a complete Index of Subjects, a Concordance, a Dictionary of Proper Names, and a series of Maps. Pearl 16mo, *cloth*, 1*s.*

ECCLESIASTICAL HISTORY, &c.

Baedae Historia Ecclesiastica. Edited, with English Notes, by G. H. Moberly, M.A. Crown 8vo. *cloth*, 10*s*. 6*d*.

Chapters of Early English Church History. By William Bright, D.D. 8vo. *cloth*, 12*s*.

Eusebius' Ecclesiastical History, according to the Text of Burton. With an Introduction by William Bright, D.D. Crown 8vo. *cloth*, 8*s*. 6*d*.

Socrates' Ecclesiastical History, according to the Text of Hussey. With an Introduction by William Bright, D.D. Crown 8vo. *cloth*, 7*s*. 6*d*.

ENGLISH THEOLOGY.

Butler's Analogy, with an Index. 8vo. *cloth*, 5*s*. 6*d*.

Butler's Sermons. 8vo. *cloth*, 5*s*. 6*d*.

Hooker's Works, with his Life by Walton, arranged by John Keble, M.A. *Sixth Edition*, 3 vols. 1874. 8vo. *cloth*, 1*l*. 11*s*. 6*d*.

Hooker's Works; the text as arranged by John Keble, M.A. 2 vols. 1875. 8vo. *cloth*, 11*s*.

Pearson's Exposition of the Creed. Revised and corrected by E. Burton, D.D. *Sixth Edition*. 1877. 8vo. *cloth*, 10*s*. 6*d*.

Waterland's Review of the Doctrine of the Eucharist, with a Preface by the present Bishop of London. 1880. crown 8vo. *cloth*, 6*s*. 6*d*.

ENGLISH HISTORY.

A History of England. Principally in the Seventeenth Century. By Leopold Von Ranke. 6 vols. 8vo. *cloth*, 3*l*. 3*s*.

Clarendon's (Edw. Earl of) History of the Rebellion and Civil Wars in England. To which are subjoined the Notes of Bishop Warburton. 7 vols. 1849. medium 8vo. *cloth*, 2*l*. 10*s*.

Clarendon's (Edw. Earl of) History of the Rebellion and Civil Wars in England. 7 vols. 1839. 18mo. *cloth*, 1*l*. 1*s*.

Freeman's (E. A.) History of the Norman Conquest of England: its Causes and Results. *In Six Volumes*. 8vo. *cloth*, 5*l*. 9*s*. 6*d*.

Vol. I. and II. together, *Third Edition*, 1877. 1*l*. 16*s*.
Vol. III. *Second Edition*, 1874. 1*l*. 1*s*.
Vol. IV. *Second Edition*, 1875. 1*l*. 1*s*.
Vol. V. 1876. 1*l*. 1*s*.
Vol. VI. Index, 1879. 10*s*. 6*d*.

Rogers's History of Agriculture and Prices in England, A.D. 1259—1793. Vols. I. and II. (1259—1400). 8vo *cloth*, 2*l*. 2*s*.
Vols. III. and IV. (1401-1582) 8vo. *cloth*, 2*l*. 10*s*.

The Vision of William concerning Piers the Plowman, by William Langland. Edited, with Notes, by W. W. Skeat, M.A. *Third Edition.* Ext. fcap. 8vo. *cloth*, 4*s*. 6*d*.

Chaucer. The Prioresses Tale; Sire Thopas; The Monkes Tale; The Clerkes Tale; The Squieres Tale, &c. Edited by W. W. Skeat, M.A. *Second Edition.* Ext. fcap. 8vo. *cloth*, 4*s*. 6*d*.

Chaucer. The Tale of the Man of Lawe; The Pardoneres Tale; The Second Nonnes Tale; The Chanouns Yemannes Tale By the same Editor. *Second Edition.* Extra fcap. 8vo. *cloth*, 4*s*. 6*d*.

Old English Drama. Marlowe's Tragical History of Doctor Faustus, and Greene's Honourable History of Friar Bacon and Friar Bungay. Edited by A. W. Ward, M.A. Extra fcap. 8vo. *cloth*, 5*s*. 6*d*.

Marlowe. Edward II. With Notes, &c. By O. W. Tancock, M.A., Head Master of Norwich School. Extra fcap. 8vo. *cloth*, 3*s*.

Shakespeare. Hamlet. Edited by W. G. Clark, M.A., and W. Aldis Wright, M.A. Extra fcap. 8vo. *stiff covers*, 2*s*.

Shakespeare. Select Plays. Edited by W. Aldis Wright, M.A. Extra fcap. 8vo. *stiff covers*.

The Tempest, 1*s*. 6*d*.	King Lear, 1*s*. 6*d*.
As You Like It, 1*s*. 6*d*.	A Midsummer Night's Dream, 1*s*. 6*d*.
Julius Cæsar, 2*s*.	Coriolanus, 2*s* 6*d*.
Richard the Third, 2*s*. 6*d*.	Henry the Fifth, 2*s*.

(For other Plays, see p. 7.)

Milton. Areopagitica. With Introduction and Notes By J. W. Hales, M.A. *Third Edition.* Extra fcap. 8vo. *cloth*, 3*s*.

Milton. Samson Agonistes. Edited with Introduction and Notes by John Churton Collins. Extra fcap. 8vo. *stiff covers*, 1*s*.

Bunyan. Holy War. Edited by E. Venables, M.A. *In Preparation.* (See also p. 7.)

Addison. Selections from Papers in the Spectator. With Notes. By T. Arnold, M.A., University College. Extra fcap. 8vo. *cloth*, 4*s*. 6*d*.

Burke. Four Letters on the Proposals for Peace with the Regicide Directory of France. Edited, with Introduction and Notes, by E. J. Payne, M.A. Extra fcap. 8vo. *cloth*, 5*s*. *See also page 7.*

Also the following in paper covers.

Goldsmith. Deserted Village. 2*d*.

Gray. Elegy, and Ode on Eton College. 2*d*.

Johnson. Vanity of Human Wishes. With Notes by E. J. Payne, M.A. 4*d*.

Keats. Hyperion, Book I. With Notes by W. T. Arnold B.A. 4*d*.

Milton. With Notes by R. C. Browne, M.A.

Lycidas, 3*d*.	L'Allegro, 3*d*.	Il Penseroso, 4*d*.
Comus, 6*d*.	Samson Agonistes, 6*d*.	

Parnell The Hermit. 2*d*.

Scott. Lay of the Last Minstrel. Introduction and Canto I. With Notes by W. Minto, M.A. 6*d*.

A SERIES OF ENGLISH CLASSICS

Designed to meet the wants of Students in English Literature; by the late J. S. Brewer, M.A., Professor of English Literature at King's College, London.

1. **Chaucer.** The Prologue to the Canterbury Tales; The Knightes Tale; The Nonne Prestes Tale. Edited by R. Morris, LL.D *Fifty-first Thousand* Extra fcap. 8vo. *cloth*, 2*s*. 6*d*. See also p. 6.

2. **Spenser's Faery Queene.** Books I and II. By G. W. Kitchin, M.A. Extra fcap. 8vo. *cloth*, 2*s*. 6*d*. each.

3. **Hooker.** Ecclesiastical Polity, Book I. Edited by R. W. Church, M.A., Dean of St. Paul's. Extra fcap. 8vo. *cloth*, 2*s*.

4. **Shakespeare.** Select Plays. Edited by W. G. Clark, M.A., and W. Aldis Wright, M.A. Extra fcap. 8vo. *stiff covers*.
   I. The Merchant of Venice. 1*s*. II. Richard the Second. 1*s*. 6*d*.
   III. Macbeth. 1*s*. 6*d*. (For other Plays, see p. 6.)

5. **Bacon.**
   I. Advancement of Learning. Edited by W. Aldis Wright, M.A *Second Edition*. Extra fcap. 8vo. *cloth*, 4*s*. 6*d*.
   II. The Essays. With Introduction and Notes. By J. R. Thursfield, M.A

6. **Milton.** Poems. Edited by R. C. Browne, M.A. In Two Volumes. *Fourth Edition*. Ext. fcap. 8vo. *cloth*. 6*s*. 6*d*.
   Sold separately, Vol. I. 4*s*., Vol. II. 3*s*.

7. **Dryden.** Stanzas on the Death of Oliver Cromwell; Astraea Redux; Annus Mirabilis; Absalom and Achitophel; Religio Laici; The Hind and the Panther. Edited by W. D. Christie, M.A., Trinity College, Cambridge. *Second Edition*. Extra fcap. 8vo. *cloth*, 3*s*. 6*d*.

8. **Bunyan.** The Pilgrim's Progress, Grace Abounding, and A Relation of his Imprisonment. Edited, with Biographical Introduction and Notes, by E. Venables, M.A., Precentor of Lincoln. Extra fcap. 8vo. *cloth*, 5*s*.

9. **Pope.** With Introduction and Notes. By Mark Pattison, B.D., Rector of Lincoln College, Oxford.
   I. Essay on Man. *Sixth Edition*. Extra fcap. 8vo. *stiff covers*, 1*s*. 6*d*.
   II. Satires and Epistles. *Second Edition* Extra fcap. 8vo. *stiff covers*, 2*s*.

10. **Johnson.** Select Works. Lives of Dryden and Pope, and Rasselas. Edited by Alfred Milnes, B.A. (Lond.), late Scholar of Lincoln College, Oxford. Extra fcap. 8vo. *cloth*, 4*s*. 6*d*.

11. **Burke.** Edited, with Introduction and Notes, by E. J. Payne, M.A., Fellow of University College, Oxford.
    I. Thoughts on the Present Discontents; the Two Speeches on America, etc. *Second Edition*. Extra fcap. 8vo. *cloth*, 4*s*. 6*d*.
    II. Reflections on the French Revolution. *Second Edition*. Extra fcap. 8vo. *cloth*, 5*s*. *See also p.* 6.

12. **Cowper.** Edited, with Life, Introductions, and Notes, by H. T. Griffith, B.A., formerly Scholar of Pembroke College, Oxford.
    I. The Didactic Poems of 1782, with Selections from the Minor Pieces, A.D. 1779-1783. Ext. fcap. 8vo. *cloth*, 3*s*.
    II. The Task, with Tirocinium, and Selections from the Minor Poems, A.D. 1784-1799. Ext. fcap. 8vo. *cloth*, 3*s*.

II. LATIN.

An Elementary Latin Grammar. By John B. Allen, M.A., *Third Edition.* Extra fcap. 8vo. *cloth*, 2*s*. 6*d*.

A First Latin Exercise Book. By the same Author. *Fourth Edition.* Extra fcap. 8vo. *cloth*, 2*s*. 6*d*.

A Second Latin Exercise Book. By the same Author. *In the Press.*

Reddenda Minora, or Easy Passages, Latin and Greek, for Unseen Translation. For the use of Lower Forms. Composed and selected by C. S. Jerram, M.A. Extra fcap. 8vo. *cloth*, 1*s*. 6*d*.

Anglice Reddenda, or Easy Extracts, Latin and Greek, for Unseen Translation. By C. S. Jerram, M.A. Extra fcap. 8vo. *cloth* 2*s*. 6*d*.

Passages for Translation into Latin. Selected by J. Y. Sargent, M.A. *Sixth Edition.* Ext fcap. 8vo. *cloth*, 2*s*. 6*d*.

First Latin Reader. By T. J. Nunns, M.A. *Third Edition.* Extra fcap. 8vo. *cloth*, 2*s*.

Caesar. The Commentaries (for Schools). With Notes and Maps &c. By C. E. Moberly, M.A., Assistant Master in Rugby School.
The Gallic War. Second Edition. Extra fcap. 8vo. *cloth*, 4*s*. 6*d*.
The Civil War. Extra fcap. 8vo. *cloth*, 3*s*. 6*d*.
The Civil War. Book I. *Second Edition.* Extra fcap. 8vo. *cloth*, 2*s*.

Cicero. Selection of interesting and descriptive passages. With Notes. By Henry Walford, M.A. In Three Parts. *Third Edition.* Ext. fcap 8vo. *cloth*, 4*s*. 6*d* *Each Part separately, in limp cloth*, 1*s*. 6*d*.

Cicero. De Senectute and De Amicitia. With Notes. By W. Heslop, M A. Extra fcap. 8vo. 2*s*.

Cicero. Select Letters (for Schools). With Notes. By the late C. E. Prichard, M.A., and E. R. Bernard, M.A. Extra fcap 8vo. *cloth*, 3*s*.

Cicero. Select Orations (for Schools). With Notes. By J. R. King, M.A. *Second Edition.* Ext. fcap. 8vo. *cloth*, 2*s*. 6*d*.

Cornelius Nepos. With Notes, by Oscar Browning, M.A. *Second Edition.* Extra fcap. 8vo. *cloth*, 2*s*. 6*d*.

Livy. Selections (for Schools). With Notes and Maps. By H. Lee Warner, M.A. *In Three Parts.* Ext. fcap. 8vo. *cloth*, 1*s*. 6*d*. each.

Livy. Books V—VII. By A. R. Cluer, B.A. Extra fcap. 8vo. *cloth*, 3*s*. 6*d*.

Ovid. Selections for the use of Schools. With Introductions and Notes, etc. By W. Ramsay, M.A. Edited by G. G. Ramsay, M.A. *Second Edition.* Ext. fcap. 8vo. *cloth*, 5*s*. 6*d*.

Pliny. Select Letters (for Schools). With Notes. By the late C. E. Prichard, M.A., and E. R. Bernard, M.A. *Second Edition.* Extra fcap. 8vo. *cloth*, 3*s*.

Catulli Veronensis Liber. Iterum recognovit, apparatum criticum prolegomena appendices addidit, Robinson Ellis, A.M. 8vo. *cloth*, 16*s*.

Catullus. A Commentary on Catullus. By Robinson Ellis, M.A. Demy 8vo. *cloth*, 16*s*.

Catulli Veronensis Carmina Selecta, secundum recognitionem Robinson Ellis, A.M. Extra fcap. 8vo. *cloth*, 3*s*. 6*d*.

Cicero de Oratore. With Introduction and Notes. By A. S. Wilkins, M.A., Professor of Latin, Owens College, Manchester.
Book I. Demy 8vo *cloth*, 6*s*. Book II. Demy 8vo. *cloth*, 5*s*.

Cicero's Philippic Orations. With Notes. By J. R. King, M.A. *Second Edition.* Demy 8vo. *cloth*, 10*s*. 6*d*.

Cicero. Select Letters. With English Introductions, Notes, and Appendices. By Albert Watson, M.A., Fellow and Lecturer of Brasenose College, Oxford. *Third Edition.* Demy 8vo. *cloth*, 18*s*.

Cicero. Select Letters (Text). By the same Editor. *Second Edition.* Extra fcap. 8vo. *cloth*, 4*s*.

Cicero pro Cluentio. With Introduction and Notes. By W. Ramsay, M.A. Edited by G. G. Ramsay, M.A., Professor of Humanity, Glasgow. *Second Edition.* Ext. fcap. 8vo. *cloth*, 3*s*. 6*d*.

Livy, Book I. By J. R. Seeley, M.A., Regius Professor of Modern History, Cambridge. *Second Edition.* Demy 8vo. *cloth*, 6*s*.

Horace. With Introductions and Notes. By Edward C. Wickham, M.A., Head Master of Wellington College.
Vol. I. The Odes, Carmen Seculare, and Epodes. *Second Edition.* Demy 8vo. *cloth*, 12*s*.

Horace. *A reprint of the above*, in a size suitable for the use of Schools. Extra fcap. 8vo. *cloth*, 5*s*. 6*d*.

Persius. The Satires. With a Translation and Commentary. By John Conington, M.A. Edited by H. Nettleship, M.A. *Second Edition.* 8vo. *cloth*, 7*s*. 6*d*.

Plautus. Trinummus. With Introductions and Notes. For the use of Higher Forms. By C. E. Freeman, M.A., and A. Sloman, M.A. Extra fcap. 8vo. *cloth*, 3*s*.

Sallust. With Introduction and Notes. By W. W. Capes, M.A. Extra fcap. 8vo. *cloth*, 4*s*. 6*d*. *Just Published.*

Selections from the less known Latin Poets. By North Pinder, M.A. Demy 8vo. *cloth*, 15*s*.

Fragments and Specimens of Early Latin. With Introduction and Notes. By John Wordsworth, M.A. Demy 8vo. *cloth*, 18*s*.

Tacitus. The Annals. I–VI. With Introduction and Notes. By H. Furneaux, M.A. 8vo. *cloth*, 18*s*.

Virgil. With Introduction and Notes. By T. L. Papillon, M.A., Fellow of New College. 2 vols. Crown 8vo. *cloth*, 10*s*. 6*d*.
The Text may be had separately, *cloth*, 4*s*. 6*d*.

A Manual of Comparative Philology, as applied to the Illustration of Greek and Latin Inflections. By T. L. Papillon, M.A., Fellow of New College. *Third Edition, Revised and Corrected.* Crown 8vo. *cloth*, 6*s*.

The Roman Poets of the Augustan Age. *Virgil.* By William Young Sellar, M.A. *New Edition.* 1883. Crown 8vo. 9*s*.

The Roman Poets of the Republic. By the same Author. Extra fcap. 8vo. *cloth*, 14*s*.

III. GREEK.

A Greek Primer, for the use of beginners in that Language. By the Right Rev. Charles Wordsworth, D.C.L., Bishop of St. Andrews. *Seventh Edition* Ext. fcap. 8vo. *cloth*, 1*s.* 6*d.*

Greek Verbs, Irregular and Defective. By W. Veitch. *Fourth Edition.* Crown 8vo *cloth*, 10*s.* 6*d*

The Elements of Greek Accentuation (for Schools). By H. W Chandler, M.A. Ext. fcap. 8vo. *cloth*, 2*s.* 6*d.*

A Series of Graduated Greek Readers:

First Greek Reader. By W. G. Rushbrooke, M.L. *Second Edition.* Ext. fcap. 8vo. *cloth*, 2*s.* 6*d.*

Second Greek Reader. By A. J. M. Bell, M.A. Extra fcap. 8vo. *cloth*, 3*s.* 6*d.*

Fourth Greek Reader; being Specimens of Greek Dialects. By W. W. Merry, M.A. Ext. fcap. 8vo. *cloth*, 4*s.* 6*d.*

Fifth Greek Reader. Part I, Selections from Greek Epic and Dramatic Poetry By E. Abbott, M.A. Ext. fcap. 8vo. *cloth*, 4*s.* 6*d.*

The Golden Treasury of Ancient Greek Poetry; with Introductory Notices and Notes. By R. S. Wright. M.A. Ext. fcap. 8vo. *cloth*, 8*s.* 6*d*

A Golden Treasury of Greek Prose; with Introductory Notices and Notes. By R. S. Wright, M.A., and J. E. L. Shadwell, M.A. Ext. fcap. 8vo. *cloth*, 4*s.* 6*d.*

Aeschylus. Prometheus Bound (for Schools). With Notes. By A. O. Prickard, M.A. *Second Edition.* Ext. fcap. 8vo. *cloth*, 2*s.*

Aeschylus. Agamemnon. With Introduction and Notes. By Arthur Sidgwick, M.A. *Second Edition.* Ext. fcap. 8vo. *cloth*, 3*s.*

Aristophanes. In Single Plays, edited with English Notes, Introductions, &c. By W. W. Merry, M.A. Extra fcap. 8vo.

The Clouds *Second Edition*, 2*s.* The Acharnians, 2*s.* The Frogs, 2*s.*

Cebetis Tabula With Introduction and Notes by C. S. Jerram, M.A. Ext. fcap. 8vo. *cloth*, 2*s.* 6*d.*

Euripides. Alcestis (for Schools). By C. S. Jerram, M.A. Ext. fcap. 8vo. *cloth*, 2*s.* 6*d.*

Euripides. Helena. Edited with Introduction, Notes, and Critical Appendix. By the same Editor. Extra fcap. 8vo. *cloth*, 3*s.*

Herodotus. Selections. With Introduction, Notes, and Map. By W. W. Merry, M.A. Ext. fcap. 8vo *cloth*, 2*s.* 6*d.*

Homer. Odyssey, Books I-XII (for Schools). By W. W. Merry, M.A. *Twenty-Seventh Thousand.* Ext. fcap. 8vo. *cloth*, 4*s.* 6*d.*

Book II separately, 1*s.* 6*d.*

Homer. Odyssey, Books XIII-XXIV (for Schools). By the same Editor. *Second Edition.* Ext. fcap. 8vo. *cloth*, 5*s.*

Homer. Iliad. Book I (for Schools). By D. B. Monro, M.A., Provost of Oriel College, Oxford. *Second Edition.* Ext. fcap. 8vo. *cloth*, 2*s.*

Homer. Iliad. Books I-XII. With an Introduction, a Brief Homeric Grammar, and Notes. By D. B. Monro, M.A. Extra fcap. 8vo. *cloth*, 6*s.*

Homer. Iliad. Books VI and XXI. With Introduction and Notes. By Herbert Hailstone, M.A. Extra fcap. 8vo. *cloth*, 1*s*. 6*d*. each.

Lucian. Vera Historia (for Schools). By C. S. Jerram, M.A. *Second Edition.* Extra fcap. 8vo. *cloth*, 1*s*. 6*d*.

Plato. Selections from the Dialogues [including the whole of the *Apology* and *Crito*.] With Introduction and Notes by J. Purves, M.A. Extra fcap. 8vo. *cloth*, 6*s*. 6*d*.

Sophocles. In Single Plays, with English Notes, &c. By Lewis Campbell, M.A., and Evelyn Abbott, M.A. Extra fcap. 8vo.
Oedipus Rex, Philoctetes. *New and Revised Edition*, 2*s*. each.
Oedipus Coloneus, Antigone, 1*s*. 9*d*. each.
Ajax, Electra, Trachiniae, 2*s*. each.

Sophocles. Oedipus Rex: Dindorf's Text, with Notes by the present Bishop of St. David's. Extra fcap. 8vo. *cloth*, 1*s*. 6*d*.

Theocritus (for Schools). With Notes. By H. Kynaston (late Snow), M.A. *Third Edition.* Ext. fcap. 8vo. *cloth*, 4*s*. 6*d*.

Xenophon. Easy Selections (for Junior Classes). With a Vocabulary, Notes, and Map. By J. S. Phillpotts, B.C.L., and C. S. Jerram, M.A. *Third Edition.* Ext. fcap. 8vo. *cloth*, 3*s*. 6*d*.

Xenophon. Selections (for Schools). With Notes and Maps. By J. S. Phillpotts, B.C.L., Head Master of Bedford School. *Fourth Edition.* Ext. fcap. 8vo. *cloth*, 3*s*. 6*d*.

Xenophon. Anabasis, Book II. With Notes and Map. By C. S. Jerram, M.A. Ext. fcap. 8vo. *cloth*, 2*s*.

Xenophon. Cyropaedia. Books IV, V. With Introduction and Notes. By C. Bigg, D.D. Ext. fcap. 8vo. *cloth*, 2*s*. 6*d*.

Demosthenes and Aeschines. The Orations on the Crown. With Introductory Essays and Notes. By G. A. Simcox, M.A., and W. H. Simcox, M.A. Demy 8vo. *cloth*, 12*s*.

Homer. Odyssey, Books I–XII. Edited with English Notes, Appendices, &c. By W. W. Merry, M.A., and the late James Riddell, M.A. Demy 8vo. *cloth*, 16*s*.

A Grammar of the Homeric Dialect. By D. B. Monro, M.A. Demy 8vo. *cloth*, 10*s*. 6*d*.

Sophocles. With English Notes and Introductions. By Lewis Campbell, M.A. In Two Volumes. 8vo. *each* 16*s*.
Vol. I. Oedipus Tyrannus. Oedipus Coloneus. Antigone. *Second Edition.*
Vol. II. Ajax. Electra. Trachiniae. Philoctetes. Fragments.

Sophocles. The Text of the Seven Plays. By the same Editor. Ext. fcap. 8vo. *cloth*, 4*s*. 6*d*

A Manual of Greek Historical Inscriptions. By E. L. Hicks, M.A. Demy 8vo. *cloth*, 10*s*. 6*d*.

IV. FRENCH.

An Etymological Dictionary of the French Language, with a Preface on the Principles of French Etymology. By A. Brachet. Translated by G. W. Kitchin, M.A. *Third Edition.* Crown 8vo. *cloth*, 7*s*. 6*d*.

Brachet's Historical Grammar of the French Language. Translated by G. W. Kitchin, M.A. *Fifth Edition.* Ext. fcap. 8vo. *cloth*, 3*s*. 6*d*.

A Short History of French Literature. By George Saintsbury. Crown 8vo. *cloth*, 10*s*. 6*d*.

Specimens of French Literature, from Villon to Hugo. Selected and arranged by George Saintsbury. Crown 8vo. *cloth*, 9*s*.

A Primer of French Literature. By George Saintsbury. *Second Edition, with Index.* Extra fcap. 8vo. *cloth*, 2*s*.

Corneille's Horace. Edited, with Introduction and Notes, by George Saintsbury. Ext. fcap. 8vo. *cloth*, 2*s*. 6*d*.

Molière's Les Précieuses Ridicules. Edited with Introduction and Notes. By Andrew Lang, M.A. Ext. fcap. 8vo. 1*s*. 6*d*.

Beaumarchais' Le Barbier de Séville. Edited with Introduction and Notes. By Austin Dobson. Ext. fcap. 8vo. 2*s*. 6*d*.

L'Éloquence de la Chaire et de la Tribune Françaises. Edited by Paul Blouët, B.A. Vol. I. Sacred Oratory. Ext. fcap. 8vo. *cloth*, 2*s*. 6*d*.

French Classics, Edited by GUSTAVE MASSON, *B.A. Univ. Gallic. Extra fcap. 8vo. cloth, 2s. 6d. each.*

Corneille's Cinna, and **Molière's** Les Femmes Savantes.

Racine's Andromaque, and **Corneille's** Le Menteur. With Louis Racine's Life of his Father.

Molière's Les Fourberies de Scapin, and **Racine's** Athalie. With Voltaire's Life of Molière.

Regnard's Le Joueur, and **Brueys** and **Palaprat's** Le Grondeur.

A Selection of Tales by Modern Writers. *Second Edition.*

Selections from the Correspondence of **Madame de Sévigné** and her chief Contemporaries. Intended more especially for Girls' Schools. By the same Editor. Ext. fcap. 8vo. *cloth*, 3*s*.

Louis XIV and his Contemporaries; as described in Extracts from the best Memoirs of the Seventeenth Century. With Notes, Genealogical Tables, etc. By the same Editor. Extra fcap. 8vo. *cloth*, 2*s*. 6*d*.

V. GERMAN.

German Classics, Edited by C. A. BUCHHEIM, *Phil. Doc., Professor in King's College, London.*

Goethe's Egmont. With a Life of Goethe, &c. *Third Edition.* Ext. fcap. 8vo. *cloth*, 3*s*.

Schiller's Wilhelm Tell. With a Life of Schiller; an historical and critical Introduction, Arguments, and a complete Commentary. *Sixth Edition.* Ext. fcap. 8vo. *cloth*, 3*s*. 6*d*.

—— *School Edition.* Extra fcap. 8vo. 2*s*. *Just Published.*

Lessing's Minna von Barnhelm. A Comedy. With a Life of Lessing, Critical Analysis, Complete Commentary, &c. *Fourth Edition.* Extra fcap. 8vo. *cloth*, 3*s*. 6*d*.

Schiller's Historische Skizzen: Egmonts Leben und Tod, *and* Belagerung von Antwerpen. *Second Edition.* Ext. fcap. 8vo. *cloth*, 2*s*. 6*d*.

Goethe's Iphigenie auf Tauris. A Drama. With a Critical Introduction and Notes. *Second Edition.* Ext. fcap. 8vo. *cloth*, 3*s*.

Modern German Reader. A Graduated Collection of Prose Extracts from Modern German Writers :—

Part I. With English Notes, a Grammatical Appendix, and a complete Vocabulary. *Third Edition.* Extra fcap. 8vo. *cloth*, 2*s*. 6*d*.

Lessing's Nathan der Weise. With Introduction, Notes, etc. Extra fcap. 8vo. *cloth*, 4*s*. 6*d*.

Halm's Griseldis. In Preparation.

LANGE'S *German Course.*

The Germans at Home; a Practical Introduction to German Conversation, with an Appendix containing the Essentials of German Grammar. *Second Edition.* 8vo. *cloth*, 2*s*. 6*d*.

The German Manual; a German Grammar, a Reading Book, and a Handbook of German Conversation. 8vo. *cloth*, 7*s*. 6*d*.

A Grammar of the German Language. 8vo. *cloth*, 3*s*. 6*d*.

German Composition; a Theoretical and Practical Guide to the Art of Translating English Prose into German. 8vo. *cloth*, 4*s*. 6*d*.

Lessing's Laokoon. With Introduction, English Notes, &c. By A. Hamann, Phil. Doc., M.A. Ext. fcap. 8vo. *cloth*, 4*s*. 6*d*.

Wilhelm Tell. By Schiller. Translated into English Verse by Edward Massie, M.A. Ext. fcap. 8vo. *cloth*, 5*s*.

VI. MATHEMATICS, &c.

Figures made Easy: a first Arithmetic Book. (Introductory to 'The Scholar's Arithmetic.') By Lewis Hensley, M.A., formerly Fellow of Trinity College, Cambridge. Crown 8vo. *cloth*, 6*d*.

Answers to the Examples in Figures made Easy. By the same Author. Crown 8vo. *cloth*, 1*s*.

The Scholar's Arithmetic. By the same Author. Crown 8vo. *cloth*, 4*s*. 6*d*.

The Scholar's Algebra. By the same Author. Crown 8vo. *cloth*, 4*s*. 6*d*.

Book-keeping. By R. G. C. Hamilton and John Ball. *New and enlarged Edition.* Ext. fcap. 8vo. *limp cloth*, 2*s*.

Acoustics. By W. F. Donkin, M.A., F.R.S., Savilian Professor of Astronomy, Oxford. Crown 8vo. *cloth*, 7*s*. 6*d*.

A Treatise on Electricity and Magnetism. By J. Clerk Maxwell, M.A., F.R.S. A New Edition, edited by W. D. Niven, M.A. 2 vols. Demy 8vo. *cloth*, 1*l*. 11*s*. 6*d*.

An Elementary Treatise on Electricity. By James Clerk Maxwell, M.A. Edited by William Garnett, M.A. Demy 8vo. *cloth*, 7*s*. 6*d*.

A Treatise on Statics. By G. M. Minchin, M.A. *Second Edition, Revised and Enlarged.* Demy 8vo. *cloth*, 14*s*.

Uniplanar Kinematics of Solids and Fluids. By G. M. Minchin, M.A., Crown 8vo. *cloth*, 7*s*. 6*d*.

Geodesy. By Colonel Alexander Ross Clarke, R.E. Demy 8vo. *cloth*, 12*s*. 6*d*.

VII. PHYSICAL SCIENCE.

A Handbook of Descriptive Astronomy. By G. F. Chambers, F.R.A.S. *Third Edition.* Demy 8vo. *cloth*, 28*s*.

Chemistry for Students. By A. W. Williamson, Phil. Doc., F.R.S., Professor of Chemistry, University College, London. *A new Edition, with Solutions*, 1873. Ext. fcap. 8vo. *cloth*, 8*s*. 6*d*.

A Treatise on Heat, with numerous Woodcuts and Diagrams. By Balfour Stewart, LL.D., F.R.S., Professor of Physics, Owens College, Manchester. *Fourth Edition.* Ext. fcap. 8vo. *cloth*, 7*s*. 6*d*.

Lessons on Thermodynamics. By R. E. Baynes, M.A. Crown 8vo. *cloth*, 7*s*. 6*d*.

Forms of Animal Life. By G. Rolleston, M.D., F.R.S., Linacre Professor of Physiology, Oxford. *A New Edition in the Press.*

Exercises in Practical Chemistry. Vol. I. Elementary Exercises. By A. G Vernon Harcourt, M.A., and H. G. Madan, M.A. *Third Edition.* Revised by H. G. Madan, M.A. Crown 8vo. *cloth*. 9*s*.

Tables of Qualitative Analysis. Arranged by H. G. Madan, M.A. Large 4to. *stiff covers*, 4*s*. 6*d*.

Geology of Oxford and the Valley of the Thames. By John Phillips, M.A., F.R.S., Professor of Geology, Oxford. 8vo. *cloth*, 1*l*. 1*s*.

Crystallography. By M. H. N. Story-Maskelyne, M.A., Professor of Mineralogy, Oxford. *In the Press.*

VIII. HISTORY.

A Constitutional History of England. By W. Stubbs, D.D., Regius Professor of Modern History, Oxford. *Library Edition.* Three vols. demy 8vo. *cloth*, 2*l*. 8*s*.

Also in Three Volumes, Crown 8vo., price 12*s*. each.

Select Charters and other Illustrations of English Constitutional History from the Earliest Times to the reign of Edward I. By the same Author. *Fourth Edition.* Crown 8vo. *cloth*, 8*s*. 6*d*.

A Short History of the Norman Conquest. By E. A. Freeman, M.A. *Second Edition.* Extra fcap. 8vo. *cloth*, 2*s*. 6*d*.

Genealogical Tables illustrative of Modern History. By H. B. George, M.A. *Second Edition, Revised and Enlarged.* Small 4to. *cloth*, 12*s*.

A History of France, down to the year 1793. With numerous Maps, Plans, and Tables. By G. W. Kitchin, M.A. In 3 vols. Crown 8vo. *cloth*, price 10*s*. 6*d*. each.

Selections from the Despatches, Treaties, and other Papers of the Marquess Wellesley, K.G., during his Government of India. Edited by S. J. Owen, M.A. 8vo. *cloth*, 1*l*. 4*s*.

Selections from the Wellington Despatches. By the same Editor. 8vo. *cloth*, 24*s*.

A History of the United States of America. By E. J. Payne, M.A., Fellow of University College, Oxford. *In the Press.*

A Manual of Ancient History. By George Rawlinson, M.A., Camden Professor of Ancient History, Oxford. Demy 8vo. *cloth*, 14*s*.

A History of Greece. By E. A. Freeman, M.A., formerly Fellow of Trinity College, Oxford.

Italy and her Invaders. A.D. 376–476. By T. Hodgkin, Fellow of University College, London. Illustrated with Plates and Maps. 2 vols. demy 8vo. *cloth*, 1*l.* 12*s.*

IX. LAW.

The Elements of Jurisprudence. By Thomas Erskine Holland, D.C.L. *Second Edition.* Demy 8vo. *cloth*, 10*s.* 6*d.*

The Institutes of Justinian, edited as a Recension of the Institutes of Gaius. By the same Editor. *Second Edition.* Extra fcap. 8vo. *cloth*, 5*s.*

Gaii Institutionum Juris Civilis Commentarii Quatuor; or, Elements of Roman Law by Gaius. With a Translation and Commentary. By Edward Poste, M.A., Barrister-at-Law. *Second Edition.* 8vo. *cloth*, 18*s.*

Select Titles from the Digest of Justinian. By T. E. Holland, D.C.L., and C. L. Shadwell, B.C.L. Demy 8vo. *cloth*, 14*s.*

Also in separate parts:—

Part I. Introductory Titles. 2*s.* 6*d.* Part II. Family Law. 1*s.*
Part III. Property Law. 2*s.* 6*d.*
Part IV. Law of Obligations (No. 1). 3*s.* 6*d.* (No. 2). 4*s.* 6*d.*

Elements of Law considered with reference to Principles of General Jurisprudence. By William Markby, M.A. *Second Edition, with Supplement.* Crown 8vo. *cloth*, 7*s.* 6*d.*

International Law. By W. E. Hall, M.A., Barrister-at-Law. Demy 8vo., *cloth*, 21*s.*

An Introduction to the History of the Law of Real Property, with Original Authorities. By Kenelm E. Digby, M. A. *Third Edition.* Demy 8vo. *cloth*, 10*s.* 6*d.*

Principles of the English Law of Contract, etc. By Sir William R. Anson, Bart., D.C.L. *Second Edition.* Demy 8vo. *cloth*, 10*s.* 6*d.*

X. MENTAL AND MORAL PHILOSOPHY.

Bacon. Novum Organum. Edited, with Introduction, Notes, etc., by T. Fowler, M.A. 1878. 8vo. *cloth*, 14*s.*

Locke's Conduct of the Understanding. Edited, with Introduction, Notes, etc., by T. Fowler, M.A. *Second Edition.* Extra fcap. 8vo. *cloth*, 2*s.*

Selections from Berkeley. With an Introduction and Notes. By A. C. Fraser, LL.D. *Second Edition.* Crown 8vo *cloth*, 7*s.* 6*d.*

The Elements of Deductive Logic, designed mainly for the use of Junior Students in the Universities. By T. Fowler, M.A. *Eighth Edition*, with a Collection of Examples. Ext. fcap. 8vo. *cloth*, 3*s.* 6*d.*

The Elements of Inductive Logic, designed mainly for the use of Students in the Universities. By the same Author. *Fourth Edition.* Ext. fcap. 8vo. *cloth*, 6*s.*

A Manual of Political Economy, for the use of Schools. By J. E. Thorold Rogers M.A. *Third Edition* Ext. fcap. 8vo. *cloth* 4*s.* 6*d.*

XI. ART, &c.

A Handbook of Pictorial Art. By R. St. J. Tyrwhitt, M.A. *Second Edition.* 8vo. *half morocco,* 18*s.*

A Treatise on Harmony. By Sir F. A. Gore Ouseley, Bart., M.A., Mus. Doc. *Third Edition.* 4to. *cloth,* 10*s.*

A Treatise on Counterpoint, Canon, and Fugue, based upon that of Cherubini. By the same Author. *Second Edition.* 4to. *cloth,* 16*s.*

A Treatise on Musical Form, and General Composition. By the same Author. 4to. *cloth,* 10*s.*

A Music Primer for Schools. By J. Troutbeck, M.A., and R. F. Dale, M.A., B. Mus. *Second Edition.* Crown 8vo. *cloth,* 1*s.* 6*d.*

The Cultivation of the Speaking Voice. By John Hullah. *Second Edition.* Extra fcap. 8vo. *cloth,* 2*s.* 6*d.*

XII. MISCELLANEOUS.

Text-Book of Botany, Morphological and Physiological. By Dr. Julius Sachs, Professor of Botany in the University of Würzburg. *Second Edition.* Edited, with an Appendix, by Sydney H. Vines, M.A. Royal 8vo. *half morocco,* 1*l.* 11*s.* 6*d.*

A System of Physical Education : Theoretical and Practical. By Archibald Maclaren, The Gymnasium, Oxford. Extra fcap. 8vo. *cloth,* 7*s.* 6*d.*

An Icelandic Prose Reader, with Notes, Grammar, and Glossary. By Dr. Gudbrand Vigfusson and F. York Powell, M.A. Extra fcap. 8vo. *cloth,* 10*s.* 6*d.*

Dante. Selections from the Inferno. With Introduction and Notes. By H. B. Cotterill, B.A. Extra fcap. 8vo. *cloth,* 4*s.* 6*d.*

Tasso. La Gerusalemme Liberata. Cantos I, II. By the same Editor. Extra fcap. 8vo. *cloth,* 2*s.* 6*d.*

A Treatise on the Use of the Tenses in Hebrew. By S. R. Driver, M.A., Fellow of New College. *New and Enlarged Edition.* Extra fcap. 8vo. *cloth,* 7*s.* 6*d.*

Outlines of Textual Criticism applied to the New Testament. By C. E. Hammond, M.A., Fellow and Tutor of Exeter College, Oxford. *Third Edition.* Extra fcap. 8vo. *cloth,* 3*s.* 6*d.*

A Handbook of Phonetics, including a Popular Exposition of the Principles of Spelling Reform. By Henry Sweet, M.A. Extra fcap. 8vo. *cloth,* 4*s.* 6*d.*

The Student's Handbook to the University and Colleges of Oxford. *Seventh Edition.* Extra fcap. 8vo. *cloth,* 2*s.* 6*d.*

The DELEGATES OF THE PRESS *invite suggestions and advice from all persons interested in education; and will be thankful for hints, &c., addressed to the* SECRETARY TO THE DELEGATES, *Clarendon Press, Oxford.*